Thirteen Bones

By Tom King

August, 2009

First published by Dog Ear Publishing
4010 W. 86th Street, Ste H
Indianapolis, IN 46268
www.dogearpublishing.net

ISBN: 978-160844-185-3

To the Memory of
Harry E. Maude, Gerald B. Gallagher,
And the Colonists of the
Phoenix Islands Settlement Scheme,
This book is dedicated
with respect and admiration

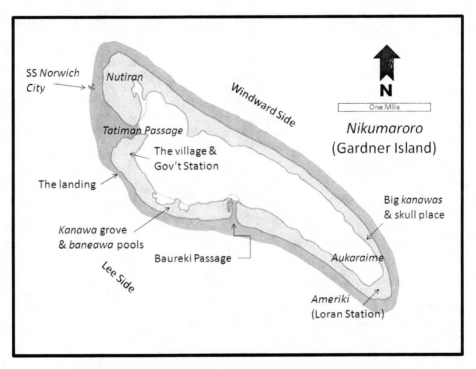

SS *Norwich* City

Nutiran

Windward Side

N

One Mile

Nikumaroro
(Gardner Island)

Tatiman Passage

The village & Gov't Station

The landing

Big *kanawas* & skull place

Kanawa grove & *baneawa* pools

Baureki Passage

Aukaraime

Lee Side

Ameriki (Loran Station)

Nikumaroro, in the Phoenix Islands, Republic of Kiribati.
Lat. 4°39'59" S, Long 174°31'06 W

People and Places
A Guide to Key Actors, Place Names and Terms
Used in *Thirteen Bones*

Note: In the written Tungaru ("Gilbertese," Kiribati) language, "ti" is pronounced as a soft "s," as in the English word "attention."

- Aana: Wife of Magistrate Koata, Tungaru elder, traditional doctor
- *Ameriki:* After 1944, name given to the US Coast Guard station site at the southeast end of the island.
- *Anti*: Ghost, dangerous spirit
- Aram Tamia: Gerald Gallagher's Tungaru houseboy, later magistrate
- *Ata:* Human skull
- *Aubunga:* Giant clam (<u>Tridacna</u> spp.)
- *Aukaraime:* Large land parcel comprising southeast end and most of windward side of island; split in two when *Ameriki* was recognized.
- Baiteke: Son of Takena and Karirea, from Onotoa Atoll.
- *Baureke* Passage: Small, southern entrance into the Nikumaroro lagoon.
- Boikabane: Mother of Keaki, wife of Ieiera.
- Babera: From Arorae Atoll, member of original working party, London Missionary Society missionary/teacher (my speculation).
- *Baneawa:* Small lagoon fish.
- Beiaruru: From Rotima Atoll; older man with young daughter, teenaged granddaughter.
- *Buka:* The tree <u>Pisonia grandis</u>, large, spreading indigenous softwood; special tree of Nei Manganibuka.
- Eddie: Son of Tumuo, brother of Segalo
- Edwin: Son of Jack Kimo Petro
- Eneri: Native medical dresser (my speculation), from Nonouti Atoll.
- Era: Daughter of Beiaruru and Teaneue

- Gallagher, Gerald B. (Mister Karaka): Second Administrator, Phoenix Islands Settlement Scheme
- Gardner Island: Colonial name applied to Nikumaroro before 1938, and sometimes thereafter.
- Holland, F.G.L., Resident Commissioner, Gilbert and Ellice Islands Colony.
- Ieiara: Father of Keaki and Taberiki, from Temeroa in Arorae Atoll.
- *I-Kiribati:* People of Kiribati ("Gilbert Islands," Tungaru). Used only since Kiribati attained independence in 1979
- *I-Matang:* Literally, "people of Matang," the traditional origin place of the first people. Honored and powerful ancestors. Since the 19th century applied to Europeans.
- Iokina: Second Magistrate of Nikumaroro
- Isaac, Dr. Lindsay: Member of the colonial medical service based in Fiji; during war changed name to Verrier.
- John: Son of Jack Kimo Petro
- *Kanawa:* The tree Cordia subchordata. A large tropical hardwood.
- Karaka: "Gallagher" as pronounced by Tungaru people; name given to the Nikumaroro village after Gallagher's death.
- Karirea: Baiteke's mother; wife of Takena.
- Keaki: Son of Ieiara and Boikabane of Arorae Atoll
- Kimo: Jack Kimo Petro, Tuvaluan-Portuguese Public Works Officer, expert builder, equipment operator, designer, construction manager
- Kirata: Member of original working party, from Onotoa Atoll. Friend of Takena's (my speculation)
- Koata: First Magistrate of Nikumaroro, from Onotoa Atoll
- *Komitina:* "Commissioner" as pronounced by Tungaru people; euphemism for government.
- Little Koata: Grandson of Koata and Aana.
- Luke, Sir Harry: Governor of Fiji and High Commissioner of the Western Pacific
- MacPherson, Dr. D.C.M.: Assistant Director of Medical Services, Fiji; Lecturer in Forensics at Central Medical School.

- Manganibuka: Traditional ancestress, believed to have brought navigation and other skills to the Tungaru people from her island of Nikumaroro; the *buka* is her special tree.

- *Mao:* The shrub <u>Scaevola frutescens</u>; very dense, hard to penetrate brush.

- Maude, Harry (Mister Mauta): Gilbert and Ellice Islands Colony Lands Commissioner, father and first Administrator of the Phoenix Islands Settlement Scheme.

- Nei: Article customarily placed before proper feminine noun; similar to "Miss," "Mrs.," or "Ms." in English.

- *Noriti:* "Norwich" as pronounced by Tungaru people; name of wrecked ship, also ascribed to land parcel south of the village, from which the shipwreck could be seen.

- *Norwich City:* Freighter wrecked 1929 on *Nutiran* reef.

- *Nutiran:* "New Zealand" as pronounced by Tungaru people: Land parcel at northwest end of the island, where the New Zealand Pacific Aviation Survey team camped in 1938-39.

- Reef flat: The coral shelf, of varying width and smoothness, that typically surrounds a coral island, submerged at high tide, usually not at low tide; terminated to seaward by the sharp drop-off of the reef edge.

- PISS: Phoenix Islands Settlement Scheme.

- *Ren:* The tree <u>Tournefortia</u> sp., a medium-sized tropical hardwood

- *Ritiati:* Land parcel occupied by colonial village, named for Sir Arthur Richards, the high commissioner before Sir Harry Luke.

- Segalo: Daughter of Tumuo, nurse in training.

- Taberiki : Keaki's sister

- Takena: Father of Baiteke and Terema, from Onotoa Atoll.

- Tarema: Baiteke's sister

- *Tatiman* Passage: The main passage into the lagoon, named after the Tasman Sea during the visit of the New Zealand Pacific Aviation Survey team.

- Teng or Ten: Article customarily placed before proper masculine noun; similar to "Mister" in English.

- Tumuo: Tuvaluan master carpenter, canoe-builder, fisherman; father of Segalo and Eddie.

- Tungaru: Traditional name for the people and language of the "Gilbert Islands," now the Republic of Kiribati
- Vaskess, Henry Harrison: Permanent Secretary to the High Commissioner of the Western Pacific, based in Fiji.
- WPHC: Western Pacific High Commission.

Prologue:

Nikumaroro – 13th October, 1937

The face of death was purple.

With beady red eyes on stalks, a dark, shiny lump between them that resembled a nose but wasn't, wiggling feelers on top, a bulbous body trailing along behind.

"Bigger than my head," she thought mildly, and shifted her eyes – aware of the effort – to examine the creature's huge, battered pincers.

The giant crab – purplish-black, she decided – sidled out of her field of vision, clattering over the rubbly ground. She tried to keep it in sight, but found she couldn't lift or turn her head.

Decided she didn't need to.

"Going for my gut," she thought, with relentless practicality.

Smaller crabs, clattering in a different key, dragging the pilfered sea shells in which they lived, were already nibbling at her legs and arms. Tiny ones too, hardly bigger than insects, but so many of them, so very many. She no longer felt them as more than an itch.

Hermit crabs, she thought fleetingly, eating a hermit. Alive.

Was she alive?

The ground seemed to be. Everything around where she lay, by the cold remains of her fire, seemed to pulsate with crabs.

So intent on their business. Eating her.

Alive, she thought, turning the word over in her mind. What was it to be alive, and how did it differ to be dead?

And which was she, now, under this tree, on this island, covered in crabs?

Alive, she decided, if barely so. And certainly – her brain began replaying it – she had *been* alive.

The memories, fragments, glimpses, fluttered across her dimming consciousness. Banking through canyons of cloud, skirting rain squalls and thunderstorms, watching the farms and roads and oceans, jungles and deserts pass under her wings. Seeing the great cities rising up on the horizon – San Francisco, New York, Mexico City.

The freedom she had felt, the sheer fierce joy of it, would have brought tears to her eyes, but she was far too dehydrated to produce them.

With an almost academic curiosity, she wondered what was killing her – besides the crabs.

Dehydration, of course, but something had made her too sick to move around and find water, and had brought on the explosive diarrhea that had left her so drained, weak, delirious. It was good the delirium had passed.

Or had it? It didn't matter.

Had it been the fish? The pretty little fish, caught on the retreating tide in the pools she had blocked off with the window screen from the shipwreck? Cooked on the coals, torn apart by hand? They had tasted all right. Or the bird, caught by hand, plucked and cooked? It had been a fishy tasting thing, but why would it have made her sick? The baby turtles? The canned food from the pile near the shipwreck?

Or was it her infected foot? She couldn't feel it now, but it had been swollen and horribly painful at times, ever since she had cut it on the way down here from the other end of the island. Thank goodness for Fred's shoe when the foot got too big to fit in her own.

Her mind flickered. What would dying bring? For a moment she felt fear, but with a familiar act of will she put it away. She found it replaced by regret, especially for Mommie. Wished she could speak with her one last time, reassure her.

George would see to it, though; George had a way, and he was kind....

And he cared so for her life's work, her story. She wondered vaguely who, if anyone, would find its last chapter, the scribbled pages stuffed in Fred's sextant box. The last words marked in big block letters with pieces of dried-up rouge from her compact, after her pencil had gone missing.

Fred's sextant box. For what he called his "preventer" – the nautical sextant tricked out with a bubble level to use in the air. She could almost see his face, his wry smile. Wondered if he would stay buried in the grave she had scraped out with her hands and a piece of wood. Or would the crabs get him, too?

With a sigh – had she sighed? Was she breathing? — she put it all aside, let herself sink away into her surroundings. The coolness of the coral gravel after the heat of the day. The darkening sky beyond the glowing green-gold leaves. The boom of the surf, unseen but so near. The squabbling cries of birds settling for the night, the vaguely felt nibbling of the crabs. A light misting of rain as a small shower passed over.

Another adventure.

The clouds were parting, and the sky was endless and glowing.

Her body's last act was to smile.

"Wheels up," she whispered.

Koata touched the gray bark of a gnarled tree at least two metres in diameter. He peered into the canopy, dark green with patches of bright blue sky showing through. The sounds of the birds and the feel of the wind told him that the sky in the east would soon darken with the swift onset of evening.

"Such trees," he said.

"Buka," Mautake murmured, unnecessarily. They both knew what kind of trees they were.

The two old men stood in companionable silence, listening to the bird cries and the boom of surf on the reef. And in the distance an occasional shout or laugh or snatch of song from the other Tungaru delegates as they pursued and caught birds and crabs. The animals on the island knew nothing of men, and were easy to catch by hand.

Gently, like a caress, Koata ran his hand over the thick, twisted tree trunk,

"Nikumaroro?" he asked, naming the legendary home of Nei Manganibuka, the ancestress, the mariner, the teacher.

"Not really under the lee of Samoa. More like upwind."

"But covered in *buka.* Her tree. No other island has so much."

Mautake was silent. Koata sensed his skepticism, but ignored it. Mautake was a trifle senior to him, but he would not challenge another elder, especially one not of his own island. And the ancient stories varied from island to island; each was held to be truth by those who knew it. And maybe was truth. Was there a single truth, especially about long ago in the spirit times?

Koata's gaze swung up and down the expanse of lagoon, and up into the sky, where the first pale stars were beginning to appear. Viewing as a navigator, viewing from the stars, he visualized his own location, the locations of Tarawa, Beru, Onotoa, Samoa. Shook his head.

"The old islands weren't necessarily where they are today. Sometimes they moved."

"True," Mautake said slowly. "One can't be sure...."

Koata smiled wryly. "Perhaps we'll find the bones of those people who were eaten." He paused a moment; did Mautake have the same story he did, about when the Tungaru people had lived in Samoa, had been required to feed the Samoan chiefs, and had slain firstborn children on Nikumaroro for the purpose? Surely he did.

Mautake grunted noncommittally. Koata went on, musing. "But those people were taken to Samoa, of course...."

Silence again, both old men wrapped in thought.

"It's rather smaller than I'd imagined Nikumaroro to be," Mautake said at last.

Koata snorted softly. "Big enough."

He stumped off to the lagoon shore, and Mautake followed, their bare, hard-calloused feet feeling the way through the deadfall. Small waves lapped the sand beach, the fins of young sharks cut the water, cruising this way and that. Eastward across the lagoon, the rays of the low sun in the west turned the trees a deep green-gold. White birds – *kiakia,* the small terns – whirled lazily above the treetops, looking for roosting places.

The other end of the island, off to the southeast, was briefly obscured by a rain shower that passed serenely on to the west.

Mautake squatted and began to draw random patterns in the sand with a stick.

"We should tell Mister Mauta."

"Yes...." Koata murmured, distracted, then focused his attention. Mautake was right; Mister Maude would be pleased, and interested. But not tonight. Tonight Koata wanted to be just quiet, and feel what the island had to say, what spirits moved among the trees.

"In the morning let's tell him. He and Mister Eric are tired tonight, and Mister Mauta's legs hurt. They've worked hard today, looking and planning."

Mautake stared fixedly across the lagoon, drew a straight line in the sand. "*I-Matang* are always planning."

"Yes, they have ideas about everything. Good ideas. Usually"

They watched the moon rise over the trees across the lagoon. The sky filled with stars, the Southern Cross hanging low in the south. Birds called softly to one another as they settled for the night. The cool evening breeze stirred Koata's sparse gray hair.

It was a good island, he thought, and it *felt* like Nikumaroro. Though small – it was remarkable to see the other side of the lagoon so close, less than a mile.

But lots of land for such a small atoll. Almost continuous land, all the way round. A good island for settlers. And open, entirely open for settlement.

What a novel idea – land that didn't belong to anyone.

"Except Nei Manganibuka," he murmured. Staring at the swirl of white birds settling into the treetops, Mautake slowly nodded.

Chapter 1–

Moamoa. 26th April 1939

"And lo," Teng Beiaruru gazed over *Moamoa's* starboard rail at the white-capped wave surging back from the bow, and at the sea beyond. He spread his arms wide. "The canoes of Samoa lay in the lee of that island Nikumaroro, whose people knew nothing of fighting."

Sitting on the deck in front of the old man where he squatted in the bows, the children looked at him wide-eyed. Keaki imagined the big canoes with their great woven sails furling, the warriors seizing their paddles to shoot through the surf to the beach. Teng Beiaruru's voice rose. His wiry body seemed to vibrate, his eyes sparkled under his heavy brows.

"And behold! The warriors of Samoa stepped ashore, and raced up the beach to where the people stood stupid. And they smashed their heads!" He swung an imaginary war club at Baiteke, who cowered back against the rail and then straightened up grinning, embarrassed to have reacted.

"Lo, they smashed the heads of those people, and pierced them with spears, and slashed them with shark-tooth swords. And the children, the firstborn, fled before those warriors of Samoa, into the bush all the way to the windward side, where no one lived except *te anti* – spirits." He clasped his hands, entreating. "And there they begged their ancestors to save them, but the ancestors did not heed. And behold! The warriors of Samoa come fast through the bush, with their spears and clubs and swords!" Teng Beiaruru grimaced at the children, made his hands into claws, towered over them as *Moamoa's* bow climbed a swell. Taberiki squeaked and ducked behind the capstan. Little Koata's mouth hung open. Keaki and Baiteke grinned nervously.

"And so," Teng Beiaruru went on, chuckling, "the fierce warriors of Samoa chase the children through the bush until they — *catch* them! And then they cut off their feet....." He pantomimed with Baiteke's foot; the boy scrunched up to pull it under him, but Teng Beiaruru lunged for his hand and described how the warriors cut those off next, how they lopped the heads off the children to decorate their canoes, and carried their carcasses back to the feast of the Samoan chiefs. How the fish and turtles climbed aboard the canoes to drink the blood.

"And this," he concluded, "is in truth the way it happened."

The children gaped at him, then Baiteke broke the spell, poking his sister's arm with his finger.

"Mmm, that story makes me hungry!"

"Then eat your foot," Tarema shrilled, jumping up and running aft – "if you can stand the smell!"

Baiteke shrugged. "Actually, I wouldn't want to eat her even if I was a cannibal. Icch!"

Keaki grinned. He had known this boy from Onotoa only since they had assembled on Beru a few weeks ago, but they were becoming fast friends. They had even started trading jokes about poop, pooping and eating poop – just as the older boys did. Keaki's grin broadened as he considered creative possibilities. Clam poop, fish poop, the soft slimy poop of the red-tailed tropic bird.

Teng Beiaruru cleared his throat. "This all happened long, long ago," he intoned, "on that island Nikumaroro."

Toward which, Keaki thought, with a sudden attack of seriousness, *Moamoa* was pounding through the long Pacific swells. The elders had decided its identity a year ago when they had landed on the uninhabited island with Mister Maude. They recognized it because it was covered, as the ancient legends said, with Nei Manganibuka's own *buka* trees. It had to be the island from which the great ancestress had come in the distant past, bringing the arts of navigation, weaving, and fishing to the I-Tungaru.

The *I-Matang* called it Gardner Island after some ship's captain. The Niue Island people who had planted coconuts there two generations ago had called it *Motu Aonga* in their language – "island of the coconut crabs" – because of all the giant crabs that rattled through its trees and deadfall. But Teng Koata and the other elders knew where they were, and they respectfully called the island by its ancient name – Nikumaroro.

"Where I will live – from now on," Keaki thought, feeling strangely at war with himself. All his ten years had been spent on Temeroa; all his memories were there, with all his friends and most of his family. The elders and the *I-Matang* said Temeroa was too crowded, but it just felt like home to Keaki. His mother and father were excited about getting good land on Niku-maroro, planting coconuts and pandanus. They dreamed of getting land for Keaki, and bringing in other family members. They spoke of being in Niku-maroro's founding generation, and having a privileged seating place in the *maneaba* – the meeting house. All those things were good, Keaki knew, and most of the time he was excited about it all, too. Sometimes he felt like one of the ancient navigators who had guided the people up from Samoa, adventuring across the dangerous sea to make a new home on unknown islands, finding a better life. But at other times he felt like a scared, lonely little boy, who missed his home, his friends, and wondered about the future. With an effort, he forced himself back to thoughts of the names he could call his new friend Baiteke. Manta Ray poop, lobster poop....

He slept on the deck as usual, on a pandanus mat near his mother and father, but was troubled by dreams in which he was lost on the windward side of an island – the side where some families still had secret shrines occupied by their ancestral *anti*. Where *te anti* – ghosts – tarried after leaving their bodies, before traveling on toward *Matang,* the island of the dead. In his dream he was running through the brush, tripping, falling, pursued by unnamed, invisible forces that he knew were cannibal ghosts. The ground was covered with the bones of people slain before him, and he knew that his bones would soon join them. He tossed and moaned on his mat, and Boikabane, his mother, patted him and rubbed his arm until he quieted.

A change in noise and vibration woke them all as the engine slowed. Keaki felt and heard the passage of feet on the deck by his head, felt way coming off the ship. Throwing off the thickness of sleep, he jumped up and ran to the rail, peered into the darkness.

The not-quite darkness. The eastern sky was beginning to turn faintly pink, shading higher up to a blue that was slightly lighter than black. But there was a dense, low black shape on the water between the ship and the sunrise, with shining white motes – birds on the wing – swirling above it, catching the light that had not yet penetrated the darkness below.

"Nikumaroro," he whispered.

Mister Maude appeared at the rail, the slender, round-faced *I-Matang* in charge of everything. Everyone listened to Mister Maude, and did as he said. He usually smiled and joked with people; he spoke better than almost any other white man, and was always pleasant with the boys and girls – though sometimes his mind seemed far away. Now he was frowning around his unlit pipe, furrowing his brows.

"Not a sign of human life," he muttered to Mister Stanley, the *Moamoa* 's Engineer, who had just come up from belowdecks and was leaning on the rail beside him. "It hasn't been that long since we left them. Surely....."

"I shouldn't fret," Mister Stanley said with a slight yawn. "It's early morning, and they've no dogs or chickens to wake 'em. We could give 'em a tootle on the whistle."

"Yes, maybe... oh wait, look, off there to the right. Below the passage!"

Mister Stanley, and Keaki, followed Mister Maude's pointing finger. The sun was high enough now to see the trees that crowded the shoreline, the waves lapping quietly on the beach, and closer to them, the streaming edge of the reef. Behind the trees, rising almost straight up in the calm air, a thin column of smoke pierced the sunrise.

Chapter 2

Coming to the Island. 27th April 1939

Moamoa lay just off the reef edge in the lee of the island, her engine turning over slowly to keep her in place. The reef flat, a broad platform of algae-covered coral now under high tide's several feet of water, stretched away a hundred yards to a short, steep beach. Behind that, the island was a rich variegated green – great spreading *buka* trees with their gnarly gray trunks, tangled thickets of the shrub *mao* along the foreshore. To Keaki's left as he scanned the shore, a broad passage cut through to the lagoon. He caught a glimpse of its aquamarine water every time *Moamoa* rode up over a swell.

But the great sight was further left still – further north. The giant broken hulk of a wrecked steamship. She stood upright, on the reef flat north of the passage, her bow almost on the beach, her stern hanging off the reef edge. She looked stricken and helpless, Keaki thought, stuck there where nothing bigger than a canoe should go, with her back broken, the stern falling away at an odd angle, twisted somehow. It made him feel uneasy, bad, like something was out of order.

"You see that ship?" his father asked, unnecessarily since they both were staring at it.

"Yes."

"It is called *Noriti*. It wrecked years ago in a storm. Many died."

"Did any survive, Father?"

"Yes. Your mother's sister's husband – the one that went with that Tuvaluan woman to live in Funafuti – he was on the crew of one of the ships that rescued those men who survived. He said they were very thirsty, and tired, and afraid of the *ai* – the coconut crabs."

"Are the *ai* so big, father, really?"

"Very big. Their bodies are bigger than my head, and their arms, their claws – they go out like this!" Ieiera held his arms out in a big circle. "They're very fast, too, and very strong. But very good eating."

"Are they only on this island?"

"No, no, other islands too, but not so many. Very few on Temeroa. All eaten up. On this island they've lived all alone for years and years – nobody to eat them but each other, so they've gotten very numerous, and very big. Or so it's said."

"How do you catch them?"

"Come up behind them, slowly, cautiously, and grab them by the – the shoulders, you know, where the arms meet the shell. Tie them up with cord. But look out for the claws, or they'll eat you!"

Keaki gazed at the shore with its thick, dark green trees, and tried to imagine crabs big enough to eat him. Could they get into a house? Would he wake up some night and find a foot gone?

How would you stop an animal like that? Nobody seemed worried, so there must be ways.

"Once we get settled, son, we'll go hunting crabs together – make sure you know how to catch them without being caught yourself. But look, here comes a canoe. Ha-ha, there's old Kimo!"

Jack Kimo Petro, a friend of Ieiera's even though he was from the Ellice Islands, and a great man. Kimo's grandfather was *I Matang*, a sailor shipwrecked in Tuvalu from someplace called *Bortigall*, but his grandmother was from Funafuti. Mister Kimo was known throughout the Gilberts and the Ellices because he could make anything, build anything, make anything work. Houses, roads, wells, breakwaters, piers, outhouses. He could use dynamite and operate cement mixers, desalination plants and electric generators. In Fiji, it was said, he sometimes drove a *kaᵎ*. There was nothing that Mister Kimo couldn't do. That's why he was the commissioner's public works officer, and why Mister Maude had sent him here. Now his wife and sons were coming to join him, too; the boys were leaning over the rail, hollering to their father in Tuvaluan, the language of the Ellices. Down in the canoe, Mister Kimo spread his arms wide, as though to embrace them across the water. He stood on the canoe's midships platform while his two grinning companions paddled strongly. He wore short pants, and a brass chain around his neck. He was built like the trunk of a *buka* tree – broad and solid, firmly attached to whatever he stood on, in control, in command. He said something to the paddlers and they brought the canoe smartly alongside, grabbing the rail and the friendly hands thrust over it. Mister Kimo bounded aboard, grinning from ear to ear.

"*Tautata, tautata!* Welcome, welcome to Nikumaroro!" he bowed to the crowd and laughed. "What are you all standing around for, like coral heads? Get your things, lower the boat, come ashore!" He gestured at the lifeboat hanging on its davits. "That boat can take six on the first travel to shore, as long as you're not carrying cows!" His boys came running down the deck and he embraced them both – Edwin on one side, John on the other.

Mister Maude came down the ladder from *Moamoa*'s bridge, smiling broadly. "Jack Kimo!" he said in English, extending his hand. "It's good to see you! Is everything all right on shore, then?"

"Mister Harry!" Mister Kimo shouted, with a smile to match Mister Maude's. "Yes, all's well. We're all alive, and there's plenty of water now!" He laughed again, a booming laugh. "We just had to dig in the right place!"

"We saw the smoke. Are you camped below the passage then?"

"Yes, yes. Come ashore and see. Not camped. We've built our great capital city! Next to our fine flowing well!"

It took many trips with the *Moamoa*'s whaleboat and several canoes to get everyone and everything ashore – all forty-eight people who were to stay on Nikumaroro, their canoes, their clothes, tools, living things, food. Five thousand seed coconuts, many bales of palm thatch for houses, lumber, bags of cement, sheets of metal and some light coloured stuff Mister Maude called "*asapestos*." Some of the people going on to Orona and Manra came ashore too, just to look around. There were over a hundred of them on the ship, and Mister Maude sternly ordered them to stay there, out of the way, but some came along anyway. Soon the beach was crowded with people and things.

Keaki and Baiteke went ashore on the boat's fourth trip, with their families. Mister Maude and Mister Kimo had gone on the first boat, and walked back into the forest. Baiteke's father Takena, a big, burly man who had greeted his family with hugs and uproarious laughter, handled the tiller now, calling to the rowers to back their oars as they approached the reef. They held position as swells passed under them, while Takena watched for the big one – usually the sixth or seventh in series – to rise up behind them. As the boat lifted on its back he shouted *aibai!* – "pull!" – and the rowers dug in with their oars. The whaleboat shot ahead, rode the wave over a low spot in the reef, bumped a few times on the coral, and slid into the natural channel along the shore. Keaki and Baiteke went with the others over the side into the water, and helped drag the boat ashore amid shouts and laughter.

Ieiera was among the first on the beach. He knelt there in the wet sand, said a short, silent prayer, and then patted the sand. Facing the island, he brought his sand-covered hand up and patted the sand onto his cheeks. All the other new arrivals followed suit. Keaki felt strange; it was the first time he had arrived on a new island and put sand on his cheeks, so the spirits when they smelled him would know he was of that place, and be kind to him. He wondered what would happen if a spirit smelled his shoulder instead, or his stomach. He rubbed some sand on his stomach, just in case.

The island seemed very different from Temeroa. There you could see from the beach straight into the village, where the thatched houses stood in neat rows under the palms. Here there were almost no palms, and the *buka* forest began just behind the fringe of low brush and small trees – *mao* and *ren*. It was dark, dense, and the gray trunks of the trees seemed to float in the darkness like ghosts. Nei Manganibuka's trees, Keaki reminded himself, and wasn't sure whether that made him feel good or a little scared.

The boys stayed on the beach as the boat returned to the ship for another load and then another. Every time it returned to the beach, riding the high wave over the reef edge while everyone shouted and laughed, they helped drag it up on the beach and unload it. A man of the working party – obviously a friend of Takena's to judge from the jokes they traded – pretended to supervise, but the women really took charge. Soon the beach was studded with piles of goods – one for each family, and separate piles for the village and government.

Teng Beiaruru and his family were on the last boat. The boys raced each other to grab the boat's gunwales and drag it ashore, shouting. Era, Teng Beiaruru's ten-year-old daughter, smiled at them from the bow and they worked harder, shouted louder. Why were they acting this way, Keaki wondered to himself, but kept doing it.

They held the boat steady while Teng Beiaruru eased his old limbs over the side and down to the beach, where he promptly slapped great handsful of sand on his cheeks and murmured something that Keaki was sure was addressed to Nei Manganibuka or one of the other *anti*. He and Era, who had joined him on the sand, took bundles of their goods from Era's mother Teaneue – a pretty young woman who didn't seem much older, really, than Baranika, Teng Beiaruru's teenaged granddaughter. Baranika's mother and grandmother must not have come along, Keaki guessed, or maybe they had died. Since the family had lived on Rotima, on Onotoa atoll, who could say?

But now, he thought, we're all part of the same village. It made him feel a little strange, to think that of himself and Era.

Who was now helping Kimai out of the boat, with little Ratimiti, just two years old. The big man supervising the unloading brightened, and Keaki realized that he must be Kirata. He had heard Kimai telling his mother – many times – about her husband, and how much she missed him. Kirata looked happy but not sure what to do, until Ratimiti yelled *"Baba!"* and held out his arms. With a whoop Kirata swept him up and tossed him into the sky, caught him, roaring with laughter.

"Quickly, my son! Sand on the cheeks! Let the *anti* know you're one of us! You too, Kimai, my love! Then I'll show you the palace I've built for you!"

Mister Maude and Mister Kimo came out of the bush onto the beach. Kirata turned to Mister Maude to report everyone ashore.

"Good, good, Teng Kirata. Very well done indeed. But is everyone aboard who should be?"

Kirata laughed. "Yes, Mister Mauta. I had to drive them like chickens, but they're back on board. I'd better take you there quick before they sneak back ashore."

"Can't have that." He turned to the stately older man who had just come out of the bush holding Little Koata by the hand. "Mister Magistrate, are the returnees ready?"

So this was the famous Teng Koata, Keaki thought. The magistrate, the boss.

"Yes, Mister Mauta, more than ready, I think. Here they come."

"Who are those guys?" Baiteke whispered as five men came down the beach, carrying bags that Keaki guessed contained their clothes. Their eyes were downcast, and no one said anything to them.

"The Arorae men," Keaki whispered back. "The ones who don't like it here." Why had they not liked it, he wondered – not for the first time. Was there something about this island that was hostile to people from his home atoll? True, none of them were from Temeroa, or directly related to his family, but still...

Five men from Arorae, half the original working party, who had, his father said, just "not liked it," and were going home. This was what made it possible for Ieiera and the others to come, with their families, along with those of the remaining workers.

Whatever their problem had been, Keaki thought, it wasn't *his* problem.

"We're the first real settlers," Keaki thought, with a burst of pride. He felt the sand drying on his cheeks and stomach.

"Come on, *anti,*" he thought; "come smell a man of Nikumaroro."

"Hey, dogshit, why are you grinning like that?" Baiteke asked.

Chapter 3

U.S.S. Swan: 28th April 1939

"The Limey's got no shoes!" It was Williams, at the gig's tiller. Greenslade glared at him over his shoulder.

"Pipe down, Williams, you wanta cause an international incident?"

"Aye-aye, Sir – er, no, Sir."

"Looks snappy enough otherwise," Griffin murmured.

"The coral must be hell on shoes."

The British officer was dressed in tropical khaki slacks and a white shirt, head protected by a pith helmet. And his feet wrapped in rags. Neatly wrapped, Geeenslade observed. He was standing on the coral shelf next to the little beach that apparently served as Sydney Island's boat landing – to judge from the whaleboat and several canoes pulled ashore there. Behind him was a large thatched building without walls – the copra drying shed, Greenslade knew – and around him, a cluster of native men in shorts, women in colorful mu-mus or grass skirts, and children in shorts or nothing at all. Behind and all around this tableau, the island presented its riches of white sand and coral, green brush, swaying coconut palms, and the deepest of blue skies. The gig crunched on the coral sand and the island men swarmed out to steady it and pull it farther up the beach. Greenslade and Griffin clambered over the bow.

The Britisher put out his hand. "Welcome to Sydney, Leftenant."

A firm handshake, callused hand; Greenslade thought approvingly. "Thank you, Mr. – Maude?"

"Ah, my apologies. Mr. Maude is away; I'm his deputy. Gerald Gallagher, Deputy Administrator, Phoenix Islands Settlement Scheme."

Greenslade matched his formality. "Lieutenant John Greenslade, Sir, commanding U.S.S. *Swan*. And my Executive Officer, Lieutenant J.G. Tom Griffin."

"Very good to meet you both; will you walk this way? We can get out of the sun. Your coxswain's welcome to come ashore, of course."

"Thanks. Williams, find a place out of the sun and wait for us."

Williams saluted – a bit sloppy, Greenslade thought – and set about securing the gig. The officers walked up the steeply sloping coral gravel beach toward the copra shed. There were a few bags of the dried coconut meat inside, Greenslade saw, and nearby, more cut coconut spread out on thatch mats to dry.

Gallagher cleared his throat. "We – were quite surprised when your aeroplane flew over this morning."

It was Greenslade's turn to be surprised. "I'm sorry we startled you. Weren't you advised we were coming?"

"I'm afraid not. We've been having a touch of trouble with our wireless; it's possible – likely, even – that a message was lost. You contacted Ocean Island, then?"

They were coming into what was apparently the colonial village – neatly laid-out thatched houses along broad graveled streets lined with coral slabs. Gallagher led them toward a somewhat larger building with verandas and a peaked roof of coconut thatch. Greenslade struggled to recall exactly what he had been told about the message traffic.

"Pacific Fleet did – telegrams to the – Resident Commissioner, right? Gilbert and Ellice Islands Colony."

"Quite so. I'm sure it's all right. We're a bit isolated here, and often enough don't – well, we're just getting established, so protocols aren't entirely set. In any event, it was a great relief when your ships appeared flying the Stars and Strips rather than Swastikas."

"Well, I am sorry, truly...."

"No harm done. The natives were – well, entranced. Most've never seen an aeroplane, or an automobile for that matter. They were quite fascinated when your pair flew over. Taking aerial photographs, I fancy?"

"That's right, sir. We're on a photoreconnaissance mission, shooting all the islands of the Phoenix group for mapping purposes. Which will be shared with your government, I'm sure."

They mounted the steps to the veranda of the peaked-roofed house, and Gallagher spoke in the native language to a tall, slender youth standing in the shadows within. He motioned them to be seated on hand-crafted wood and coconut-thatch chairs, and the boy brought glasses of water.

"Heaven knows improved charts will be welcome. The existing ones date from the last century, most of them. Frightfully inaccurate. You'll photograph all the Phoenix Islands, then?"

"The main ones – Canton and Enderbury, which we've done. Hull next, then Gardner."

"You're finished here at Sydney, then?" The boy appeared next to Greenslade with cups of tea and a pot on a tray.

"We think so, yes – thank you, son. The darkroom's on our other ship – the *Pelican* – and our photography guys are busy there right now. They're pretty sure we've gotten a good sequence for a photomosaic, though, and if that's so then we'll be ready to move on. But we won't know for sure till after our evening meal, so we'll be here at least that long. We'd be honored if you'd join us."

"Why, thank you. I'd be delighted. The ladies of the village make fine food, but a change would be most welcome. May I contribute something?"

"No, no, it's our treat, though I can't guarantee how much of a treat it'll be. Plain sailor's chow, is all."

"It'll be different, and that will be a blessing. I'll bring coconuts, though; we've plenty of coconuts."

Gallagher's canoe bumped the *Swan's* landing stage promptly at 1800, and he ascended the short ladder with remarkable ease considering his rag-wrapped feet. Shows no embarrassment, Greenslade thought; that's class. But why no shoes? Dunham's boatswain's pipe squealed as the administrator reached the deck. Gallagher briskly saluted the ensign where it hung limply on the fantail. Greenslade strode forward and offered him his hand. A smiling islander in the canoe was handing up a bag woven of pandanus, full of coconuts.

After a brief tour of the ship, the officers and Gallagher squeezed into the small wardroom and took places around the table – like the seats, bolted to the deck. Ramon, the *Swan's* one and only steward and cook's helper, had dressed the table as well as the little ship's supplies allowed; at least there was a white tablecloth and napkins. With elaborate courtesy, he began to serve the cook's freshly-baked rolls.

Gallagher bowed his head and began to murmur a prayer; at a glance from Greenslade, the officers self-consciously followed suit, more or less. Greenslade noticed that Gallagher crossed himself when he finished. Catholic; why did that seem strange in a British colonial officer? Irish name, after all. Maybe that was what seemed strange, an Irishman in the British colonial service.

"A very handsome ship, Captain," Gallagher offered, with a grateful look at Ramon as he brought out the roast beef.

"She can turn fourteen knots in calm water, and she's pretty steady in heavy weather for a ship her size. Damn good ship for these survey cruises, but I wouldn't want to take her into a fight with anything much bigger than a canoe."

"Have you been in these waters before, Captain?"

"No, I only took command at the beginning of this cruise, up in Hawaii. The *Swan's* been here before, though."

"Has she, though?"

"Yes – well, in the neighborhood. She was part of the search for that woman pilot, Amelia Earhart. Do you – er – know who I'm talking about?"

"Oh yes. Actually I quite admired Miss Earhart – or should I say Mrs. Putnam? I'm a bit of a pilot myself, and was quite interested in the press when she flew the Atlantic. Landed on the farm of a fellow named Gallagher, but no relation, I'm sorry to say."

"You don't say? Well, anyhow, the *Swan* sailed into the Gilberts and around Howland looking for her. None of us were aboard then, though."

"Dunham was, Sir," Hull piped up. Hamilton Hull was an aviation cadet, an enthusiastic kid. "He was telling me about it just the other day. The most boring deployment ever, he said."

"Oh, the Bos'n. Yeah, Hull, I meant none of the officers."

"What do you suppose happened to her, Captain?" Gallagher asked.

"Couldn't find the island ran out of gas, into the drink. What else?"

"I left England just as the search was winding down, so what I know of it is mostly anecdotal – our chaps did what they could to help, and that's the odd thing. Nothing drifted up in the Gilberts – no bodies, no life preservers, no fragments. And usually the current brings all manner of things to the beaches."

"It's a big ocean and a little plane. So you're a flyer, Mr. Gallagher?"

"Yes, haven't got to do it much, but obtained my license back in England."

"How long you been out here?"

"In the Pacific, since August of '37. On Sydney, since last December."

"Since December?" Hull squeaked. "All by yourself?"

"Well, hardly. We've over 260 souls on the island, all told. But yes, as white men are concerned, quite alone."

"Without shoes all that time?" Hull blurted out. Greenslade glared at him, but Gallagher laughed.

"No, no, my shoes wore out only about two weeks ago. My fault entirely – underestimated what the coral would do, and brought too few pair. And I'm hard to fit, unfortunately. Size thirteen foot."

Greenslade turned to Griffin. "Tom, let's see if we can help Mr. Gallagher out of ship's stores before we weigh."

"Yes Sir. It may be a stretch, though – so to speak. British size thirteen is our size – um..."

Gallagher waved his hand dismissively. "Fourteen, I believe. Much appreciated, Captain, Leftenant, truly, but I've actually got quite accustomed to my rag footwear. There are certain advantages, when you're constantly getting your feet wet."

"Still," Griffin said, "I'll check with the Quartermaster. But Mr. Gallagher, if you don't mind telling us – I'm really in the dark about your work here. Can you fill us in?"

Gallagher sat back and wiped his mouth with his napkin, cleared his throat.

"Well, despite what some in your government may think, Mr. Griffin, the Phoenix Islands Settlement Scheme isn't an effort to deny any U.S. rights in the Central Pacific – though of course, we're quite firm that His Majesty's jurisdiction over the area is thoroughly grounded in law."

"Luckily for us," Greenslade smiled, "that's for our governments to sort out."

"Quite. In any case, the PISS – Mr. Maude is ever so proud of that acronym, by the way – the PISS was Harry Maude's brainchild. A brilliant man, and very witty conversationalist. Wish he were here; he has the most astounding knowledge of the people... In any event, Mr. Maude is the Senior Lands Commissioner, you know, and in that capacity is keenly aware of the land hunger that's growing in the Southern Gilberts and Ellices."

"Land hunger?"

"Correct. Before 1892 — that is, before His Majesty undertook jurisdiction at the request of the kings of the various islands, there was quite endemic warfare in the Gilberts – and to a lesser degree in the Ellices."

"Which are the two island groups...." Griffin began.

"...that make up the colony. Quite – plus Ocean Island off to the west, where the Resident Commissioner is headquartered, and the Line Islands east of here, and the Phoenixes. Only the Gilberts and Ellices are permanently inhabited, apart from Ocean, which is rather another matter. The Gilbertese are Micronesian, the Ellices Polynesian – somewhat different racial stock, languages, and cultures, different histories, dispositions...."

"And Ocean?" Greenslade wanted to know.

"An isolated raised coral island – not an atoll like most in the Gilberts and Ellices. Natives are Banabans – essentially Gilbertese but... Anyway, it's rich in phosphates – bird guano, you know? So it's the colony's prime economic asset. The Germans would love to have it, I fear."

"Or the Japs."

"Too busy in Manchuria, I think – or at least hope. Though they're quite active up in the Marshalls, we hear.

"See anything of them down here?"

"The occasional fishing boat. And their trading company has representatives at Tarawa in the Gilberts and on a few other islands. They're good enough neighbors. If secretive. Perhaps just quiet."

They had finished the beef, and Ramon began clearing off and serving coffee. Gallagher was effusive in his praise for the meal.

"I'll pass that on to Frenchy, our – er – chef," Greenslade smiled. "He gets few enough compliments from the crew. But you were explaining land hunger."

"Oh my, yes. Well, indigenous warfare, for all its horrors, kept the population in check – together with disease, losses at sea, and unfortunately some infanticide and abortion. But since we've been here, population has increased quite dramatically, and on some islands land's got very scarce. Hence land hunger."

"Oh. Of course." Greenslade was from Nebraska, where there was no land hunger, but the Highland clearances had sent his great grandparents over from Scotland, and stories persisted in his family folklore.

"So, Harry's – Mr. Maude's – inspiration was to establish agricultural colonies here – copra plantations – on the uninhabited but habitable islands of the Phoenix, and give people on the land hungry islands of the Gilberts and Ellices the opportunity to emigrate.

"Makes sense if the agriculture is productive enough."

"That's the big question, together with the social and cultural issues of bringing people from different islands together and creating new governance systems. Coconuts grow tolerably well on Hull and Sydney, and we think they'll do even better on Gardner once we have it cleared and planted. We've established island governments on Hull and Sydney, and have pretty full complements of people living on them, busy planting. Even starting to harvest and cut copra."

"And Gardner? "

"Very few coconuts on Gardner at present – just a few groves planted by Arundel – a businessman hereabouts – back in the 1890s. But the land where the *buka* forest grows – that big oak-like tree – we think that land is good for coconut, and there's lots of *buka* on Niku – Gardner. So we've some dozen men there now, clearing and planting. More men and their families should be en route, with Mr. Maude."

"White man in charge there?"

"No, we're very keen on native administration. A chap named Koata is the Native Magistrate, from Onotoa in the Gilberts. Roman Catholic, very disciplined. Our Public Works Officer is there right now, too – Jack Kimo Petro. Half Tuvaluan – Ellice Islander, that is – and half Portuguese. Very skilled builder, mechanic. We've had trouble developing water on Gardner, so Jack's there to help in the search, and to keep the distilling units up to snuff."

Hull looked puzzled. "What do you mean, developing water, Sir?"

"You have to dig for it. Most coral islands have fresh water, but down in the rocks, you know? No springs, no rivulets."

"The fresh water lens," Griffin said knowingly. "I've read about it. Rides on top of the salt."

"Right. It's rainwater that percolates down through the coral, and since the salt water that percolates in from the sea is heavier...."

"So you just dig." It clearly didn't seem so hard to Hull.

"Not so easy, though. The lens isn't continuous, so you have to find the right place, then dig – sometimes a couple of meters."

"Through rock?"

"Rather loosely consolidated rock, luckily. But nonetheless, quite an enterprise. They've had a devil of a time on Niku – Gardner. Hence the distillery, and when we get the cement we'll build cisterns to catch rainwater."

"Plenty of that, I suppose," said Griffin.

"Highly variable, actually. It'll pour like Noah's flood, then go dry for months. Squalls, of course, but nine times out of ten they march right past, out over open ocean."

Greenslade thought about squalls at sea, the way they looked like living things crawling over the ocean on legs of rain. Imagined being on a drought-struck island, watching them go by.

"Incidentally," Gallagher was saying, "the natives have given all the islands their own names, in lieu of their European ones – which all derive from whaling captains that no native ever met, or if they did they wished they hadn't. So Sydney is become Manra to them, named for one of their legendary homelands. Hull is Orona – actually named by some Nieue Islanders who were doing plantation work there when we arrived. And Gardner's Nikumaroro. You'll hear them refer to it if you meet up with the working party.

"What's Niku – Nikumoro mean?"

"Nikumaroro – in myth, a mysterious island with many *buka* trees. Home of Nei Manganibuka, a legendary ancestor ghost."

"So Gardner's haunted?

Gallagher laughed. "To the Gilbertese, Captain, all islands are haunted."

Chapter 4–

On Nikumaroro: 30 April 1939

Keaki peered right and left as he staggered along the path from the landing, laden with a huge roll of sleeping mats. What colour were these crabs, anyhow? And how aggressive were they? Did they lurk along the path waiting for unsuspecting travelers?

Soon the path broadened, with the *buka* cleared on each side. Piles of ash and charred wood showed where the cut trees had been burnt, and in the clear areas, seed coconuts were sprouting in neat rows. So different from the broad open spaces of Temeroa, but Keaki decided he liked it. It was a place of adventure, of discovery. A place to be made, to be built, where anything could happen, anything was possible.

The village, when they reached it, was tiny – just a single line of thatched houses facing the beach near the mouth of the lagoon passage. Keaki gratefully dumped his roll of mats in front of a house near the northern end of the line, assigned to his family by Teng Koata. Such a dignified old man. He must have been happy to see his wife, Nei Aana, but neither of them said anything about it. They had greeted each other gravely on the beach, where she had patted sand on her face with the others and stood for a long time in silence, gazing into the trees. He had spoken quietly with her, for just a moment, and gravely greeted his grandson, the six-year old everyone called Little Koata. Then he had turned to organizing the families to carry their gear to the village.

No one had moved far from the landing, however, until Jack Kimo and the rowers returned from taking Mister Maude and the returnees to the ship, and *Moamoa* spouted black smoke and blew a long blast on her whistle. The ship had seemed so stately, Keaki remembered, turning slowly to the north along the island's lee shore, blowing another blast while everyone aboard waved and shouted. She gathered way and passed out of sight behind the bulk of the *Noriti*. Orona, her next stop, was away somewhere to the east, and she was wasting no time making for it.

Everyone had looked at one another then, probably all thinking what Keaki was thinking; they were alone with the island. Whatever happened now would be their own doing.

"Well," Jack Kimo had said, with satisfaction, "shall we...." He seemed about to pick up a parcel and lead the way up the beach, but a look and a wave of the hand from Koata stopped him. It was the magistrate who led the way to the village, with Nei Aana and Little Koata a step or two behind him, hand in hand. It still seemed strange to Keaki, thinking back on it, how silent Mister Kimo had become, and how silent Teng Koata was. How silent they all were, as they passed along the path through the *bukas.*

But now that they had reached the village everyone's spirits had revived. The men of the working party showed off the houses they had built, especially to their wives. Wives and other new arrivals extolled the fine workmanship the houses displayed – though, Keaki thought, they were really quite ordinary houses – and the beauty of the setting. White terns – *kiakias* – swooped and glided overhead, and the fins of small sharks rippled the water of the lagoon, out beyond the newly constructed pier with the outhouse on its end. Everyone admired the well, and the men drew up a bucket of water for everyone to taste.

"Aack..." Keaki gagged; the water tasted salty, brackish. His father touched his arm.

"Shhh," he whispered, and turned to Mister Kimo.

"Excellent water," he said.

"It's a little brackish; it comes and goes, and you get used to it. May give you the runs for awhile."

"Water is different on every island."

"You've no idea how hard we all worked to find a place where the water was any good at all."

"Mister Mauta told us about how hard it was."

"Ah," Mister Kimo laughed. "Those magic *I-Matang!* He knows how hard it was, and he wasn't even here! Let me tell you...."

The men retold the story around the fire that night on the lagoon beach, and on many evenings thereafter. The great search for water; if it had not been successful, Nikumaroro would not have been a good place, even a possible place, to live. And the men all might have been dead when *Moamoa* arrived, rather than healthy and vigorous. It had been a great accomplishment, finding the water, and the men never tired of telling about it, and adding verses to the song they were composing about it.

"It really is awful water," Baiteke whispered to Keaki, as the singing voices rose and fell.

"Like chicken shit! Especially compared to back home – back on Arorae. They say our water there is some of the best."

"Well, we'll drink it till the cistern is built, or dry up. Of course, there's always *karewe.*" Baiteke very much liked *karewe* – toddy – the beverage made from the sap of coconut palms. Keaki was indifferent about fresh toddy, and didn't much like the fermented, "sour" version of the drink.

"Hard to make without coconut trees."

"Hey, Teng Scholar, you're right! What a brilliant..."

"Have you seen any?"

"A few, over near the lagoon."

"Right. Exactly ten. That's one grove. The other's up across the channel, on that Nutiran place. A couple of dozen trees, my father says. Mister Kimo told him"

And that, of course, was one of the things that made this island feel so strange. Almost no coconut trees – just the ones planted long ago by those Nieue Island people.

Baiteke looked stricken. "Crab shit! No toddy?"

"Not till we get some trees growing. Have you seen any of those crabs?"

"No. My dad says there were lots here when they first came, but they ate them all. He says there are more across the channel, and down to the south away from where they've cleared."

"I wonder what they're like."

"Tasty, is what I hear. But I just hope Mister Kimo doesn't waste any time building that cistern. I'm going to get really thirsty."

Mister Kimo didn't waste any time, and neither did Teng Koata. The next morning they organized the men and boys into working parties to haul the building material that *Moamoa* had brought. Lumber, corrugated metal and *asapestos,* and bag after bag of cement. Keaki and Baiteke had never worked so hard – none of the boys had. They carried big pieces of lumber between them, staggering under the weight, trying to keep up with the men who marched along with bags of cement on their shoulders. Pick up at the landing, stagger the half-mile to the site where the cistern would be built, drop their load, march back to the landing for another. And nothing to drink but the brackish water, or the flat, strange-tasting stuff from the condenser that Mister Kimo kept running.

"I'm going to die," Baiteke groaned, flat on his back on the rocky beach. Koata had called a midmorning halt to the work, a half-hour of rest.

"Me first," Keaki murmured, shielding his face with his arm from the brilliant sun. "You think we're half done?

"Quarter. Maybe."

Baiteke started to groan again, but Keaki sat up suddenly, punching him in the arm to be quiet.

"What's that?"

"That what? Oh, that noise?"

The men were getting up and hurrying out from under the trees, look-ing round. There was a buzzing in the air, like some great insect. Keaki imagined some gigantic, vengeful dragonfly, sent by Nei Manganibuka.....

And there it was! Right over the treetops, going so fast, roaring and whining.

"Shit!" the boys whispered in unison, and ran for the shelter of the *mao*.

The men were shouting: *wanikiba!* – canoe that flies! – and as a second one of the things whished overhead, Keaki saw that it really was a built thing, not an animal. Something made of sticks and – was it cloth? Metal? With something in front that seemed to be stirring up the air, making a strange fuzzy hole in it. Four big wings, a rounded tail, and men in it! Looking down at them. What sort of men, he wondered, wildly, and where did they come from? Keaki found that he couldn't speak, realized he was whimpering, and that he was wet between his legs. He wanted to bury himself in the sand, but he wanted to look, too. What <u>were</u> these things?

"Aeroplanes!" Mister Kimo shouted, and waved at the things. "R.A.F!" The words meant nothing to Keaki. Most of the men were cowering under trees and bushes, but Mister Kimo and Koata stood out on the beach – Mister Kimo waving and calling, Teng Koata standing tall and dignified, silent.

The *wanikiba* passed out of sight toward the southeast, but before long they were back, much higher now, seeming to go more slowly. By this time Teng Koata had called everyone out from their hiding places.

"Those are aeroplanes," he said sternly. "*I-Matang* machines in which people can fly. They probably belong to the King, and come from a ship which will shortly make its appearance. We will post a watch and prepare to welcome the ship."

Abera interjected: "Why didn't Mister Mauta tell us about this ship? These... aero... aero..."

"He must not have known. When we first came, there were other people here he didn't know about. He doesn't know everything."

Teng Bueke, standing nearby, tore his eyes from the sky to look hard at Teng Koata. "Other people, Teng Koata?"

"*Kain Nutiran,*" Koata murmured, as much to himself as to Bueke.

"Navy men, from New Zealand," Mister Kimo explained. "They were living up there on the land you Tungaru call Nutiran. That's why you call it that."

"Maybe they've come back," Teng Koata speculated. "They said they were looking for a place to land aeroplanes."

"Perhaps so," Kimo nodded. "Or perhaps...."

Everything paused. Everyone looked at him. Koata broke the silence.

"Yes, Mister Public Works Officer? Perhaps what?"

"Mister Magistrate, my first thought was that they were Royal Air Force aeroplanes, but now that I consider... What if they're – you know – German?"

Koata stood stock still, looking at Kimo. Raised his hand to his ear, pulled on it. Muttered.

"*Kain* Germany. Oh....."

Keaki was thoroughly confused. He understood *kain Nutiran* – people from that island called New Zealand – but here? Why? Something about sky canoes landing? And who were *kain* Germany – people of Germany?

Whoever they were, the thought that they might be flying the sky canoes made Teng Koata stand silent on the beach, pulling on his ear. Then he turned abruptly to Kirata, standing nearby with his mouth open.

"Teng Kirata! Please close your mouth and go cut a long stick – longest you can find – long enough to be a flagstaff."

Kirata snapped to life. "Yes, Mister Magistrate!" He grabbed his bushknife and ran off.

"Where are the administrative supplies!"

Mister Kimo grinned lopsidedly. "Ah. Very good, Mister Magistrate. Over there under that *ren,* I think. He picked up his own knife and strode to the wooden crate, pried it open, began rummaging inside. Kirata came back with a long pole – a *kanawa* trunk – just as Mister Kimo produced a small Union Jack.

"Fix it in the sand there," Koata told Mister Kimo. He gestured for the others to gather round. Faced them with his back to the sea. Mister Kimo and Teng Kirata were tying the flag to the end of the pole, digging the other end into the beach, piling rocks around to hold it erect.

"Listen!" Koata hissed fiercely. "There are big things going on in the world that we in the government know about. Usually they have no effect on us here, but sometimes they can. We must be prepared, and do the right thing."

Everyone looked at him dumfounded. Baiteke leaned over to whisper to Keaki: "What the shit is he talking about?"

"Where His Majesty the King lives..." Koata started to explain. Stopped, started again.

"There are many countries in the world. Great Britain, Australia, Tonga. On the other side of the world where His Majesty lives, besides his nation... our nation, Great Britain, there is another country called Germany. That country has a king ..."

"Called Hitler," Mister Kimo called out from the base of the flagstaff.

"Called Hitler, who has lots of soldiers and warships with guns and other weapons, and wants to conquer other people. Many of the *I-Matang* – our *I-Matang* on Ocean Island and Tarawa and Beru, and even in Fiji, think he may start a war, at any moment, and he may decide to attack His Majesty."

Keaki felt weak in his knees. Attack His Majesty the King? Attack *Engiran?* With guns?

"If war comes," Koata continued, "it could happen here as well as ... there. And it could start without our knowing it."

"Could have already started," Mister Kimo said, slapping the sand from his hands. The jack cracked in the wind behind him.

"So those sky canoes," Teng Koata was saying, "could be from a Germany ship, which could be coming here...."

"It just came," Mister Kimo said, nodding toward the north.

Chapter 5 –

The Sky Canoes. 30th April 1939

The ship was just coming into sight, rounding the hulk of the *Noriti*. A steamship, longer and lower than the *Moamoa*. A pointed thing – a gun, Keaki realized with a start, a huge gun, bigger than a man – on the bow. And there was another ship, a little smaller. Both gray, serious looking. Men were walking around on the decks, perching like big birds in the rigging. Keaki felt a shrinking in his chest, like he wanted to draw into himself and hide.

Koata whipped back round to face the people.

"If they land and are polite, we will be polite; we will welcome them in the name of His Majesty." Several men nodded vigorously.

"Maybe they just want food," Kirata offered lamely. Teng Babera snorted and spat into the sand. Koata looked from one to another, sharp-faced.

"But if they attack us, we will defend our island."

"How?" someone blurted out.

Koata stood for a moment with his mouth open, but was spared the need to respond. Mister Kimo let out a whoop.

"They're not Germans!"

Koata shaded his eyes with his hand, peered at the ships. "What are they?"

The lead ship was turning, and its flag stood out straight. The same colours as those on the Union flag, but arranged in stripes with a blue square in one corner.

"Kain Ameriki," Jack Kimo said. "United States."

Koata stroked his chin. "Indeed," he agreed. "And that may not be good."

Keaki was tired of being confused. What did "Ameriki" mean? It must be like "Germany," but different somehow. But not good – so, another enemy? Or what?

"Look at the flag." Baiteke pointed to the lead ship. "What a dumb flag. All the stripes run in the same direction."

"Who are they?" Keaki asked, glad to have someone to question even if he wasn't likely to believe the answer.

"

Kain Ameriki – they're from another island," Baiteke said authoritatively. "Big island, like Australia, but not under the King. I learned about it in school."

"Are they with that – that Germany?"

"I guess so. Kimo and Koata don't seem very happy."

Mister Kimo and Teng Koata were standing side by side on the beach, looking fixedly at the ships. Across the water everyone could hear the sound of a bos'ns pipe and some kind of voice from the lead ship, and then the rattle of the anchor chain. Mister Kimo chuckled.

"That'll slow them down."

Koata stroked his chin. "They don't know there's no anchorage. Maybe they won't come ashore."

"Mister Magistrate, I request your permission to visit them, before they visit us."

"No, Mister Petro. I am the magistrate; I shall go."

"But think, Mister Magistrate; you're needed here, and – with respect – my English is better."

Koata was silent, watching the lead ship, which had come about and was steaming back toward the north just outside the reef, with a leadsman in the bow looking for bottom. Mister Kimo went on.

"And I know machinery. I can see what they've got, report back."

"If they let you come back."

"Mister Mauta says they want these islands, but they don't want us. No reason for them to keep me. Besides, I met Ameriki sailors on Kirimati. They were good fellows."

Koata was silent; Mister Kimo pressed his case.

"They're not with the Germans. I heard they may join our side. Mister Gallagher said..."

Koata held up his hand. "Very well, Mister Petro. Take two men and my canoe. Be back inside three hours."

Mister Kimo grinned and put his hand to his forehead. "Very good, sir. Inside three hours." Gesturing at Kirata and Bueke, he sprinted toward Koata's canoe; the other men whooped and followed.

As the canoe shot over the reef edge in a sheet of spray, Teng Koata tried to get people organized and back to work. But it was hard – as much for him as for the others. They all stopped to watch Kimo and the others pull alongside the lead ship, and climb over the rail. It appeared that the sailors greeted them in a friendly way – at least they didn't shoot them.

Then the sky canoes came back! Came in low over the *Noriti* and landed on the water! Soon they were being lifted by the ships, using big cargo booms like the ones on the *Moamoa,* and taken aboard.

"Like lifeboats!" Baiteke shouted. "Just like lifeboats! They really are flying canoes!"

It was mid-afternoon when Jack Kimo and the other men returned, and as they crossed the reef the American ships blew their whistles, puffed black smoke from their stacks, and got underway. Keaki was a little disappointed; he had wondered what *kain Ameriki* looked like. But if they were enemies..... He marveled at the bravery of the men who had paddled right out there and gone aboard the strange ship.

The women had gotten a big fire laid on the beach, and as it roared to life and the darkness gathered around them, Mister Kimo crossed his arms and told his story, with the other men adding bits and pieces he left out.

"They're all right, the Ameriki. They were at Manra two days ago, and visited Mister Gallagher. Said they gave him some shoes! They're not here to take anything, just flying over the islands to make photographs."

Keaki wondered what "photographs" were, but didn't feel like he could ask. Luckily, Mister Kimo was a thoughtful man, and saw the blank looks on several faces.

"Photographs – you know, pictures, with a machine. You point it at something and 'click!' it makes a perfect—ah – picture, you know, like a drawing or carving – of whatever it is."

"I-Matang," someone said with a shake of the head.

"Mister Bevington has one," said someone else. "He used it to make a picture of us in Beru once."

"Anyway," Kimo went on, "that's what they're doing with the aeroplanes – taking pictures from right overhead, very high – so they can make maps.."

"Government gave them permission," Kirata assured them solemnly.

"What about their guns?" someone asked.

Kimo shrugged. "The ships have guns. They're warships. HMS *Achilles* has much bigger guns."

That must be one of our warships, Keaki thought. Naturally, Mister Kimo would know.

"How was the food?"

"Good! They gave us tinned meat and bread, and canned beans."

"No bones in the meat," Bueke scratched his head. "Funny stuff."

"Not goat?"

"No, thank goodness!"

"Did you see it when the sky canoes landed?"

"Sure! The aeroplanes landed on the smooth water that the ships made by putting themselves crossways to the wind. Very clever! They came down..." Kimo showed with his hands how the sky canoes had swooped down "... and landed so neatly on the water, then motored right up to the side of the ship. And they hooked on the boom, and whoop! Up she went, neatly as you please."

"How do they fly?" Only after he blurted it out did Keaki realize he had spoken. His mother looked at him sternly, but Mister Kimo laughed.

"It's their engines, and propellers, and wings. The engine's round, with its pistons arranged in a circle, and they fire – boom! boom ! boom! — and make the propeller spin very fast. That drags the aeroplane through the air just like the screw drives a ship, except the other way round. It pulls the aeroplane, yes? And they can move parts of the wings to go up, or down, or left, or right – like the rudder on a ship, or .... or the way you can make a canoe go different directions by the way you hold your paddle."

"But they're in the air!" Keaki protested, emboldened by Mister Kimo's attention.

"Yes, yes; you can't see it, but the air's just like the water, only thinner."

Keaki considered that, breathing and thinking about the air that flowed through his nostrils, down into his chest. Like water but thinner? Lots thinner. But Mister Kimo knew these things. What an exciting place to live! He hoped the sky canoes would come back.

Chapter 6–

Water. May 1939

They learned to drink the brackish water, and worked with a will on the cistern. It rained almost every day, but only briefly, so they had plenty of time to build. They put up forms using the lumber that *Moamoa* had brought, and then mixed cement and poured it in the forms, building the walls higher and higher. Mister Kimo and some of the men then cut up the lumber to build the gables and the roof itself, which they covered with sheets of *asapestos* to catch the rain.

There was a big squall just before they finished the roof, but they couldn't catch much of it. The boys stood under the cistern's overhanging eaves with their mouths open, and caught the sweet rain water that flowed so readily off the *asabestos*. The men admired its efficiency; it caught the rain so much better than thatch would. When the rain stopped, the men hung gutters off the eaves to carry water round and in through holes into the building, where they had poured a thick cement floor. They cleaned out all the cement dust, made the inside sparkling clean, and waited. The sky had turned blue and cloudless.

The squall seemed to have drained the heavens. Days passed, and the inside of the cistern remained dry. The well water seemed to get saltier, and it seemed to Keaki that it was farther down in the well than it had been. The few mature coconut palms had been stripped of their nuts; there was no more coconut water. All the old trees had been tapped for their juice, too, dripping into bottles hung under severed flower stalks. They drank some of the juice fresh and fermented some to make toddy. But no one could live on toddy, and the men tended to horde it anyway.

"I don't want to die of thirst," Baiteke whimpered, as they dragged *buka* limbs to the fire. The clearing of the forest had to go on, water or no water. There were thousands of seed coconuts to get into the ground. Of course, they needed water, too, if they were ever going to sprout. And the sky remained cloudless.

They prayed. Teng Koata led the Catholics in prayer, and Teng Babera led the Protestants. They tried to outdo one another with the urgency and sincerity of their prayers. Keaki asked for God's mercy, and wondered it he should ask the old spirits and *anti* as well.

"Might as well," Baiteke shrugged. "It can't hurt."

Maybe he was right, Keaki thought, but he knew that Teng Babera wouldn't approve. There's only one God, the missionary always preached every Sunday – though he had three parts. Jesus was part of him, but the *anti* very definitely were not; Teng Babera made that very, very clear. Maybe it was different for Catholics, since they had the Virgin and all those Saints. Weren't they kind of like *anti?*

Keaki kept his prayers directed to God and Jesus, but they – and the Virgin, the Saints, and even the *anti* must have been busy elsewhere. A week had passed since the cistern was finished, and it was still dry, dry as dust.

Nei Aana began going off by herself in the bush, looking grim. The adults seemed to know why, but they didn't talk about it. They acted like no one was missing at the Catholic prayers, or at meals, but Nei Aana was never there. The boys would see her leaving the village in the early morning, as dawn was creeping up the sky, walking one direction one day, another the next. Sometimes it would be dark night before she returned.

Keaki and Baiteke worked with the other men and boys to clear the *buka* and *mao,* drag the cut branches and tend the fire – oh my it was hot, under the bright, white sun – and plant the seed coconuts, giving each one a little of their precious water. And drinking very little themselves.

"My gut hurts," Baiteke moaned, sitting on a buka log with his legs splayed in front of him, idly tossing twigs at the fire.

Keaki nodded glumly. "Mine, too. When's the last time you made poop?"

"I don't know. Days ago. Nothing comes out but little balls. My aunt used to have an animal that made shit like that. Long ears. Got it from an *I Matang"*

"All black and hard. You could shoot 'em with a sling."

"Kill rats with 'em." Baiteke grinned faintly.

"Feed 'em to fish, and the fish would choke and float to the surface." A week ago they would have been falling off the log by now, shrieking with laughter. Now they smiled vaguely and held their stomachs.

"And then you could knock 'em in the head with your dong."

"Oh, I don't have the energy."

"It'll come back, when you see Era again."

Keaki's face felt even hotter. "Era is... a nice girl. For a girl."

"Ha! You'd prefer an *ai!"*

Keaki was glad to change the subject. "To eat, yeah, if I had something to wash it down with." He had seen his first giant coconut crab two days before, in a buka tree the men were cutting down. As promised, a body bigger than his head, and a long, nasty-looking set of pincers. All dark brown and black, almost purple, and so mean looking. Bueke had grabbed it behind its arms, and Kirata had tied it up with a length of twisted creeper. They had all tasted it around the fire that night, and it would have been delicious if it hadn't been for the water accompanying it. He had seen two more since then and was no longer afraid of them. They never stayed to fight the men who jumped so eagerly to catch them, and they didn't seem interested in sneaking up on anyone.

"Down it goes!" Abera shouted, and the boys jumped up to watch another giant *buka* crash to the ground. The men and boys went silent; the men murmuring words that Keaki knew were meant for Nei Manganibuka. Words of thanks for allowing them to take the tree, of hope that she did not object. Teng Babera stood by himself and was silent, but didn't protest. Keaki wondered about this, but then the men began to chop up the trunk and limbs, and the boys hurried to drag them to the fire.

The women brought their food to them at midday – rice and fish, and a little brackish water. Era brought food to her father, and stayed awhile. Keaki, feeling funny in his guts – was it gas? – stood and watched her. Her long black hair, so shiny, with a shiny *co:m*— a hair comb— holding it back. Teng Beiaruru gestured to the boys to come share his fish; Baiteke punched Keaki lightly on the shoulder.

"How's your dong?"

"I'll beat you to death with it if you don't shut up."

Baiteke giggled; Keaki tried to look adult as they walked over to where Beiaruru and his family sat in the shade of a straggly *mao*. Era smiled at them, and Keaki felt his chest go tight. His dong, too. He had to say something! What could he say?

"That... that's very pretty in your hair, that... *co:m*." Era rewarded him with a smile.

"Thank you. I found it on the reef up by *Noriti* when we were looking for clams – that is, I found the thing it's made from. My father made it into a *co:m*, as you can see."

It was easier to talk now, especially about something someone had found. "Is it clamshell?"

"No, I think it's wood or something. It's very light and thin."

"Well, it's a nice color. Kind of like a shark's skin."

"I think it's like water."

"That... that, too. I wonder what it is.

She laughed – such a happy sound, itself like water, falling off the reef edge and gurgling over the coral. "Well, now it's a *co:m*."

Chapter 7–

Rain – Late May 1939

Night. Cooler, but still so dry. So many stars in the dark, dry sky. Keaki sat in the outhouse at the end of the pier, straining every now and then, but all to no avail, between times looking at the sky through the open thatched doorway. How many stars? How would anyone begin to count them?

What were they, really? He had asked his parents, when he was much younger, and their answers had been vague. He had asked his teacher back on Arorae, and he had said that each one was like the sun. But if that were true, didn't that mean there were thousands and thousands of other worlds? Could that possibly be? Maybe. There were so many other places, so many things he didn't know about, places he'd never been. He felt a rumble in his guts and strained again, but no luck. And yet he felt so ready.

Were the stars really *anti?* His father had said something about that, and Teng Beiaruru had said so, very much as a matter of fact. He had named some of them, the old people and spirits from Samoa and *Matang* and the time when the earth and the sky were as one. What about the ones that flashed through the sky so fast? *Anti* coming to earth? To lurk on the windward side of some island?

Voices.

Someone else wanting to use the outhouse; he'd have to get out. He twisted around to peer through a gap in the thatch, back toward the beach. No one coming along the pier, but still he heard voices. His flesh crawled. *Anti!*

There they were – on the beach next to where the pier connected with the land. Blacker shapes against the blackness. Muttering voices. A splash. Someone was launching a canoe. He felt his bowels churning and was frantic for them to stop. It was no longer time to poop.

Anti don't launch canoes, he told himself, and then wondered why he thought that. He held his stomach, willing his guts not to let go. Had they seen him? Sensed him? How did *anti* sense things?

One of the voices came more loudly, the speaker facing him, facing away from the village, out into the lagoon.

"Go back and pray to your virgin, old man."

Nei Aana's voice. She was wading out alongside the pier, pushing her canoe. A wave of relief flooded over him, and his bowels almost let go. But wait, what was she doing out here in the night, with a canoe?

The mumbling figure splashing along next to her must be Teng Koata. He said something, and Nei Aana's answer was an angry hiss.

"A great deal of good your God has done!"

Another mumble.

"You can die of thirst on your knees, but I won't, and I won't let these people, these children." He could hear Koata now, barely, as they came almost abreast the end of the pier.

"Very well, then I will...."

"You will go back and pray to your Virgin. It's I who has business with her over there."

Nei Aana rolled into the canoe with surprising agility and dug in with the paddle, shooting out through the winding channel toward the open lagoon. Koata stood watching her for awhile, shook his head, turned and walked slowly back to shore.

Keaki's bowels finally let go. First it was hard, then very soft, watery. Beneath the outhouse, little sharks churned the brown water to froth with their tails.

Just before dawn, a great clap of thunder shocked him out of sleep. With the rest of the family he jumped up to see the rain come crashing down, filling the air. Thunder exploded, lightning burned images into his eyes. Images of the trees across the lagoon, shaking wildly in the wind. Images of Mister Kimo, Abera, Kirata, dancing wildly in the rain, turning their faces and hands to the sky. Images of Nei Aana, paddling wearily up to the beach, walking slowly toward her house, her hair and dress soaked, hanging limp.

Chapter 8 –

The Nutiran Reef, Late May 1939

If there was one thing everyone on Nikumaroro could agree on – Catholics and Protestants, from every island, men and women and children – it was that Sunday was a day of rest. A day for church, for singing, for visiting, for relaxing and handicrafts, for rambling and exploring, fishing and catching coconut crabs. The Sunday after the storm felt especially blessed – clear and bright, not too hot, the northeast trade wind gently rustling the trees and rippling the water.

The cistern wasn't full, but it was far from empty. Mister Kimo measured with a stick and said it contained 3,000 gallons – over a quarter of its capacity. Everyone drank the sweet, clean water, but sparingly. Who knew when rain would fall again?

The village didn't yet have a *maneaba* – a meetinghouse – or a church, so worship services had to be held elsewhere. The Catholics gathered at the Magistrate's house, the Protestants under a thatched sunshade behind Teng Babera's house.

As Teng Babera droned on, reading from the apostle Bauru's epistle to the whats? Epeesians? — Keaki wondered about Catholics. There were some on Arorae, but not many; almost everybody worshiped at the London Missionary Society church with the Samoan pastor. Did Catholics really believe in God? They seemed to think they did, but what was all that stuff about Jesus' virgin mother, and all those saints? Baiteke had told him some wild stories about Catholics on Onotoa years ago, provoking Protestants to riot; they said one man got killed, and that Teng Koata had been threatened. But then Mister Maude had arrived and put things right.

Why would anyone get so mad at Catholics for being Catholic? It didn't make sense. Catholics seemed pretty much like everybody else – quite like everyone else, actually. Their elders were less strict than the LMS elders about things like dancing and belief in *anti,* but nobody really paid a lot of attention to the elders on those scores anyway. And Baiteke was Catholic, and there was nothing wrong with him.

Both services ended at about the same time, and he met Baiteke at his father's canoe on the lagoon beach. Tossing their spears into the canoe, they shoved off and worked their way out through the coral heads to open water, then turned left and entered the passage to the open sea called Tatiman. Huge white clouds piled up over Nutiran, but they weren't storm clouds.

They both grinned and dug in with their paddles, anticipating what they might find. It wasn't that the fish were any bigger or better off Nutiran; it was just so different from the village, and there were so many interesting things to see. The *Noriti,* of course, though they were under strict orders not to go into the wreck and were cautious when they did. There was the campsite of the *Nutiran* men – not really much there that they'd found so far – and nearby, a mess of cans and bottles that people said had been left by the castaways from the *Noriti.* Not much left there either, when it came right down to it; all the unbroken bottles had been collected for use in the village, and the cans were – well, cans. But who could tell? And there were *keta* – the red-footed birds that nested under the bushes along the shore, and....

"Tatiman – What does that mean?" Baiteke asked as they glided across passage. "Something to do with fish?"

"No, Mister Kimo says it's named after a big channel where *kain Nutiran* live."

"Nutiran's a pretty stupid word, too."

"It's where those men were from."

"It's a stupid word, anyhow."

They paddled along the north side of the passage, only a canoe's length off the Nutiran shore. The tide was going out, so it was easy going; they could rest most of the time and watch the shore go by, dipping a paddle from time to time to steer or change direction. Keaki thought about *kain Nutiran*, trying to recall what Mister Kimo had said. They were the King's people, part of the great Empire that included England and *Autralia* and the Colony of the Gilbert and Ellice Islands, and they'd been trying to decide whether they could land aeroplanes – Keaki no longer thought of them as sky canoes – on Nikumaroro or in the lagoon. They had set out the big steel barrels that stood in the lagoon, marking passageways through the coral heads. Mister Kimo said they had taken lots of photographs and made maps. Then they'd gone away, shortly after he and Koata and the other men of the working party arrived. He wondered if they'd ever come back. Mister Kimo said they hadn't thought the island was very good for aeroplanes. He wondered what was wrong with it.

The passage opened up onto the Nutiran reef flat, with the bulk of the *Noriti* looming in the distance. They paddled quietly north, drifting with the tide that flowed over the reef, looking for the right fish. There were so many – great swarms and crowds of them, in every imaginable colour, some cruising alone, stately and slow, others darting in groups like fractured sunbeams. Fishing was the easiest thing in the world on Nikumaroro; what was hard was choosing which fish to spear.

His mind wasn't entirely on the fish. It kept turning back to Era's *co:m* – that strange, lightweight, fish-coloured material that wasn't shell. She said she'd found it around here. Maybe he could find another piece, and give it to her so her father could make another *co:m.* Maybe he could even make a *co:m* and give it to her! It couldn't be too hard. Cut it with a knife, smooth it with a file, or a piece of pumice. He thought briefly about pumice – such strange stuff, floating stone. Good for smoothing things, though, and he had found a nice piece on the beach just the other day. Sure, he could make a *co:m* from the silvery stuff. He smiled as though the funny material was already in his hand.

But the afternoon went by, and nothing turned up other than the usual fish and shellfish, and whirling, crying birds. He and Baiteke rolled over the side of the canoe from time to time to spear a fish, bringing it up and letting it flop in the bottom of the canoe, covering the growing pile with a piece of burlap that they wetted from time to time. They paddled up close to the *Noriti* wreck, and tried to make out the letters on the bow.

"N-O-R-W-I-C-H-C-I-T-Y," Baiteke spelled out. "Too many letters!"

"I-Matang put extra letters in their words when they write them, I think."

"How do you pronounce that 'double-you' thing?"

"Double-You."

"I know that, clam shit, but there's nothing like that in *Noriti.* Why's it there?"

"Maybe it's silent. Some letters are, in English. Don't hurt your head thinking about it; we can ask Mister Kimo or someone."

"Yeah, my father will know."

"Your father can't read."

"So? That doesn't mean he's not smart. Come on, let's go look at the toddy palms."

Coconut toddy held a never ending fascination for Baiteke. They paddled on along the shore until they came to one of the few places on the island where there were mature coconut trees. Neat rows of them, twenty or thirty feet high, with younger ones growing up between, from nuts that had fallen. Beaching their canoe, each boy ran to a tree. Grinning, they yelled in unison.

"Race you!"

Footholds were cut into the trees, but they were spaced for a man. The boys had to use the pressure of bare feet on smooth bark between steps. Even so, both were up among the fronds in less than a minute. Here selected fronds and flowers had been cut close to their bases, and metal tubes inserted to collect the sap. Glass bottles hung below the ends of the tubes.

"This one's about half full."

"Mine's close to three quarters."

They slid down the trees and climbed others, usually with the same result.

"My father will be so happy," Keaki grinned, slapping his hands.

"Mine too. And me too!"

"I wish I liked the stuff."

"You'll learn. It's for men, you know."

"If you like it, it must be for the poop-holes of barracuda!" Keaki chased him back to the canoe, both of them whooping and laughing.

While the tide was at its ebb, and the reef flat mostly dry, they splashed around in tide pools, speared a few more fish, and rested in the sun. Then as water began to flow over the reef again, they paddled slowly homeward through the rough coral near the beach. They were just north of the *Noriti* when Baiteke pointed toward the reef edge with his paddle.

"Look at that!"

"What?"

"I don't know. Maybe a huge dead fish."

It did look like that, flashing in and out of view as the waves broke over it – a long, smooth silvery fish-side, several yards long. Hung up on the reef edge, waiting to break free and sink into the depths, or be eaten up by sharks. Strange it hadn't been eaten already.

"Let's take a look!" Keaki dug in with his paddle and the canoe shot out toward the reef-edge, where the surf was shooting up in walls of spray. There was barely enough water on the reef flat to float the canoe, but the flat out here near the edge was very smooth and the boys were light. The canoe bumped every now and then, but there was nothing to stop it.

"Not so fast, boobie!" Baiteke bellowed, backing on his paddle. "You'll go over the reef!"

Keaki brought the canoe broadside to the reef edge and its tumultuous surf, and to the fish. Which, he could now see, was not a fish. It was a big – well, maybe an inverted canoe? A piece of a boat hull? He wasn't sure, but it was all smooth, and silvery-gray and kind of shiny, with funny lines of bumps on it, like the heads of nails. He realized with a shock of recognition that it was the same kind of stuff as Era's *co:m*, but a huge hunk of it! Enough for a thousand combs.

He tapped the thing with his paddle; it made a sort of clunking sound, but didn't move. He tried to move it and couldn't. Enlisted Baiteke to help, but there was no way to really get a grip on it, or hold the canoe in place while they tried to move it. And the tide was getting higher by the minute.

"Forget it," Baiteke panted. "What would you do with it anyway?"

"Oh... I don't know. But you're right; we can't move it. Let's come back when the tide's really low."

"Tomorrow we have to work."

"Well, in a few days. And – Baiteke, let's keep it a secret."

"Why?"

"Well.... I'd just like to know what it is before we tell anybody. I don't want the men taking it from us."

"Oh. All right; sure, why not?"

They paddled back into the channel. Keaki's mind whirled. He thought of himself setting up a business, selling combs made from that mound of stuff. Getting people to pay him for it from the wages they got for clearing and planting the land. Getting enough money – real English money! – to .... well, maybe to travel, to Australia, or even England, and to get books, and.....

But wouldn't' this cheapen Era's *co:m*, make the one he gave her less special? Maybe he should just keep the thing hidden, and only make the one *co:m*. Then everyone would marvel over it, and Era would be so proud. But did this mean he would never travel, never go all those places he wondered about dreamed about? Was he going to spend his life on this island, fishing and farming? It was a nice island, but...

He was pondering this quandary when the canoe grounded on the village beach.

Chapter 9 –

The *Noriti*, Early June 1939

Another squall blew through that evening, and another the next day. It was the following Sunday before they got back to the Nutiran reef edge, and the fish-coloured thing was gone. Like it had never been there – just gone.

It felt to Keaki like a hole had opened in his soul. Both the futures he had suddenly, astonishingly, begun to imagine and find contending within him were gone in a single moment. Impress Era, play with her, enjoy her, have babies with her .... Or get rich, travel, see places, learn about things.... All week he had been tossed back and forth between futures, and now suddenly there was no choice to make, nothing he could do.

Baiteke thought it was funny.

"Poor Keaki, lost his comb tree!"

"Shut up, crab poop."

"He'll just have to find some other way to impress Era. Maybe with his eloquence, or his strength, or his manly dong..."

"Shut up. Maybe I had other plans. But it doesn't matter now." He felt tears pushing on his eyes. Baiteke put his arm around his friend's bare shoulders.

"It's OK, manta-shit, we'll find another piece of that stuff. Maybe when we go with Edwin and John to the *Noriti*."

Keaki and Baiteke had begun to make friends with Mister Kimo's sons John and Edwin. Of course their native language was Tuvaluan, so they pronounced some Tungaru words in funny ways, but they were learning fast, and at school they were among the best at reciting in English. They both played guitars, as did Mister Kimo, so there seemed always to be music around their house in the evenings – even though they were Protestants. But during the day Mister Kimo kept them pretty busy helping him; he talked about how they were going to learn everything he did, and one day be far better builders and fixers than he was. That was pretty hard to believe, Keaki thought; there was nothing that Mister Kimo couldn't fix, or build.

He had asked Keaki and Baiteke – or rather, their fathers, and the boys were tagging along – to go with him and his boys to salvage machinery from the *Noriti* shipwreck. It wasn't clear to Keaki just what Mister Kimo wanted – indeed, he didn't seem sure himself – but Keaki didn't care and neither did the other boys. Getting to search the wreck was too exciting to worry about details.

They got into the hull through a gaping hole broken in the port bow. Enough sunlight filtered through other holes in the ship to allow them to make their way slowly aft and upward, climbing ladders and metal staircases to upper decks. Finally they came out on the main deck and the sun was so bright that for a moment Keaki couldn't see at all.

"Careful, son," Mister Kimo put his hand on Edwin's shoulder and pointed to the deck right in front of him. It was all black and charred.

"These burned parts of the deck may be very thin; you could fall through and disturb the fish."

Ieiera showed the boys how to work around the burned areas by walking close to the gunwale and holding on to the rail. They looked around at what was left of the *Noriti 's* superstructure – almost all the wood burned away, metal twisted and blackened. One funnel was askew and looked like it might fall off at any moment. The whole aft part sloped down at a more acute angle than the forward part of the ship. Waves broke right over the stern.

Almost in unison, Edwin and John asked the question the other boys were thinking.

What happened to this ship, Father?"

Of course, Keaki and Baiteke knew it had grounded in a storm, and that some men had died whilst the others were rescued after a few days – and that this was long ago, before most of the boys had been born. But the boys had ventured by themselves only into the lower parts of the hull; this was the first time they had seen the topside, and they were astonished at the devastation.

"It burned, son. This was a steamship, of course; down below we can see its boilers, and the big firebox where they put the coal to burn and make the steam. So there was lots of fire down there, and lots of bunker oil. When they hit the reef, Boom! Fire everywhere!"

Edwin looked stricken. "Did everybody burn up?" Apparently he hadn't heard the story of the wreck.

"No, no," Baiteke said authoritatively. "Only eleven or ten men died. The rest jumped overboard and got on the island."

"And then did they get away?" John looked like he was wondering if the sailors were still wandering around Nutiran.

"Yes, some ships came and took them away. They all lived."

They had been moving carefully aft, and now they had reached the superstructure – what was left of it. Everything was badly burned, and the bridge and wheelhouse had collapsed right down to the deck. Inside, there were instruments like clocks and a compass, fallen down to the deck when the wooden bulkheads burned. Baiteke picked up a brass clock.

"Oh, can I take this?" He asked his father.

"What'll you do with it? It doesn't work."

"Maybe I can fix it. Maybe Mister Kimo can fix it."

"Yes, that would be good. The clock could tell you when to get up in the morning."

The boys laughed heartily at the joke. Who would use a clock to get up? When the sun came up, you got up; what good would a clock do?

"Well, I still like it, anyway. It's interesting."

His father shrugged and went forward to help Mister Kimo collect some turnbuckles.

They paddled home that afternoon with their canoes loaded with gear – turnbuckles, hawsers, blocks, machine parts, buckets, an oil can, some pots and pans, Baiteke's clock, and hundreds and hundreds of nuts and bolts that Mister Kimo especially prized. Others came down to the lagoon shore to help, and they hefted all the stuff up to Mister Kimo's house, where it would be divided and most of it stored for use later. The boys rested under a buka tree near the shore, throwing rocks in the water. John was still worried about the men who had died on the ship.

"Do you think their ghosts are about? What do you call them, *ans?*"

"Anti," Keaki said, pronouncing the "ti" like a soft "sh." I suppose they might be. I wonder, were they buried there?

"Anti can't hurt you," Baiteke proclaimed, throwing a rock at a gannet that was flying by. "Only old grandmothers believe in *anti*. Grandmothers and girls. And besides, they don't live on this side of the island."

"That's true," Edwin said. "It was my grandmother who told me about *tupua* – what you call *anti* – and she said they usually live on the windward side."

"Well," Keaki mused; "maybe they live there, but I'll bet they come over on this side sometimes to find people to eat."

At the end of May, a wireless message came through from Mister Maude on Manra, summoning Mister Kimo there to build another cistern. The next day a sail appeared on the western horizon. Everyone gathered on the shore to watch the colonial schooner *Nimanoa* heave to in the lee, while Kirata and Takena paddled Mister Kimo and his family out with their gear. The last of them – Edwin – had barely gone over the rail when the schooner came about and tacked off to the south to round the island and set a course for Manra. It seemed strange to have Mister Kimo and the boys gone, like a hole had opened up in the little community.

Chapter 10–
Nei Manganibuka, July 1939

Keaki followed Nei Aana through the *kanawa*. Tall, wide-spreading trees with roots that snaked all over the ground and a dense, high canopy. It was dark in their shadow, but for dancing beams of sunlight that filtered through the leaves. Keaki had never been to the *kanawa* grove before, and he felt proud that Nei Aana had selected him to go with her, but he was shy around her. The old woman walked purposefully through the woods with her staff, letting Keaki follow along with the fish net and bags.

The *kanawa* grove stood on a small peninsula jutting into the lagoon. On the side away from the village were the pools with the *baneawa* fish that Nei Aana was after. Quick, flashing little fish, but not quick enough to escape Nei Aana. With surprising grace for one so old, she dipped the net in just the right place to intercept their flight, and bring them up in their multitudes for Keaki to scrape out and drop in the bags. The bags filled quickly, and Nei Aana called for a stop. She sat to rest, and lit a pipe, while Keaki prowled the shoreline.

"Nei Aana," he asked. "Who do you suppose ate all these *aubunga*?" The coral shelf that formed the shore was littered with the big clam shells, as big as two or three of his hands, if he had had three hands.

"I don't know, child," Nei Aana said distantly, looking out over the lagoon. Keaki waded into the water and found a few *aubunga* living there, but not many.

"Whoever it was, they must have eaten most of them. I wonder why they brought the shells out of the water." It was simpler to just sneak up on the clam when it had its shells open, reach in quickly and cut the big muscle that closed them, then cut out the meat and leave the shell on the reef. "Maybe they were too clumsy...."

Nei Aana didn't answer, but she looked at him and scowled. Leaned on her staff and rose to her feet, began walking purposefully toward him, still scowling. Had he done something? Was she going to hit him? He searched his brain for something he'd done wrong, started to back away.

"Stay!" she said, and walked right past him.

Keaki watched where she walked; she'd seen something hanging in the *mao*. Something kind of pink, light red, maybe faded. A piece of cloth. He started toward her as she detached it from the branch and looked at it. Shook it out, held it up. Keaki could see that it was a shirt of some kind.

"Stay!" she said again, gesturing with her left hand. Keaki stopped, stood still, watched wide- eyed. Nei Aana was holding the cloth in her hands, close to her drooping breasts, looking into the *mao* thicket. Keaki opened his mouth to speak, closed it again.

"Go!" Nei Aana hissed. "Go home, right now! I'll be along. Go!"

Keaki started to back away. She turned to face him.

"Go!" she shouted at him. "Have you no ears?"

Keaki spun around, grabbed the bags of fish, and scampered away through the trees. Glancing back, he saw Nei Aana still standing, still clutching the shirt, still staring into the *mao*.

Back at the village, Keaki delivered the fish and his news to Teng Koata, who seemed unperturbed by his woman's strange behavior. "She is a doctor," he said, as though that explained everything. He divided the fish, and sent Keaki home to his mother with a basketful.

As the swift twilight spread across the sky, Nei Aana came out of the bush and walked slowly into the village, saying nothing to anyone. The people were beginning to gather on the lagoon beach, where a fire was crackling.

"We should build a *maneaba*, " Mereke said, reflectively. Keaki thought he was right; a village just wasn't complete without its meeting-house, with its assigned places for all the families. It was disorienting not to have one. He looked at Era, sitting with her family on the other side of the fire. Would her family's seating place, her *boti*, be close to his? Would he be able to look at her like this?

"Not enough thatch," Kimai murmured, "and anyway, who would sit in which *boti?* "

"That's true. But still....."

Nei Aana appeared in the circle of firelight. Teng Koata nodded a greeting to her. She seated herself on his mat. It seemed that she had something to say, but she was in no hurry to say it.

"Maybe everyone from Onotoa could take the first several *boti* in the *maneaba*, " Kirata answered Kimai's question, "because there are more of us than others. And then...."

"I saw Nei Manganibuka," Nei Aana broke in. Everyone stared at her in silence.

"Where?" Koata asked evenly.

"Near where we caught the *baneawa*, in the *mao*."

"Ah."

Kirata strode purposefully into the firelight. "Who has tobacco? It's time for a smoke!" Nei Aana ignored him, and Koata scowled.

"This woman has seen the ancestress," he snapped; "the *anti*. She is explaining."

Kirata grunted, sat abruptly on a log. Nei Aana went on.

"The ancestress, that woman who taught us navigation, that woman of the *buka*...."

"Eng!" several people murmured. "Yes."

"That woman was sitting in the bush, but the bush was a *maneaba.*"

"Eng! A maneaba!"

"A big, handsome *maneaba* with a tall peaked roof."

Keaki searched his memory and couldn't recall any building at all near the *baneawa* pool. If there had been, whose would it have been? Who would have built it? Why hadn't he seen it? But Nei Aana was a doctor, and doctors saw things that other people couldn't see. Maybe the people from the *maneaba* had eaten the *aubunga*.

Nei Aana went on. "She was talking with some old men, and a few children." She fell silent. It was full dark now. Sparks whirled up from the fire. Everyone waited. Finally Teng Babera, who had been sitting a bit back from the fire looking uncomfortable, cleared his throat.

"This is not a Christian thing...."

Nei Aana cut him off. "She was speaking with those people, those old men and children, telling them of the future. She was in the future, and they were in the future, and she could see farther into the future."

"Eng, " Koata murmured, crossing himself.

"It was the future of this island, of Nikumaroro, of which she spoke."

"That is good," Koata said quietly. Nei Aana looked at him for a long time before she sighed and spoke again.

"She said the island would prosper, and one day thousands of people will live here and – and be happy."

"That is good," Koata said again, slowly, looking carefully at her.

"Eng." Nei Aana was silent then for a long time, looking into the fire. People drifted away to their houses, until only she and Koata were left, watching the glowing embers.

The next day, Keaki found it hard to concentrate on his work. He was helping his father plant seed coconuts, but he kept finding himself stopping, forgetting what he was doing, his mind drifting away. After awhile, Ieiera sat down on a log and lit his pipe, patted the log next to him.

"Come over here, son. Have a seat. Rest."

"Oh. OK, thank you, baba, but I'm not...."

"Where are your thoughts?" Ieiera smiled, raised an eyebrow.

"I'm.... Baba, what do you think...?"

"What do I think Nei Aana saw?"

"I didn't see anything, baba – just an old red shirt, and then she got so – so fierce."

"She's an old, fierce woman, and she knows a lot. And sees things the rest of us can't see."

"A *maneaba?* Nei Manganibuka?"

Ieiera shrugged. "If she says it, I believe it."

"So there really are *anti?*"

"I don't know, son. I've never seen one. But the old people have always said so."

"But Teng Babera...."

"Teng Babera is a young man, and a man of little experience, though he knows his bible.. He can teach you a lot, son, but he doesn't know every-thing."

"Nei Aana said she was in the future."

"Yes, she did."

"Can Nei Aana see the future, then?"

"Well, she said that's what she was seeing, and the future people were talking about the future."

"How can that be?"

"I don't know."

"You know what I think, baba? I think maybe time is kind of like water – just like air, like Mister Kimo said. And sometimes when you're in the water, you know how what you see through it sort of shimmers, gets longer and shorter, fatter and skinnier? Well, maybe time is like that, and some-times somebody who can see, like Nei Aana, looks through it and sees....."

"Ho, you're losing me, son." Ieiera clapped his son on the shoulder. "All I know is that Nei Aana is a woman of power, and if she says she saw something, I believe her."

"But there's got to be a reason....."

"Sure there is," Ieiera chuckled, rising from the log. "Nei Manganibuka wants us to make this a thriving, prosperous island, so she showed herself to Nei Aana. And we'd better get to work planting those coconuts, or she'll be pissed off and then we'll be in trouble."

"OK, baba." Keaki pulled himself to his feet and went back to patting mulch around the coconut in its hole, but he kept looking out across the lagoon, wondering what it would be like to see through time. And why nobody else seemed to wonder.

Chapter 11 –

The Wreck of the *Nimanoa*, Mid—June 1939

For Keaki and the other boys, the days fell into a routine. Up with the sun, and the stirrings of birds in the trees. Frigate Birds and Red-Tailed Tropic Birds sailing out to the deep ocean to fish; *kiakia* swooping among the trees and along the beaches. A little food, a little talk around the cooking fires, and then on to the day's work. Cutting and burning *buka* and *kanawa,* hacking away *mao*. Digging up the gravelly coral ground, mixing in chopped-up leaves, bark, and seaweed to fertilize it, planting the seed coconuts in neat rows. A rest when the sun was high and the women and girls brought food – usually fish, and some *babae* or rice. Then a quick swim and it was time for school.

Their schoolhouse was an open-sided thatched shelter, and they sat on logs with their slates, boys on one side, girls on the other. Teng Babera stood or sat in front and called on them to read and recite. Reading was in English, from the bible – they had several copies to pass around. Teng Babera was careful not to use the LMS Tungaru or Tuvaluan bible, or do anything that a Catholic would find offensive. Considering the matter, Keaki couldn't imagine what such a thing might be, other than slandering the Virgin or one of those saints, but Teng Koata often sat in on the classes, and the rumor was that he was watching to make sure Teng Babera didn't try to convert anyone. They also did sums, and multiplication, and sometimes Teng Babera would talk to them about history, but that was mostly from the Bible, too. School adjourned while the sun was still high in the sky, and there was time for some fishing, work around the village, and games. Evening was a time for visiting around the cook fires as the moon rose and the birds made soft rustling and cooing noises in the branches.

And on the Sabbath, after church, Keaki and Baiteke explored. Sometimes paddling down the lagoon, sometimes up along the edge of the mudflat in the middle of Nutiran – a filled-in part of the lagoon, alive with crabs. But most often up along the Nutiran reef flat. They marveled at the things they found there, coming out of the *Noriti* as the waves broke around and through the hulk. Steel barrels and boxes, hatch covers, life rings. Bottles, pieces of machinery, dinner plates, grappling hooks. And finally, one day, another piece of the fish-coloured stuff.

It wasn't going to make Keaki's fortune; it was about as big as his two hands put together. Longer one way than the other, and very thin – almost as thin as paper. It could be bent, but not easily. It didn't seem like it would break very easily. It had obviously been torn off something bigger, perhaps the big thing they had seen before. It had a couple of the nail-like things along one edge, together with holes where some others had been ripped out by whatever....

"Whatever ripped it up, whatever it was." Baiteke turned the thing over in his hand. "I don't think it's natural."

"Birdshit, of course it's not natural," Keaki scoffed. "It's a piece of...."

"Yes indeed, a piece. A piece of some weird *I-Matang* thing. Maybe it'll skip." He started to throw it low and flat across the reef flat.

"No!" Keaki grabbed the thing from his hand. "I'm going to take it and – make something out of it."

"Ah. Lucky Era."

"I didn't say anything about Era"

"No, no, but I can see it in your eye. Still thinking of a *co:m?"*

"Maybe. It's for me to decide."

"Maybe you could make a little something to tickle her with – Oh, but you already have one of those."

"Shut up, you puny pile of tern poop!" Keaki chased Baiteke across the reef flat, both of them shrieking with laughter, lifting their feet high out of the water. Fish scattered in all directions. But as he splashed Keaki thought about the decision that was no longer his to make, and what that meant. That he should make the comb, and one day lie with Era and make a baby, and have a farm? Was his future set? Was he looking through time?

"Come on, boobie droppings," Baiteke called to him. Keaki had stopped, was staring across the reef unseeing. "What did you do, trip on your dong?"

One day it was Era herself, with two or three other girls, who came running breathlessly into the village, yelling that a ship was coming.

"I think it's the *Nimanoa!"* Era told Keaki, her face flushed, eyes flashing. Keaki felt weak and flustered. Era whipped around and ran back toward the landing, the whole village running after her – except the old people, who walked and chuckled about the youngsters.

It was indeed the *Nimanoa,* sails furled here in the lee of the island, little puffs of smoke coming from her small stack. She came abeam the landing and turned to steer in closer to the reef edge.

"Coming awfully fast," Katoi murmured.

"Why don't they stop?" his wife, Nei Tekatin asked, her hand to her mouth.

Shouted commands rang across the water, the sound of the anchor chain clattering out of the hawse. Kirata pulled his pipe from his mouth and looked around wide-eyed.

"Dumb shits don't know there's no bottom!"

Shouts, nervous laughs, and a couple of screams were cut short by an awful crunching as the schooner drove up onto the reef.

"Holy Mary Mother of God!" Koata exclaimed, with more emotion than Keaki had ever seen him show, crossing himself abruptly. "Get canoes! Get out there and help!" Within minutes four canoes were in the water and flying toward the schooner, which was heeling over on her starboard side. Several men jumped off her stern and swam for the reef.

"Good job it's a pleasant day," Mister Maude commented an hour later, sitting on a log in his soaked, salt-encrusted clothes. "Not the first time I've had to swim for it, coming ashore, nor the last, I suppose."

By now it was apparent that the ship was not in immediate danger of sinking or being broken up on the reef. The engineer and his mate were aboard, fussing with the machinery – Mister Maude said the engine hadn't been willing to stop. The bosun and his hands, and half a dozen men from the island, were on the reef and aboard the ship, holding her steady with lines running in all directions. Others were offloading the supplies meant for the island, into canoes to be brought ashore. And everyone waited for the tide to finish coming in, lifting the hull free.

"And then we'll see how she floats," Mister Maude said complacently, stuffing his pipe and lighting it. "If she floats."

Mister Gallagher, a tall, slender, long-faced *I-Matang,* stood up and brushed the sand off his legs, grimaced at his wet feet, encased like Mister Maude's in the things they called "shoes."

"If you think things are in hand here, Harry, I'd like to take advantage of the time..."

"And see a bit of the island. Quite, quite. Go along the road there. The men are rather occupied, but perhaps one of these boys can show you around. You, son... eh..."

"I'm Keaki, Mister... — I'm son of Ieiera and Boikabane...."

"Quite. From Temeroa, yes? You're looking healthy here on Niku-maroro, and I see your father out there holding the ship together. Will you show Mister Gallagher around the village?"

Mister Gallagher smiled and stuck out his hand to shake. "Teng Keaki, eh? You look like a — " he glanced up, apparently seeking the Tungaru word in his mind – "like a strong young man. I hope you're ... helping your parents." Keaki nodded vigorously, grinning. The trouble Mister Gallagher had with the Tungaru language made him seem more human than other *I-*

Matang; it had never occurred to Keaki that *I-Matang* might find it hard to speak. He's like me trying to speak English, Keaki thought — startlingly. Somehow it made him feel a sort of bond with the tall, white administrator.

Holding Mister Gallagher's hand, he led him up the path, with Baiteke and two or three other boys tagging along. He felt shy, but the *I-Matang* smiled encouragingly and he soon began to enjoy showing off his island.

"You see, there's one of our *ai* — coconut crabs." There aren't too many around the village any more, but there are lots and lots out in the *mao."*

"Oh yes. A – a big one, yes?. And here are the – the plantations, eh?"

"He's not so big, Mister … Karaka; otherwise we'd have eaten him. Yes, these are where we've planted the coconuts, and the only reason there aren't any coconuts planted over there is that we're going to dig a *babae* pit."

"Very — foresightful. And what's this?"

"That's our cistern, sir. Twenty thousand Imperial gallons. Mister Kimo built it. Well, we built it, but Mister Kimo showed us how. Do you know Mister Kimo, sir?"

"Oh yes, very well. He's just built one – a cistern, much like this one on Manra, and he's building one on Orona."

"Will he come back here soon?"

"Yes. I expect so; he and his family. There's much still to build here."

"Oh good. And here is our village!"

The afternoon flew by, but Keaki was beginning to run out of things to show Mister Gallagher by the time the *Nimanoa* blew her whistle. Mister Gallagher thanked Keaki and shook his hand. He strode briskly toward the beach, with Keaki and the other boys following behind.

"I thought you were going to show him the crappers," Baiteke murmured behind his hand. Keaki smiled sheepishly, which encouraged Baiteke to continue, making grand gestures to the right and left.

"And here, Mister Karaka, you see our shitting places. Four hundred Imperial gallon capacity...."

To everyone's surprise – not least that of her master, Mister Harness, *Nimanoa* was not badly damaged. "We'll take her slow and gentle," he said, "but the wind's on our quarter and we should have no trouble fetching Tarawa."

With which, the canoes took to the water again to ferry the *I-Matangs* and ship's crew out over the reef, and with a blast of her whistle *Nimanoa* hoisted her sails and glided west on a long port tack.

Life returned to normal on Nikumaroro. Keaki worked every evening on the comb he was making for Era – though of course Era didn't yet know about it, and he had no idea how he was going to give it to her. At his father's suggestion, he cut a rectangular piece out of the fish-coloured stuff using a hack-saw blade. It wasn't hard at all to cut. Then he cut a series of parallel slits, and now he was using the blade like a file to work them into the teeth of the comb.

How would he give it to her? Just walk up and hand it to her? Wrap it in leaves so she could open it and be surprised? Have someone else give it to her? He frowned and puzzled as he worked, but nothing he thought of seemed right.

Then Mister Kimo reappeared.

Chapter 12–

The Return of Mister Kimo, August 1939

How many stars were there?

Keaki lay on his back and tried to count them. How many times had he tried, here and back on Temeroa? He tried holding his hands and thumbs out to make a square, counting just the stars within the square. Then he could move his hands over and.... He kept losing count, and mistaking sparks flying up from the fire for stars burning in the sky. Did they really burn? How could anyone know? How could one find out? Or were they really *anti*? He yawned...

"Who's there?" It was Teng Koata, in his most authoritative magistrate's voice. Everyone around the fire was struggling to their feet. In the commotion, Keaki couldn't tell what had upset them, but then he looked where everyone else was looking, and – there were torches – burning fire torches, coming along the road from the landing!

"Who's there?" Teng Koata called again, gruffly. The answer came back through the darkness on a wave of laughter. A very familiar voice.

"We're the cannibal warriors of Samoa, coming to eat you all!"

Even Koata was speechless. Everyone stared as Mister Kimo strode into the circle of firelight, with half a dozen grinning men behind him.

"Here, you mannerless Tungarus. Have you no food? No tobacco to offer this crew of fearless mariners?"

"*Mauri,* Jack Kimo Petro." Koata shook Mister Kimo's hand. "Welcome back to Nikumaroro. We... were not expecting you."

"But we are here, as you see! These are my mates, my working partners. We have just finished building the cistern on Orona, and decided to come back here and build some more."

"But... how..." Everyone was asking – "Where did you come from; how did you get here?" Men were clapping Jack Kimo on the back, women were running for food, offering the men places to sit close to the fire. Jack accepted a half coconut shell of water.

"Fine water," he said, wiping his mouth. "You must have a good cistern."

"An excellent cistern," Teng Koata said, "but Teng Kimo, where are the others?"

"Others?"

Teng Koata looked at him with a raised eyebrow, as everyone else took up the questions: "The ship's crew? Mister Mauta? Mister Karaka?"

"Ship? Englishmen? We are navigators, are we not? Were not our ancestors the greatest navigators in all the world?"

"Well..."

"Did they not sail great canoes up from Samoa, or from your homeland *Matang,* to settle all these islands?"

"Of course, but..."

"Did not great war fleets carry hosts of warriors into fierce battles across hundreds of miles of the sea?"

"Yes, but..."

"Well, so, we just sailed here from Orona in two canoes."

Everyone stared. Mister Kimo struck a dignified pose. His men doubled over with laughter.

"Two canoes...." one of them choked out, "... and a cement mixer."

Some of the other men hooted with derision; women laughed. Some just stared. Old Kimo with his outrageous stories! Unable to get the truth out of him, the whole group finally took up torches and trooped down to the landing.

And there they were – two sailing canoes, pulled up on the sand and tied to *buka* trees, their sails neatly furled, and between them a raft of big *kanawa* logs, on which stood – the very same cement mixer they had used in building the cistern.

"We had it on Manra, you see," Mister Kimo explained as though it were the most natural thing in the world. "And we took it to Orona on that schooner *Nimanoa.* And when we finished building there – well, we didn't know when the Englishmen were coming back, and we had nothing to do but fish, so we thought – it's only one hundred and sixty miles, and all downwind....."

"How did you manage to tack?" Koata, the navigator, went straight to the practical question – "with that thing dragging behind you?"

"We didn't have to very much, sailing before the wind. But when we did we traded off. When it was time for one canoe to tack we'd throw off the tow line on a float, and the other canoe would swoop in" – Kimo stuck out his arms and swooped – and grab it up on the other tack. It really worked very well, most of the time."

"Except that time...." one of his men began, and another took up the story, and the rest of the night was given over to telling, retelling, and embroidering stories and songs on the great voyage of the cement mixer.

Almost everyone slept most of the next day, but having fallen asleep during the third recounting of how the cement mixer had tried to sail away on its own, Keaki was up with the sun. He trotted through the sleeping village to Baiteke's compound, where he found his friend snoring softly on a mat under the shade arbor. He sat for awhile watching him breathe, and wondered about wakening him. When he had gone to bed, Baiteke had been sitting with Mister Kimo and his men, and Kirata and Takena, sharing their coconut toddy and joining in their songs. Now he was sleeping like the dead.

"Stretched out like a big long turd," he murmured, and wished Baiteke were awake to hear. "Good one," he thought, and filed it away in his mind for future use. He drifted over to Teng Beiearuru's compound, but there was no sign of Era. Perhaps she was at the beach, washing her hair, he thought with a surge of interest, and ran to the lagoon shore. No Era, no one at all but the gannets and *kiakias,* and the cruising sharks.

Back at his own compound, everyone was asleep except Taberiki. He certainly didn't want to spend the day with his little sister, but she wanted to go look at the cement mixer.

"Oh, all right. Since everyone else is dead."

They walked hand in hand down the path toward the landing, Taberiki stretching out her short legs to match her big brother's long strides, and talking non-stop.

"I think that's Mareta's chicken. Do you think she knows it's out?"

"Um, probably."

"What's Mister Kimo going to do with his cement mixer?"

"Probably make cement."

"But what's he going to make with the cement?"

"Canoes for little girls to use crossing the lagoon."

"They'd sink!"

"Most likely."

"You're mean. Be serious. Is he going to build houses?"

"I guess. Or maybe sky canoes."

"Are they made of cement?"

"Oh yeah, that's what I've been told."

"Wow! That's ..... oh, what happened to that dog's leg?"

They reached the landing, where Mister Kimo's men were sleeping in, under, and around their canoes and the cement mixer. Taberiki wanted an explanation of how it worked, and Keaki found himself enjoying the role of teacher, which worried him a little.

"So," he brought the lesson to an end, "the tank goes round and round and you put in water from time to time, and then you pour the cement out when it's all wet and gloppy, and it makes your house. I'm going to walk up the beach to the boathouse."

"Me too!"

They walked along the high water line, darting out from time to time to grab a pretty shell or try to catch a fish.

"Keaki, help me!"

"Help yourself. What are you doing out there?" Taberiki was up to her waist in the water, peering into a crevice in the coral.

"I've found something! Come help me get it out!"

"Probably a nice friendly moray eel. Let him kiss your finger."

"Come on, Keaki, help me!"

Keaki struggled through the incoming surf to where his sister had almost disappeared in the foam. "If you wash away and get eaten by a whale, it won't be my fault when he gets indigestion."

"Look at that thing! What is it?" Taberiki pointed into the crevice.

"Piece of glass, I think."

"But wouldn't it make a nice plate?

"Oh, yeah, I guess so."

"Get it for me, please?"

"OK, why not?" Keaki crouched and held his breath as a wave rolled over him, reached gingerly into the crevice and got his fingers around the thing. It was slippery, but had some kind of border around the edges that gave him a pretty good grip. It came rather easily out of the crack.

"Here it is, sister," he handed it to her, shaking the water out of his eyes and wishing he could think of something more clever to say.

"Oh thank you! Look how it shines in the light! Is it a shell?

"I've never seen a square shell, or one you could see through." He took the thing from her and held it up in front of his face. It was rectangular with rounded corners, about as long as his arm and almost as wide, rimmed about with black stuff. And he could see through it, in a distorted sort of way; it was badly scratched and pitted.

"I don't know what it is, but I'll bet I could make some good dive goggles out of it."

"But it's mine!"

"I picked it up!"

"I saw it first!"

"And that's all you'd have done if it hadn't been for me."

"You wouldn't even know about it if it hadn't been for me."

They argued all the way home, but in the end Keaki gave in. Despite his bluster, he couldn't resist his little sister.

Chapter 13 –

Mister Kimo's Sentence, September 1939

The boys ran along the shore in a pack, whooping and leaping over the rough-surfaced coral shelves and ledges. But the canoes outpaced them, and when the shore curved off to the east and the *mao* grew out close to the water the boys stopped, panting, laughing and waving. Mister Kimo waved back as the canoes tacked gracefully, their crews smoothly moving the feet of their V-shaped yard-set from one end of the hull to the other. They carried on, growing smaller and smaller until they disappeared behind the curve of the land. The boys started back toward the village.

"I wish they'd stayed longer," Kaeki grumbled.

Ngauta tossed a rock at a small shark cruising the waters just off shore. "Well, Mister Kimo said he missed his wife, and Edwin and John."

"Yeah," Baiteke chimed in. "And there wasn't much for him to build."

"Without cement." Everyone giggled.

"Yeah, what's the use of having a cement mixer if you have no cement?"

"I guess it's up to us to find out, since we've got it now."

"Maybe we could cook something in it."

"Mix up coconut toddy."

"Keep crabs in it, and fatten them up."

"I wonder why he brought it."

Kaeki shrugged. "Didn't know there wasn't cement, I guess."

Baiteke grinned crookedly. "I think they just did it for fun."

They walked on in silence for awhile. Kaeki thought about a grown man doing something for fun. Something as ambitious, and dangerous, as sailing to Nikumaroro from Orona, and now back to Manra. Decided he could imagine Mister Kimo doing something like that, just to see if he could. Realized he was imagining himself doing it.

He smiled at the memory of Mister Kimo's punishment.

Everyone knew, of course, that interisland canoe travel was forbidden under colonial law. Everyone knew that people did it back home, though, from time to time – to visit relatives, hunt turtles, trade. Most people thought the law was silly, and just didn't talk about violations. But as magistrate, Teng Koata had to enforce it.

People had speculated about what Teng Koata would do. He couldn't very well put Mister Kimo in gaol, because there was no gaol. Teng Kirata had suggested solemnly that Koata could have Mister Kimo build one, and then collapsed with laughter at his own joke. Others speculated that Koata could report him to Mister Maude and Mister Gallagher, so they could put him on trial, but everyone knew that that was not Teng Koata's way. He would do something himself, and not involve the *I-Matang* unless he had to.

So no one had been surprised when Mister Kimo and his workmen began cutting trees and leveling the ground out near the end of the point at the edge of the lagoon – land that they all knew was reserved for construction of the government station. It was work that anyone could do – far beneath the capacity and dignity of a man like Mister Kimo – but Mister Kimo was his usual lighthearted, hard-working self, and he treated the work with respect. He never complained, and when friends like Kirata and Takena stopped to talk, he explained his own vision for the government station.

"Of course, there will be a parade ground," he explained, "with nice straight streets all round, and a big flagstaff in the middle. Maybe a stone wall along there" – he waved his hand across the width of the island – "running right across, at the edge of the ground. Government buildings all round – treasury, gaol, hospital, dispensary. All nice and square and straight."

"The cooperative store will need to be there, too," Takena put in. He wanted to be the storekeeper when the co-op was set up, like the ones back on Onotoa, and on Manra.

"Sure, the cooperative store, too, with a big sign over the door and a counter inside."

"And a steel safe for all the money."

"What about houses?" Kirata asked. "Will we all live in the store, or in the gaol?"

"Or on the beach, under our canoes?"

"Houses," Mister Kimo said with great certainty, "will begin just outside the wall that will run across the island. They'll be on the ocean side and lagoon side of the streets, equal distances apart, all the same size."

"With cookhouses behind, and pigpens."

"Of course. But the staff will have houses inside the wall. So – ha! – my house can stay where it is, and be the official residence of the Public Works Officer whenever he's in residence!" Kimo puffed out his chest and laughed. His house, with its shelves of parts from the *Noriti* and its collection of tools and equipment, stood near the shore of Tatiman Passage at the east edge of the village.

"That's good," Kirata grinned. "I'd hate to have to move all that crap."

"And there'll be a big, beautiful rest house for Mister Mauta and Mister Gallagher and other Englishmen who come to visit."

"Ha! Kirata exulted, "a rest house fit for the King to sleep in, with an indoor shitter!"

"We could do that." Mister Kimo put down his shovel as a dreamy look slipped over his face. "If we made it all of concrete, it'd hold a big steel tank on top. We could pump the water up and let it fall down to flush the toilet, just like in Government House in Suva. Wouldn't that be something?"

"It should be in a beautiful place."

"Right, and set off from the other buildings by – ah — by being at an angle to them." Mister Kimo gestured in the air, then squatted down and drew in the dirt with a stick. "See, the parade ground is here, with the streets around it, and it's all square, but then the rest house is here at the corner, on the diagonal – 45 degrees to the square formed by the parade ground....."

All of one mind, the men strode off to the northeast until they got to the spot that they calculated would be the corner of the quadrangle. Looked through the remaining *bukas* toward the lagoon.

"Right then," Mister Kimo exclaimed, "this is the place! A beautiful view out across the lagoon, and when the sun comes up in the morning it'll fill the place with light. There'll be big wide verandas, a great tall thatched roof, like the District Officer's house on Beru."

"But the shitter will be concrete," Kirata reminded him.

"Ah, but the concrete shitter will be inside, with thatch covering everything. It'll be a masterpiece."

Apparently the sentence Teng Koata had imposed was two weeks hard labour, and by the end of that time, the government station site was mostly clear of big trees. The ground was still rough and studded with coral outcrops, but smoothing it and putting in the streets could wait – would have to wait until Mister Kimo's plan was approved by Mister Maude and Mister Gallagher. In the meantime, several of the family heads proposed, and Teng Koata agreed, that they should build a temporary *maneaba* on the cleared land just outside where Mister Kimo estimated the government station's boundary wall should go. Mister Kimo and his team cheerfully helped frame up the building and cut planks for the floor.

It was at this time – resting at the end of the work day – that Mister Kimo told Kirata and Tekena of his plan to sail back to Manra to be with his family.

"Won't you be punished again?" Kirata passed him the bottle of coconut toddy he had kept cool all day in the lagoon. Mister Kimo took a long drink and wiped his mouth with his arm.

"Ah yes, and that's a problem. There's a gaol on Manra." He shook his head as though concerned, but no one thought he was. After all, he had built the gaol.

"It's probably got a secret tunnel," Baiteke said.

So that morning Mister Kimo and his workers had gotten in their canoes, supposedly planning to do some trolling in the lee of the island. Everyone knew what they were really doing, of course, but not talking about it saved Teng Koata from embarrassment. All the supplies and water they took aboard might have seemed excessive for a day-long fishing trip, and everyone coming down to the shore to see them off, but no one commented on this, and Teng Koata slept late that day – the only time anyone had known him to do so.

Chapter 14–

USS *Bushnell*, November/December 1939

A few weeks after Mister Kimo returned to Manra – Keaki worried about him, wondered if he'd gotten there safely, but had no way to find out – Teng Koata announced that they should stop clearing and planting for a few days and finish the temporary *maneaba*.

"Soon it will be Christmas," he said, "and we will need a place to hold our holy mass."

"Very true, Mister Magistrate," Teng Babera interjected politely, "and our services as well."

"Of course, Teng Babera," the magistrate said in a flat voice. "That goes without saying."

He wishes it had, Keaki thought..

It was not a large *maneaba* – they didn't have enough thatch to cover the roof of a big one – but it was big enough for the community, and after all, it was only temporary. Building it raised questions, however. Every Tungaru village had a *maneaba* in which everyone met to discuss the village's work and needs. Every family had its own place to sit in the *maneaba* – its *boti* – arranged strictly by rank, with the highest ranking families farthest from the door. But here – with this ragtag group made up of families from multiple villages on different islands....

"Where will we sit?" Kirata blurted out the question, sitting on the ridgepole.

Keaki's father mumbled something around the strip of coconut cordage in his mouth.

"Eh?"

Ieiera extracted the cord and began wrapping it around the juncture of a support post and a roof joist.

"I said, Koata will obviously sit at the high end."

"That takes care of Koata then. And the rest of us will just wiggle around like crabs, I suppose?"

"Maybe we can just see, when we get it built. There are so few of us, maybe each family can sit more or less where we're used to at home."

"And all jabber together like a bunch of *kiakias,* eh?"

Keaki, handing up more rope to his father to secure the roof, pictured everyone squawking like the little white birds that so fiercely defended their territories in the *buka* forest. It really is a problem, he thought. The order of the *boti* determines the order in which people speak on any subject. His family was number six in the *maneaba* back at Temeroa; it would be remarkable if there weren't another number six family....

"There are so few of us," Ieiera said again. "Maybe it won't be a problem. After all, I'm number six back home, out of almost fifty families. Here we've only sixteen families."

In the event, when the *maneaba* was built and they had their first meeting, they worked out their relationships with remarkably little trouble and only a few embarrassed silences. Teng Koata sat at the high end, of course, with Nei Aana and Little Koata. Babera and his family sat next on one side, Abera and his wife on the other, and for the moment they left it at that, everyone else sitting where they wished, with much talk of how it was all just temporary. Luckily there wasn't much to talk about – just plans for constructing a new latrine pier and the cistern's puzzling unwillingness to fill up completely – and they had gotten used to informal talk at their evening meetings on the beach. Koata was careful to call on people by name, and that masked the lack of a hierarchy of speakers. But some of the adults weren't happy; they talked among themselves about how such a lack of structure made them feel nervous, unsure of themselves.

"Why's it such a problem?" Baiteke wondered. They were sitting on the beach near the landing, twisting strips of leaf into strings and idly watching the waves break on the reef edge. "I always used to think it was pretty shitty, back home, that father almost never got to speak at all."

Takena had relatively low status on Onotoa.

"The old people are just used to the old ways, I guess. It makes them comfortable. But it does seem like a lot of trouble."

"I kind of like the way it's been on the beach – nobody better than anybody else."

"Except Teng Koata."

"And now Teng Babera."

"Well, yes, but ..... dog crap, what's that?" He pointed out to sea, beyond the *Noriti*.

A ship had come into view, around the *Noriti*'s drooping stern. A ship with a long, rakish prow, two masts, a smokestack belching black smoke. A low, serious-looking gray hull. Flags flying.

"It's those – those Germany people, I'll bet! Oh shit, what'll we do?"

What they did was run, as fast as their legs could carry them, all the way to the village, crying out the news. Koata listened to them impassively, arms folded on his chest.

"Very well," he said at last. "Let's all go to the landing and see if they come ashore. Let no one speak unless I say to."

When they got to the shore, the strange ship was trying to drop anchor but – like every other ship that came to Nikumaroro – finding no bottom. Finally her captain must have given up, because the ship lay to and began putting boats in the water.

"So many boats," Kirata said with a nervous laugh. There was a whale-boat, and two other boats that looked like whaleboats but must have had engines, because no one was rowing them and they moved about. And a long, low, boat, pointed at both ends like a canoe. And they began hoisting things out of the ship into the bigger boats – it looked like long sections of pipe.

"Are they Germany people?" Nei Timou asked in a whisper. With three children, she worried especially about anything that might mean danger.

"Be quiet!" Koata hissed, but then went on. "I don't think so. Their flag looks like the one on the sky canoe ships, I think. Ameriki."

The whaleboats with their cargos poked at the edge of the reef, but couldn't find a way through. The thin, pointy boat was more maneuverable; the men on the shore commented appreciatively on its qualities, and the skill of its crew.

"Pretty good, for *I Matang,* " Takena mused, sitting down on the beach and lighting a pipe.

"Good boat, too," Eneri chimed in. "Almost like a canoe."

The long boat coasted along the reef edge. One man in a blue shirt and dungarees stood in its stern steering with a sweep oar, four men were row-ing, and a man in a brown uniform crouched in the bow. The steerer pointed, said something; he had found the low place on the reef edge that led in to the natural boat channel along the shore. The rowers rested on their oars while the man on the sweep studied the waves. He and the watchers on the beach all saw the big one mount behind the boat. He shouted something undistinguishable, while everyone on the shore sucked in their breaths and a couple of the men muttered "now!" The rowers dug in, spinning the boat to point dead at the shore, and they rode the wave up over the reef edge and in to the channel. The boat came up on the gravelly beach with a long, sat-isfying swish, and several men from the beach were immediately in the water pulling it to security. The man in brown jumped over the bow, nod-ding thanks to the men in the surf. He came puffing up the beach with a sailor's roll, and stopped in front of Koata.

"Anyone here speak English?" he asked, speaking English himself with a funny accent.

Koata spoke with great formality in English: "Welcome to Niku-maroro, sir. I am ... Magistrate. Name Koata. Speak a little English."

"That's a relief, for sure." The officer did something with his hand above his eye that was kind of like a salute, Keaki thought. "Lieutenant Devereaux, Sir, United States Navy, Third Officer of U.S.S. *Bushnell*."

Koata smiled broadly. "Good, good. Afraid might be ... Germany."

"No, sir; we're from the United States, here to make – uh — surveys and – uh – write things down." He mimed writing on a piece of paper. "You've been advised..."

Koata shook his head. "Regret... No, sir, not know. Wireless..." He spread his hands in a gesture of resignation.

"Well, we've cleared it with your government. We're on a mission to map all these islands, for the good of your – er – both England and America if – well...."

"Understand, yes, map. We – welcome, will help. Will visit village? We have – food."

"Thank you. We'll drop by in a little while, if that's OK. And I wonder... we're never going to get those whaleboats over the reef with the tide so low. D'you think some of your men could help us offload at the edge and bring the stuff ashore? We can pay."

Koata was nodding his head when Teng Babera stepped forward, holding up his hands.

"No, no, sir. Very sorry, but – Sunday. Sabbath."

Koata looked from the American to the Aroraean and back again, inclining his head to peer fiercely under his brows at the latter. He turned back to the man in brown.

"Teng Babera is ... LMS – our schoolteacher. He is... right, correct about day, but..." He turned to face Babera and went on in Tunguran: "Teng Babera, these men are on government business."

"With respect, Mister Magistrate, government business does not excuse dishonoring a solemn and holy commandment from the Lord God himself, given to Moses...."

"Yes, yes, Teng Babera, of course, but we must render unto Caesar..."

"We'll pay fifty U.S. cents per man," the American threw in, looking puzzled at the rapid-fire exchange between the two men. "And we can provide some food, too, if...."

"Thank you, sir," Koata switched back to English. "We... our village is... poor. Just started... Food and money very... good, but.... We very ... believe in God – both Catholics and Protestants... honor Sabbath.... " Teng Babera looked smug, and the faces of the other men fell; the prospect of money had excited everyone. They might not be able to spend it readily now, but some day...

"We will have to have a meeting," Koata told his people, "in the *maneaba*. These things must be discussed; it is neither for Teng Babera nor me to say."

"But God...." Teng Babera began.

"Is a merciful god and will understand his poor children," Koata snapped, turned back to the brown suited man. "Please wait, sir. Women will bring water. We have meeting, decide. Try to help." He walked up the beach, gesturing for the others to come along. The American lifted his visored hat and scratched his head.

Chapter 15–

The Towers, November/December 1939

No one could really argue with Teng Babera. It certainly was Sunday, though for awhile Kirata insisted that it was actually Monday, or perhaps Saturday; after all, who paid attention?

"I pay attention," Teng Babera informed him. "I who teach school, and lead prayers on the Lord's Day. I keep a calendar."

Koata raised a hand for silence. "It is Sunday," he said, "and with gratitude to Teng Babera for recalling us to our duty, I suggest that he lead Protestant services here in the *maneaba* right now. I will supervise Catholic services in a couple of hours.

Babera smiled broadly and hurried off to get his bible. The men all looked toward Koata, but he was impassive as he got to his feet and shuffled away. Kirata smiled crookedly and whispered something to his wife, who looked mildly shocked, but nodded her head. He punched a couple of other Protestant men on the shoulder and walked quickly away.

Teng Babera was well into his homily before he realized he was speaking only to women and young children. .

The pipes the Americans needed unloaded from their boats at the reef edge – along with barrels and boxes and big canvas-wrapped parcels – turned out to be pieces that fit together to make towers, or so the sailors said. Once they were ashore with the rest of the cargo the boats were lighter and the tide higher, so the Tungaru and Americans worked together to push the boats over the reef edge into the boat channel. Another long skinny boat came along from the ship, together with a broad, flat-bottomed one. One of the whaleboats was damaged on the reef edge, but not too badly. The Americans stood on the shore among their piles of equipment and waved as the ship turned round and got underway, steaming north with black smoke pouring out down the wind.

"Where it going? Someone asked in stammering English. A sailor said "Corondolet," which someone said meant a reef off to the east. No one knew why the Americans might want to go there. Those left on Nikumaroro set up camp on the beach and warped most of their boats around into the lagoon. The next day they were hard at work, and had arranged for about half the men of the village to work for them.

"Where are they going with that thing, I wonder?"

Baiteke and Keaki were sitting on the end of the latrine pier, watching the Americans on the other side of the lagoon. They had unloaded a lot of pipes over there, and disappeared with them into a trail they had cut across to the ocean beach. After awhile a pipe appeared above the trees, then another and another, gradually creating a structure. Now men were clambering over it, building it still higher.

Baiteki shrugged. "I don't know. To heaven, maybe."

"Where did they take the rest of the pipes?"

"Across the channel to Nutiran and up the shore. I guess they're building another one up there."

"What for, do you suppose?"

"Some *I Matang* thing. It looks like maybe they're finishing this one."

The Americans – little bug-sized silhouettes above the trees – were putting together what looked like some kind of platform on what now appeared to be the top of the tower. The thing was much higher than the *buka* trees – maybe twice as high, Keaki thought. And some of the men had come out of the bushes on the lagoon side and gotten in their boat.

"Well, I guess they're not building it to heaven," Baiteke giggled a little. A clever rejoinder came to Keaki's mind – something featuring Teng Babera and going to hell – but he thought better of it. Teng Babera had been awfully angry at the village's Protestant men and boys, including Ieiera and Keaki. Joking about going to hell seemed disrespectful toward Teng Babera, especially joking with a Catholic.

Koata had done little to conceal his scorn for Babera and his rigid beliefs. He had not encouraged the village's Catholics to help the Americans, but he hadn't discouraged them either. It was not his place, he said; he represented secular authority. But he had let it be known that he had little sympathy for narrow interpretations of Scripture, and he dropped hints that the secular authority might do something about such interpretations getting in the way of government business.

"You don't think Koata will send you away, do you?"

Keaki started; it was like Baiteke had been reading his mind.

"Why would he do that?"

"My father said that Katoi told him Teng Koata wanted this island just for us Catholics."

"Oh...."

"And Mister Karaka is Catholic."

"He is?"

"Yeah. I don't want you to leave."

Keaki didn't want to, either, but he couldn't think of anything to say that wouldn't seem unmanly. Luckily the Americans in the boat – the flat-bottomed one, with an engine – were speeding across the lagoon toward them, giving him a diversion. He nodded toward them as he scrambled to his feet.

"Let's go ask the *I Matang* what their tower is for."

The sailors were friendly, and even had some American candy that they gave the boys. They tried to explain the towers, but spoke such funny English it was hard to understand them – especially when they tried to talk like babies, as though the boys couldn't understand anything else.

"So they're making a map," Keaki mused, as the boys joined the other young people tending the coconut shoots. Every day the seed coconuts had to be carefully, sparingly watered, and the soil around them had to be mounded up to keep them fresh. This was work for children, and as more and more coconuts went into the ground, it took more and more of their time.

"I think that's what he meant. What did he mean, 'shootum sightings'?"

"I guess it has something to do with making maps. I don't know. And there was something about stars and planets."

"I think that's something for navigation. Old men know about that stuff, but maybe the *I Matang* are just learning."

"Maybe so. But they must know how to navigate; they seem to get around the ocean well enough."

"*I-Matang* do strange things."

"Yeah," Keaki mumbled, finding it very unsatisfactory. Why should they just accept that *I-matang* did things they couldn't understand?

In the days that followed, the Americans did more strange things. They went up on the towers and peered through shiny pieces of pipe with glass on the end, looking at this part of the island and that and waving flags in the air. These seemed to be signals to men on the other side of the lagoon. They also went up at night, and spent long hours there in the dark, or with just some dim red lights.

They didn't all work all the time, though; some of them were always in their camp near the landing. They were friendly, gave the children candy, and had lots of things to trade – knives and cigarettes and good tobacco, as well as American money that the adults said traders would take when they started visiting the island. Many people got to work making things for them – leaf mats, old-type swords of wood lined with sharks' teeth, feathered fans, models of canoes, carved boxes. Keaki tried his hand at making boxes and canoes, but found he had no aptitude for the work. Baiteke, however, was really good at it.

"How do you keep from making big gouges in the wood?" Keaki asked, watching his friend swing the small adze with which he was working the surface of a box. The box was carved out of a single piece of *kanawa,* and would have a fitted lid when it was done.

"I don't know; it's just easy. Of course, I'll smooth it all with rocks when I'm done, and make it all shiny."

"I wish I could do it, but I just can't seem to get it right."

"I know. Some of us have talent, and some of us just don't." Keaki ignored him

Baiteke had to hurry to finish his box, because after a few days the Americans took all their towers apart and hauled the pieces back to their camp. They said they were all done with their "sightings." And the next morning the long gray ship was back, and again most of the men and boys helped carry things across the reef flat to load in the boats and be taken aboard. It was Sunday again, but everyone got to work before Teng Babara even knew the ship had arrived. Not wishing to embarrass himself running around exhorting men who were already spread out in lines across the reef passing gear to one another, Teng Babera stalked back to his house and stayed there.

"Probably praying for our souls," Baiteki said, "or against them." Keake felt a little worried.

Though the "sightings" were done, the American sailors apparently had more work to do, because the men who took gear out to the boats brought other gear back, and another flat-bottomed skiff. The captain himself came ashore – a careworn looking man in a brown suit and officer's hat, and talked earnestly with Koata about taking care of the things they were leaving, against the time they would come back to work some more. Koata's grandson – everyone still called him Little Koata, though he was now almost as tall as the magistrate – said his grandfather had been polite in his talk with them, but was deeply affronted that the Americans would think the people of the village might steal.

The Americans weren't gone long. After about a week the *Bushnell* appeared again in the lee, and put more men ashore. These were as industrious as the others had been, but they worked in the lagoon, attaching the flat bottomed boats together to form a broad platform and cruising back and forth from one side to the other. They dropped weighted chains into the water at intervals and hauled them up again.

"Leads," Keaki mused. "They're taking soundings."

"Funny thing to do. They're not going to run into anything with that flat bottom boat that they can't get off." Baiteke was working on another box, and hadn't looked up.

"I'll bet they're making another map. First they mapped the land, now the lagoon. They're mapping depths."

"I guess so."

"I wonder why."

"I-Matang..."

Just before the long gray ship came back again and the sailors loaded everything up, Baiteke finished his second box and traded it for a sweet-tasting dark coloured drink in a bottle, called Coca-Cola. The captain and some other officers came ashore in one of the pointy boats and had another meeting with Koata; there was lots of hand shaking, and they paid him some money. Lots of the adults went aboard the ship, some paddling in canoes, others going in the long pointy boats, and had a last opportunity to trade. Then the ship steamed away and life returned to its normal rhythms. But Koata and Babera continued to be coldly polite and formal on the rare occasions when they talked. And Keaki continued to wonder about a world in which adult men traveled around in big ships building towers and making maps and sailing away again.

"Over the horizon," he muttered, sitting on the beach throwing stones into the sunset-reddened sea.

"What?" Baiteke skipped a stone; it made five skips.

"Everything."

Chapter 16 –

The Canoe Builder, January-March 1940

Early in the new year the little schooner *Kiakia* appeared in the lee and the whaleboat brought Mister Gallagher ashore. The Administrator didn't stay long – just long enough to tour the village with Koata, inspect the coconut plantings, and peer into the cistern through the little door that Mister Kimo had let into the gable end. Koata explained that the water caught by the structure was sufficient for present needs, but that it never got more than half full, no matter how hard or long it rained.

"Probably needs to be re-rendered," Mister Gallagher opined, and promised to send Jack Kimo to see to it. Keaki and Baiteke, watching with all the other boys and girls, grinned broadly and punched each other; Mister Kimo would be coming back!

Kiakia also brought a new family – a Tuvaluan carpenter named Temou, his wife, son, and daughter. With Koata's acquiescence they moved into Jack Kimo's house, unoccupied since the cement mixer navigators had sailed away. He and Jack were some kind of cousins, but as Kirata said with a shrug, all Tuvaluans seem to be cousins.

Temou had barely unloaded his gear before he was off with Kirata – an old friend from some previous adventure – to fish on the Nutiran reef. They came back with a canoe-load of fish and distributed them gaily to all the families.

"What a reef!" Temou exulted; he spoke Tungaru fluently. "I've never seen so many fish! And they just swim up and look at you like they're saying 'oh Mister Temou, please spear me!'"

Kirata laughed and clapped his friend on the back. "It was good of you, Teng Temou, to so graciously accommodate them." He turned to Eneri; "You should see this guy! He spears a big grouper – stab! Before the grouper even knows he's dead, Temou flips around and spears a jack – stab! Then in one smooth movement he gathers them both up and zips right up to the canoe before the sharks even know he's there!"

"Sharks," Temou scoffed. "Sharks and I have an understanding. Temou doesn't bother them, and they don't bother Temou. You people have a fantastic reef here. Tomorrow – with your permission, Mister Magistrate – I'd like to walk all the way round it and scout out good fishing spots. I'll bet there are turtle, too."

Koata nodded his agreement, and several of the men volunteered that there were lots of turtles, especially at the southeast end of the island. Soon all the men in the village, except Koata who pronounced himself too old and feeble, had decided to accompany Temou and show him all the best spots.

They set out right after breakfast, walking along the shore southeast from the landing. The tide was out, so they walked the reef flat, examining tide pools and every now and then jumping off the edge of the reef to check the ledges and crevices. Fish were everywhere; birds soared overhead, a pod of dolphins played offshore. All the older boys had gone along, of course, and even little Eddie, Temou's son. Unfortunately in Baiteke's eyes, his sister Segalo hadn't come with them – none of the women or girls had.

"Whoaa," Baiteke shook his head, "she is SO beautiful!"

"She's much too old for you. And too pretty. And probably too smart."

"So you say. I'll bet she'd appreciate a wood carver like me – her father being a carpenter."

"Well, you do make quite a box, so I guess if she wants boxes, you're the man for Segalo."

For quite a way southeast from the landing, the shore was hard, shelving coral that merged with the reef flat. Some of the rocks had shellfish embedded right in them, as though the rock were hardened mud. Inshore was a low surge ridge, made up of broken coral thrown up by long-ago storms. It was black with sun-loving algae, and nothing grew on it but a little *mao*.

"But on the other hand," Keaki mused, hopping down from the surge ridge to the shore next to his friend, "she may be sick of living with a carpenter. All those shavings, and chop, chop, chop all night and day."

Baiteke ignored him. "I'll make her such a beautiful box. But maybe first something to hang around her neck."

They reached the smaller of the two passages connecting the lagoon with the sea, which someone had named "Baureke." The shore was coarse sand now, interspersed with cobbles and intervals of hard coral. They began to see turtle tracks – trench-like marks where turtles had dragged themselves out of the waves and up across the beach to make nests and lay their leathery eggs. A couple of the men who had gotten tired gathered armfuls of eggs to take back to the village, loading them in burlap sacks they had brought along. The rest of the party carried on around the far southeast end of the island, skirting a fine *buka* forest.

The windward side was a long sand beach, with never an embayment or cove, running straight all the way to the northwest cape, four miles away. Where the beach ended there was a wall of solid *mao*, punctuated by a few coconut palms whose parent nuts had washed up from somewhere. Behind the *mao* the land was heavily wooded with *buka*. And Temou spotted something else.

"Look at that *tou!*" He pointed to a cluster of tall trees just behind the *mao*.

"That's *te kanawa,*" Baiteke volunteered.

"Right, right, that's the Tungaru word for it. I've never seen one so tall and straight. I guess nobody's been here to cut these trees since... forever."

"That's true," Kirata said, puffing out his chest and tapping it with his finger. "We are the first men of Nikumaroro."

"Since the time of Nei Manganibuka," Eneri warned; "Don't commit the sin of pride, Kirata."

"Nor," Teng Barbera began, "the sin of worshiping false gods..."

"Of course not, *te minita*," Kirata said humbly. "I was only joking. But Temou's right; those are very big *kanawa*."

Temou was already on his way across the beach to look at the trees up close. Kirata ran up with his knife and began cutting a path through the beachfront *mao*. Soon they were all through the *mao* fringe and up the surge ridge that lay behind it, standing under the trees. There were four really big trees on the ridge crest, and more – not as big – on the slope down toward the lagoon. Temou walked around the base of the largest, slowly, awestruck.

"What a canoe this will make!" he whispered. "Whose land is this?"

"Nobody's," Babera informed him. "Not yet assigned."

"None of the land's really been assigned," Ieiera explained. "Since we're all just government employees, and nobody's really decided to stay here. Though as far as I'm concerned...."

"You're the First Man of Nikumaroro!" Kirata whooped. "Somebody make a crown for the First Man! Adam! Where's Eve?"

"I'm looking for her up in this tree, but seeing nothing but birds. Anyway, Temou, if the magistrate agrees, I'm sure you're welcome to this *kanawa*."

"It'll be the village's canoe," Temou said, "or maybe for Mister Gallagher."

It took some time to pull Temou away from his tree, and the rest of the way around the island he seemed distracted, barely able to evince interest in the fish that crowded the tide pools, or in the interwoven turtle tracks. He and Baiteke fell into animated conversation about trees and wood and carving. Keaki was surprised that his friend actually knew so much.

Chapter 17 –

The *Kanawa* Expedition, April 1940

The sky seemed endless, Keaki thought, endless blue behind the clouds, so white they almost hurt his eyes. As the teacher said, in school back on Temeroa — endless space, sprinkled with stars that are really suns. Endless, but what is endless? What has no limits? God's love, the teacher would say....

"If you keep gawking at the sky like that," Teng Kirata laughed, "you'll get an eye full of bird shit."

"And we're lucky he's not steering," Teng Abera added; "we'd be hung up on a coral head by now. Paddle, lazy boy!"

He'd *been* paddling, Keaki thought. Nothing hard about paddling while thinking of something else. But he stabbed the murky lagoon water and pulled hard; the canoe shot ahead. The others followed suit, laughing and hooting, and a race was on with Teng Takena's outrigger, off to the right. The Onotoan and his fellow paddlers – Baiteke, and Temou– shouted thanks to them for waking up, digging in with their own paddles and sending their canoe flying. Little sharks fled in all directions.

The lagoon shore slid past. *Buka* forest, dark in shadow. From beyond came the boom of surf on the windward reef.

The windward side, home of the *anti*. Keaki frowned. The island had been uninhabited until Teng Koata and the working party got here. If no people had died here, could there be *anti?*

But people had lived here, hadn't they? The people whose firstborn were stolen by the Samoan warriors to feed their nobles? Angry *anti,* those would be.

But had they really been here? If so, why weren't there any signs of them? No grave markers, no stone house platforms?

Were *anti* always the ghosts of ancestors? Every one he could recall hearing of had been – or hadn't had a known identity, was just a fearsome thing encountered in the forest or on the shore, on the reef sometimes, or at sea. Especially on the windward sides of islands.

And Nei Manganibuka had been here, if no one else. And though she loved and took care of the people, if she were angered....

How did she feel about the *bukas* they'd been cutting in such numbers? Her special trees. But Nei Aana had heard her say that she was pleased with them, and wanted the colony to thrive. To do that, they had to cut trees and plant coconuts, didn't they?

Of course, that had been on the lee side of the island, on the point of land by the *baneawa* fish ponds. Those ponds, and the grove of *kanawa* between them, were far behind now. Ahead of them in the distance was Temou's *kanawa* – or *kou,* as he called it, and another that Teng Koata wanted. On the windward side.

Keaki mused that he and the others had walked all the way up the windward side that day, a month or so ago before the latest rains, and no *anti* had bothered them.

But they hadn't been cutting trees.

Well, he thought, at least it's not *buka* we'll be cutting. Maybe Nei Manganibuka doesn't care about *kanawa.*

Teng Takena's canoe was pulling ahead. Teng Abera shouted at Keaki to paddle harder. Crap of a serious octopus, he thought, what did these men want of him? This was hard paddling, with the canoe all loaded up with metal. He glanced again at the sheets of rusty corrugated iron riding the platform between the hull and the outrigger. What was Temou going to do with that ugly stuff?

He dug and pulled, through the tiredness and pain in his shoulder. They came even with the other canoe, edged ahead. Teng Takena shouted something about paddling like old women with overused cunts. Keaki wondered what a cunt felt like, when one was using it. Thought of Era, her smile, the way her hair shone in the sun. Considered hair, where it grew, its character. Shook his head to drive away the pictures that his mind began to construct.

He concentrated on his paddling, but his mind drifted again, this time to the metal that weighed them down. He thought about the old house they had torn down to get the rusty stuff, up on Nutiran. Koata said it had been built by the Neiue islanders who'd planted coconuts here, many years ago. "You've them to thank for the trees and nuts we have now," he said, "few as they are." They must have cut down *buka* to plant those coconuts, Keaki thought now. He wondered how they had made out, and then realized that, of course, they hadn't.

So what had happened to them? Did they go back to their home islands, disappointed with Nikumaroro? Or did they, perhaps, never leave? Were their *anti* prowling Nutiran? Or did they live on the windward side, like other *anti*? Could an *anti* be said to "live," exactly? Did birds become *anti* when they died? Pigs? Coconut crabs?

Teng Takena shouted and pointed toward shore. A small bay, lined with shelving coral, one piece broken off forming an island about the size of a large sleeping mat, its flat top dipping into the water on one side. *Mao,* some *ren,* a few *kanawa* along the shoreline, and behind them, on the slopes and crest of the surge ridge, the really big *kanawa*. They rested on their paddles, dipped them to slow the canoes and turn them toward the shore.

The canoes grounded a few meters from the shelving coral that lined this part of the lagoon. They waded ashore through soft whitish sludge, part coral sand and part bird shit, pulling the canoes. There was a narrow beach backed by a coral ledge, with overhanging *mao* to which they tied off the canoes' painters. Up on the ledge, the actual shore, the tangled thicket of *mao* blocked their view of the trees beyond.

Kirata took charge, bowing extravagantly to Temou.

"Mister Temou, your tree is waiting for you. Will you lead the way?"

"Indeed I shall, Teng Kirata, but first we should unload the iron."

"Ha! My canoe will be grateful to get rid of that ugly stuff!" Kirata motioned to the others to follow and waded back to his canoe, his feet stirring up milky clouds on the bottom.

The old sheet metal was heavy and awkward, and dotted with rusted-through holes. It had been a struggle to get the pieces off the ruins of the collapsed building up on Nutiran, and to get them down to the lagoon shore. Now they had a lot fewer people to carry the stuff, and they tottered and slipped in the slimy mud. Kirata fell down and bobbed back up, sputtering and laughing.

"Bird poop soup!" he shouted. "It cures all sickness!"

With the metal piled up on the coral ledge, they rested awhile and drank some water.

"I'd hoped there'd be some coconuts down here," Kirata said, shaking his head. "It seems like they'd float down here and seed."

"There were several on the ocean side, remember? They didn't have any nuts, though." Takena jerked his head toward the *kanawa* grove and the ocean shore beyond. "Maybe they do now."

"Why don't we send these boys over to see? They won't be any help to us anyway, until we get a tree down."

Takena grinned. "Good idea! You hear the man, boys. Run over to the shore and bring us back a bunch of coconuts!"

"And tap the trees for toddy while you're about it!" Abera laughed.

Takena joined in the joke. "Right, boys, find a tree that spurts sap like...."

"My prick!" Kirata roared, leaning against a tree and shaking with mirth.

Keaki looked dubiously at the wall of *mao* confronting him, and thought about *anti,* but there was nothing for it. He took his knife and began hacking at the branches. Baiteke came along behind, cleaning up the cut stalks he left. The *mao* was a tangled thicket of interwoven stalks two or three meters high. The boys slashed on, swearing as colorfully as they knew how.

Actually, Keaki thought, stopping to rest and pant, if it weren't for the *anti* this would be a welcome mission. Even if there weren't coconuts, the wind would be fresh and cool in their faces on the ocean shore, and perhaps there would be interesting things to see.

But between here and there was another matter. It was steaming hot, and no wind penetrated the thicket.

"Maybe there'll be *ai"* Baiteke gasped hopefully, slashing at a wall of *mao.*

Keaki grunted, and fell to considering coconut crabs, why they congregated in some places and not others, their relative scarcity and shyness near the village, how much his father liked them and how he, on the other hand, had eaten about as many as he cared to, ever. Musing, he slashed down a curtain of *mao* and stepped into a clearing. And stopped so abruptly that Baiteke ran into him.

"Ow! Did you decide to stop and shit?"

Keaki put out his arm to stop Baiteke from blundering into the clearing. Pointed.

The *mao* had ended because the *kanawa* grove was beginning, its canopy depriving the shrubs of sun. The relatively clear ground ahead was shady and rather gray compared to the brilliant green of the *mao* thicket. The land under the big trees sloped sharply upward – the inland slope of the surge ridge. At the foot of the slope, directly in front of them not ten feet ahead, lying on its side looking at them with big vacant eye sockets, was a very round, very white skull.

"Is it – a person?" Baiteke whispered.

"I think so."

"Who?"

"I don't know, stupid!" Keaki stood transfixed, afraid to move or speak above a whisper for fear the thing would see him, hear him. Rise up out of the forest floor dragging its bones behind it, grinning like Teng Beiaruru on *Moamoa 's* moonlit bow, with finger bones reaching, grabbing....

Without another word, the boys turned back along their trail, first creeping silently, then running, jumping over stumps and piles of cuttings.

They burst out onto the shore and found – no one! The men were gone!

Keaki looked around wildly. The canoes were there, and the piles of metal, but where were the men? Had the *anti*.....?

"There they are," Baiteke pointed down the shore, where someone had just dumped a double armload of cut *mao* into the lagoon. The boys scampered over the shelving coral and turned into the broad cut the men were making through the *mao,* heading straight for the heart of the *kanawa* grove.

"Ho, you're back fast!" Teng Abera exclaimed. "And no coconuts, either."

"We... we..." Baiteke stammered, "we found a head."

"A bone head," Keaki clarified. "Maybe it's...." he stopped, deciding he didn't want to guess who it was, didn't want to speak the ancestress' name. Started to get lost in his thoughts – if the ancestress were dead... Well, then she'd be an *anti,* so...

"You found an *ata? —* A skull?" Teng Abera asked, embedding his knife in a thick *mao* stalk and leaving it there, vibrating. They nodded.

"Do you think it's a person's skull?"

Well, yes, Keaki was quite sure, though he didn't know exactly why.

"Not a turtle?"

No, he had seen turtle skulls. They were smaller, and more like boxes. The eyes were different. He shook his head.

"Well," Temou swung his knife. "We'd better go look."

Unable to admit how little they liked this decision, the boys followed the men back up the shore and along their narrow trail. Temou, in the lead, stopped just where Keaki had.

"Well," he said, looking at the skull. Which hadn't moved, Keaki was grateful to see.

"We shouldn't touch it," Teng Abera said softly.

"It's only a bone," Teng Takena objected. "We'll take it back, show it to Tutu next time he visits. He can..."

"No!" Teng Abera was vehement. "Not to the village! Too dangerous!"

"Bring Tutu here," Teng Kirata suggested. Tutu was the colony's Native Medical Practitioner, living on Manra as far as they knew.

"Bring Koata," Teng Kirata added; "it may be months before Tutu comes around."

"And ask Mister Karaka to send a warship, perhaps? What old women!" But Teng Takena made no move to pick up the skull. Keaki exhaled.

Chapter 18 –

Koata Decides, April 1940

Koata crouched in Keaki's trail where it opened into the clearing. He pondered the skull. He was alone. He had left Abera and the others back on the lagoon shore, smoking and looking uncomfortable. No one liked to be around the bones of an unknown person.

His mind drifted back to the skull of his grandfather, who had a prominent place in his family's house when he was a boy. Grandfather sat up high, just under the thatch of the roof, so that no one could stand above him and embarrass him by letting him see their genitals. He remembered standing on tiptoe and whispering in Grandfather's ear-hole, asking him about things that puzzled him, asking for answers, for wisdom, and sometimes for things – like the girl Aana, who became his wife. But almost no one – on Onotoa or any other island he had visited lately – kept ancestor skulls in their homes any more; it wasn't Christian. His father had buried Grandfather's skull, put it in the ground with garlands of flowers, after blowing pipe smoke into his mouth one last time.

Had someone discarded an ancestor's skull out here in the bush, on this unpeopled island? Why?

Or had there been a house here once, that had fallen down, and all that was left was the ancestor skull?

Unlikely, he decided. Not a good place for a house, here on the windward side, on the back side of the surge ridge, and besides, he saw no sign of anything that would indicate a house site – pandanus trees, maybe coconuts, signs that trees had ever been cut here.

He shifted his weight off the *mao* stump that was poking his butt. Why couldn't the young ones learn to cut a trail properly?

If it was an ancestor, he thought, it certainly wasn't *his* ancestor, or the ancestor of anyone in the party. So it, or its *anti,* wasn't likely to do them any harm; it would be wandering around looking for the family members who had dishonored it.

But could they be sure it wasn't a relative? The working party had been drawn from different islands and different *utu* – families. Every *utu* had stories about ancestors who had sailed away, never to return. This could, he imagined, be his own great-great grandfather, Pialoi, who had gone away in his sailing canoe with five friends to find new land, and never been heard from again. Perhaps he had come here, and died somehow.

Maybe that was it; this was someone who had come here and died, and never been buried. If that was so, the best they could do would be to bury him with the most respect they could, not knowing who he was or what his *utu* was.

But, he considered, this was Nikumaroro. This was Nei Manganibuka's island, and the island of the great cannibal wars with Samoa. And this was the windward side, the place of spirits. Maybe it was someone special.

He thought about Riki the eel, he who had raised heaven from earth in the beginning time. In some stories the first ancestor Nareau found Riki mostly buried, with only his head protruding, but when asked – there in the darkness under the rock of heaven-attached-to-earth – he had risen up and pushed heaven up and up, whilst Nareau chanted and Na Kika the octopus, Tabakea the turtle, and the others cut the ties that connected it to the earth's surface. If he were to chant, perhaps chant Nareau's creation song, would this skull stir, rise up with the rest of its body behind it and...

And do what? He shook his head. This wasn't Christian. What would Jesus say about such thinking?

But Jesus could raise the dead. Remember Lazarus.

But Jesus had reason to raise Lazarus, and anyway, so what? Whatever Jesus could do, he, Koata, couldn't raise the dead, and he didn't want to.

Jesus, he thought, would say a prayer and bury the poor fellow, send him on his way to judgment with all the respect owed a fellow man. Even if he was some criminal, like the other fellows on Calvary. That was what they should do.

"*Teuana...,* " he muttered "So..." Where should they bury him? Back at the village? He shook his head.

"*Tiaki* – no, not there." He didn't belong to them – as far as anyone knew – so why have him around? Don't tempt his *anti* to come bother their dreams, drive someone mad. Why not bury him here on the spirit side of the island?

"*Teuana!*" he said again, this time with conviction. So! That's what he'd do. He rose to his feet, joints creaking a bit, and duck-walked over to the skull to avoid showing it his genitals. Picked it up. Was relieved that nothing came after it out of the ground.

The crabs had been at it, of course; it was all rough from the nips of their claws and pincers. Its right cheekbone was missing, and its lower jaw, and all its teeth. He scanned the ground, searching for the jawbone. No sign of it. But about three meters away he saw the sunlight glint off something shiny, almost buried in the leaves and bark. He shuffled over and looked at it. A bottle, brown, with a long neck.

Setting the skull down, gently, murmuring to it to please be patient, he pulled the bottle out of the detritus. His fingers felt something on its shoulder – embossing of some kind. He held it at an angle in the dappled sunlight to get a better view. It was a word – a word in English, he thought. He had seen this word before, perhaps, but that didn't bring it to his lips. He ran his fingers over the letters, sounding them out.

"Bee-Eee-En-Eee..." sometimes the second "Eee" was not voiced in English, he thought, but only at the end of the word, and there were more letters...

"Dee—Eye-See... Benedic... Tee..." He stopped, startled.

"Benediction?" Was this a church thing? When he had just been thinking of Jesus, and what he would have him do? Was this a sign? But that wasn't quite what the letters said.

"Benedict-Eye-En-Eee...BENEDICTINE!" That was it, Benedictine! The order of the Sisters from *Aotiteria* – Australia – who had visited Onotoa last year, inviting his much-loved niece Lyidia to come to their boarding school. His brother was inclined to send her – at least that had been his thought just before Koata sailed for this island. Surely this was a sign, not about the skull – nothing to do with the skull – but about what Lyidia should do, what her father Lokona should do. Koata smiled. No, it *was* about the skull. He wouldn't have received such a sign, such a blessing, had his thoughts about the skull not been right. He turned his smile to the skull.

"Kantaninga," he said. "Wait, father. I need to go get a shovel and some men to help, and prepare for your burial. Then I'll be back to make your path straight." Taking the bottle by the neck, he stumped off along the trail.

Chapter 19 –

The *Ata* Catches His Canoe, April 1940

The four men and two boys paddled down the lagoon before dawn, so as to be at the place of the skull when the sun rose. Koata told Keaki and Baiteke to spread a pandanus mat at the end of their trail and remain there while he and the other men approached the skull. Gently, he picked it up. Murmuring words meant to be soothing, he placed it on the branch of a bush where it could watch the proceedings. He spread a mat and sat down next to the bush, still talking quietly to its occupant, explaining what was going on.

Kirata, Takena, and Abera took shovels and, taking turns, swiftly dug a hole about a meter deep in the gravelly coral rubble, at the precise spot where the skull had lain. Koata signaled to them when it was deep enough.

Sitting cross-legged on his mat, Koata took the skull in the crook of his arm, as though he had his arm around the skull's nonexistent neck. He pointed the vacant eye sockets toward the rising sun. With the back of his left hand he rubbed the skull's brow gently, then knocked softly on it and began to chant.

> *N mangi tiba tabekia, kaetia, kawain áei mæ ti, b e nangi nako abama ba Innang, ma Roro, ma Mouru ma Marira. Ao k na toua Manra; ma kanoa ni wam te ungira ma te taitai...*
>
> *I am about to lift and straighten the path of this dead person, for he is about to go to his land of Innang, and Roro, and Bouru, and Marira. And you will tread Manra, and the contents of your canoe will be pandanus...*

He sang on about what the dead person would take with him to Manra – the land of the dead in the west, not the island the *I Matang* called Sydney – and how he would get there. He sang the same song three times, gently rocking the skull and occasionally knocking on it. Kaeki felt his nervousness about the place and the dead person subside. Everything would be all right, he thought, now that they were sending this poor person on his way.

Koata handed the skull to Takena, who carried it carefully, with measured tread, to Abera, who crouched at the edge of the hole. Abera in turn handed it gently to Kirata, who stood in the bottom of the hole. Kirata, murmuring a prayer, set the skull on the necklace and amulet of *kanawa* bark he had already coiled there – the offering that would have gone around the dead person's neck had there been one. The four men took turns dropping handfuls of coral into the grave until the skull was almost covered, and then took up their shovels and finished filling it. They all ate some fish that they had brought along, and the thing was done. The poor man, whoever he was – or, Keaki thought, who knows? – maybe it was a woman – was on the way to the islands of the dead. Keaki hoped the *anti* would not trouble his dreams.

As they picked up their mats, tools, and food containers and started to make their way down the trail, a little squall swept out of the east and passed over the island, dropping a light misting of rain. Everyone smiled, and laughter ran through the group.

"Ráoirói!" Koata exclaimed. "Excellent! He caught his canoe!"

Koata remained in an excellent humor all the way up the lagoon to the village, and readily agreed that Temou and the other men could continue with the tree cutting the next day if they wished. "Just stay away from the *ata 's* grave," he said; "show respect for him."

Keaki slept that night untroubled by *anti* or anything else. He enjoyed a quiet, comfortable dream in which Era played a big role, though in the morning he couldn't quite remember what she had done besides smile. He was still puzzling about it when he joined Baiteke and the men on the beach. Everyone was in high spirits as they sailed and paddled down the lagoon.

They went to work finishing the broad path from the lagoon to the *kanawa* grove, and the boys finally learned what the sheets of metal were for. Kirata and Takena positioned each piece to smooth out some rough portion of the path, to speed the logs down from the ridge to the water.

"Our road, eh?" Kirata laughed. "Those logs will just go 'whoosh!' down to the water! Don't get in their way; you'll get crunched like eggs!"

As the sun rose, it got hotter and hotter in the pathway, where the boys – sternly warned not to find any more bones – labored to remove stones and snags, throwing them into the brush on either side. At about mid-morning Teng Takena and Teng Kirata passed through, heading back to the canoes. Shortly they were back, carrying the big two-man saw. Temou called for everyone to come up to the trees.

Teng Abera was sitting in front of the biggest tree, facing it. As everyone settled down he closed his eyes, held out his hands to the tree, and began to mutter under his breath. He went on for some time, giving thanks to the tree and the spirits of the place, and apologizing, in a way, to the tree for disturbing its life. Keaki found himself smiling. The windward side *anti* didn't seem quite so threatening.

"*Teuana...,* "Abera said, grunting and leveraging himself up from the ground. Temou took his place and spoke to the tree in Tuvaluan, making graceful gestures with his hands. Then he, too, got up and nodded to Kirata.

Temou and Teng Kirata took the ends of the big saw, and with a shared grunt began to slice into the *kanawa.* Several of the men began to sing, and soon they had all joined in.

"Rise up, rise up, oh people of Nikumaroro,
And cut down this great, good tree for Temou's canoe.
He will carve and build it with skill
And it will never break or sink..."

Kirata and Temou grinned and leaned into their saw strokes, keeping time. Before long the great *kanawa* shuddered, and in one swift move they pulled the blade out of the cut and leaped backward.

"Look out, everybody!" Kirata roared, as Temou jumped back at the tree and pushed it. It creaked, groaned, leaned, and as men and boys scattered in all directions it crashed to the ground.

Now the real work began for everyone; cutting off limbs and branches, smoothing out the log. Abera and Takena took the saw, and soon had dropped a second tree. By this time the sky to the west was turning color, and Kirata called a halt to the work. Wearily but in high spirits, they paddled back up the lagoon as the sunset turned the world red and gold.

"Ow! Ow! Ow!" Baiteke yelped, but didn't move. He was lying on his back under a small *ren* tree. Keaki didn't move either, but curiosity finally impelled him to speak.

"What's the problem, Brains-in-your-butt?"

"I'm lying on something that hurts my back."

"Try moving."

"I'm too tired."

It was the middle of the second day of work in the former *kanawa* grove. They had helped the men heave on the cable dragging the first two logs – for the canoe and the flagpole – down the slipway; they had not exactly gone "whoosh." The men had tied them together in a sort of raft, and then Temou and Abera had begun the long, laborious paddle up to the village, hauling the rafted logs behind. Kirata and Takena were resting and smoking on the lagoon shore, and had sent the boys back to the grove to finish trimming the remaining logs. This seemed grossly unfair to them both, and after half an hour of work they had grown weary and collapsed on heaps of leaves and branches. The sun blazed down on the new clearing, which seemed to shimmer in the heat.

"Ow! Ow!"

Keaki lifted his hands in mock prayer to the sky. "Please, God, save my friend Baiteke from his torment. Cause him to roll over before his back breaks in two."

"You torment me," Baiteke grumbled, rolling onto his side. "What *is* this thing?"

"What thing?"

"This thing I was lying on – well, crab shit, it's a box!"

"You've been lying on a box all this time and...."

"It was under all these leaves and twigs; I thought they'd be nice to lie on."

"Let me see." Keaki rolled over, folded into a crouch to see what Baiteke was pulling out of the deadfall.

It was certainly a box, made of wood, with a hinged top. Rather a nice box, something over a foot on each side, half a foot deep.

"Pretty box," Keaki said admiringly. "What's in it?"

"I don't know. How am I supposed to know?"

"Try opening it."

"Yeah, all right." Baiteke didn't move. "Do you think it *is* all right?"

Well, Keaki thought, that was a good question. Not far from where they'd found the skull, and here was a box. What might be in it? More to the point, what might come out of it?

"Maybe not. Maybe you should....."

"Oh, well, what can it hurt? Here's a catch...."

Baiteke threw back the lid, wrinkled up his forehead. "Bunch of paper."

"Paper?"

"Yeah, but all brittle; look, it falls apart when I touch it."

Keaki stood up and looked over Baiteke's shoulder. The box, he saw, had a lot of pieces of paper in it, with handwriting on them, but they were crumbling away right before his eyes. Some of the writing was gray, like pencil lead, some of it was red and smudgy.

"I wonder what the words say. Can you.....?"

"I don't know, but nobody can read them if they can't even pick them up. Look..." He held up a piece of the paper, crumbled it in his fingers.

"Wait... don't..."

"I wonder if there's anything else." Baiteke held the box upside down and the fragments of paper fell out, blew away in the wind.

There was nothing else inside.

Keaki watched the fragments of paper scattering through the forest. What had the writing said?

"Shall we keep it?"

"Not me. I wish those papers....."

"You could give it to Era with her comb in it."

"I don't think so. But the paper..."

"What could you do with some old crumbling paper? The box is pretty useful, though...."

Keaki shuddered, felt a sudden revulsion for the box, for everything associated with this place.

"Baiteke, I don't think we should keep anything from this place – you know, with the *ata*. And the men told us not to find anything else."

"Yeah, I guess you're right. It's not really all that nice a box anyhow; I'm sure I could build a better one." He pushed the box back into the deadfall under the *ren* tree, and pulled vegetation over it. The men were coming up the skidway, calling to them. The boys exchanged a glance and hurried back to the logs and their knives.

Chapter 20 –

The Sickness, April/May 1940

As he woke the next morning Keaki tried blearily to reconstruct the dreams that had made him spend the night tossing and turning. He found a strange mixture of Era and the skull. What did they have to do with one another? And the paper pieces with their writing; in his dreams he had seen them drifting together in front of his eyes, and the words – were they Tungaru or English? – the words made sense, and told him something terribly important, perhaps about Era, or the skull, or both, but try as he might, he couldn't organize the message in his waking mind. It hovered somehow, just outside his reach.

"Shit!" He slapped his sleeping mat, realized where he was, rolled over and scooted on his bottom out the door into the gray light of dawn.

He sat for awhile listening to the birds waking up, watching them begin to circle up into the sky out of the lightening treetops. Like the pieces of paper, he thought, but it didn't help him recapture the dream.

Stretching, yawning, he blinked his way to the lagoon shore to wash. Across the lagoon, the dark trees were gold-tinged, and *kiakias* were rising out of the branches, whirling pure-white specks against the endless blue. As usual in the early morning, there was little breeze; the lagoon reflected the trees and the puffy clouds, disturbed only by little shark fins coursing back and forth.

Baiteke was already there, floating on his back with his arms outstretched.

"Kang butae!" Keaki shouted, shaking off his dreams with a sudden grin, "Eat shit!"

Baiteke started, flailed his arms and got water up his nose, sputtered. He dropped his feet to the bottom and stood up, shaking his fist.

"Eat your own, you sea cucumber! What do you mean, sneaking up on me like that?"

"Sorry. I thought since you were up so early, you must be wide awake. Didn't mean to disturb your dream." He trotted into the water, fell forward, and flipped onto his back. Baiteke splashed him; he ignored it, contemplated the sky.

"Shall we fish today?"

Baiteke splashed him again. "No, let's fight."

"Don't want to. What if we go to Nutiran, look for more gray stuff?"

"I don't feel like that much trouble. That was a lot of paddling and tree cutting. And you haven't finished the piece you've got; why look for more?"

Keaki pondered the clouds. "Do you think the *ata* really found his canoe?"

"Teng Koata said so; he ought to know."

"Shh. There he is."

Koata had come out of the path from the village, walking down toward the lagoon. Moving slowly, Keaki thought, and looking strangely at his arms. Ignoring the boys, he pissed in the water, washed his arms and hands, examined them some more, and then did the same with his legs.

Keaki was still feeling bold. "Good morning, Mister Magistrate," he said. "I hope you are well?"

Koata looked at him, then over at Baiteke. Furrowed his brow. "You boys; are you well?"

Keaki couldn't remember the magistrate ever before inquiring after his health, or the health of any child other than those very sick and in danger of dieing.

"I am well, Mister Magistrate."

"Me, too, Teng Koata," Baiteke chimed in.

"No itches? No boils? Skin eruptions?"

"Uh... no." They both began examining themselves, finding their skins unblemished. Now, though, Keaki could see that Koata had big red pustules on his wrists, and up along his lower arms. Some of them were white in the middle; some had burst, and were oozing pus.

"Good, good," Koata nodded, turned, and went slowly back to the shore and up the path to the houses. The boys looked at each other.

"Maybe we should stay close to the village," Keaki said. "Something's happening."

By midday, the thing had materialized. Koata was not the only one with boils. Kirata, Takena, and Abera had them, too, as did Teng Iobi and Nei Ariti, though not so seriously. The boils were not especially painful, but all the sufferers felt tired and weak.

Koata called all the people to a meeting in the temporary *maneaba*. He held up his puffy, oozing forearms.

"You all can see that I have a sickness. So do Kirata, Abera, Takena, Iobi, and Nei Ariti." Up until now, we do not know the cause of this sickness, but I suspect that it is from eating too much tinned food, and not enough of our native plants and fish."

Nei Aana snorted softly, but said nothing.

"However," Koata went on, "this sickness may be contagious, so for the moment everyone not affected will stay away from us, the sick ones. We

will work as usual, but separate from other people, and because the sickness
makes us tired, we may have to rest a good deal. Do you all understand?"

Heads nodded, murmurs of assent.

"Anyone else who gets this disease, who finds boils on the body, will
report immediately to Teng Eneri for treatment. Do you all understand?"

More nods, murmurs. Teng Eneri, trained as a medical dresser and
therefore the island's medic between visits by the Native Medical Practitioner, looked at his feet and fidgeted with his hands in his lap.

"Thank you, then, and may God preserve us." Koata crossed himself, as
did the other Catholics, and the meeting was over.

Keaki and Baiteke drifted over to sit on a log lying across the beach.
Baiteke fiddled with the spine out of the center of a young palm leaf. Keaki
stared at the horizon. A tiger shark cruised by just offshore, its fin slicing
the gentle surf; a Frigate Bird swooped low along the beach.

"That *ata*..." Keaki began. Baiteke cut him off.

"Teng Koata says it's the food."

"Funny we all eat the food, and only those four get it."

"Teng Iobi, too, and Nei Ariti, and they weren't there."

"They're not as bad. But then, if it was that... if it... They wouldn't have
it at all."

"Thank you, Grandfather. Your wisdom sustains us all."

"Fuck you. What about us?"

"Well, we don't have boils?"

"Wait and see; we may get them. But we didn't handle it."

"Neither did...."

"I know!" They lapsed into silence and watched as Nei Aana emerged
from the house she shared with Teng Koata and Little Koata. She strode
purposefully toward them, but didn't seem to notice them, started to pass
them, eyes on the ground.

"*Mauri,* Grandmother," Keaki said politely. She stopped and looked at
them.

"You really have no boils?"

"No boils, Nei Aana."

"Do you feel well? Not weak, tired?"

"Maybe a little tired," Keaki mumbled. "Or maybe not; I'm not sure."

Beiteke shook his head. "I'm all right."

Nei Ana stared at them quizzically, considering.

"Did neither of you touch the *ata?*"

There, it was out. Both boys shook their heads.

"No, Grandmother. Just the men...."

Nei Aana sighed. "Just the men with the boils. Indeed."

"Do you go to get medicine, Grandmother?" Keaki blurted out.

"I do. But do not speak of it."

"May we help?"

"You may not. It is woman's work, old woman's work, medicine woman's work. You boys go fishing, do boys' work. It will be all right."

She didn't seem convinced, and neither were the boys.

Chapter 21 –

Mister Gallagher, Late May 1940

Nei Aana's medicine – compresses of boiled leaves applied to the out-breaks, as far as Keaki could tell – had a good effect on the boils. Teng Iobi and Nei Ariti pronounced themselves entirely cured, except maybe still a little tired. The men who had buried the skull had no new outbreaks, and the old boils started to dry up and scab over, but the men continued to feel tired and weak. Koata hid it better than the others, Keaki thought, continuing his visits to working parties clearing brush and planting coconuts, circulating around the village checking on the health and welfare of the families. But he seemed to sit down a lot, and even lie on the ground with his balding gray head on his muscular arm.

By a week after the boils had erupted, no one new had become infected, and Iobi and Ariti said they felt fine, so Koata relaxed his quarantine. The village returned to something like its normal condition, though things moved at a slower pace than before; no one wanted to overtax the sick men.

Temou worked on the canoe almost every day, under an arbor of buka leaves next to his house, shaping it, adzing out its interior, smoothing it with coral and pumice sanders. Baiteke helped every chance he got – perhaps to learn how, Keaki thought, but more likely to moon around Segalo. Baiteke had decided he was going to marry her, and nothing – including her utter indifference – could dissuade him.

Keaki scowled. It was the hot part of the day, and they had left off tending the young coconuts, strolled up to Temou's house to lie on the beach and nap. Temou was working on the canoe, and just as they came up the path Segalo came out of the cookhouse with some fish for her father, so Baiteke just had to stop and talk, with his dewy eyes fixed on the carpenter's lithe-some daughter. Who showed no interest in him whatever. Obviously – Keaki thought – she viewed him as a mere child. So there he was, peering over the canoe's hull at the object of his obsession, while her father instructed him in fine points of woodworking and canoe design. And here was Keaki, leaning bored against a post, trying to ignore Segalo's little brother Eddie, who wanted him to play. What on earth was he saying? It was hard enough to understand an adult talking in Tuvaluan, but a little kid? And who cared anyway?

"Go play with yourself, child," he spat at Eddie, and unfolded himself to stand and stride off to the beach, where he sat under a *ren* tree and looked moodily out toward the *Noriti* baking in the sun. It had lost its funnel in the last storm, and its stern seemed to have settled. Someday, he mused, perhaps it would be completely gone. What a strange thing to imagine. Why did things change? He stared at the ship and tried to imagine time rippling like the view of a coral head through the water. Could he see the ship as it was when it struck? Whole, intact, but on fire, exploding? No, he could imagine it, but not see it. Not like Nei Aana in the *kanawa*.

Eddie, who had of course followed him, waded out in the water and started trying to catch fish with his hands. He sat on a round flat thing that lay on the coral a few meters offshore, so that just his head and chest were out of the water, splashing his hands and shrieking. Keaki mused vaguely about what the thing was; it had appeared after the last storm had stripped away some of the beach. It looked like one of those things that held the anchor chain on *Noriti*, but much smaller. Mister Kimo would know what it was, he thought.

The sound of a whistle startled him out of his reverie. A ship's whistle! A ship must have come up from the south to lie in the lee, and was announcing its arrival. He jumped up and started to scamper down the beach, then remembered Baiteke and ran to join him, but found him and Temou already gone.

"Couldn't have waited for me, I suppose," he hissed, and joined the rest of the village hurrying toward the landing.

The ship was the *Moamoa*, en route – they learned later – from Manra to Tarawa. Her captain was in a hurry. The whistle had served its purpose – two canoes were alongside before Keaki reached the landing. He could see people aboard the ship lowering down big bundles of thatch, loading up the canoes. Then a whaleboat came round under the bow from the other side, with four strong men rowing and several passengers. Keaki shaded his eyes with his hands and tried to make out who was coming ashore. He felt a smile breaking over his face as he recognized Mister Kimo, standing as always like a great tree, with John and Edwin on either side of him. His wife was there too, and lots of bundles and packages, so they must all be coming back to stay!

It was only as the boat circled off the reef edge waiting for a big enough wave that he noticed the tall, slender *I-Matang* officer in white uniform and topi[3] sitting unobtrusively in the sternsheets.

Mister Gallagher was a lot browner than he had been before, Keaki thought, and even skinnier. But agile; he vaulted over the bow of the boat as it ground on the gravelly beach. He shook hands warmly with Koata, and then spoke and shook hands with everyone else – even the boys and girls.

---

[3]Pith helmet

Keaki felt shy about shaking his hand, wondering if the *I Matang* would recognize him. He did.

"Teng Keaki!" he exclaimed with a broad smile. "You're bigger!"

Keaki grinned and stuck out his hand for a vigorous shake. Later Baiteke said he'd looked like a fish flopping on a slack line.

Mister Kimo, of course, had been mobbed by men wanting to shake his hand, boys and girls just wanting to be close to him. Keaki had a million questions for him, but his irritation with Baiteke kept him away; Baiteke was there in the midst of the crowd, which now was sweeping away toward Temou's compound, carrying the Kimo family with it.

Introductions complete, Koata took Mister Gallagher on a quick walk through the village and the cleared plantation lands. Most of the adults politely left them alone, but several boys and girls followed the two men, giggling and teasing each other. Every now and then Mister Gallagher would smile at them and all the smaller children would burst into laughter. Teng Koata frowned, or ignored them. Keaki couldn't figure out what else to do, so he tagged along.

The men talked as they walked, in a combination of English and Tungaru; Keaki was pleased with himself to understand so much of what they said.

"You've done well, Teng Koata." Mister Gallagher waved his arm at the neat rows of seed coconuts sprouting where the *bukas* had been cut. "That's a lot of land to have cleared, and planted too."

"It was just a little work, but we did our best, Mister Administrator."

"Indeed you have, and the houses all look shipshape."

"I'm not sure we've put them in the right place. When the wind turns round and comes from the southwest, the water piles up and gets very close to the houses."

"Well, we can move them when we get the government station built. Did you say you'd started to clear the land for the station?"

"Um... yes. We ... had some men with a little time, and..."

"Good, good. We can make a fast start then, when I relocate here from Syd – Manra. Now I see how well you've done, how well the trees are coming on, I've no doubt that this island should be the headquarters for the Phoenix district."

"That will be an honor for us, sir. May I ask when you'll be moving here?"

"Well, I've got to make this trip back to Tarawa and Beru, confer with Mister Maude, and get more settlers for Manra and Orona, and supplies. Then I'll come back and directly relocate here. Maybe two, three months from now."

Koata shook his head slightly. "Sir, we may not be able to finish your house...."

Mister Gallagher laughed. "Please don't worry, Mister Magistrate. I can live temporarily in a tent, or whatever we can throw together. And now Jack Kimo Petro's here to supervise the work. As you know, he can build anything in no time at all."

Keaki smiled to himself. So not only had Mister Kimo made it safely back to Manra, he seemed not to have gotten into any trouble for the voyage of the cement mixer. Koata, however, changed the subject.

"Uh... you should know, sir, that some of the men have been sick. Myself, even."

"You don't say? A serious sickness?"

"No, no, just some boils and rashes, and we have – cured with native medicine. But we still feel tired, weak."

"Oh dear, and no NMP. Look here, Koata, should you come with us to Tarawa, to hospital?"

"No, no sir. My duty is here, and I am feeling better. Maybe when you come to stay, if I am still feeling bad, maybe then I will go to hospital. You will have... Kimo to help you, and maybe you can name another magistrate."

"Only temporarily, I hope. But we'll cross that bridge... we'll decide about that when I come back. If you're sure you're well enough to stay here now...."

In the distance, *Moamoa* 's whistle sounded. Offloading was complete; it was time for Mister Gallagher to board. They turned toward the landing, Koata shaking his head.

"I think we got sick from eating too much tinned food, sir. So we fish more, and eat more native plants, and now you've brought us pandanus and coconut from Manra, we will all soon be well, I think."

"If you're sure....."

"Yes sir. We will be strong and healthy, and if any of us are not, well, we can go to hospital when you get back, or build a hospital here."

"There's the spirit!" Mister Gallagher clapped him on the shoulder. "We'll have a hospital here indeed, and a store, a school, churches.... This will be the model island of the Phoenix!"

Chapter 22 –

Temou's Canoe, June 1940

"No one can make a canoe like you, brother!" Mister Kimo ran his hands over the smooth hull. "Where did you find such a tree?"

Temou grimaced at such praise from his famous relative – his mother's sister's son. "Across the wind," he said, waving to the southeast, "down the lagoon. I didn't cut it by myself. Those Onotoa and Aroraia men helped. There's another even longer, but thinner, and it belongs to the magistrate."

"Whew! You don't see trees like that on other islands. Will you sail around the world, brother?" Mister Kimo laughed his mighty laugh and clapped the smaller man on the shoulder.

"I think," Temou said modestly, "that I shall be satisfied with the lagoon and the reef front."

"Look out, fish! Flee for your lives! The mighty Temou comes in his giant canoe!"

Temou cackled a wry laugh. "They need have no fear if I don't get back to work, brother. But all these poor Tungaru people will starve. Where are you going to put the wireless?"

Mister Kimo had come from Manra to advance construction of the Government Station, and he had brought with him a wireless set and a dozen batteries, charged from *Moamoa's* generator. These were piled outside the house that he, his wife, and their boys would now share with Temou and his family.

"Right over there." Kimo waved toward the shore a short distance away. "Line of sight toward Tarawa, and a pretty good line toward Ocean. Can you tear yourself away from your beautiful canoe long enough to help me put up a shelter, brother?"

"Very well; these people can stifle their hunger awhile longer. Let's call your industrious sons, too, shall we?"

Kimo shouted, and John, Edwin and Jack came running from where they had been helping the other children chase down a gannet. Keaki and Baiteke came with them, with Little Koata close behind.

"Boys," Kimo boomed, "we're going to build a little house for the wireless, eh? We'll need a lot of thatch, so go fetch it. Understand?"

"We haven't much thatch," Keaki volunteered. "Not many coconut trees yet."

"What do you think those long brown things were that we took off the ship, eh? Bundles of bird wings? They're thatch, foolish children, thatch from the old houses we took apart on Orona. Go fetch a bundle of it, if it hasn't all been taken by these thieving Tungaru."

This seemed awfully much like work, but it was for Mister Kimo, so the boys set about it with a will, while Kimo and Temou picked out a place on the shore upwind from the carpenter's house and began digging holes for house posts. It took most of the afternoon, but by evening the wireless was set up in a snug shelter, wired to an array of batteries, with an antenna stretched from tree to tree. Mister Kimo tapped out a test message to Tarawa and got a response. Almost everyone was gathered around the little hut, and they burst into cheers. Nikumaroro was no longer quite so lost in the vastness of the ocean.

"Where does it come from?" Little Koata wanted to know. He and Keaki were sitting under the thatch at the edge of the wireless shack, listening to the funny sounds – beeps and boops – coming out of the machine. Mister Kimo sat at the table Temou had built, on a bench Temou had built, concentrating on a piece of paper he was covering with short and long lines.

"Shh," Keaki whispered. "Mister Kimo will miss something."

"But..."

"Shut up!"

The wireless carried on beeping and booping for awhile and then fell silent. After a moment Mister Kimo put down his pencil and turned around.

"Whew! That's not so easy! Now let's see what it all means." He opened a small book that Keaki knew – he had looked through it – matched up combinations of long and short lines with letters of the alphabet.

"Where do those sounds come from?" Little Koata persisted. Keaki was irritated, but only partly by the boy's insistence. He also didn't know how to answer him.

Mister Kimo closed the book on his pencil and looked at the little boy.

"Well, they come from Beru, from Mister Gallagher, but I think you mean how do they get here, eh?"

Little Koata nodded, and Keaki almost did, too. Mister Kimo looked at them appraisingly.

"Well," he began. "You see, the batteries carry an electric charge, eh? And when that electric current flows through the coils – the copper wire coils – in that wireless set, they make a magnetic charge, yes? And that charge propagates – um, it sends out, goes out, in waves through the air, and..." he stopped, frowning. Keaki and Little Koata looked at him blankly.

"The waves have – er – a frequency and.... Well, when another wireless set's coil is hit by the waves..."

Keaki shook his head, smiling crookedly at Little Koata. "It's an *I-Matang* thing."

Mister Kimo scowled at him, slammed his hand down on the table.

"Boy! Don't you <u>ever</u> let me see you – hear you – snap your brain closed like that! Like a fucking clam!" He seized Keaki by the shoulders and shook him; Keaki wanted to flee, go bury himself somewhere, but he couldn't. His mouth hung open and he felt tears in the corners of his eyes.

"There is nothing – <u>nothing</u> – that you or Little Koata or any of us can't understand because it's an *I-Matang* thing. There's nothing the precious *I-Matang* know or do that we – that you – can't know and do. Look at me! Am I *I-Matang*?"

The boys shook their heads. Keaki thought, "well, he is part *I-Matang*," but he didn't say it aloud.

"No, I am an island man, just as you'll be island men. Do I know how to operate this wireless?" The boys nodded vigorously.

"There, then. And can I make a distillery work? Build a house with cement? Build a cistern? Fix an engine?" Nods, nods, nods.

"There is nothing, <u>nothing</u> you can't do. Nothing magic about the *I-Matang*. Nothing!" He started to turn back to his papers, but wheeled around again, shaking his finger at them.

"And another thing! Your parents, your elders, know things no *I-Matang* knows, can do things no *I-Matang* can do. Can any *I-Matang* build a canoe like Temou can? No! Fish like Temou? Like any of your fathers? Build a house..." He leaned down to put his face in Little Koata's. "You, Little Koata, do you know how your grandfather navigates? Let me tell you a story. When we were first coming to this island, on that little *Kiakia*... We planned to go first to Sydney – Manra – but the wind turned against us and we altered course for this place. We called it Gardner then. Your grandfather had gone to sleep on the foc'sle before we altered course, and it was all cloudy; you couldn't see the sun or anything. And the *I-Matang* – Mister Maude and Mister Bevington – laughed and said, he'll be confused because we've changed course.' But – you can guess – he wasn't confused at all! He woke up, and looked at the waves and the clouds, and then went back to the helmsman and said he needed to come to port if he wanted to fetch Sydney. He knew exactly where he was, eh? Because he knows the old ways of the navigators, the ways that brought your ancestors and mine across the greatest ocean in the whole world..... No *I-Matang* knows those things."

He looked from one startled boy's face to the other's, the anger draining out of his own features.

"You respect your elders, you boys, and respect yourselves, too. Don't ever think the *I-Matang* are better than you are. Never!" He turned back to his papers, and the boys slipped out of the wireless shack as the setting sun smeared the sky with flowing patterns of red and pink and orange. Little Koata was crying, just softly, tears running down his cheeks.

"I'm sorry, Little Koata," Keaki mumbled, feeling odd about apologizing to the younger boy, but like he had to. "That was my fault. I should never have said that."

Little Koata sniffed. Keaki went on, to no one in particular.

"But the wireless! Shit, how can anybody … how did anybody figure it out?"

I-Matang or not, how could anybody find out how to send words through the air? And what was it about a coil, and an electric charge? Electricity was what made lights work aboard ships, and – well, how did that work?

"So much to know...." He put his arm around Little Koata's shoulders. "But it's OK, little man. We'll learn it all, you and me."

The night had gone black before they saw Mister Kimo again. The boys had lit a fire on the beach; Edwin and John were playing guitars and singing, Keaki, Beiteke, and Eddie were lying around talking and looking at the stars – and in Keaki's case, sanding his *co:m* with a piece of pumice he had found on the beach. Temou and a couple of other men were planning the next day's fishing, the women were in the cookhouse doing something with food. Teng Babera had just walked past along the beach and glared at them; the songs Edwin and John were singing weren't hymns. Mister Kimo stumped over from the wireless shack, sat down next to Temou and lit his pipe.

"I will be so glad when a regular wireless operator gets here! My hands are made for bigger tools than that little clicker key."

"So an operator is coming?"

"With Mister Gallagher, yes. What a relief!" He flexed his hand and looked mournfully at Segalo, who smiled sweetly and brought coconut oil to massage it. Mister Kimo lay back with a sigh until Temou tapped him on the side with a toddy bottle.

"Ah, thank you, girl. With hands like yours you're going to make a fine, fine nurse." Segalo smiled graciously and slipped away, while Kimo sat up and took a long drink, wiping his lips with the back of his hand. Turned abruptly to Temou.

"Brother, I almost forgot. Our administrator wants to know how many of those *tou* we have here."

"Four," Temou said, around his pipe. But one will soon be a canoe, and another...."

"No, no, I mean *tou* trees, growing, standing, you know, with roots and leaves and birds."

"Oh. Plenty. Two big stands at least – maybe eighty-ninety trees on the point by the pools with the little fish, and another handful down where the canoe and the flagpole came from."

"Ah. More than one hundred, then. Mister Gallagher wants some for the sawmill at Rongorongo."

"It will be a big job to cut them, and then float them up and out through the passage..."

"But we can make them up into rafts, yes? And put an engine on them and a screw...."

As happened with almost everyone, Temou began to be caught up in Kimo's enthusiasm. "Yeah, and in the shallows men could walk alongside the logs, to help 'em along if they get stuck."

"All right, brother! I'll tell Mister Gallagher he'll have his logs, and tomorrow we can talk with the magistrate about some serious logging."

"It's done." Keaki held up the *co:m* and turned it this way and that, watching how it sparkled in the firelight.

"It's been done," Baiteke yawned. "You've just been scared to give it to her, so you keep screwing around with it."

"Am not!"

"Yes you are..... OK, if you're not, why don't you just go over there right now and give it to her?"

"Well.... I have to do the thing right, you know?"

"Ah! Yes, of course! Edwin! John! Bring your guitars! We need to sing a serenade while..."

"Shut up, barf of a putrid octopus!" Luckily, Edwin and John were busy composing a song, and ignored them.

"All right," Keaki growled. "I'm leaving now for Teng Beiaruru's house."

"We'll all go with you, and sing a lovely fucking song."

"I'll stick your fucking song up your fucking ass so far it'll come out your fucking ear. *Kang butae!*" He clenched the *co:m* in his hand as he marched off into the darkness.

Halfway to the home of old Teng Beiaruru and his lovely daughter, he sat down in the middle of the road to calm his spinning mind and churning stomach. He needed a plan.

"I can't just walk in there and hand her the *co:m*. How would that look? What would I say? How would they look at me? Shit, what if somebody made a joke?"

Stars were shining behind the trees, *Nei Aiabu,* the Milky Way, dusted her path across the sky. Keaki lay back on the ground and watched, wondered.

"Maybe I just shouldn't do it. Maybe it's a mistake." But if he didn't do it, how could he ever face Baiteke? How could he explain?

"I'd look like such a child to him...."

Something was tickling at the edge of his mind. He lay on the coral gravel and looked at *Nei Aiabu,* trying to seize the thought. Calmed his mind, and shortly smiled, jumped up and ran to find some pandanus fronds.

Chapter 23 –

The Secret, June 1940

Jack Kimo Petro felt like kicking something. And he was puzzled, too. Teng Koata had said no to his *kanawa*-cutting plan. He couldn't spare the men, he said, and he had no orders from Mister Gallagher.

"Spare the men?" Kimo ran his hand through his hair, pacing up and down across Temou's canoe yard. "What does he need men for? I'm the one in charge of building the government station. There aren't any more coconuts to plant, until another shipment comes, so there's no real need for any more clearing. Why is he saying no?"

"It's probably..." Kirata began, then stopped himself.

"Probably what?"

"Umm..... probably ... he's listening, maybe, to his woman, to Nei Aana."

"What's she got to do with cutting *tou* — *kanawa*?"

"Well, like I told you, she had that talk with – that lady."

"Manganibuka? Oh, right, near the *kanawa* by the pools with the little fish. I guess that's possible. But I'd start with the trees down where you got the flagpole, and the canoe."

Kirata fell silent, studying a frigate bird that had just landed in a tree on the shore.

"Kirata? What's the bar to cutting the trees down there?"

"Um.... Maybe.... I think that land isn't good."

Kimo ran his hand through his hair, scowled at Kirata through narrowed eyes.

"The land isn't good? What does that have to do with anything? It's been good for growing *kanawa,* and that's all that matters."

Kirata squinted out to sea, paying close attention to the set of the swells.

"Kirata? What aren't you telling me? Eh?"

"Me? Nothing. It's.... it's something... something not for me to say, you know? It's – er —- it's for the Magistrate to say."

"So, clam crap, did you give your lovely lady her *co:m?*" Baiteke had found Keaki on the lagoon beach, tossing rocks at little sharks.

"What's it to you, poop-of-a-tropic-bird?"

"Seriously, did you?"

"I did."

"Wow! What did she say? What did she do?"

"Well..... I'm waiting to find out."

"Uh... "

Keaki's eyes sparkled; he tossed another rock and hit a shark, who flipped around and bit the water.

"I gave it to her the Chuukese way."

"The... what?"

"You remember Mister Kimo talking about the way his friend from Chuuk got his wife?"

"No."

"Oh, well, you were probably mooning around Segalo. The guy stuck this special carved stick through the thatch of her house and tickled her with it. She grabbed the end and pulled it, and then came out to him in the night, and they were married."

"So you got a stick...."

"Well, not exactly. I waited till everyone at her house was asleep, and then I reached in through the thatch with a stick, with the *co:m* hanging off the end in a nice pandanus bundle, and dropped it on her mat. So by now she's found it, and if she likes it she'll wear it, and start asking who gave it to her, and....."

"What about pulling the stick?"

"She never woke up. She wasn't supposed to. This isn't Chuuk, shithead. It's just the same principle."

"Ah. So she's going to start asking who gave her this nice *co:m,* and every boy in the village will say 'I did,' and what do you do then?"

"Well, I'll....."

"When God handed out the brains, he really did give you crab shit, you know?"

"*Mauri,* Mister Magistrate."

Koata looked up at Kimo's greeting, and moved to rise from the mat in front of his house. Kimo quickly seated himself, and Koata settled back into his place. Both men pulled out pipes and concentrated for a moment on filling and lighting them.

"The wireless reports," Kimo began, "that Mister Gallagher is on his way to Sydney, and intends to relocate his headquarters to this island."

"That has been his plan from the start, I know."

"May I inquire, Mister Magistrate, as to your health?"

"I am strong, Mister Kimo, but for the last of the skin sickness, and feeling tired."

"Maybe Tutu will be with Mister Gallagher; he'll be able to put you to rights, eh?"

"Perhaps. Or perhaps I'll go to Tarawa, to hospital. See Dr. Steenson."

They smoked awhile in silence, while Kimo composed his thoughts. A gannet cruised past, parallel to the shore.

"Mister Magistrate – Mister Gallagher has asked – in his wireless message – that you consider where next to clear for planting."

Koata nodded. "Ah."

"He inquires..." Kimo took a breath; he disliked bending the truth. "He inquires about that land you call Aukaraime, on the windward side."

Koata, he thought, jumped a bit – twitched, rather – but he remained composed. "Aukaraime," he said, noncommittally.

"The windward part of Aukaraime. Where we've discussed logging. This could be very – efficient. From the public works point of view...."

"Indeed," Koata said noncommittally, looking into the distance through his pipe smoke. Kimo groped for his next tack, found one.

"Is there anything about that land we should be careful about, Mister Magistrate?" Koata contemplated the trees across the lagoon, stroked his chin.

"Some of the soil is not good, I think, Perhaps we should start in the north – by Taraea" – he pointed with his pipestem – "then work gradually down along the shore."

"Ah yes, very wise." What to try next? Kimo racked his brain.

"The southeast end of Aukaraime, Mister Magistrate – I've not yet been there. Can you tell me about it?"

Koata knocked the ashes out of his pipe. "Two pools of salt water with some fish. Some *buka*. Some *kanawa*. Land is pretty – skinny, narrow."

"Twelve or ten *kanawa,* eh?"

"Yes, perhaps that many"

Kimo waited. So did Koata. There was no question which of them had the greater staying power; Kimo began to feel twitchy.

"Well...." He started to rise, defeated. Noticed something leaning against the wall of the house. Seized on the opportunity to continue the conversation.

"That's a handsome bottle. Did you find it here – on this island?"

"Yes. It has letters – words on it. Benedictine." Koata smiled. "A Catholic name."

"Ah. True. I wonder where it came from."

"Out of the ocean, I suppose."

Koata looked at him politely, noncommittally. Kimo nodded and rose to his feet, gave a slight bow as he backed away, leaving the old man contemplating his bottle.

Chapter 24 –

Koata Reconsiders, June/July 1940

With Mister Kimo on the island, although clearing and planting continued, most of the men and boys went to work expanding the cleared area for the Government Station, and removing rocks and roots. Koata exhorted everyone to work hard, and spoke of how fine Nikumaroro would be once the improvements were complete. But Keaki overheard his parents talking about how pensive and thoughtful the magistrate seemed to be, and Keaki noticed that he and Nei Aana seemed to spend a lot of time sitting by themselves, talking.

Most of the sick men soon seemed fully recovered, but Koata continued to say he was weak, and Nei Aana continued to treat his arms with leaf compresses. She also gave him massage, straddling his legs as he lay face down on a mat, pushing the pain and sickness out from his midpoint into his arms, out through his hands, chanting under her breath. Then doing the same with his legs, pushing the evil out through his feet.

"You are a foolish, inconsistant old man," she observed, wiping the coconut oil off her hands with a rag.

"You have the hands of an angel," he murmured, eyes closed, smiling, "but the mouth of a booby."

"It is a good island. Nei Manganibuka...."

"...told you. I have heard you. I don't believe it any more."

"Disturbing the *ata*..."

"Was a mistake. I've heard that, too. Do you think I'm deaf?"

"Well?"

"Maybe it was; I don't know. Maybe it was the food."

Aana snorted. Koata rolled over, sat up, pulling a piece of towling up over his drooping penis. "But whatever it was, I no longer feel – right, in this place. So we should go back."

"To Onotoa, where they have a new magistrate. What will you do? Climb trees and cut copra? Being so young and lithe."

"I never promised to stay here. I always reserved the right to return."

"So you believe. Do the Protestants agree?"

Koata gazed out across the lagoon. There, she had said it. The Protestants. Why did they exist? Why couldn't there be an island with only Catholics? Why couldn't it be *this* island? Why had Mister Gallagher turned down his request for such an arrangement – difficult as it had been to transmit the telegram to him without anyone finding out?

How did things stand back on Onotoa between the religions? What would happen if they returned? Surely Mister Maude would support him, as he had before, but would Mister Maude even be there? Was the government going to keep him on Pitcairn forever? He wondered what Pitcairn was like. They called it a high island....

"This time they may hit you with more than magic fists," Aana went on. Young Koata came in with an armload of wood; she nodded to him to dump it next to the fire, jerked her head to tell him to go join the other boys playing in the lagoon. He scampered away. Koata began to stuff his pipe.

"The Swords of Gabriel have been disbanded," he said. Silently acknowledging to himself that something like them could rise again, without the least warning. Protestants got such strange ideas.

His mind slid inexorably back in time, away in space. Back to Onotoa, six years into the past. He could see and hear them coming, a good sixty or seventy of them, men and women, chanting and dancing, convinced that they had received special word, special power from God, that they had a mission, were invincible. He saw the charismatic preacher Barane in front, urging them on, a mad light in his eyes. He recalled how, as he sat on a mat on the ground, wondering if he was going to die in service to the government and the King he had never seen, he had felt the weave of the mat on his backside and found it so pleasant, so enjoyable. How the thought of losing all that, the texture of living in the world, made him want to weep.

Aana remembered too. "You were a coral head," she smiled.

"No, no, I was not. But you were, you crazy old woman."

He had sat, feeling the revolver in his pocket but intent not to use it. He had told Aana to go away, to be safe, and she had responded by sitting next to him, commenting dryly that she might as well die there with him as anywhere else. And so with her at his side he had faced Barane and in a calm voice – he thought it had been calm – told him in the name of the King to disband his people, give up his revolt, go home. Withstood the blows that Barane delivered to his chest, watched the mad preacher turn dumbfounded when God did not strike him dead, saw the confusion enter the faces of his people.

But nevertheless, people had died, and many more might have if Mister Maude and the Reverend Eastman hadn't come when they did. Reverend Eastman, a Protestant. He still turned it all round in his mind, wondering at the complexity of men and history, the will of God.

"But that was long ago," he shook off the thoughts. We will be welcome to return, and take up our old duties. We are no longer needed here."

"If a Catholic teacher had come, you...."

Would feel differently, he thought. Yes, maybe. It was a great disappointment that the Bishop in Fiji had not yet seen fit to send a Catholic missionary, while the London Missionary Society had empowered Babera to teach Protestantism. And with Jack Kimo here again – that barely Christian man, with his power to inspire the people....

As usual, Aana knew his thoughts. "Jack Kimo is not Barane," she said softly.

"Of course not. He's a fine man. We would be dead without him. But Jack Kimo has nothing to do with it. We will go to Tarawa, to hospital, and then if God lets me live, we will return to Onotoa."

Nei Aana sighed and began splitting a fish for supper.

"*Mauri,* Teng Beiaruru. I've brought you a jack." Keaki shyly laid the fish on the mat at the edge of the family's cookhouse.

"Ah, thank you, young Keaki. You're a good boy." The old man smiled around his missing front teeth. "Era, you lazy girl, prepare this fish for me."

Eyes cast down, Era scooted across the mat and took the fish. She rose to her feet once she was in no danger of seeming to elevate her head above her father's, and went near the fire to fetch a gutting knife. She favored Keaki with a brief smile, and her hair fell around her face. There was no *co:m.*

Chapter 25 –

Aram, August 1940

Keaki enjoyed working on the Government Station. As he dragged buka limbs to the fire he visualized how Mister Kimo's great plans for the place, which he explained at every opportunity, would work out — the wide streets, the parade ground, the Rest House. He imagined Mister Gallagher in the Rest House, smoking his pipe and... well, what did *I-Matang* do besides smoke pipes and give orders? They had many skills, of course, most notably reading and writing so easily, but what did they do during the day? During the night? Well, when Mister Gallagher came, maybe he'd find out.

In the meantime, he spent much of his free time at the Tuvaluan compound, talking with Edwin and John, helping Mister Kimo, and learning a little Tuvaluan. He found that the language came easily to him, and somehow learning it helped with his English, too – though Mister Kimo talked to him in English a lot. Baiteke was there too, of course, but most of his time was spent on the canoe, or deep in technical conversations with Tumuo.

All the while ogling Segalo, who continued to ignore him. "Just like Era ignores me," Keaki grumped to himself. "Doesn't she like the *co:m*? Or is she trying to figure out who made it before she wears it?" Worrying about it was beginning to get tiresome, like it was more trouble than it was worth. But then, every now and then Era would smile at him, and laugh.....

Mister Kimo continued to be frustrated in his efforts to cut *kanawa,* and as the clearing of the government station site progressed, the need for *kanawa* houseposts became more and more apparent.

"Especially for the Rest House," he complained to Tumuo, slamming his fist into his hand. "How can I build a house so big without good, strong hardwood?" *Buka* was far too soft, and *ren* not big enough.

But Koata wouldn't hear of cutting *kanawa* without Mister Gallagher's permission, and Kimo's discrete wireless message requesting just that did not bring useful responses, from Kimo's perspective.

"Will bring tent for quarters until Rest House completed," Mister Gallagher had telegraphed.

"What makes me crazy," Kimo went on as Tumuo sighted along the hull of the canoe and found another rough spot to sand down, "is that he had no objection to your cutting this tree and the others, but now...."

"He's an old man," Tumuo grunted, "set in his ways. And his superstitious wife has influence over him...."

"And she thinks she saw a ghost in the trees. Maybe that's it."

"Well, there's still work to do leveling the site, isn't there?"

"Yes, but..."

"And you could pour concrete for the floors, eh?"

"Well, to some extent, but until we have the corner posts to set in the cement...."

"You have that concrete bathroom to build."

"That's true; that'll take some time." Kimo began to relax, drumming his fingers on the table.

"And tomorrow we'll start work on the flagpole, yes?"

Kimo laughed. "All right, brother, I give in! No doubt you're right; there's work enough to be done. And if I'm right in my guess, we aren't going to have Mister Koata to give us orders much longer."

It was the very next morning, just as the work day was beginning, that someone saw smoke on the horizon. Soon the dumpy little freighter *John Bolton* was in view, steaming in toward the landing. Mister Gallagher had come.

It took many trips for the *Nei Manganibuka* and the canoes to bring everyone and everything ashore. Crates of supplies, furniture, cement, batteries, a great deal of thatch, and so many people! Besides Mister Gallagher there was a wireless operator named Tirosi. And Mister Gallagher's clerk and translator, Bauro – a short, thin, taciturn man – and six men from Mister Kimo's public works team on Manra, with their families — ten people in all. Mister Kimo welcomed his friends warmly – especially Iokina, a short, barrel-like Tungaru Protestant man who was second-in-command of the public works party.

And there was Aram. Aram Tamia was Mister Gallagher's houseboy, who kept house for him, took care of his clothing and supplies, and made sure there was food; two women of the village would do the actual food preparation for the administrator. Aram was a slender young man of about sixteen, with a quiet manner and ready smile.

Keaki helped carry the bulky canvas tent – Mister Gallagher's temporary headquarters – in to the village, for erection near the site where the Rest House would be built. Was, in fact, already being built, in the form of the corrugated *asepestos*-walled cookhouse and the massive concrete bathroom. Aram was very impressed with the bathroom.

"So, the rain from the roof runs into the water tank on the ground, and then this hand-pump sends it up to the tank on top of the walls....."

"That's right," Keaki said, feeling very adult to be explaining this to the older boy. "And then it runs down to some kind of tub...."

"Yes, we brought it with us. A bathtub just like in England, with feet on it and everything."

"Have... have you been to *Engiran?*

Aram laughed. It was a nice laugh, and it didn't sound like he was laughing at Keaki, but rather that he was sharing something funny.

"No, but I've been to Fiji, and to Funafuti. And here to Gardner – er, Nikumaroro, too."

"Really, here before? I don't remember..."

"Before you got here. Mister Karaka left me with others on his staff and Mister Mauta's, to help look for water. Several days and nights, and things were rough! Almost no thatch for shelters, and we had such a hard time finding water!"

"Yeah, the men still sing about it."

"The Great Search for Water song – I remember. I wonder if my marker's still here...." He looked around. "It's hard to tell... everything's changed so much."

'What marker?"

"Just some concrete that the *Nutiran* men spilled. I wrote my name and the date in it. I think it was right around here somewhere; this is where we camped at first."

"I haven't seen it."

"Doesn't matter. Help me with this tent, will you? The big post goes in the middle, and the shorter ones around the sides to make walls...."

The tent was a fascinating construction. Keaki marveled at the way the poles and the canvas with its grommets fit together and became a three-dimensional structure. "Just like a house!" he exclaimed with delight, and Aram laughed. Aram laughed a lot at what Keaki said, and it made Keaki feel very clever.

He helped Aram unpack Mister Gallagher's things and arrange them in the tent. A package of sticks and canvas folded out into a bed. A flat wood thing folded out into a table, another made a chair. There were things to cook in and things to put food on, and there were many, many clothes, most of which remained packed for now. There were Tilley lamps for light, and a big electric torch.

"This is Mister Karaka's flying hat," Aram said, holding up a strange leather bag with goggles hung on the front. He slapped it on his head, with the goggles over his eyes, and grinned as Keaki giggled.

"You look like a grouper!" Keaki laughed, holding his sides.

"But I'm really a flyer!" Aram held his arms out from his side and pretended to soar like a frigate bird. Keaki realized that he didn't know what his new friend was talking about.

"You mean some kind of bird?"

"No, silly boy, a man who flies aeroplanes. You know, sky canoes?"

"You fly sky canoes?"

"No, no." Aram took the hat off and carefully put it back in a trunk. "But Mister Karaka does, or did when he was in England. And look..." he opened another trunk and unwrapped a box with what looked like a clock or compass on the front, and some round black things.

"This is Mister Karaka's personal wireless."

"What's it for?"

"Listening to, of course. Every evening Mister Karaka listens to the Bee Bee See, and it tells him about the war back in England."

"There's a war in *Engiran?*"

"Of course, with that Hitler guy. I guess you haven't heard. Hitler has thousands of sky canoes, maybe millions, and..."

"Keaki!" It was Ieiera, coming across the village with Kirata and Baiteke. "Come on, lazy boy! We're going fishing!"

Keaki grimaced at Aram. "I have to go. I'll see you... later...?"

"Good. You come any time."

They fished on the other side of the lagoon, off the point of land called Taraea, first spearfishing and then, as the sun began to go down, trawling with hook and line. By the time the moon rose, they had a good catch of reef fish and a couple of small sharks.

They sat for awhile watching as the moon broke free of the *buka* trees and soared up into the sky against the vast field of stars. Then Kirata broke the spell with a loud slap on the canoe's hull.

"Wake up, dreamers! Time to go home, and impress our women with these magnificent fish!"

They steered easily in to the beach through the twisting channel among the coral heads, and pulled the canoe up near one of the latrine piers. Ieiera and Kirata divided up the fish, making a pile for each family and for friends and relatives. Ieiera handed Keaki a big rainbow runner.

"Here, boy. Take this to that Aram, and tell him to cook it for Mister Karaka."

Keaki flashed a grin at Baiteke and trotted off up the beach.

When he came under the trees it was very dark, and alive with sound – birds settling in to roost, crabs scuttling. His sense of direction was good, but he had to be careful not to stumble. Ahead he could see a point of light, which he realized was from a Tilley lamp. He steered for it, and soon the tent came into clear view – looking ghostly white, though it had been light green in the sunlight.

"Woo!" he called, but no one answered. But he could hear someone talking inside, and remarkably it did not sound like either Aram or Mister

Gallagher. Curiosity overcoming politeness, he pulled back the flap from the tent opening.

Aram was asleep on a mat, just inside the doorway. Beyond him, at the back of the tent, Mister Gallagher was sitting at the folding table, turning knobs on the boxy thing that Aram had called his "personal wireless." The strange voice, speaking in English, was coming out of it!

Hundreds upon hundreds of bombs are raining down on this stricken town; there seem to be no end to them.... The whole target area is a sea of flames and smoke. Great clouds of black and purple smoke...

The voice dissolved into a strange screeching sound that reminded Keaki of crabs in a bucket. Mister Gallagher was staring fixedly at the canvas of the tent wall. His fist clenched on the table.

"Oh, God damn, God damn, God damn!" he muttered. He seized a glass of pale liquid on the table and drank it in a single gulp, shook his head violently.

"Mister...." Keaki began. Mister Gallagher jumped like he'd been struck, spun around. His face was twisted as if with unbearable grief, and tears stood out on his cheeks. He hastily turned a knob and the noise from the wireless was stilled. Keaki watched in amazement as the Administrator's face rearranged itself into a smile.

"Yes, young man? Don't waken Aram; he's had a long day. What do you want?"

"I have ... fish, Mister Karaka. For you.... Aram cook... for breakfast, yes?"

Mister Gallagher smiled – a smile with no happiness behind it, Keaki thought – dabbing his eyes with a piece of cloth.

"Oh, jolly good, young... Keaki. From your father...?"

"Yes sir. Ieiera, sir. And also Teng Kirata. We went fishing by Taraea."

Mister Gallagher took the fish and wrapped it in some pieces of paper, being careful for some reason not to awaken Aram. Keaki was amazed at an adult being so thoughtful of a child. Charged with conveying Mister Gallagher's thanks to his father and Kirata, he walked slowly through the dark toward his home. Behind him, he heard the wireless voice begin again.

Chapter 26 –

The Government Station, August 1940

"Two hundred feet on this axis, then, Jack?" Mister Gallagher peered under his hand across the Government Station site, cleared of trees but still cluttered with roots, stumps, deadfall and rocks. Keaki tried to visualize what the parade ground would look like, all clear and paved with coral gravel, the flag snapping at the peak of the staff. He couldn't quite imagine it.

"Yes sir, two hundred by one hundred, I think, with streets twenty feet wide all round, fronting the government buildings, and your house...."

"Can we afford to leave so much land out of production, Jack? What do you think, Mister Magistrate?"

Koata stared inscrutably at a point somewhat below the administrator's chin. "If government desires a parade ground, sir, it can be done."

"If we need this land in future," Mister Kimo added, "it can always be planted."

Mister Gallagher's eyes flicked back and forth between the two men – Mister Kimo shifting from one foot to the other, Teng Koata immobile. "I suppose that's so," the administrator said at last.

"And sir, if this is to be the capital of the Phoenix Islands, it needs an impressive parade ground. A place to assemble, round the flag, to march, to make speeches, have games, races...."

Mister Gallagher laughed, clapped Mister Kimo on the shoulder. "And assemble the firing squad when the administrator overspends his budget without due authorization. All right, Jack, I surrender to your vision. A parade ground it is. Carry on. Agreed, Mister Magistrate?"

"It is not for me to say, Mister Administrator. It is Mister Kimo's...vision."

"Very true, Teng Koata, but the magistrate should approve what he will administer."

Koata looked steadily at the administrator. "Mister Karaka, I am growing old, and as you know, I am sick. Who knows if I will live or die, or ever come back from Tarawa?"

Mister Gallagher looked for a time at the magistrate, pursing his lips. Nodded sharply. "Ah, well. God grant you a speedy recovery, Mister Magistrate. We need you."

Later, helping Aram unpack Mister Gallagher's books and check them for mold, Keaki put the question to his friend. "Do you think the magistrate will come back from Tarawa?"

Aram flipped the pages of a volume and handed it to Keaki to put back in the box. "You've lived with him longer than I have. What do you think?"

As always, it pleased Keaki when Aram treated him like an adult, and he felt required to offer an opinion. "I don't think so. He seems very – tired. Maybe because of the sickness."

"That may be."

"And you know – maybe I shouldn't say, but – I don't think he likes Teng Babera."

"Well, he's Catholic, and Teng Babera is LMS. That's another one by Mister Kipling; put it in that other box. I'll be glad when the Rest House is built, and we can put 'em on shelves."

Keaki glanced at the gold letters on the leather cover – He could make out the words "the writings," then a couple he didn't know, then Rud-something Kipling . "I guess it's just because I'm young, but I can't figure out why it makes such a difference which religion you are."

Aram gave him a wry smile. "You know, I can't figure it out, either, but Mister Karaka has told me that in one part of England – well, it's not exactly England, it's another island nearby – people kill each other because some of them are Catholics and others are Protestants."

"That's crazy!"

"Yeah, but the same thing almost happened on Onotoa, you know."

"It did?"

"Yes, I heard Mister Mauta and Mister Karaka talking about it. Teng Koata was magistrate there, and a Protestant missionary from Samoa talked and talked to all the Protestants and they decided to kill the Catholics."

"Like Koata? And Nei Aana?"

"Yes, and they marched up to Koata and started hitting him, but he was brave and told them to go home."

"Did they?"

"No, they chased him and the others into the Catholic church, and who knows what might have happened, but Mister Mauta sailed in with the boss of all the LMS missionaries, Mister Goodman, and they stopped them."

"Woo – I can see why Teng Koata doesn't like Protestants."

"I'm afraid he doesn't even like Mister Kimo much."

"Yeah, I've noticed that. Aram?"

Aram took another armful of books out of their crate and piled them on the table. "Um?"

"How do you get to know so much?

Aram chuckled. "I don't know much; I just hang around with young boys who don't know anything. Oh, don't look like that, Keaki. I'm sorry; I was just joking..."

Keaki had felt a sudden catch in his chest, a surprising tear in his eye. He flopped down in one of the folding chairs and stared moodily out at the lagoon. Aram turned from the table and stood in front of him, looking him in the face.

"Don't be a silly little boy, Keaki. I was just teasing."

"But you're right, Aram. I don't know anything. I've never been anywhere, never done anything...."

"You're only twelve years old, Keaki."

"Eleven, actually."

"Eleven. So, you have lots of time to learn stuff."

"Not here."

"Of course here. You've already learned about the island, and the fish and birds, where things are...."

"Everybody knows that stuff."

"I don't."

"But I can't use any of that stuff anyplace else, and I can't stay here forever."

"Where do you want to go?"

"I don't know. Fiji, maybe, maybe Tonga. Even *Engiran*. I don't know, I just.... It isn't enough to just sit here and fish and plant coconuts."

"You're ambitious." Aram said it in English.

"What does that mean?"

"You want – oh, I don't know, you want to do something besides being a farmer and a fisherman."

"I guess that's right."

"Well, you're right, you know? If you want to do that, you've got to get smart. And you have a great chance to do that." Aram held up one of the heaviest of Mister Gallagher's books – its gold leaf said something about the Roman Empire, and a picture of Jesus being crucified flipped through Keaki's head. "You can start by reading these."

"Mister Karaka's books?"

"Sure. That's what I started to do, on Manra – my wife and I. I'd read about half of them when we left to come here, and she...."

"Your wife?" Keaki stared at him wide-eyed, clutching the Roman Empire book.

"Uh – yeah."

"You have a wife?"

"Well, yes, but she stayed on Manra with her family."

"But you're..."

"Young? Oh, not much younger than lots of other guys who get married."

"Why didn't she come with you?"

"Well, she's even younger, and she has the baby...."

"You're a father?"

"Yeah, that's – er – why we got married."

"I don't understand."

"It's an *I-Matang* thing, you know? Mister Karaka insisted."

"That you have a baby?"

"That we get married, when he found out she was pregnant, and it was...because of me."

"That's...." Keaki was interrupted by the sound of quick footsteps outside. Mister Gallagher ducked in under the tent's propped-up door flap.

The administrator looked at Keaki with the big book, and his eyebrow went up in that startling way he had.

"Reading, Teng Keaki? Jolly good! I shan't discourage you from Gibbon, but you might want to try something with a bit more action – and shorter." He picked a slim volume off the table and handed it to him. "Try this, eh? One of my favorites, when I was your age." He ducked back into the sunlight where Mr. Kimo and Teng Koata waited. "You know of Stevenson, Jack? Lived and died in Samoa, and for awhile in the Gilberts, too. Wrote very amusingly about Abemama – my copy got water soaked in Funafuti and I had to throw it away." The three men walked toward the beach. "He died in Samoa, you know? Has the most lovely grave monument; I rather aspire to one like it...."

"He really likes that Stevenson," Aram smiled. "If you like that book there are lots of others. That *Kidnapped* is about Scotland, pretty near where Mister Karaka lived before he came here."

"I can't believe you're married, and have a baby."

"Yeah, a little boy. I named him Bernard, after Mister Karaka. That's his middle name," he continued, seeing Keaki's blank look. Ger-ald – it's hard to pronounce – Bernard Karaka."

"It makes you seem so old."

"Well, I am old, compared to you. But I won't really be married until I go back to Manra, or Alicia – my wife – and Bernard come here."

"A real .... Married the *I-Matang* way?"

"Yeah, yeah, with promises and things, and the bible. The magistrate on Manra did it, but Mister Karaka wants me to have a priest do it again if one ever comes here, or if we all go to Fiji or Tarawa."

"Wow...."

It wasn't long before Mister Gallagher and Mister Kimo returned, sitting in folding chairs outside the tent. Apparently Teng Koata had gone away.

"He's very strong on the law," Mister Kimo was saying. "He was the scribe in Taboiaki for awhile."

"And he did well as a policeman on Manra, certainly. Perhaps you're right, Jack. He just doesn't seem a very – um – forceful individual."

"He's quiet, that's all. But you know, when there was too much toddy drinking on Manra that time, he helped put a stop to it."

"Yes, so I've heard." Mister Gallagher sighed. "I don't know of a candidate who's obviously better."

"Another thing is that he's new to this island. He hasn't had time to pick sides."

Mister Gallagher leaned back in his chair; Keaki heard it squeek. "Are there truly sides being picked, Jack?"

"Oh, just the usual, sir. Catholic and Protestant, Tungaru and Tuvalu. Nothing we're not all used to."

"Old ways and new?"

"That too, but with Aana leaving there won't be anyone who really believes in the old gods and ghosts."

"Umm, I doubt if that's true, but there may be nobody who can actually communicate with them." Mister Gallagher glanced into the tent; Aram and Keaki quickly became industrious and concentrated on flipping through and re-boxing books.

"Jack," he said, reaching for his hat, "let's walk around the station again. We need to develop a full list of supplies for you and Bauro to collect in Tarawa." Mister Kimo looked in at the boys and winked before following the administrator out into the sunlight.

Chapter 27 –

Revelation, September 1940

Mister Kimo was leaving! Of course, he had to. He had duties all over the islands, and now Mister Gallagher wanted him to go to Tarawa. Keaki wasn't quite sure why – something to do with dynamite. And of course, his boys would go with him. He said they'd be back soon, but who knew what "soon" meant?

Koata was going, too, with Nei Aana and Little Koata. Going to hospital on Tarawa, because of those sores on his body that wouldn't quite go away. Iokina would move into his house and act as magistrate, as well as being acting public works officer.

Keaki felt a sort of vacancy within him. He'd gotten used to thinking of Koata as the boss of the island, and Mister Kimo – well, there was nobody like Mister Kimo. He liked the excitement that Mister Kimo brought with him, the excitement of the work he did. The work would go on, of course, but no one, surely, could conceive of plans, and make them real, like Mister Kimo. And Iokina didn't seem very friendly. Keaki might no longer be able to hang around when the men were planning the work, watching how the dreams of Nikumaroro were conceived and made concrete.

He leaned back against the corner of the Tuvaluans' house, cradling his bowl of reef fish and rice in his hands. The low, red rays of sunset flooded the village, no longer sheltered by *bukas*. The rows of coconut seedlings cast long, spindly shadows. Mister Kimo was finishing his own supper, telling a funny story about fishing at Manra.

Temou motioned from his place near the doorway. Eddie sprang up and got the oil lamp out of the house, lit it with a twig from the cooking fire, set it where it would illuminate Temou's work. Temou set aside his food bowl and took up the canoe paddle he was carving. Segalo collected the food bowls and took them to her mother, outside the cookhouse.

A pale shape moved along the path over toward the lagoon, trailing smoke. Mister Gallagher with his pipe, walking toward the wireless, where Tirosi had just lit his lantern. Mister Kimo rose with a grunt and went to join him, and Keaki followed. He loved these evening talks among the men – the strange things they discussed, the challenging mix of languages. Maybe Aram would come, too, if he'd finished cleaning up after Mister Gallagher's supper.

The wireless house was dark but for a kerosene lamp. Battery power was far too precious to waste on lighting, or anything else but wireless operations during the prescribed times for communication with Tarawa, Ocean Island, and sometimes Suva. Tirosi got up from his chair in front of the tappy-tap key as Mister Gallagher came in, offering it to Mister Gallagher. As always, Mister Gallagher tried to decline but finally accepted it. Tirosi and Mister Kimo sat down on spent batteries, while Keaki squatted near the door. Aram slipped in with a smile for Keaki.

"Any further news, Tirosi?" Mr. Karaka asked it in English. It was his custom to be at the wireless early in the time for sending and listening, to read any urgent directives or queries from Ocean Island or Suva and to supervise the transmissions, then to take his light supper and evening turn around the village while Tirosi transcribed messages and monitored signals from other stations.

"Not so much, Mister Karaka," Tirosi said, passing him several typed pages. "*John Bolton* is on schedule at Onotoa, so we should soon see our thatch."

"Thank goodness for that. And you'll have your transport to Tarawa, Jack."

"Five or four days, then," Jack grunted.

"Assuming fair weather and moderate winds."

"We'll have time to finish the bathroom in your house..."

"The Rest House."

Jack smiled. "Just so, sir. The Rest House. And finish lining the sunken garden, so if *John Bolton* brings the bananas...."

"Not the highest priority, Jack."

Jack shook his head mildly. "Nothing more important till we get the *kanawa* posts, sir, and the dynamite. And if the bananas thrive in the sunken garden, we'll know the *babae* will, too."

Keaki grinned at Aram and signed a silent "Boom!" Digging the big pits for growing *babae* – taro and other water-loving plants that needed to tap the atoll's fresh-water lens – was the major reason for getting dynamite. The small sunken garden between the Rest House and the shore was justified as a pilot project, a test. Never mind how beautiful it would be from the Rest House veranda.

But Mister Gallagher was no longer listening. He looked intently at the last of the sheets of typescript.

"News of England?" Jack asked Tirosi in Tuvaluan. Tirosi nodded, as did Mister Gallagher.

"More air raids," he murmured in English. "Almost every night on London."

"But RAF shoot them down!" Tirosi grinned fiercely.

Keaki wondered what an air raid was, what the RAF was, what "shooting down" meant. Nobody volunteered to tell him, but whatever they were, to judge from Mister Gallagher's face they must be something really bad.

Mister Kimo cleared his throat.

"And Koata, Mister Karaka – He'll be going?"

Mister Gallagher's head came up and he looked at Mister Kimo quizzically. "Yes, as you know; to hospital. See if Steenson can determine what ails him. And Bauro, too – he needs to see his family after all this time on Manra, and he can help you with the paperwork."

"And you no longer need a translator," Mister Kimo chuckled. You can talk like a native to these Tungaru savages now."

"Hardly so, but I'll get by, with Aram's help" He smiled crookedly at Tirosi. "I know you'll all help me."

"Yes, sir. All help."

Mister Gallagher looked thoughtful for a moment, turned back to Mister Kimo. "Jack, I know you're concerned about getting the *kanawa*. I think tomorrow you should take Iokina, show them to him, so he can get started cutting them as soon as..... possible." Even Keaki knew that this meant "as soon as Koata is gone."

John Bolton blew a long blast on her horn and gathered way to round the north cape and make for Manra. The crowd on the beach was quiet, the Nikumaroro people alone again. And this time, for the first time, without both Teng Koata and Mister Kimo. Keaki felt the hollow feeling again, the future vast and empty.

He walked back from the landing behind Mister Gallagher, who was talking with Kirata. Trying to speak Tungaru, but still with some difficulty, Aram helping him. Keaki listened, pleased to understand so much when they spoke English.

"Koata seemed very attached to that bottle," Mister Gallagher said with a chuckle. What did he mean, "attached?" Had Koata somehow been connected to a bottle? Tied to it? Was it sewed to his shirt somehow?

"He is taking it to his niece," Kirata muttered. Oh, Keaki thought, they're talking about that bottle from the skull place.

"Ah," Mister Gallagher nodded, understanding. "The one who's gone to the Sisters at Rockingham." Keaki marveled at how much Mister Gallagher knew. "Found the bottle on the beach, did he?"

"Something like that."

Keaki frowned. Didn't Kirata know where Teng Koata had found the bottle? Maybe not, and surely Mister Gallagher wanted to know about such things.

"Not on beach!" he volunteered. "From *kanawa* forest, near *ata*."

"Yes, yes," Kirata said quickly, shooting a dark look at Keaki. "He found it near the *kanawa* we cut for the flagpole and Tumuo's canoe – where we'll cut..."

Mister Gallagher had stopped walking, and was looking back and forth – Kirata to Aram to Keaki. How did he make his eyebrow go up like that? Keaki wondered if he could do it, and thought he'd practice when he was alone. But why did Kirata look so unhappy?

"Your English is quite good, Teng Keaki," Mister Gallagher said, "but I don't know the last word you used. *Ata?*"

Keaki felt his face get warm. He stammered.

"Uh – *ata*. It means – uh – head?" He patted the side of his own, and used what he thought was the right English word. It was.

"So Koata found the bottle near someone's head?"

"Not someone. Well, yes, someone. But ... not one of the people." Why did Kirata look so agitated, opening and closing his mouth? He switched back to Tungaru. "A head we found on the ground." Aram translated.

"You found a head? You and Koata? What kind of head?"

"No, me and Baiteke, son of Teng Takena. Mister Koata find bottle when he" – pantomiming digging – "when he put head in ground."

Kirata turned away, peering up into the trees as though concentrating on ripening coconuts – except they were *ren* trees. Mister Gallagher looked at him closely.

"Aram, please ask Teng Kirata if he can shed some light on this. I need to understand what this boy is talking about."

Aram considered. "Teng Kirata," he began, "the administrator needs to know about... this head."

Kirata seemed reluctant to drag his gaze down from the treetops. He spoke toward them.

"When we were cutting *kanawa,* down there" – he waved his hand vaguely to the southeast – we found a – uh – you know, *ata."*

"Ah." Aram turned to Mister Gallagher. "This man says they found a – skeleton head."

"Skeleton head. A skull?"

"Skull. Yes. *Ata* in Tungaru language."

"A human skull?"

"I think so..." Kirata nodded glumly. "Yes."

"That's very interesting. Why didn't Koata report it?"

Aram translated. Kirata shrugged. "I don't know."

"Where is it now?"

"Buried. Koata... we...buried it."

"Ah. Where? Here in the village?"

"No, where we found it. Where the *kanawa* is, where we were cutting them, at the other end of the island." The words rushed out of Kirata, almost too fast for Aram to translate. "Koata looked at it, decided to bury it, so we did. That's when he found that bottle – about then. It had that word on it – Benedictine – and his niece will be going to the Benedictine Sisters in *Aoti-teria,* so he thought he should give it to her and that's why he kept it and took it with him onto *John Bolton,* and....."

Mister Gallagher put up his hand. "I see, I see. Teng Kirata, will you come with me, please? We have some things to discuss. Teng Keaki, will you excuse us, please?"

Chapter 28 –

Back to the *Ata* Place, 23 September 1940

Mister Gallagher swung over the canoe's gunwale as they approached the sloping beach. "Oh! Too early!" Aram exclaimed, as the Administrator sank into the oozy mud of the bottom. The bath-warm water of the lagoon lapped around his waist.

He laughed. "No harm done! But maybe we should mine here for phosphates!"

They all smiled at his enthusiasm, and unconcern for having just sunk up to his knees in a combination of sand and bird shit. Mister Gallagher grabbed the prow of the canoe and dragged it toward shore, Kirata, Takena and the boys jumping out to help.

"He doesn't wait," Kirata murmured to Takena.

Ashore, Mister Gallagher pulled off the things he wore on his feet – Keaki marveled at how narrow and white his feet were – and drained the water out, hauled them back on as the men secured the canoe to an overhanging clump of *mao*. He picked up a straight *kanawa* branch as a walking stick.

"Right, then. This way, is it?" He started up the path down which they had dragged the logs. "That goes to the *kanawa* place," Kirata said. "Boys, your trail was more to the left, yes?"

Keaki's path had disappeared in the resurgent *mao* – or rather, would have been invisible to the unknowledgeable eye, but Keaki and Baiteke found it easily and began clearing the new growth. They said nothing as they worked to re-open the trail. Keaki noticed that the men weren't saying anything either; ordinarily they would have been offering insulting remarks about the boys' knife techniques.

He stopped cutting. "This is the place, isn't it?"

Baiteke looked around. "I think so, but it's really changed." With so much of the canopy removed upslope on the surge ridge, the whole area was growing up in *mao*.

Kirata cut around them to the left, Takena to the right. Mister Gallagher and Aram came up to look over their shoulders.

"Found the spot, then?" Mister Gallagher gestured into the fresh *mao*.

"Yes Sir." Baiteke and Keaki nodded vigorously.

"And you – Teng Koata and the other men, that is – buried it in the same place?"

"Yes, Sir. The same."

"Can you show me exactly where? Mark the spot?"

Aram translated. Keaki looked at the clearing with dismay. With the *mao,* and the deadfall, and leaves, and the time that had passed, he had trouble being sure. The light was different, the shadows.

"Right about there," Baiteke volunteered, pointing with the end of a long stick. Takena and Kirata nodded.

"No marker, then?"

"No Sir."

"No marker."

Mister Gallagher looked from one boy to the other, then back at the clearing. Raised an eyebrow, scratched his head.

"Right, then," he sighed, and waded into the young *mao,* which came up only to his waist. Tied a red cloth to a bush right on – well, close, anyhow –the skull place. The men murmured and Keaki cringed. The man had no fear!

"Here, then? Correct?"

"Yes, Sir."

"Right." Mister Gallagher looked up the slope of the surge ridge. "So it could've rolled...." He took a step toward the slope, stopped, turned back to the boys.

"Did you see the bottle that Teng Koata found?"

"Yes, Sir," they said, in unison.

"Here, on the ground, I mean."

"No, Sir."

Mister Gallagher smiled crookedly. "Fit for the Royal Fusiliers, you two." He sighted toward the apparent crest of the ridge.

"What do you make it, Kirata? The ridge. Perhaps two meters elevation from this point?"

"A little more, I think. We can survey."

"No, no, we needn't do that. But look, the land slopes down from the ridge crest to about here, and then levels off. There can't be more than half a meter drop from here to the lagoon."

"Maybe a meter."

"Still, it's a lot steeper that way –" he pointed northeast "—and that way –" southeast, "than that way" – pointing behind himself, southwest toward the lagoon.

The two men nodded. "Yes, much steeper."

"So if the skull rolled, it would roll from up there to down here, and stop when the slope flattened out, no?"

Takena looked dubious. "Surely, if it rolled."

"And if a crab dragged it, it would be easier to drag downhill than up?"

Takena shrugged. "Yes, I suppose."

"You didn't look farther up the ridge, then?"

"Well, we cut the trees right over there." Takena gestured into the clearing where the canoe and flagpole trees had stood.

"But you didn't look for – bones or anything?"

"I didn't, no. We stayed around the trees."

"Kirata?"

"That first day I walked up there a little distance to piss, but..." he shrugged, grinned "... but I wasn't looking for anything."

"Besides your prick," Takena volunteered.

Kirata grinned weakly. "Found it, too."

"Well, then, off we go." Mister Gallagher began to pick his way up the slope through the *mao*.

Reaching the crest of the ridge – only, as they had estimated, a couple of meters higher than the skull's burial place– they found the trade wind full in their faces. Their sweat dried almost at once, the refreshment made them smile. The roar of the surf on the windward beach was loud in their ears.

Mister Gallagher began walking back and forth along the ridge crest, stirring up the leaf litter with his stick. The others followed suit with a good deal less definite purpose.

"What are we looking for?" Baiteke whispered to his father.

"More bones, of course," Takena said, a little louder than was really necessary.

"Yes, more bones," Mister Gallagher said, a bit absently. "And artefacts – things the poor – uh – person might have used before she passed on."

"Or he," he added.

Keaki nudged Baiteke as they walked together along the slope of the ridge, eyes on the ground.

"Keep quiet about that box."

"Yeah, I've had to answer enough questions already. Besides, maybe it's gone."

Keaki glanced toward the base of the ren tree. Was that possible? Did things just come and go like that? In and out of the world? Or did Baiteke mean that someone might have taken it? If so, who?

The ridge crest curved round from northwest to southeast and then almost due south, forming a small wooded dryland cove near whose centre was the place where the skull was buried. On the crest almost directly above the skull's resting place, Mister Gallagher began brushing away deadfall with his walking stick.

"Hmm. This is interesting."

They all gathered round him and looked blankly at the ground.

"Aubunga," Kirata said, to everyone's solemn nods.

"Right. And they didn't crawl up here by themselves. Someone's brought these clams up from the reef or the lagoon."

Keaki shivered, remembering the last time he had seen *aubunga* on land. He glanced uneasily into the *mao,* but no one seemed to be there. What would Nei Aana see, he wondered.

Takena was counting. "About thirty shells. So fifteen clams. That's a pretty good meal."

"And spread out in front of this log." Mister Gallagher said when Aram translated, tapping his stick on a rotting kanawa trunk that lay next to the pile of shells. "Like someone sat here on this log and opened the clams."

Kirata scratched his head. "I wonder why they'd bring the shells up here? Why not open 'em up down on the shore, or in the water?"

Takena nodded. "Why not just cut the muscle there in the water, and then cut the meat out?"

"Well," Mister Gallagher said briskly, "we're not likely to find out by standing here. Onward."

Following the ridge in a northerly direction, they were perhaps twenty meters northeast of the skull's resting place and getting close to the *ren* tree when Mister Gallagher stopped again, this time dropping to his knees.

"Ah-ha!"

"Ra?" Kirata and Takena asked in unison. "What?"

"A leg bone – femur, I think. Yes, and look there, that's... a humerus. No, no, don't crowd too close! Be careful where you step! Mind we don't break anything." He began to pick up leaves and twigs. Aram saw everyone's quizzical looks and translated quickly, puzzling himself over the bone names.

Mister Gallagher was all business. "Here, let's be organized. Let's line up over... here..." still crouching, he duck-walked backwards about six feet. The others – Aram included – backed up further, looking at each other, thoughts of boils and rashes running through their minds.

"Come on, then, get down and pick up all the leaves and twigs, get them off the ground, toss them well behind you. We'll clear the whole area and see what's to be seen." Everyone still hesitated. Mister Gallagher looked from one to another.

"Ah, you don't want to touch the bones." The boys nodded vigorously, the men shook their heads, Aram looked embarassed.

"Well, just carefully pick up the leaves and sticks, eh? And if you see anything underneath, you don't have to touch it; just call me. Aram, can you make that clear?"

Still with considerable reluctance they began to pick up leaves and twigs, staying a safe distance from the bones. Only Mister Gallagher worked right among them, murmuring to himself.

"Here's... something," Baiteke murmured reluctantly, pulling back some leaves. Mister Gallagher and Kirata leaned over him.

"Taimano ," Kirata said.

"Mosquito net, yes?" Something like that, but metal. For a window, I think. Strange thing to find. Must've been a house here – Arundel, most likely."

They looked at him quizzically.

"John Arundel," he explained. "The man who planted the coconuts – or rather, got the Niue Island men to plant them – forty years ago. He must've had a house.

Keaki and Baiteke looked at each other. So that was who lived in the old house they had torn down up on Nutiran.

"Do you want it, Mister Karaka?"

"No, I shouldn't think so. Let's carry on looking for bones, and things that might go with bones."

They returned to work, making their way carefully over the ground, raking gingerly through the leaves and twigs.

"Oh!" Takena jerked backward. "It's a... *kete!"*

"A box? Really?" Mister Gallagher jumped over to look.

"Yes, a box, of wood."

Keaki and Baiteke tried to look interested but not too interested. Luckily no one cared how they looked.

"Indeed." Mister Gallagher carefully brushed it off, picked it up. "An instrument box – for a sextant, I'd say. In jolly good condition for having lain out here...."

"Nicely made," Takena murmured, leaning over to look closely at the box's carefully fitted dovetailed corners and hinged lid.

"A nautical sextant box," Mister Gallagher mused, rocking back on his knees with the box in his hands. "So the person here was a navigator, perhaps. Or at least was navigating. I wonder what Mrs. Putnam used to navigate....."

"Missus – Missus Put... who?" Kirata wanted to know.

"A woman pilot, who – uh – got lost flying over the ocean near here."

"So that box...." Kirata smiled. "That box would have held her... sextant?"

"Yes, possibly, a sextant like Captain Harness uses on *Nimanoa.* You've seen it, yes?"

"Yes, of course." Kirata looked rather embarrassed, ran a hand through his hair. Mister Gallagher arched an eyebrow.

"What is it, Kirata? Is there ..."

"Well, Mister Karaka, you see... When I went up... came up this hill to piss, during when we bury that *ata,* I... uh... I find something."

"Something?"

---

[4] Mosquito net

"I think maybe part of that sextant."

"Really? What part?"

"That little glass thing that you flip over to look through, to make things upside down go rightside up. Captain Harness showed me once, because my father was a navigator...."

"An inverting eyepiece?"

Kirata had a short, fast conversation with Takena in Tungaruan, turned back to Mister Gallagher with a glance to Aram for help.

"Yes, I think it was an inverting eyepiece, or part of it. Very shiny, black, with screw-things, you know?"

"Threads? What did you do with it, Kirata?"

"I – uh – took it home with me."

"Jolly good, then. We'll look at it when we get back."

Kirata was silent, looked up into the trees.

"I'm afraid I – lost it."

"Lost it?"

"Yes sir. I didn't know it was anything important....."

Mister Gallagher looked at him for a moment, then shrugged.

"Well, what's done is done. If it turns up, you let me know, eh? Or if you remember where you lost it?" Kirata nodded sheepishly.

Mister Gallagher turned back to clearing the deadfall. The others continued working around the edges and in a short time they had an area of about thirty square feet cleared of leaves and twigs.

"So here's what's left of the poor – chap," Mister Gallagher mused, looking at the scattered bones. "An arm, part of another arm, most of two legs. Part of the pelvis, the lower jaw. And with him – or her – a sextant box and – what's that?"

"I don't know. I don't think it's wood." Baiteke was pointing; he didn't want to handle anything.

"It's like the tire of a *ka*," Kirata said.

"Quite so." Mister Gallagher turned the thing over in his hand. "Most of the sole of a shoe, or maybe a sandal. And – from the size and shape of it, I think... maybe it's a woman's shoe."

"That woman aeroplane flyer?" Kirata asked curiously.

"Perhaps. Oh bother, who else could it be? A woman with navigation instruments here, the bones lying here perhaps three years? Heavens!"

Kirata and Takena looked quizzically at one another, and back at Mister Gallagher. What was so special about this woman flyer? Kirata scratched the ground with a stick.

"Hmm... someone had a fire here."

"Really?" Mister Gallagher bounced over, still squatting. "Oh yes, I see! Charcoal, and ash, it looks like. And bird bones, and – here's a piece of turtle carapace! Remarkable!"

It didn't seem so remarkable to Takena and Kirata, or to the boys. Someone – that woman aeroplane flyer, maybe – had gotten stranded here, caught some birds and a turtle, cooked them, but then died. There had been no one to bury her until now. Sad, but only for her *utu,* really. The only issue for the people of Nikumaroro would be how to be sure her *anti* was settled.

"Right then," Mister Gallagher was summing up for himself. "Body was lying at the base of this tree, next to a fire where she'd been cooking birds and turtles. She had a sextant, or at least its box and an inverting eye-piece – so perhaps the sextant too, and presumably a Benedictine bottle. Died, was mostly consumed by crabs, cranium came detached from lower jaw, rolled or was dragged down the slope." He stood up, stretched, took off his hat and ran his hand through his hair, looking out toward the lagoon.

"So... Kirata, Takena, are there particular – precautions we should take – about the *anti,* I mean – in carrying these bones back to the village?"

Telegram 23 Sept. 1940: Gallagher to Resident Commissioner, CCGEI[5], Ocean Island

Some months ago working party on Gardner discovered human skull - this was buried and I only recently heard about it. Thorough search has now produced more bones (including lower jaw) part of a shoe a bottle and a sextant box. It would appear that (a) Skeleton is possibly that of a woman, (b) Shoe was a womans and probably size 10, (c) Sextant box has two numbers on it 3500 (stencilled) and 1542- - sextant being old fashioned and probably painted over with black enamel. Bones look more than four years old to me but there seems to be very slight chance that this may be remains of Amelia Earhardt. If United States authorities find that above evidence fits into general description, perhaps they could supply some dental information as many teeth are intact. Am holding latest finds for present but have not exhumed skull. There is no local indication that this discovery is related to wreck of the "Norwich City". Gallagher.

Chapter 29 –

Reluctance to Dig, October 1940

Gilbert and Ellice Islands Colony: 6th October 1940 Your telegram No. 71.

Information has been passed on to the High Commissioner particularly with a view to identifying number of sextant box. Information on following points, where possible, would be of interest: (a) How deep was skeleton buried when found, (b) How far from shore, (c) In your opinion does burial appear deliberate or could it be accounted for by encroachments of sand, etc., (d) Is site of an exposed one (i.e. if the body of Mrs. Putnam had lain there is it likely that it would have been spotted by aerial searchers)? (e) In what state of preservation is shoe, (f) If well preserved does it appears to be of modern style or old fashioned, (g) Is there any indication as to contents of bottle. Do you know anything of wreck of "Norwich City" — e.g. when did it takes place, were any lives lost and how long were survivors marooned at Gardner Island?   Resident.

6th October 1940Your telegram No. 66.

(a) Skeleton was not buried - skull was buried after discovery by natives (coconut crabs had scattered many bones), (b) 100 feet from high water ordinary springs, (c) Improbable, (d) Only part of sole remains, (f) Appears to have been stoutish walking shoe or heavy sandal, (g) "Benedictine" bottle but no indication of contents, There are indications that person was alive when cast ashore - fire, birds killed, etc.,

```
"Norwich City" wrecked and caught fire 1930
or 1932. Number of crew sailed to Fiji in
lifeboat, remainder picked up later at
Gardner by "Ralum". Think Board of Enquiry
held Suva - loss of life not known. This
information derived from gossip only. Gal-
lagher.
```

The midday sun seared the tree-shorn government station site, but it was shady in front of Mister Gallagher's tent, where Iokina stood in silence, shuffling his feet and fiddling with the tail of his shirt. Keaki looked up from *Kidnapped* – what in the world did "ca cannie" mean, and why did Uncle Ebenezer keep saying "hoot?" – glancing quizzically at the hesitant magistrate, at Aram sweeping the ground around the tent, at Mister Gallagher and his typewriter.

Mister Gallagher looked up, smiled at Iokina. "*Mauri,* Mister Magistrate."

"*Mauri,* Mister Karaka." Iokina lapsed into silence. Politely, Mister Gallagher waited awhile before speaking again.

"May I help you?"

Iokina straightened his shoulders, tightened his lips.

"Mister Karaka, with your permission, I will go and dig up that ... head."

Aram stopped sweeping, leaned on his broom. Keaki peered over the top of his book. Like Mister Gallagher, they stared at Teng Iokina. Mister Gallagher steepled his fingers, peered over them at the fidgeting magistrate.

"Mister Magistrate, it is... of course ... your decision, but may I ask why you will do the work instead of those men?"

Keaki and Aram looked at each other. Those men, they knew, were Kirata, Abera, and Takena, and the boys knew very well why Iokina had to do their work.

Something on the ground seemed to have seized Iokina's attention; he stared down at it fixedly. The silence stretched out.

"Mister Magistrate?"

Iokina shook his head, mumbled something. Realized he hadn't been understood, blurted— "They won't do it!"

Mister Gallagher raised an eyebrow. "Won't do it, Mister Magistrate?"

"No one will do it, Mister Karaka. So I will do it! It is my duty as magistrate!"

Teng Iokina is a brave man, Keaki thought, but maybe not very wise. He pretended to concentrate on his book. Aram started sweeping again, slowly and quietly. Mister Gallagher cleared his throat.

"Mister Magistrate..... It will not do for the men to refuse your orders."
Iokina swallowed hard.

"Perhaps, Mister Karaka... Perhaps I should not be magistrate."

The boys caught their breaths in unison, almost inaudibly but not quite.
Mister Gallagher started to turn toward them, stopped, was silent again.
Then he turned to them and spoke in a kindly voice.

"Aram, would you and Keaki be good fellows and go... go ask Tirosi if
he's had any messages from Ocean Island?"

Aram started to open his mouth, thought better of it. He grabbed
Keaki's hand, and the boys walked slowly out into the sunlight.

"Messages?" Keaki asked when they were on the path to the wireless.
"At this time of day?"

Aram shrugged. "There are no messages."

There weren't. Tirosi was asleep. They woke him, bore his irritation,
apologized for disturbing him, and walked back to the tent. Teng Iokina was
gone, and Mister Gallagher had turned his chair to face the lagoon. He was
smoking his pipe and looking fixedly at the trees on the other side. The
leaves of the *buka* trees shimmered as usual in the wind, under the sun.

Iokina did not resign as magistrate. Nothing was said about the men's
refusal to dig up the skull. Over the next few days, as the men rather shame-
facedly went about the work of cutting the *kanawa* down by the *baneawa*
ponds and rafting the logs to the village, Mister Gallagher conferred with
Temou and Aram and gathered some supplies. Soon everyone knew that
Mister Gallagher was going to go spend some time by himself, with only
Aram, at the other end of the lagoon. He had requisitioned Temou's new
canoe; the Tuvaluan assured him it was his as a gift, but Mister Gallagher
demurred; he was only borrowing it, he said. He and Aram loaded their
supplies, hoisted the sail, and tacked away down the lagoon. Everyone
thought it was strange – why would anyone want to be alone with only his
servant for days at a time? But everyone knew that *I-Matang* were different.

Baiteke looked up with a thin smile from the piece of *kanawa* he was
carving. Keaki crossed his legs and sat on the mat next to him under Takena's shade arbor.

"Mauri, poop of a bilious grouper."

"Mauri, excreta of a diahretic eel, what are you carving?"

"I'm not sure. We'll see. Maybe a toy for Merina's new baby."

"Want to go fishing?"

"Not right now."

"Oh, well....."

"Keaki, I'm – um – I'm sorry about that girl."

Keaki started. "What girl?"

"Era, you dumb pile of cat shit. I'm trying to...."

"What about Era?"

"You haven't heard?"

"Haven't heard what?"

"Oh shit, you haven't. I really am sorry!"

"About what? Tell me before I hit you on the head!"

Baiteke carefully set down the *kanawa* and his knife. "Era's.... *mena bunaki*. She's going to marry Abitai."

Keaki sat very still, puzzled at the feelings that ran through him. Shock, regret, but a funny feeling of relief, too. He shook himself.

"How do you know this?"

"Abitai told me, this morning. It's all arranged. As soon as they both turn fifteen, or maybe thirteen."

"Oh."

"I'm sorry."

"It's all right. Maybe.... It's all right."

"You still want to go fishing?"

Keaki stared out across the lagoon, sorting through his feelings. He should be crushed, shouldn't he? And he was, wasn't he? But if he was, then why this giddy sense of relief, of release?

"Yeah," he said, a smile spreading over his face. "Let's go fishing!"

Chapter 30 –

It Doesn't Mean Piss, October 1940

The wind was brisk out of the northeast. Close-hauled, the canoe sliced the lagoon, its outrigger barely skimming the surface despite the two boys who scrambled out to weigh it down. Their fishline trailed behind, bisecting the wake.

"Come about, eh?" Baiteke shouted. Keaki shook his head. "Let's keep on."

"You'll run us into the end of the lagoon!"

Keaki shook his head and held the sheet steady. Baiteke, who had been chattering ever since they put out from the village beach, fell into a puzzled silence, then brightened and laughed.

"What a strange accident! This evil wind!" Keaki said nothing, gazing fixedly ahead.

"Blowing us right to Aram and Mister Karaka!"

"So it is!" Keaki let go the sheet; the sail lost its belly of wind and the canoe slowed as the boys collapsed the scissor yards. They stowed the yards and furled sail on the outrigger, dug in with their paddles. The canoe curved smoothly in to shore behind the broken-off coral shelf, beaching next to Tumuo's handsome craft.

"It would be not polite," Keaki said flatly, "to be down here and not pay our respects." He was puzzled by his own feelings – the strange sense of steadiness he felt, mixed almost with giddiness. He felt, he realized with puzzlement, like he had once when he almost fell over the rail aboard *Moamoa,* in the darkness on the way from Beru, and was saved only when the ship rolled to port and threw him back across the deck.

The canoe ground into the soft sand a short distance from shore. Baiteke vaulted over the bow, laughing.

"You're right. And we should make sure they're healthy. After all, they've been all alone for over one day and one night."

Keaki hopped up onto the coral shelf. Fuck Era, he thought. Or rather, don't bother. I'm a man of Nikumaroro, I'm an explorer, I don't need a fucking woman.

Setting foot on the trail to the skull place, however, he felt a cold thrill run up his spine. Had coming here really been a good idea? What was Mister Gallagher doing in this place? And what was the skull doing? What might it do?

"I didn't really mean to come here," he found himself saying, rather more loudly than he'd intended. "It was the strong wind."

"And all the fish we were catching," Baiteke snorted, his eyes darting here and there into the dappled shadows.

"If we'd caught a lot of fish we'd have gone back."

"But now we're here...."

Approaching the end of the trail, their pace slowed. Baiteki put up his hand and they stopped, listening. A sound – out of place amid the bird cries and the distant boom and hiss of the surf. A metallic scraping sound. Baiteke made a face.

"He's doing it."

They crept forward to the end of the trail. Baiteke crossed himself.

As they had known, but really not allowed themselves to believe, Mister Gallagher was digging! Digging up the skull! Shirtless, his shockingly pale skin was almost as frightening as what he was doing. For a moment Keaki wondered if it was really Mister Gallagher in the flesh, or his *anti*. But there was Aram, cooking a fish on a small fire a few feet away, in front of a little canvas-topped arbor, and *he* didn't look like an *anti*.

Mister Gallagher looked up, flashed them a surprised smile, put down his shovel and reached for his shirt.

"Hullo, boys. Come to visit, then?"

Keaki nodded, speechless. Aram jumped up with a broad smile on his face. Mister Gallagher stepped up out of the hole he was digging, buttoning his blouse.

"Well, it's a good job you're here. I'm not sure I'm digging in quite the right place."

Keaki looked at him wide-eyed, stammering. Baiteke was only slightly less tongue-tied. Aram quickly translated.

"The... .uh... right place...?"

Mister Gallagher looked from one boy to the other, lifted his topi and wiped his brow, motioned toward the little arbor.

"Come and rest, boys. Have some water."

In the shade of the arbor, Mister Gallagher seated himself on a biscuit tin. He gestured toward a mat on the ground, and both boys sat as Aram gave all three of them half-coconut shells full of water from another biscuit tin.

Keaki's eyes were still wide, fixed on Mister Gallagher's face as he wrestled with his feelings. How could he express his fears, put his warning into words? What was his warning?

Mister Gallagher cleared his throat and leaned forward, talking slowly, sometimes pausing while he searched for a Tungaru word, or turning to Aram for help.

"Boys, I think you're wondering – why am I digging up that *ata* that Koata and the other men buried. Am I right?" Baiteke nodded; Keaki started to shake his head, changed his mind, did nothing.

"I'll tell you, then. Do you remember when you first showed me this place?" Both boys nodded.

"And we went up there –" he motioned toward the ridge – and we found those bones, and the box?' Nods.

"And a shoe, eh? You understand shoe?" The boys shook their heads at the English term. Aram looked puzzled, seeking a Tungaru word.

"That's a shoe," he said, pointing to Mister Gallagher's foot. *"I-Matang* wear them almost all the time."

"Right," Mister Gallagher said. "That's because our feet are just weak, get hurt easily."

Of course, Keaki thought. I knew that. Shoe.

"There are different kinds of shoes, you see. Shoes of women are different from shoes of men, and there are different sizes, because some feet are big and some feet are little."

The boys nodded. That made sense.

"The shoe we found up there" – he gestured again to the ridge – "was a woman's shoe, and it came – I think – from America. You remember the men of America who came on that ship..."

"With the sky canoes!" Baiteke rolled his eyes as though he were watching them again, soaring above the trees.

"Quite. Well, America is a land far away, much like England, where many things are made. The shoe we found had marks on it that showed it was from a factory – a place where shoes are made – probably in America."

Keaki thought of things he'd seen with marks showing where they had been made. Tilley lamps, for one, with little metal signs on them. With a start, he realized that the stuff he'd found on the Nutiran reef looked a lot like the metal of a Tilley lamp's base. Why would Tilley lamps be broken up on the Nutiran reef, he wondered. Had someone been out there night-fishing, and lost his lamp? Who would that have been? Or were other things made of the same kind of thin metal? Some cooking pots, he thought, and maybe some things he had seen aboard the *Moamoa*.... But then there was that big thing – so much bigger than a lamp....

But Mister Gallagher was still talking.

"So you see, I think perhaps the skull rolled down the slope from where the other bones and the shoe were. If so, we ought to put it with the other bones, and send them all to her family for a proper Christian burial."

Her family? What had he missed? Oh, of course; the shoe was a woman's. And now he remembered Mister Gallagher talking, that first day, about a woman flyer, somebody who rode sky canoes. So – yes, of course, the right thing to do would be to send the bones to her family.

"This is why I'm digging, then – to find that *ata* and put it back together with the rest of that person's bones, so her ... remains can be sent to her family in America."

They'll be sad, Keaki thought. Did people in America have *anti?* Surely they did, but were they like Tungaru *anti?* Anyway, the skull's *anti* shouldn't be mad about being dug up to be sent home for proper burial, should it? Maybe – it came to him in a flash – maybe it was mad about being buried! Separated from the rest of its bones and kept on the island, and that's why Koata and the others got sick! So maybe it was good that Mister Gallagher was...

Baiteke must have been thinking the same thing. "Mister Karaka," he said, "I think you're digging a little too much north."

Mister Gallagher smiled crookedly. "Thank you, Baiteke. I won't ask you boys to help me dig, or to touch the *ata,* but I'm grateful for your advice. There may be a reward for finding that woman, and if there is, I'm sure.... Well, never mind. No use getting ahead of events."

"Reward?" Baiteke again. Mister Gallagher frowned.

"A – ah – a prize, a present. But don't let's get hopes too high. We don't yet know.... I shouldn't have..." Mister Gallagher looked strangely uncomfortable. He glanced at Aram for help.

"In any event, whoever this was, her death here – or his, we can't be sure – is very sad. And she or he certainly should have a proper Christian burial."

"Will her family come here?" Baiteke, Keaki could see, was still thinking about a reward.

"I shouldn't think so. And again, we don't know for sure...." Mister Gallagher sighed, turned to Aram, back to the boys.

"I suppose I can..... You see, I think this... person may have been a woman who's very ... well, that many people admire. A very..." he struggled for a word. "A woman many people, all over the world, would like to ... many women would..."

Baiteke broke in: "Was she from that sky canoe ship?"

Mister Gallagher shook his head. "No, no. No women there, and the captain didn't report losing anyone. No, I think it – she – may have been a woman from America called Amelia Earhart."

Meira? What a funny name. Keaki thought about it in silence; Baiteke did not.

"Meira? Piss? Why would anyone..."

"No, no," Aram interjected – "it's an English name; not Tungaru."

"Quite right" Mister Gallagher went on. "A-meelia Air-heart. She was – is – a flyer, of sky canoes, but not on ships. She flew – very fast, won races, and flew long distances, clear across oceans. A very strong woman, very... respectable. But she got lost, not far from here, in an aeroplane, a sky canoe. Not long before some of our men – your father, Baiteke, and the others – came and started living here, clearing the bush. No one knows what happened to her."

Like the ancestors, Keaki thought, who sailed off over the horizon and never came back. But it's good that her name isn't piss.

Mister Gallagher seemed to have thought of something new.

"I say, boys. Uh – Aram, please ask them – he spoke a sentence or two, and Aram puzzled for a moment, then translated.

"My master – Mister Karaka wants to know whether in traveling about the island, you've seen anything that might be part of a sky canoe. It would be quite big, all shiny metal. Much bigger than the ones on the ship, and with two engines."

The boys looked blankly at him and at each other. Keaki tried to visualize the thing Mister Gallagher was asking about, but couldn't. Big, shiny, two engines. How would that work? One at either end? Wouldn't they work against each other? Wouldn't they tear the sky canoe apart? He and Baiteke both slowly shook their heads. Mister Gallagher sighed.

"No? Well, not surprising, I suppose. Could've landed in the water off the lee side, swum ashore. Probably what I'd have done." He got up from the biscuit tin, and the boys jumped to their feet.

"Well, back to work, eh? And you boys had better be starting back. Don't want your parents to worry. It's a long run upwind. But show me first just where you think I should dig, eh, Baiteke? Under where I've been throwing the dirt, I imagine....."

Western Pacific High Commission. 15 October 1940 Confidential.

Please telegraph to me particulars of finding of skeleton in Gardner Island, including where found and state reason for believing it to be that of a woman and whether this belief based on anatomical characteristics. State dental condition and whether any evidence of dental work on jaw, length of skeleton from vertex of skull to arch of foot, approximate age and condition of bones and whether any hair found in the vicinity of skeleton.

What have you done with skeleton? It should be carefully cared for and placed in a suitable coffin and kept in secure custody pending further instructions.

Keep matter strictly secret for the present.

Secretary,
Western Pacific High Commission

17ᵗʰ October Confidential.

Complete skeleton not found only skull, lower jaw, one thoracic vertebra, half pelvis, part scapula, humerus, radius, two femurs, tibia and fibula. Skull discovered by working party six months ago — report reached me early September. Working party buried skull but made no further search.

Bones were found on South East corner of island about 100 feet above ordinary high water springs. Body had obviously been lying under a "ren" tree and remains of fire, turtle and dead birds appear to indicate life. All small bones have been removed by giant coconut crabs which have also damaged larger ones. Difficult to estimate age bones owing to activities of crabs but am quite certain they are not less than four years old and probably much older.

Only experienced man could state sex from available bones; my conclusion based on sole of shoe which is almost certainly a woman's.

Dental condition appears to have been good but only five teeth now remain. Evidence dental work on jaw not apparent.

We have searched carefully for rings, money and keys with no result. No clothing was found. Organized search of area for remaining bones would take several weeks as crabs move considerable distances and this part of island is not yet cleared.

Regret it is not possible to measure length of skeleton. No hair found.

Bones at present in locked chest in office pending construction coffin.

Gallagher

Chapter 31 –

Organized Search, October 1940

The rain swept across the government station, whipped by a wind that made the Union Jack on the stubby temporary mast strain at the halyard, cracking like pistol shots. It rustled in the thatch that partly covered the Rest House veranda, and a thin mist drifted over Mister Gallagher and Teng Iokina where they sat on Tumuo's first two new *kanawa* chairs. Aram unobtrusively cleaned up nearby, like the others preferring the unfinished veranda to Mister Gallagher's tent. With several other men and boys escaping the downpour, Keaki sat on the veranda with his back against a post, comfortably watching the rain. It would soon pass, he knew, the clearing would steam in the suddenly reappearing sun, and they would get to work again lining the roads and parade ground with coral slabs. For the moment, everyone had taken shelter under the thatch of half-finished buildings and the veranda, or had gone home for a rest awaiting the squall's passage.

"The work is going well, Mister Magistrate." Mister Gallagher waved his pipe at the scene in front of him.

He had found the skull, and dug it up – he acknowledged as much when he returned from his digging and Baiteke blurted out the question – but no one saw him bring it to the village. Everyone knew that he'd put it with the rest of the bones, in the locked trunk under his cot, but everyone pretended to believe he had left it down at the other end of the island. Everyone – except perhaps Babera – was on the lookout for ghosts, but so far if an *anti* were in the area, it hadn't bothered anyone. Everything seemed to go on as usual in the village, on the reef where the men were fishing, and on the land where they were clearing *mao* and *ren,* and planting coconuts and pandanus.

Teng Iokina nodded, replied in halting English. "Yes, Mister Karaka. When we get the – flagstaff up, it will look – good."

"Like a real city."

Keaki looked furtively at Mister Gallagher. No signs of sickness – yet. He and Baiteke – and Aram, he thought – had been watching the administrator closely. He looked tired, and he spent a lot of time sitting quietly and looking off into the distance, occasionally mumbling to himself, waving his hands, even pounding one with the other. But no boils, no scabs, no lesions.

Iokina squinted at the fast-moving clouds. "I hope rain stop soon."

"Never say no to water, though."

Across the veranda, Kirata rumbled deep in his chest. "Very true, Mister Karaka, but my wife makes unhappy noises when our roof leaks." Aram quickly translated for Mister Gallagher, who brightened and chuckled.

"Never a good thing, when a wife makes unhappy noises. But here, it seems to be passing." The rain was tailing off, the squall sailing out to sea. Tirosi, who had run to his wireless station to stay dry, came splashing up the neatly lined coral-pebble path, shielding a piece of typing paper under a *buka* leaf.

"Message from Suva, Mister Karaka."

"Ah, from Vaskess, I'll wager. Thank you, Tirosi." Henry Harrison Vaskess was the Permanent Secretary to the High Commissioner. Tirosi turned back to the parade ground, which was already beginning to steam. The sun always seemed brighter after a rain, Keaki thought comfortably.

Mister Gallagher skimmed the paper Tirosi had given him – how easily *I-Matang* did such things! A wry look crossed his face; he shook his head. "Ah, yes, whilst keeping it all strictly secret, we're to leave no stone unturned." Kirata looked at him quizzically. Mister Gallagher read:

"Your telegram of 17th October. Organised search should be made in the vicinity and all bones and other finds, including box, sextant and shoe, should be forwarded to Suva by the first opportunity for examination."

Kirata grunted. "Mister Karaka, what does he mean by 'organized search?"

"Well, clear the area of vegetation, walk carefully over the ground, examine everything."

Iokina grimaced. "This will take time. Mister Karaka, with respect – the rains..."

"I understand, Mister Magistrate. We must get the buildings done, and houses secured.... And I know nobody likes to work where there may be bones. But... the High Commissioner himself, it seems – Sir Harry Luke – has taken a personal interest in these things, and..." He put the paper down on the *kanawa* table next to his chair, put a rock on it against the wind. Stared fixedly out at the steaming clearing. When he spoke it was to himself rather than to anyone around him.

"Perhaps that's it. American sensitivities...." He started, looked around at the men, all peering at him quizzically.

"Never mind. Mister Magistrate, I agree, we must make everyone's homes secure above all else. And we must also take care of the plantings. But – Aram, help me, please – I'm sure the High Commissioner has good reason to want us to search the place where the bones were – I think he has an idea who the person was, and it's important to be sure."

Some of the men nodded and made affirming grunts as Aram translated, but most stared noncommittally into space. Mister Gallagher looked around the group and added quickly:

"Of course, I know how you all feel about – those things, so I will continue to do the searching myself, perhaps with Aram's help if he's willing. Everyone else will work on the station, and the plantings." This brought smiles and many more nodding heads.

"And recall, please, that it's the High Commissioner's wish that we keep the matter — *te raba*[7], eh?" Iokina nodded solemnly.

"We can discuss it amongst ourselves, of course, but if anyone comes to visit, or if anyone has cause to communicate with family on another island – *te raba*. Everyone should understand that."

"Very good, sir. " Iokina hesitated, then slapped his knees and stood up. "Well, back to work, eh?"

As Mister Gallagher crossed toward Tumuo's compound, Babera stopped him.

"Mister Administrator, please come and look at our houses. I told that Koata..."

"Teng Babera, with respect, I've already agreed that the houses must be made more secure."

"But the need is urgent, Mister Administrator! Even this little storm we just had has made the water rise far too close to them. A big storm...."

They walked around the line of houses, and anyone could see that the teacher was right. The combination of high tide and a modest storm surge had brought the sea very close to where the houses stood. They were in no immediate danger of being swept away, but a heavier storm could bring disaster. Mister Gallagher pushed back his hat and scratched his head.

"You're quite right, Teng Babera, though the fault was not Koata's but mine and Mister Maude's. We said the houses should be built here. But anyway, you're right; they really must be moved."

Within half an hour, the men were clearing ground to relocate everyone's houses to a row along the lagoon shore, between the government station and a silted-up inlet punctured with crab burrows.

"It wasn't a good place for the houses," Teng Babara announced, for at least the tenth time. "I tried to tell him..."

"We didn't know," Kirata said reasonably, ripping up the roots of a cut-off *mao*. "We weren't expecting big winds out of the southwest, and we wanted...."

"It doesn't matter," Mister Gallagher grunted as he forced his shovel under the roots of another bush. "We – learn, yes? And we've learned that the houses should be down here, on the lagoon side."

"Not too close to the lagoon, though," Kirata cautioned. "Look at how high the water came on this side." The inlet was still waterlogged; it had been flooded during the storm.

---

[7]Secret

"It's because the lagoon has only two ways in and out," Takena observed; heads nodded throughout the group. "Both on the west side, both going east and west."

Kirata motioned with his hands; "So the water just piles in when the wind's from the west, and it can't get out."

"That reminds me of another thing we must do," Mister Gallagher said, "besides moving the houses, we need to make sure the seed coconuts are all right – and the pandanus. What do you think, Mister Magistrate?'

Iokina shook his head. "I'm afraid we should move some of them – the ones on low ground near the water are getting a lot of salt spray."

"I told him...." Babera began.

"Well," Mister Gallagher cut in, "this is how we learn, eh? I think – let all the men finish up here and then start taking the houses apart and moving them over here. Teng Babera, if you'll help me, we'll identify the coconuts that need to be relocated, the boys can do that job." He handed his shovel to Abera and walked away, as Babera earnestly explained how foolish it had been to plant the coconuts where they were.

Relocation of both homes and plants was soon underway. About half the young men and boys, including Aram and Keaki, spread out around the lagoon-ward side of the coconut plantation and began carefully digging up seed coconuts without disturbing their delicate young roots. They carried them one by one to a recently cleared inland plot. The other half of the boys were waiting there to replant them.

Coconut by coconut, Keaki made his way to Aram's side. The older boy gave him a lopsided smile as he eased a coconut out of the ground, delicately detaching the coral particles from its developing roots.

"Mauri, Keaki. Where's your buddy?"

"Baiteke? He's on the planting team with the Tuvaluans. Uh.....Teng Aram?"

Aram smiled at his formality. "Yes, Teng Keaki; may I help you in some way?"

Keaki inserted a stick under the coconut in front of him and began to wiggle it. "A few nights ago, when I brought that fish...?

"Was it you that brought it? Thank you for not stepping on me."

"Mister Karaka was doing... something... with that box....."

Aram laughed. "His wireless. You're wondering about the voice."

"Yes! Where did it come from? Who was there? Where ?

"No one, Teng Keaki; no one was in the wireless. That kind of wireless – uh – sort of collects voices out of the air, just like the other one collects the dits and dahs...."

"So someone talks someplace else...."

"In *Engiran,* yes. People called Bee Bee See. And the wireless sends their voices out all over the world, where other wireless sets can collect them and let people listen to them."

"Wow! Can Mister Karaka talk to *Engiran?*"

"No, his wireless is only good for listening to. The one Tirosi uses with the tapper is the one they use to talk to Fiji and Ocean Island and other places. But it's not really talking."

"Yeah, it's *mosscode,* Tirosi says."

"Different patterns of dits and dahs mean different words."

"But this one actually speaks!"

"Well, sort of. The guy in *Engiran,* is speaking, but...."

"Mister Karaka was really upset."

"Ah. Well, I was asleep."

"He seemed mad, and like – it was almost like he'd been crying."

Aram leaned back and wiped his forehead. "Yeah. It's that war. You know, that Hitler guy?"

"The king of that Germany place?"

"Yeah, except Mister Karaka says he's not a king; he's more like a really powerful chief. Anyway, he has huge aeroplanes – sky canoes, you know, but as big as ships, and they're flying over *Engiran,* and dropping – uh, bombs."

"Bombs?"

"Like dynamite; stuff that blows up, BOOM! And they're dropping them on houses and ... and other buildings, and people."

"Shit! That must kill people!"

"Yeah, lots of people, and that's why Mister Karaka's so sad, I think."

Keaki absorbed this, imagined what it would be like if someone were dropping dynamite things on Temeroa.

"It must be terrible for him."

"Yeah, he doesn't talk about it much, but sometimes he does, and – I don't really know what to say. He really needs to talk to a priest, I think, maybe."

"Like – uh — *bure* ? Is he Catholic?"

"Oh yes, he's very – religious. He just doesn't talk about it; keeps things to himself."

"But... if this Teng Hitler is doing the bombing, what does Mister Karaka have to *bure?*"

"Oh, nothing, really... but... well, I think.... You remember that he knows how to fly sky canoes?"

"Yeah – that funny hat."

---

[8]Confession

"Well, he has that hat because he flew those aeroplanes, and if he was in *Engiran* – he says there are men in little aeroplanes who fly up with guns and try to shoot the guys in the big ones dropping bombs. So if he was there, that's what he'd be doing."

"That sounds really dangerous."

"Yeah, but exciting, and I think he's kind of – mad that he's not there to help – you know, defend his mother, and...."

"He has a mother?"

"Everybody has a mother, shit-for-brains. He has a really nice mother, who writes him letters. He's read some of them to me. And he has a brother who's a – a warrior of some kind, fighting in the war on another island against those Germans."

"Who are dropping things that blow up – bombs – on his mother. Shit! No wonder he's upset!"

Keaki lay awake a long time that night, in the half-reassembled house on the lagoon shore, listening to it creak and rustle in the wind. Where did wind really come from, he wondered. How far was it, really, to *Engiran?* How did those sky canoes work? What would it be like to fly in one? To <u>fly</u> one? To shoot at people with one? How would it feel to be a warrior and not be able to fight? Not defend your home island, your family? Were all *the I-Matang* feeling the same way Mister Gallagher did? What if they all went home to fight? But then maybe the Germany people would come to Niku-maroro....

Chapter 32 –

Weather, October-November 1940

Keaki woke to the sound of wind in the thatch. A strong wind, shaking the house. A fine mist of rain drifted in through the mat walls. Keaki shivered.

His mother levered herself up from her mat and shuffled sleepily over to the corner where some copra bags lay in a heap. She tossed one to Keaki and another to Taberiki.

"Here. Wrap up. Stay warm."

Keaki wrapped the bag around himself, trying to ignore its sickening sweet smell. The house shook again under a blast of wind. He heard a piece of thatch break off the roof and fly away. His father pulled back the flap that covered the doorway, squinted out into the watery darkness.

"It's turned round," he said, unnecessarily. Everyone could tell that the wind was coming from the west-southwest, contrary to the usual steady northeasterly trade winds.

"Just a squall, I think," Boikabane murmured.

"Maybe not. Remember last year? This could go on for awhile."

Keaki tossed and turned for much of the night, unaccustomed to the cold and all the unfamiliar noises the new house made as it played its game with the wind. The morning dawned gray and chilly, with scudding clouds and spitting rain. Keaki abandoned his copra sack as soon as it was light, splashing through puddles to Baiteke's house, where he dragged his friend off his mat to go see what the storm had done.

"Woo!" Baiteke gasped, "That's where the houses were!" Waves had swept clear over the former village site, ripping out trees and washing away the land right down to the solid coral. Waves were still breaking there, tossing spray.

"And look at the Rest House!" The veranda roof where they had sheltered just days before had been ripped off and plastered against the frame of the unfinished main building; one end draped sadly over the concrete bathroom. They continued their circuit down the lagoon shore, where both latrine piers had disappeared. Keaki said "Shit!" at the sight, and they both collapsed laughing.

It turned out that even Teng Babera had underestimated how far the water could come inshore; some of the coconuts and pandanus were damaged or killed despite their relocation work.

The rain and wind went on, and on, for days and nights, sometimes wild and strong, sometimes abating to sullen gray clouds and scattered spits of rain. Every day – sometimes every hour, it seemed, brought new work to do, just to hold the half-finished government station together and keep the remaining plants from being swamped. Mister Gallagher was everywhere, offering suggestions, resolving questions, and lending a hand wherever it was needed. He said nothing about the other end of the island.

"Maybe," Keaki said, swinging his legs out the front of Baiteke's new house and watching the rain, "maybe he's not supposed to search the *ata* place."

Baiteke looked up abruptly from his work, sharpening his adze with a steel file. "Who doesn't want him to search? Nei Manganibuka?"

"Maybe, or maybe the *anti* of that woman."

"The aeroplane woman."

"Yeah."

"You think *anti* control the weather?"

"Maybe. Why not?"

"Don't let Teng Babera hear you talking like that."

"I don't give fish shit for Teng Babera."

Baiteke grinned, but changed the subject. "Think Mister Karaka will listen to his wireless tonight?"

"Sure, if he has the batteries."

In the last few days, the two boys had begun to hang around Mister Gallagher's tent and cookhouse in the evening, chatting with Aram and helping him clean up, waiting for Mister Gallagher to turn on his fascinating machine. He usually did so for about half an hour each evening, conserving the supply of big black *ka* batteries that powered both his wireless and the one that Tirosi operated. He didn't seem to mind their being there, and the second evening when they looked bewildered by what they were hearing, he had tried to explain. This emboldened them to ask questions, and he had tried to respond in Tungaruan. It was becoming a sort of evening tradition. Mister Gallagher said they were helping him expand his Tungaru vocabulary, and Keaki hadn't seen him clenching his fists or weeping since the night of the fish.

What the boys learned astounded them. The German aeroplanes with their bombs had done terrible things, Mister Gallagher said, blown up many cities, some far larger than Beru or even Tarawa, or places they'd only heard about like Suva. They had especially attacked the city of London, where the King himself lived, and killed many people. But the brave flyers of the R.A.F. – the boys knew now that this meant his Majesty's Royal Air Force – had shot many of them out of the sky with guns in their aeroplanes. As October ended and November began, fewer raids were reported. Occasionally the reports they listened to each evening reported no bombs falling at all. But the ones that were reported seemed so monstrous, the aeroplanes pouring fire down on houses and churches and government buildings and people alike. And there was fear that the Germany chief Hitler was getting ready to bring thousands of soldiers – warriors with guns, some as large as houses, Mister Gallagher said – across the ocean from Germany to attack *Engiran.*

In early November there was another break in the weather, and all the men worked together to repair and finish thatching the Rest House. The women wove mats for the walls, and Temou built wonderfully handsome chairs, tables, and beds out of *kanawa* limbs. Around the middle of the month Aram took down Mister Gallagher's tent and they moved into the big gabled house. Each family brought food and they all celebrated with songs and dances. The next day they tipped the new flagpole into a hole the men had dug in the middle of the Government Station clearing, straightened it with guide ropes and poured cement round its base to hold it firm. Mister Gallagher hoisted the flag to its peak and made a little speech that no one really understood, and everyone sang "God Save the King." Teng Babera claimed the old flagpole for use in the church he was building.

In mid-November the Mister Gallagher's wireless reported a terrific raid on a place called Coventry, destroying much of the city and killing thousands of people. Keaki had trouble imagining thousands of people, dead or alive. Listening to the wireless, Mister Gallagher's face became rigid, and his hand clenched his pipestem so hard that it snapped in two. He didn't seem to notice; just said "excuse me, please, boys," and went outside into the darkness without even a hat, despite the spitting rain and blustery wind. Baiteke started after him.

"Mister Karaka, your hat..."

Aram caught him by the arm. "Don't bother him, Baiteke. He needs.... Just don't bother him."

The next day, Mister Gallagher announced that he and Aram were going to resume the search of the skull place. Kirata and Abera went with them in their own canoe, with a surplus steel tank still marked "Police, Tarawa" balanced on their outrigger; they also carried a roll of green and black tarpaper and some canvas. They helped Aram build a little canvas-roofed house where Mister Gallagher could escape the rain squalls, sit dry on the tarpaper, and collect water in the tank. Then as quickly as they decently could they left the administrator and his servant to their work and sailed back to the village. Both were silent and thoughtful until midway through the second tack; then Abera burst into an obscene song of his own creation. Kirata responded with one of his own. In the village, the women working in the cookhouses heard their uproarious laughter before their sail came into view; they smiled at one another, and chuckled.

Everyone now knew, and more or less acknowledged, that the bones were locked up in the Rest House. There were murmurs about *anti,* but Mister Gallagher had said the storage was only temporary, and part of the respectful treatment that any deceased person was due. He had asked Tumuo to build a good coffin for the bones, and the woodworker was busy with a piece of *kanawa* from a tree near the lagoon shore at the skull place. It would be a handsome box, cut from a single block of wood with a fitted top from the same block, and big enough to hold all the bones – assuming Mister Gallagher didn't find very many more.

"I wonder where the rest of her bones went," Keaki said to no one in particular, as he watched Tumuo working on the box with a hammer and chisel.

"Crabs," Tumuo grunted.

"Did they eat them?"

"Yes, crabs will eat anything; you know that."

"But people's bones...."

"Crabs aren't picky. Or they may have taken them down in their burrows and left them there, or put them in holes in trees, or just lost them. I don't think crabs have long memories."

"Oh, here comes Mister Karaka!" The administrator was back from the skull place, walking slowly across the station toward the carpenter's house. He stopped to speak with Kirata, and the two came on together. Keaki ran out to meet them.

"Yes," Mister Gallagher was saying, "the house was very snug when it rained yesterday, and plenty of water collected in the tank. It's really very pleasant down there."

"*Mauri,* Mister Karaka."

"*Mauri,* Teng Keaki. Have you been staying out of trouble?"

"Yes sir. Did you find more..."

"Bones? Only a couple of small ones. I'm afraid the crabs have picked the place pretty clean. But here..." He had reached the arbor, and he put down the bag he was carrying on Tumuo's work table. Keaki shuddered momentarily at the thought of what he might pull out of it, but it was only a couple of cylindrical wooden looking things with metal chains on them.

"Tumuo, any idea what these may be?"

The carpenter picked one up. "Corks," he said.

"Indeed, but what do you suppose they corked up?"

"Maybe... the drain hole in a boat."

"Pretty small for that, I think."

"Maybe Koata's bottle."

"Big for that."

"A small cask, perhaps."

"That's what I was thinking, perhaps from a lifeboat. Or perhaps water bags."

"Maybe so, but I think maybe casks."

"Well, whatever they were, they're gone now, unfortunately. Only the corks left."

"Crabs wouldn't eat a cask."

"Unless it was impregnated with wine or something."

"And then," Kirata interjected, making his eyes very wide, "they'd get drunk and fall in the ocean, and the casks would still be there." He burst out laughing, holding his sides. Tumuo slapped him on the back, laughing uproariously himself. Keaki joined in, until he thought of the poor woman, or man, stuck down there under the *ren*, waiting to be dead and eaten by the crabs. Which would come first, he wondered.

"Well," Mister Gallagher said, a crooked half-smile acknowledging Kirata's joke, "we'll pack these up with the rest of the lot and send them down for the High Commissioner to puzzle over. Perhaps he can solve the mystery."

From Progress Report of the Phoenix Islands Settlement Scheme,
fourth quarter 1940, by Gerald B.
Gallagher, Officer-in-Charge.

4. When labourers were first landed on Gardner Island in December, 1938, the site selected for their houses was the only one which, at that time, was even partially clear of the huge "Buka" (pisonia grandis) trees and the dense scrub which covers the island. Since this area was found to be waterlogged at high spring tides, however, it had long been realised that the village would have to be removed to a better site. Work on the clearing and levelling of the site for the Government Station, which was begun in September, was well advanced at the beginning of the quarter and it was decided to remove the village to this new site before the onset of the high December tides. Accordingly, some forty houses were taken down and re-erected in such a manner as to accord with the eventual

requirements of the Government Station. Each house was re-roofed with coconut thatch brought from Hull and Sydney Islands by the m.v. "John Bolton" and although the houses, for lack of material, are very small, the labourers are now considerably better housed in a more healthy situation. -

5. Coincidentally with the work on the transfer of the village, the erection of the Rest House was continued. This building was in a sufficiently advanced state of construction to be occupied in the middle of November and, soon after that, work had to be abandoned until further supplies of materials could be transported from the Gilbert Islands.

6. A new flagstaff, 59 feet high, was completed and erected at the beginning of November and a section of the old temporary flagstaff was very suitably incorporated in the little church which the more devout or, at all events, less indolent, labourers were then erecting in their spare time.

7. It had been planned to make a start on the demarcation and clearing of new lands as soon as work on the removal of the village had been completed. Unfortunately, very soon after the last house had been erected, the wind swung round to the North-West and it was soon obvious that the wet season had begun. With very little protection from the newly planted coconut trees and bereft of the windbreak formerly afforded by the "buka" trees, the gales managed to play havoc with the village in the first few days. When it was realised, however, that the gales had come to stay, houses were shored up, thatch tied down and everything made as secure as possible. The unfinished Rest

House was slightly damaged, the boat
house was partially wrecked by a whirl-
wind and a clean sweep was made of such
structures as latrine wharves and bathing
houses. The greater part of the damage on
Gardner Island, however, was caused by
the exceptional tides which were swept
into the lagoon by the high winds and
flooded considerable areas of newly
planted coconut land. Many of the coconut
trees were damaged and nearly all of the
newly planted pandanus bushes were
killed. A small area of land was washed
away and the course of the Southern
lagoon passage altered. Due to the very
heavy rain during this period, properly
organized work at any distance from the
village was impossible and advantage was
taken of the opportunity to build roads
and paths and to clean up one or two
small areas of land on or near the Government Station.

Chapter 33 –

The Coffin, December 1940

"Not much." Aram shook his head over the board where he was ironing Mister Gallagher's shirts. "I'm worried about him."

Keaki had asked what he and Mister Gallagher had done at the skull place. Aram continued shaking his head as he passed the iron to Keaki, who put it on the fire to heat up and collected one that was hot. Aram accepted the fresh iron with a nod of thanks, looking pensively out the cookhouse window at the lagoon.

"You know, before, he was the one doing the work, right in the middle of everything. This time – he told me to search down the ridge toward where the *ata* was, and then he went off to the beach. I checked on him after awhile and he was just sitting out there with his hands up like this." Aram covered his face with both hands. "I think he was crying."

"Because of the war, do you think?"

"Most likely. He finally came back and looked around a little, but he didn't seem to really be thinking about it. We found those corks, and a couple of bones. It's pretty hard – the *mao* is really growing up fast, and it's hard to see stuff on the ground. We kept stumbling over that pile of *aubunga;* I finally put a bunch of tarpaper over it so we'd see it. And the second day – well, it wasn't past noon when he said "damn it, that's enough," and we came home."

"He seemed all right when he came up to Tumuo's house."

"Maybe by then, yeah. But – I just don't think he's right in his head."

The weather was still sour as November merged into December, alternating between squalls and sullen gray clouds that swept across the sky. The water backed up in the lagoon, and it took constant vigilance to keep it out of the coconut plantings. Big pieces of the *Noriti 's* superstructure were swept away, and her stern settled deeper off the reef edge.

Men took turns going the rounds of the plantings, making sure no more water got in. When not employed this way they fished, tended their *babae* gardens, worked on the government station or their home sites, or just hung around their houses talking and sleeping. Women got together to talk in the cook houses as they prepared food and washed clothes; at least there was plenty of fresh water. Boys and girls played in the rain, but when the squalls came there was little to do but sit inside and listen to the wind whistling through the thatch.

Mister Gallagher walked around the village twice or three times a day, looking in on each family or group of workers. The rest of his time was spent fixing things up in the Rest House – rearranging books, taking care of his wireless, cleaning and oiling his typewriter, his pistol, his sextant. And every evening he listened to the BBC, and talked with Aram and the boys. It seemed incredible to them that there could be anything left to blow up or burn in *Engiran,* but there were still raids both on London and on places with odd names like Liver Pool. The RAF pilots were still bravely flying and fighting.

"And dying," Mister Gallagher said, not to the boys, staring at the flying hat he had hung on a peg.

Tumuo finished the box for the bones, and displayed it proudly to his children and the boys. Keaki thought it was a very dignified box, dark and heavy, fine-grained, with a close-fitting top, all made out of a single log.

"He should be happy in this, eh?" Tumuo asked with a wink. Keaki wasn't sure it was right to talk this way, but Baiteke laughed. Both boys walked to the Rest House with Tumuo and Eddie to deliver the box to Mister Gallagher, who expressed great admiration and appreciation for it.

"And just in time, too. *Nimanoa* should be here soon to take it to Suva."

"Will more people come, Mister Karaka?"

"I hope so. *Nimanoa* 's going to Beru first to collect more people to live here, but since I haven't been able to go there, I don't know who wants to come. But don't worry, Baiteke, I'll not let any new arrival get the land your father wants."

Much of the discussion around the village centred on who was going to remain as a permanent settler, and who was going to return to their home islands when their labour contracts were complete. About half the people intended to stay, including Takena, Ieiara, and their families. Soon, Mister Gallagher had promised, they would start marking out the land into parcels for assignment to the permanent settlers, and many were already getting greedy for their land. Takena talked endlessly about the parcel he wanted, a long piece of land already planted to coconuts that were growing healthily, stretching from the ocean to the lagoon south of the government station and the village. Each child was to be assigned land, too; it was a popular pastime among the children who were staying to debate what they would get, and what they would do with it.

"I think I want a parcel down below Baureke passage," Baiteke mused, as he and Keaki sat under the work arbor behind Keaki's house, sharpening their knives. "I'll bring in some good *kanawa* logs to build my house, and a fine cookhouse for Segalo."

"Such dreams," Keaki scoffed. "You know she's going to Fiji." Segalo had started working in the dispensary with Teng Eneri, and was talking about going to school to be a nurse. Baiteke was sure this was just a passing fancy, that she would eventually see the folly of her ways and fall in love with him.

"Better than having no dreams at all, fish crap. The trouble with you is, you have no self-confidence."

"I have plenty of self-confidence. Dreams, too. I just don't need a girl."

"Who will cook for you?"

"I didn't mean forever, shithead, just for right now. I have other things to do with my life."

"Like what? Fly aeroplanes? Fight Hitler? Daydream?"

"I don't know. Maybe.... maybe work with machines like Mister Kimo."

"You who can't carve a piece of wood?"

"Machines aren't made of wood."

"Where do you want your land?"

"Oh, I don't know. Nutiran, maybe. I like it up there."

"Oh, I thought you'd try to claim the *ata* place."

"When whales fly." Keaki pointed toward the Rest House. "There's Tirosi with a piece of paper. Let's go find out what it says."

The boys scooted out into the rain and ran for the Rest House, stepping in every available puddle along the way. Tirosi was just coming out across the veranda.

"Better leave the administrator to think, boys," he warned. "I've just given him bad news."

"More war?"

"No, *Nimanoa's* been damaged in this storm, off Abemama, won't be coming for awhile."

Nimanoa, they later learned, had torn her sails and ripped some copper off her hull in heavy seas, and was limping in to Tarawa for repairs, accompanied by *Kiakia*. There was no telling how long it would be before she – or any ship – got to Nikumaroro.

"I have consulted with the administrator," Iokina said to the villagers assembled in the *maneaba*, "and we have decided on certain austerity measures to be put into effect until a ship comes." He looked around at the expectant faces. No one said anything – they had not yet established a permanent order of priority among the *boti,* and until they did everyone was shy about speaking.

"Among the measures are these. Tirosi will operate the wireless only one hour each day in order to conserve the batteries. Everyone must limit consumption of canned food and tobacco. Tumuo will lead a party of men each day to fish for the whole village; they will be responsible for making sure that each family has enough fish each day. If necessary, we shall catch birds as well. And if need be, we can harvest *te mtea.*" *Te mtea* was a low-growing shrub[9], traditional famine food. Nobody liked it, but it was edible and fairly nutritious. "Abera will take inventory of all our kerosene supplies, and beginning now, no one should burn a lamp unless it's absolutely necessary. Finally, both Protestants and Catholics will celebrate Christmas during the daytime, so there will be no need for kerosene lights at night."

"When is *Nimanoa* expected?" someone asked.

"That is not known. We don't know the extent of the damage. But the High *Komitina* and the authorities on Ocean Island are aware of our needs; we will not be abandoned."

"Well," Keaki grumbled as everyone dispersed. "No more wireless in the Rest House, I guess."

Baiteke kicked a hermit crab into the brush. "And no nighttime Christmas party. I was hoping...."

"To sneak off in the dark with Segalo? Without light it might work; she might mistake you for somebody else."

A few days later Tirosi's wireless failed. Now Nikumaroro was well and truly cut off from the world.

Shortly after the island's quiet Christmas festivities – Catholic and Protestant religious services, some foot races and tree-climbing contests among the boys – Gerald Gallagher sat down in the gray light of another squally afternoon to compose a letter to accompany the bones, whenever they could be sent.

```
    Nikumaroro   (Gardner)   Island,   Phoenix
Islands District, 27th December, 1940.
    Sir,
    I  have  the  honour  to  acknowledge  the
receipt of your confidential telegram No. 2
of the 26th. October, 1940, and to state
that two packages are being handed to the
Master, R.C.S. "Nimanoa", for eventual
delivery to the High Commission Office in
Suva. The larger of these packages is the
coffin  containing  the  remains  of  the
unidentified individual found on the South
Eastern shore of Gardner Island; the second
package is the sextant box found in the
```

---

[9]Portulaca sp., aka purslane or pigweed

immediate locality and contains all the other pieces of evidence which were found in the proximity of the body.

The fact that the skull has been buried in damp ground for nearly a year, whilst all the other bones have been lying above ground during the same period, was probably not apparent from previous correspondence, but may be helpful in determining the age of the bones. In spite of an intensive search, none of the smaller bones have been discovered and, in view of the presence of crabs and rats in this area, I consider that it is now unlikely that any further remains will be traced. A similar search for rings, coins, keys or other articles not so easily destroyed has also been unsuccessful, but it is possible that something may come to hand during the course of the next few months when the area in question will be again thoroughly examined during the course of planting operations, which will involve a certain amount of digging in the vicinity. If this should prove to be the case, I will inform you of the fact by telegraph.

Should any relatives be traced, it may prove of sentimental interest for them to know that the coffin in which the remains are contained is made from a local wood known as "kanawa" and the tree was, until a year ago, growing on the edge of the lagoon, not very far from the spot where the deceased was found.

I have the honour to be, Sir,
Your obedient servant,
(Sgd) Gerald B. Gallagher.

Chapter 34 –

Doctor Isaac, January 1941

1941 arrived with no sign of a ship. Everyone put on a brave face, beating on tins with sticks at what they calculated to be midnight. No one said they were afraid their little island had been forgotten. Gerald spent hours with Tirosi in the wireless shack, exploring ways to jury-rig the wireless. Some ten days into the month they were successful, but the arrangement was fragile, and achieved only at the expense of Gerald's own receiver, which they had to cannibalize for parts. But sending a signal and getting a reply brought grins to the faces of everyone in the crowd around the wireless; they were not forgotten, and *Nimanoa,* they were assured, would soon be on her way.

A few days later, Tirosi was smiling broadly when he brought the transcript of another wireless message into the Rest House, and he didn't wait to deliver it by hand.

"Nimanoa, sir! *Nimanoa 's* left Beru!"

Gerald removed his pipe and returned the smile. "Good, good, Teng Tirosi. When...?"

Tirosi switched to English. "Eight or maybe seven days. Bring wireless parts, and also a doctor."

Gerald's smile widened as he read through the typed copy. "A doctor," he murmured to himself. "MacPherson, perhaps, making his rounds."

It was actually nine days before *Nimanoa* appeared in the lee, under power with her sails furled. Temou and Kirata jumped into the big canoe and paddled Gerald out to the ship. Captain Harness was standing at the rail, with a stumpy, long-faced Englishman in a kepi.

"Ah," Gerald muttered, "Isaac."

Lindsay Isaac had arrived in Fiji from England in 1938, serving as a freighter's medical doctor. Visiting the Central Medical School and finding its pathologist, Gerald's friend MacPherson, about to go on leave, Isaac had volunteered to stand in for him, and soon had become a permanent member of the medical staff.

Isaac's brother officers, on the whole, had little truck with the man. His recruitment had been somewhat irregular; though his medical background and skills seemed sound, he was not trained as a colonial officer. It was widely suspected that he had traded on his Jewish heritage – an unusual quality in the service, but one said to appeal to Sir Harry Luke, who had served for years in the Holy Land – to slide into his position. He held strong opinions on almost everything, and felt no constraints about sharing them. He had no wife, and some found him indecorously familiar with young Fijian men and boys.

"Captain Harness, Dr. Isaac," Gerald saluted. "Welcome to Gardner."

Harness' smile spread his fleshy red face wide. "Jolly good to see you, Irish. Sorry to be so long in comin'."

"Couldn't be helped, and we've got by. " Gerald swung over the rail and shook hands with the two men. "I was a trifle concerned about you, though; with my wireless out until recently, I didn't know what had become of you."

"Ran into a helluva storm trying to reach you several weeks ago, had to hole up in Tarawa for repairs."

"That much we learned before our wireless went down; I'd no idea the damage was..."

"It wasn't. Bloody Krauts, it was."

"You don't say? Germans?"

"Disguised raiders. All shippin' was ordered back to Fiji for safekeepin', but after some wheedlin' we got special dispensation, seeing you was cut off, else."

"Very much appreciated, gentlemen! Truly beyond the call.... But raiders! You didn't see them, I take it?"

"Wouldn't likely be here if we had, eh Doctor?"

"Quite; the bastards are..."

"But Irish, you've been all right, then?"

"Oh yes; suffered a bit from storms, same system that caught you, I reckon. Had to relocate the workers' houses. But everything's shipshape now. Will you come ashore?"

"I've stores for you, and also for Hull and Sydney. Time and tides bein' what they are, I'm thinking we should make straight for Hull, then touch at Sydney, then stop back here in two-three days' time. I thought you might like to make the circuit with us."

"Bless you, captain; I've been out of touch with the rest of the Phoenix since the wireless went down, and haven't been on shore in – oh, months. Half an hour to fetch my kit?"

"We can spare an hour and make Hull in daylight."

"Excellent! Dr. Isaac, would you care for a quick look at our little establishment?"

"Delighted." Isaac gave a little bow. Gerald vaulted over the rail into the canoe and reached back to help the doctor, who himself descended with considerable nimbleness. Temou and Kirata shoved off and dug in with their paddles; the canoe shot toward the shore.

"Beautiful canoe!" Isaac shouted over the roar of the breakers on the reef. Temou grinned broadly.

"Tuvaluan in design, Nikumaroro construction. Temou here is a master. Hold tight now..."

The paddlers had timed the swells perfectly, and had barely a wait before riding the big one over the reef edge and into the boat channel along the shore. The prow crunched on the beach; Gerald rolled over the gunwale and helped Kirata drag the canoe above the wave line. They both helped Dr. Isaac step out onto the sand.

"Thank you, Gallagher," the doctor said, holding his hand a little longer than Gerald thought quite right. "Let me stop and make the proper gesture." He leaned down for a handful of wet sand to pat on his cheeks. "There we are, then." He shook hands with both boatmen and followed Gerald onto the path to the village.

"Very good of you to visit, Doctor, especially considering the danger. We've quite competent dressers on all the islands, and as you know, Tutu goes from island to island, but we've never had a white doctor look at our arrangements; I'll be most interested in your opinions."

"Being the Senior Medical Officer in Tarawa, it seemed only appropriate to visit the Phoenix whilst I had the chance."

"You've replaced Steenson, then?"

"Yes, while he's in Fiji at least. Remains to be seen how long I'll be there. Quite a lot of work to do in Fiji."

"Ah. No doubt. Well, once we've seen Manra – that's Sydney, and Hull is Orona – I'll be especially happy to have your thoughts on our needs here; everything is quite new, but we've high hopes...."

They had reached the stone wall demarking the edge of the government station, and Gerald awaited Isaac's reaction to the well-ordered plantation of young coconuts, the broad, straight streets with their lining of coral slabs, the tall flagpole with its cracking jack, and the peaked-roofed Rest House. But Isaac had other things on his mind.

"You've not heard of our Kraut raiders, then?"

"Only the general cautions broadcast from Suva. Here's the Rest House then. Aram! Aram! Help me gather gear for three or four days; I'm going with *Nimanoa*. This is Dr. Isaac..."

Aram bowed as he shook hands with the doctor, and then raced to pull together Gerald's clothes. Isaac stood looking over the sunken garden toward the lagoon.

"Delightful view you have, Gallagher; you and your houseboy must be very happy."

"I can't speak for Aram, but I like the view. Very peaceful, with all the trouble in the world. "

"You haven't heard, I suppose, that the Krauts attacked Nauru."

"No! My wireless was out of commission until just the other day; I jury-rigged it with parts from my receiver..."

"Ah. Yes, the bastards sank the *Rangitane* off Queensland – a passenger ship! – and took the survivors aboard; dumped those that weren't military ashore on Nauru after sinking two phosphate ships."

"Good heavens. And did they make a landing?"

"No, no, slipped away like thieves in the night. Bloody blighters."

"Astonishing! But I suppose we have to expect to get our share. Nothing to what's happening at home."

"Or on the Continent."

Gerald stopped in the midst of collecting his toiletries, feeling a sudden stab of guilt. How had he let the sufferings of Jews under the Nazis slip his mind? When talking with Isaac? How must the man feel? He sought a way to change the subject, at least a little.

"Indeed, the Continent. What news of the war, then?"

"I imagine you know as well as I do, with that handsome wireless rig."

"As I said, I had to cannibalize some of its parts to get the station wireless working. Haven't heard BBC in weeks. Seemed we were making progress in Africa, though...."

"Yes. Good to be on the offensive somewhere. Little hard news out of Europe, though – nothing but refugees and bombers. You heard about Manchester and Liverpool."

"Sickeningly, yes. But the RAF are beating them back...."

"Seemingly. One worries about what may come from the sea, though."

Aram came out of Gerald's sleeping room with two rattan suitcases. "Ready to go, Mister Karaka!"

"Well done, Aram. Add my shaving gear and toothbrush here, eh? Doctor, we're all yours."

They hurried toward the landing as Isaac continued the conversation. "The raiders — they're disguised, you know, made up to look like Jap freighters. Understand they sometimes feign distress calls, and when a ship comes to the rescue they uncover their guns and demand surrender."

"No respect whatever for the rules of war!"

"No, the bloody National Socialists have no respect for anyone's rules. And in the case of the *Rangitane,* they let most of the civilians go in Nauru, but they took the crew back to Germany. So if they caught a British officer...."

Especially a Jewish one, Gerald thought...

They had reached the beach and Isaac stopped, turned to Gerald with troubled eyes.

"I don't mind telling you, Gerald, it worries me, especially on Tarawa where there's really no defense. If they came ashore and learned my name, I'd be en route to one of their devilish camps before I could say Solomon."

"I've only heard vague allusions to camps...."

"About all any of us have heard, but it's common knowledge that in the last couple of years, Jews have been disappearing from German cities, and everywhere else the Nazis have rolled over. And they're not all coming to England. It's said they're being concentrated in veritable prisoner of war camps, but of course they're not prisoners of war, so no Red Cross, no Geneva protocols. It's bloody frightening."

"God, yes!"

"And I'm not even observant, dammit! Haven't set foot in a synagogue in – shit, decades."

"But the name, you think, would be enough."

"I'm seriously considering changing it."

"I don't wonder you are."

They boarded the canoe and sat in silence as Kirata, Aram and Temou pushed off over the reef edge. Gerald tried once more to imagine what it must be like to be Isaac. He couldn't. Then they were clambering aboard the schooner as she got underway.

Three days later they were back, unloading and inspections complete on Manra and Orona, a few passengers taken aboard for Tarawa and points west. Isaac had expressed approval of the medical facilities on both islands, and Gerald had found most of the colonists satisfied and at work improving their lands and houses. As *Nimanoa*'s engine throttled back in Nikumaroro's lee, Gerald was gratified to see ten fine straight *kanawa* logs anchored in the boat channel, ready to be loaded for the Rongorongo sawmill. Takena, Abera, and Bueke were just entering the water to guide them out over the reef edge, while Kirata, Tumuo, Iokina and Ieiara maneuvered canoes into position to take them in tow.

"Efficient chaps," Harness commented, tapping his pipe out on the rail. "We'll have the logs aboard before you know it."

"Just so Dr. Isaac has time...."

"Plenty of time, Irish; we're ahead of schedule. And I'll make special room for your" – he winked – "other cargo."

Gerald and Aram rolled out of the canoe as it ground up onto the beach, and reached to help Isaac out.

"Welcome again, Doctor. Our dispensary...?"

"Plenty of time for that, Irish; I'd like to see your abode with a little more leisure, and I'd kill for a drink."

As they walked up the Rest House steps, Gerald was a little taken aback to see Temou's *kanawa* box sitting on the veranda, then remembered that he had left instructions for it to be prepared for shipment as soon as *Nimanoa* was sighted in the lee. Isaac paused to look at it. Gerald volunteered no information, remembering Vaskess' insistence on secrecy. He conferred briefly with Aram, then took down one of his precious bottles of Irish whiskey and poured short drinks for himself and Isaac, adding a little water. They settled in chairs on the lagoon-side veranda, looking out over the sunken garden with its vigorously growing bananas.

Isaac sighed, stretched out his legs, swirled the whiskey in his glass. "Ah, far from the madding throng, eh?"

"I hadn't realized till now just how comfortable it is, even compared with Manra and Orona."

"And the trees over there are quite special." Isaac waved his arm at the far side of the lagoon.

"Yes, *buka*. Pisonia grandis, a true indigene, replaced by coconut almost everywhere else in the Pacific. Associated by the Tungaru with the ancestress, Nei Manganibuka. The people say this was her native island."

Isaac drained his glass, leaned forward as though about to share a secret. "I say, Gerald, That's quite a handsome box you have on the other side of the house. Is it locally made?"

"Oh yes, quite. Temou, who's come recently from Funafuti – the canoe-maker, you know – is a very talented woodworker."

"I collect boxes, you know..."

"No, really?" I didn't know.

"Is it for sale, then?"

"Well, actually, I'm afraid it's.... it's going to Sir Harry, in *Nimanoa* with you."

"Oh, a gift, jolly good of you, and your woodman."

"Not a gift exactly. He... um... requested that I send it, or rather what it contains. The box is just the .... container."

"What it contains?"

"Quite."

Isaac lifted an eyebrow. "Which is...?"

"Umm... It's... Look, old man, I'm dreadfully sorry, but I'm not allowed to discuss it...."

"With a brother officer? Irish, really!"

"I'm instructed to keep the contents entirely to myself; orders direct from the HiCom. But.... I don't know, the contents are really of no importance; haven't an idea why Sir Harry wants it all kept so close. But I'm afraid you'll have to ask him, if you're that interested."

"Well, so be it. But...."

"Lindsay, I truly cannot discuss it. Terribly sorry, but orders are orders, eh? Shall we...."

Isaac snorted. "Very well, Gallagher. Let's get on with our rounds. Thank you, Aram; you're a fine host and a charming travelling companion." He squeezed Aram's shoulder as he followed Gerald out into the sunlight.

They walked in silence across the parade ground toward the dispensary, Gerald thinking madly of a way to change the subject.

"We've just finished digging these *babae* pits. They'll soon be producing..."

"Yes. Just so."

"And that's the temporary *maneaba*. The people have plans for a quite elaborate permanent one... "

"Jolly good."

Gerald was greatly relieved when the dispensary came in sight, with a couple of women sitting under its thatched porch roof waiting to be treated.

"Right, then; here's the dispensary, and this is Teng Eneri, our dresser, and our nurse-in-training, Nei Segalo... ."

Isaac and Eneri shook hands, and the doctor made a cursory inspection of the shelves of medical supplies. He made a point of discussing needs with Eneri, ignoring Gerald. Wrote a few notes in his small notebook.

Just as Gerald was beginning to worry about finding something else to keep Isaac busy, the *Nimanoa 's* whistle blew, signaling Harness' readiness to be underway. With a curt nod to Eneri and ignoring Segalo, Isaac started back toward the landing. Gerald thanked the dresser and caught up with him. Ahead on the path he could see Kirata and Abera carrying Temou's casket, slung under a pole between them. Temou himself was carrying the sextant box, in which they had packed the shoe parts, corks, and other artefacts. Better divert Isaac's attention, Gallagher thought.

"If you'd like, Lindsay, I could have Temou build you a box, and the next time ...."

"Thank you, Gallagher. Don't trouble yourself.

A mistake, Gerald thought, mentally kicking himself. Only served to rub salt in the wound. But as they reached the shore, he was relieved to see that two canoes had just left the beach, with the boxes aboard. The *Nei Manganibuka* was waiting for him and Isaac. Gerald took his time helping Isaac into the whaleboat and climbing in himself. He could see the boxes being lifted over *Nimanoa's* rail.

"Very good, Kirata; let's be off then."

The boat shot out over the reef flat on an incoming wave, the rowers pulling strongly. Reaching *Nimanoa,* Gerald climbed lightly aboard and reached back to help Isaac, who took his hand with an unintelligible grumble. Harness called from the quarterdeck.

"Sorry to hurry off, Irish, but without sail it's a long chug to Tarawa." Even with the wind fair on his quarter Harness had decided to keep sails furled to minimize the ship's profile – in the event the raiders were still about.

"Of course." Gerald walked quickly aft to where the captain stood, and asked in a low tone about the boxes.

"Packed in the hold, already, and your letter to Vaskess in my cabin."

"Capital. Uh... Captain, um... the less said about the boxes to Dr. Isaac, perhaps, the better, eh? Vaskess – well, Sir Harry, actually, is quite keen on keeping their existence quiet."

"Bones, are they?"

"Quite, but my instructions are... "

"To keep them secret. Mine, too."

"Jolly good; knew I could rely on you."

Harness winked. "Got my orders, same's you." He extended his hand. "Mum's the word, Irish, and best o' luck to you and your little colony."

"It'll be far bigger and more prosperous the next time you visit." They shook hands, and Gerald vaulted over the rail into the whaleboat. Isaac had already gone below.

Chapter 35 –

Wretched Relics, February 1941

The excitement of *Nimanoa*'s visit lingered for a day or so after her masts disappeared over the western horizon, but there was an element of sadness, too, Gerald thought, of regret and uncertainty. Unlike other visits, this time *Nimanoa* had brought no new settlers, no family members to augment and encourage those already in residence. And there was not much prospect for future infusions of new blood. Not while the war continued at home.

"Which tempts one to ask once again," he murmured, watching from the Rest House veranda as the lagoon reddened and glowed in the setting sun, with what he knew was a too-large glass of Scotch whiskey in his hand, "what earthly good one is doing here."

It had all made such sense back in Worchester, to follow his father's footsteps into the colonial service, after bashing about with no obvious purpose in life – at university, at the farm in Ireland, learning to fly. His father and mother had encouraged him, and now he wondered if – in his mother's case, at least, it had been to get him out of harm's way. Certainly, had he been at home he would have been up there in the clouds, over the Channel and the cities, facing down the waves of droning Heinkels and their shark-packs of Messerschmitts. Had he only known....

"Rubbish!" He rubbed his eyes tiredly. "You knew, you could have foreseen....." He stared at the glowing trees, the calm, placid universe of the Phoenix Islands, carrying on as though the world were not in flames. The Prime Minister's voice came to his mind, as it had come scratching over the wireless – was it over six months ago? "We shall fight them on the beaches; we shall fight them on the landing fields...."

"Fight them on the beaches...." He smiled grimly at the placid beach at the lagoon edge, imagining German troops charging ashore. Drained his glass. "Balls!"

He examined the glass, set it down carefully. "Right, then, Gerald. Here you are. England expects every man to do his duty. And this, for better or worse...."

He clenched his fist to pound the veranda rail; stopped at the soft whisper of bare feet on the wood floor. Aram had come out of the house.

"Mister Karaka?"

"Ah, Aram. Everything *bairaki raoi?*" — the words meant orderly, shipshape.

"Yes, Mister Karaka. I have taken in and folded your clothes and washed the floors. They'll be dry when you...."

"Get back from the wireless. Quite right, Aram. Come, let's see what news Tirosi has for us."

Tirosi was typing when they got to the wireless station, with the code book at his elbow. Young Keaki was sitting on the floor with his back against one of the two-by-fours that formed the structure's framing. He smiled his usual shy smile, and even in his present funk Gerald couldn't help returning it. The boy had such promise....

Tirosi rolled the paper carefully out of the machine and handed it to him. "This come from Tarawa, Mister Karaka. From Doctor Isaac."

"Doctor Isaac? I wonder....." He scanned the typescript and stifled an oath.

         6 Feb
         I understand from the Master R.C.S.
      Nimanoa, that he has certain human remains
      on board consigned to Suva. As I am in
      charge of Medical and forensic investiga-
      tion of such objects throughout the whole
      colony and have no knowledge of the matter,
      I presume that the package was intended to
      be consigned to myself?
         Isaac.

"Fucking pompous pederast!" he started to say, caught himself. Took a deep breath to regain composure. Aram and Keaki were looking at him, while Tirosi studiously examined the code book.

"It appears," Gerald said tightly, "that I wasn't quite clear in my consignment of our cargo on *Nimanoa.*"

"The logs, Sir?" Aram asked politely.

Gerald smiled. "No, those – things from Aukaraime. Dr. – the Chief Medical Officer must examine them."

"Ah." Aram nodded. "That's good."

Tirosi stood and offered his chair to Gerald, who shook his head. Tirosi sat on the floor anyway and lit his pipe. "Did I get that word right, Mister Karaka? For — forensic?"

"Quite. I suppose I should've made it clear that they were..." He stopped. No good tempting the island mind to dwell on why the bones had been where they were. Damn Isaac! Couldn't he see that the bones were old, the next things to archaeological specimens? Would he have consigned the bones of Maiden Castle's defenders to the Cornwall medical examiner?

Clever, cutting questions bubbled up in his mind and he shoved them down again. Wouldn't do to imply any disrespect for Isaac.

"Yes, Tirosi, you transcribed the word quite correctly. It means – a special examination of the bones by the CMO. Quite... uh ... routine."

Routine indeed, he thought later, alone on the Rest House veranda with another scotch, watching the moon rise over the lagoon. The calm blue beauty of the night contrasted sharply with his mood. Why did Isaac have to be at Tarawa? Steenson wouldn't have indulged in such self-righteous nonsense.

"Bloody pederast," he murmured again, and immediately crossed himself.

"The Lord works in mysterious ways," he mumbled, "his wonders to perform." But the practical problem remained; how to prevail upon Isaac to let go the bones?

But was this his problem? His responsibility? No, certainly not. It was Holland's on Ocean Island, and Vaskess' in Suva, and Sir Harry's. And they would probably bring an end to Isaac's little assertion of his nonexistent authority soon enough.

Or would they? And what if their inevitable order that Isaac stand down and send the bones on ruffled Isaac's feathers further, to the point of causing him, in his wounded pride, to take some action? Would he go so far as to arrange somehow for the bones to be lost? Yes, he just might be that vindictive.

And if the bones were Mrs. Putnam's?

"Then God intends that her fate is never to be known," he told himself, but wasn't satisfied.

Why was Isaac making such a fuss? He surely couldn't believe the bones to be a likely source of disease, could he? Or a victim of foul play? Had he some ulterior motive? If so, what could it be?

"Surely," he murmured, ridiculing the idea as soon as it came into his head, but not quite able to dismiss it. "Surely it's not – the box?" He puzzled awhile longer as the moon sailed higher in the almost- cloudless sky, then slipped quietly into the house, stepping over Aram as he made his way to the typewriter.

```
        Senior Medical Officer
        Personal should be delighted if you keep
    box but matter has been mentioned in pri-
    vate letter to High Commissioner who is
    interested in timber used and may ask to
    see it. It would be fun to make you one for
    yourself or perhaps a little tea table – we
    have a little seasoned timber left. Please
```

```
let me know whether you prefer box or table
and if former give any particular inside
measurements.
   Gallagher
```

He rolled the paper out of the machine and prepared for bed, still unsatisfied and unsure whether it would be wise to send the message.

As it happened, the next day there was a telegram from Holland on Ocean.

```
7 Feb
Senior Medical Officer repeated to me
his telegram to you regarding human remains
addressed to Suva on "Nimanoa". I am
informing him of position and there is no
need for you to take further action.
   Resident.
```

"Position." Gerald scratched his head. Was there a position? Whose? Perhaps Sir Harry's, leaving no doubt that the bones were to be shipped on?

"Well, in any event, the matter seems to be out of my hands." He folded his unsent message and put it in his pocket.

A few cloudless, breezy days passed, with Gerald bending his efforts toward the matter of land allocation. It was important to be fair, for each family, and each child, to have adequate land not only in terms of acreage but coconut trees and other important resources. It was not intellectually challenging work, but it was engaging, and for a time he could push both the war and Isaac out of his mind.

```
11 Feb Confidential
For your information remains taken from
"Nimanoa" part skeleton elderly male of
Polynesian race and that indications are
that bones have been in sheltered position
for upwards of 20 years and possibly much
longer.
   Isaac.
```

"Well," Gerald murmured, "that's that – if...." He read the text to Aram, who translated for Kirata and Takena, who had come in with the boys for the evening wireless session.

"With respect, Mister Administrator," Takena shook his head, "twenty years... well, it is not for me to question the doctor, but.... Those bones did not look that old to me."

"Nor to me, Teng Takena, but we're not the experts, eh?" But he couldn't shake his suspicions about Isaac's intentions.

```
11 Feb Confidential
```
Your confidential telegram 11th February. Many
thanks — rather an anticlimax!

On an impulse, he pulled out his folded-up earlier message and typed
it in ahead of his signature. Looked at it long and hard, then crossed it out
before handing the message to Tirosi.

```
14 Feb
    Your  telegram  11th  February.  Confiden-
tial.
    Matter  became  somewhat  tense  and  complex
after  guillotine  conversation  between  us.
As  I  had  (and  still  have)  no  information
save  presence  of  remains  and  therefore  ...
…quarantine  from ....................no
danger  infaction.  I  am  still  wondering  how
wretched  relics  can  be  interesting.
    Isaac.
```

"I'm sorry for the gaps, Mister Karaka," Tirosi shook his head. "The
reception was very bad and I could not make … sense of some of the
words."

"You did well, Tirosi. Perfectly understandable."

"There were two words I didn't know...."

"Quite all right, Tirosi, not important." Infection? No point in raising
that sort of thing with the natives, either; bones were frightening enough to
them as it was. But quarantine? Isaac had quarantined.... What? The bones?

"Afraid they'd go ashore? Have an evening on the town?" He mumbled
as he walked the path back to the Rest House, pondering the message. Or
had he quarantined the harbour? Held all shipping in port?

"My, my, wouldn't that put Sir Harry's knickers in a twist? And
Vaskess!" He couldn't help but chuckle at the idea of a confrontation
between Isaac and Vaskess, known to all as "the prince of bureaucrats."

"No wonder he's 'wondering,' poor devil, and almost apologetic about
cutting me off. 'Wretched relics' indeed!"

Chapter 36 –

Organization, March 1941

"It's a map," Aram said in response to Keaki's question.

"Oh, really? I thought it was some kind of animal." Keaki was leaning over Mister Gallagher's work table, being careful not to disturb anything. The sheet of typing paper held a pencil sketch of something roughly oval, fatter at one end than at the other. Aram looked at it over his shoulder.

"All right, smart guy. It's a map of Nikumaroro, actually. See, there's Tatiman Passage, so this thing that's shaped kind of like a dog's head is where we are – that's the Government Station, and the village."

"It is?"

"Yeah, and there's Baureke Passage down there, and Nutiran up there, and that lump on the other side is Taraea....."

"Oh, so this in the middle is the lagoon...?"

"Right."

"I didn't realize it was so long."

"Nor did anyone else," Mister Gallagher said, walking in from the parade ground with Iokina. "All the old maps showed the island as more or less round, or almost square." He leaned over the map, tapping it with his pipestem. "Now, Mister Magistrate, I suggest that we begin by dividing up the land down here south of the landing...."

The two men huddled over the map as Mister Gallagher explained his plan for land allocation. Keaki was disappointed that they weren't talking about land on Nutiran, or even below Baureke Passage where Baiteke wanted his honeymoon parcel. Iokina nodded as Mister Gallagher spoke, but said little.

"We think, I take it, that about half the labourers and families intend to remain as settlers?"

"That is what I think, yes."

"But we've no verification."

"No, sir."

"And no way to get it."

"It will be difficult without a real *maneaba* with *boti*. People are just – shy, hesitant – about making requests unless they have a ... a..."

"A system for doing so, and resolving issues that may arise. I understand, Mister Magistrate. As you'll recall, we faced a similar problem on Manra."

"Yes, Mister Karaka, and you made it right."

"Hardly my doing, but I think I do understand the problem."

Everyone knew – because Iokina and other newcomers from Manra had told them – how Mister Gallagher had solved the *boti* problem there, leading the Manra settlers to call their meetinghouse *tabuki ni Karaka* – Gallagher's accomplishment. When the dispute over whose seating places had priority in the *maneaba* – that is, the assignment of *boti* – almost reached the point of violence, Mister Gallagher had suggested that the elders of the village assign each household a place to sit that was <u>not</u> the one it had occupied on its home island. This novel idea had taken all the Manra family heads by surprise, and they had accepted it. Once everyone had a place to sit, the priority of speaking had developed fairly naturally, and decisions could be taken.

Teng Iokina looked thoughtful, rubbed his chin. "Perhaps, Mister Karaka, we could do the same thing here that we did on Manra."

Mister Gallagher looked at the magistrate with a solemnity that equaled his, cocked his head to the side quizzically. "Do you suppose that would work?"

"I think – I think it might work, yes."

"Perhaps, then – would it be best to discuss it with Teng Beiaruru, as the senior elder?"

"I think so – and with Teng Babera as the senior Protestant and Teng Takena as the senior Catholic. With your permission, Mister Karaka, I will see to it."

"I think that's a wonderful idea, Teng Iokina. Very well done indeed! Please by all means discuss it with the others. Perhaps you're right and it will work as well here as on Manra. An excellent idea!"

Iokina hurried out into the sunshine to pursue his mission. Mister Gallagher smiled broadly, but only for a moment, quickly turning back to his map.

The *maneaba* – still only a temporary structure, though the men talked often about building a permanent one — was duly organized following the model of *tabiki ni Karaka*. After a little sorting out, all the families settled into their *boti* and discussions proceeded in an organized way. One of the first subjects was agreeing on formal names for the different parts of the island. Names for most areas had been in use for some time, but had never been formalized, and boundaries had never been established. By the end of March each family had a map, laboriously copied out by Aram from Mister Gallagher's original, showing clearly where Nutiran ended and Taraea began, where the border was between Ritiati and Noriti, and so on. Then on larger maps of each part of the island, Mister Gallagher began marking the boundaries of land parcels, and people began letting him know what parcels they would like for their own. Sometimes there were arguments, or Mister Gallagher might suggest different parcels from those a person selected. For the most part all such disagreements and uncertainties were resolved amicably.

Of course, the parcels had to be mapped on the ground as well, so every day Mister Gallagher went out with a small team and a surveyor's chain, to locate and mark the boundaries of the plots, to each of which he assigned a number. Kirata and Abera hammered temporary stakes into the ground at each boundary; these were later replaced with coral slabs brought in from the shore and made to stand on end like gravestones. The cleared portions of the island began to look very orderly, if somewhat funereal, and the marked-up areas on Mister Gallagher's maps began to fill up with names.

"Did you notice," Ieiera asked Takena as they walked carefully along the reef edge in ankle-deep water, fish spears at the ready and their sons close at hand with bags for fish, "that someone put his name on that *ata* place?"

"No!" Takena exclaimed. "Who?"

"I'm not sure. I was looking at the map of Aukaraime on the south side, by Baureke Passage, and just caught a glimpse of the map showing the other side. But I'm sure it was that place Mister Karaka had marked, and there was a name on it."

"Nobody's talked about that in the *maneaba*."

"Well, maybe it's not definite – just someone's request."

"It shouldn't even be a request without discussion."

"Oh, but.... shhh...." Ieiera crouched, drew back his arm, and thrust out his spear, piercing a rainbow runner which he flipped expertly to Keaki. His son caught the fish in his bag, where it squirmed and flapped. Keaki was too preoccupied to tell his father, as he had been on the point of doing, that he knew what name was on the skull place.

"Anyway," Ieiera went on, "who'd want that place? Too many *anti* for me!"

"Good fishing, though," Takena shrugged, "and lots of turtles."

The fish quieted in death, and Keaki could get back into the conversation. "It's his own name," he said.

"His own?" his father's eyebrows went up. "Teng Karaka? Does he plan to stay here and farm?"

"No," Baiteke answered before Keaki could. "I asked him, and he said he's reserving it for government."

"Hmm. I wonder what government wants with it."

"Maybe," Keaki mused, "he's not finished searching."

But if Mister Gallagher planned to do more searching at the skull place, his plans were not realized. There was too much else to do, and too much else to worry about. Land division, land allocation, resolving disputes over land. Overseeing the cooperative store – making sure it was stocked, that prices were set, that the extension of credit was kept under control. Planning the new hospital, and finding the people to staff it. Replacing Eneri when he decided to return to the Gilberts – in the process adding to the Tuvaluan population with a dresser called Vaiaga and a nurse named Maria, and dealing with the unstated but obvious concern this raised among some of the Tungaruan settlers. And all the time keeping the coconuts growing, and planting new areas. Plantings extended down to Baureke Passage now, and he had assigned land there to some of the settlers who had come with him from Manra as members of the public works team. So much to do.

"So much to do," Gerald thought wearily, leaning over his typewriter with his chin in his hand, "and so little to do it with." He felt as though he were on a treadmill that went faster and faster the harder he tried to walk. And how much time did he have?

"The Empire," he mused, as the trees across the lagoon turned red and gold and the *kiakias* circled. "The bloody Empire. What'll be left of it if – hell, when the Nazis cross the channel?" Could there be an Empire without England, Scotland? And what of Ireland?

"What in Heaven's name is the point?"

A discrete cough; he steadied himself, built a smile on his face, turned around. Aram was standing at the door with a dishtowel in his hands.

"Excuse me, Mister Karaka. Cleaning is all done."

"Thank you, Aram." He looked at his watch. "Not quite time for BBC yet. Think your young friends will be coming?"

"Fishing, Sir." Aram jerked his head toward the lagoon, turning red under the sunset. A canoe was silhouetted there. Keaki and Baiteke, he thought, feeling strangely deprived by their being there, not scurrying up the steps for wireless time.

"God," he whispered. "I do so love this place, these people."

"Sir?"

"Nothing, Teng Aram, never mind. Light the lamp, would you? I'll spend a bit more time with this map...."

Chapter 37 –

Coastwatchers, April/May 1941

"See? It's right here – just about on the opposite side of the world." Mister Gallagher had opened a book of maps and was pointing to a brown spot in the blue Mediterranean Sea. "Malta. It's an island like Nikumaroro, but much bigger, and no lagoon."

"And that's where your brother is – Tarry?"

"Terry – Terrence; yes."

"He must be very brave." The BBC had been reporting massive almost daily German air raids on Malta.

"Indeed he is. In the letter I got the other day he was laughing about how the Germans always miss. Though they break lots of windows." He noticed the boys' blank looks.

"Windows there," he went on, "are covered in glass."

Baiteke scratched his head. "No wonder they break."

"Um... yes. Well. Here..." he pointed at a spot on the big land below the blue "Here's Benghazi, near where our soldiers have defeated the Italians, and captured so many of them..."

"Made them prisoners, yes?" Keaki was pleased to understand words like "defeated" and "captured."

"Yes, precisely, so they can't fight any more."

"Do they put them in gaol?"

"Rather like that, but with people guarding them with guns, and big fences, because we can't trust them to stay in gaol on their own, as we usually can here."

"Mister Karaka, where are the Japanese?"

"Ah, well...." He flipped several pages to another map, much of it blue. "The Japanese are over here, much closer to us. Right on the edge of the Pacific Ocean, see? And down here are the Gilbert and Ellice Islands, and we're out here on the east edge...."

"The Japanese are with the Germans, yes?"

"Regrettably, yes, but that doesn't necessarily mean they're going to go to war with us. Until recently they were our allies – that is, we were – um – friends..."

"And *Americi* is over there?" Keaki pointed.

"Exactly. On the other side of the Pacific Ocean. And they are our friends, and they've just agreed to send us guns and warships and supplies, but they're not fighting. But the Germans...." He flipped pages to show the Atlantic Ocean. "The Germans have many, many submarines – boats that go underwater – and they're sinking a lot of the cargo ships that are trying to bring us food and weapons, and some Americans are getting killed, so that may.... Well, the Americans might go to war, too. Mister Churchill..."

He broke off, looked up at Tirosi, who had come to the door and was waiting to be recognized. "Coded message from Suva, Mister Karaka; urgent and secret."

"Ah. Thank you, Tirosi. Time to clear out, boys; work to be done." As the boys gathered themselves up to leave, he turned to his desk and opened the lock-box where he kept his code books.

Wireless traffic from Suva and Ocean Island was becoming heavier all the time, and more and more of it was in secret codes that required his special book to decipher. Most of it didn't concern Nikumaroro in any direct way, but he still had to decode it all, and acknowledge receipt. This one revealed that *Nimanoa* had finally arrived in Suva.

"So," he said to himself, "now somebody trustworthy can look at the bloody bones. Wonder if MacPherson's on island." Gerald's friend "Jock" MacPherson taught forensics at the Central Medical School besides serving as chief medical officer. A big, bluff Scott who, to Gerald, virtually oozed competence and responsibility.

The message went on to its main subject. Colonies were to cooperate with New Zealand military authorities in placing coastwatchers on islands in the Ellices and Gilberts. Nothing said about why such men were needed, but nothing had to be said. Watching for the Japs.

"Risky business if they make a move," he murmured to himself, wondering what would be entailed in coastwatching, and why no one was being positioned in the Phoenixes.

"Suppose we fill the bill," he surmised, and fell back to thinking about his brother Terry, under the bombs on Malta.

"Boats that go underwater...." Baiteke shook his head as they walked toward the lagoon beach. "How do you think they breathe?"

"Maybe with a long hose or something? I wonder how they sink ships."

"Must have guns."

"Underwater?"

"I don't know. I just hope they don't sink the *Nimanoa*."

A bottle had washed up on the beach near the canoes. Baiteke grabbed it with a whoop.

"Ha! For toddy!" Bottles for collecting the juice for toddy were not common on the island, and were much sought-after along the beaches.

"I wonder where it came from."

"Oh, Wiatabo probably dropped it out of his canoe." Wiatabo was one of the island's most notorious toddy drinkers. "He'll be glad to get it back – if I give it to him"

If Mister Gallagher was aware of the drinking parties that were becoming more common as trees began to mature, he paid no attention. Teng Babera scolded them in his sermons, but was known himself to take a tipple from time to time, and none of the Catholics had any qualms about it. Toddy had always been a part of island life, and there was little enough entertainment.

The time of heavy rains and storms had passed. Almost every day dawned clear and bright, and at night the skies were cloudless and thick with stars. An occasional squall marched through on legs of rain, sometimes over the island, more often not, but there was still plenty of water in the cistern. Re-rendering it with a thin coat of cement had cured its tendency to lose water. Land clearing had proceeded to the far side of Baureke Passage, and parcels were being staked out and mapped for hypothetical future settlers as well as those already on the island.

"Will you divide up the whole island, Mister Karaka?" Keaki asked as he peered over the administrator's shoulder at his growing map.

"No, Keaki; we'll keep most of the windward side as bush reserve, for the birds and crabs and to supply firewood and such."

"So it won't be assigned to anyone?"

"No one but *komitina*." "Komitina" was the Tungaru way of saying "Commissioner," meaning the head of government. Mister Gallagher put down his pencil and began to fill his pipe.

"If you're worried about that place...."

"Oh no, sir; I'm not worried."

"No one will be expected to live there – though it's a very pleasant place. A very nice breeze, and easy walking to both the lagoon and the sea."

"Lots of turtles, too," Aram said with a smile. They had eaten turtle steaks and soup the evening before.

"Yes, lots of turtles." Mister Gallagher laughed. "Look here, boys. When I come back, maybe we'll build up that little house down

there, and plant some coconuts. I'll stay there and catch fish and turtles; you can come visit me and we'll listen to the wireless."

It wasn't until some time later, as Keaki was walking home wondering whether he would be brave enough to spend a night at the
skull place, that the full weight of Mister Gallagher's words came
home to him. He stopped in mid-step and tried to remember exactly
what the administrator had said.

"When I come back? That's what he said, 'when I come back.'"

The next day, Keaki's puzzlement was resolved. Mister Gallagher
met with the family heads and announced that he was being called to
Suva to help with a special project. No, he couldn't say anything
about the project, but it had to do with the war. While there, he
would try to arrange for more colonists, and supplies.

"When I return – in two or three months time, God willing, we'll
be able to build up the hospital and get the island really ready to
become the centre of this new colony."

"It will be good to have a real doctor," Teng Beiaruru cackled in
his cracked, high-pitched voice. "Young and strong as I am, I need
someone more experienced than these young men they send us.
Those NMPs don't know a hiccup from a fart. Maybe that Dr. Isaac
will come back."

Mister Gallagher smiled thinly. Kirata's eyes got big and round.
"Say, does he still have those ... things from the other end of
Aukaraime?"

Mister Gallagher shook his head. "No, he ... sent them on to Fiji,
after looking at them and deciding they were a Polynesian man. I
expect they've been looked at by other doctors there in Fiji, so perhaps while I'm in Suva I'll learn more about them."

"No need to bring them back here, though, eh?"

"No, Kirata, no need for that. There are cemeteries in Fiji."

Mister Gallagher wrote a long set of instructions for Iokina, all
inTungaruan, and had meetings with him and all the other men.
Aram packed up their gear, and made the Rest House secure. On 13th
June, *Nimanoa* lay in the island's lee; Mister Gallagher and Aram
went aboard. A blast of her whistle, her sails rattled up, and the
schooner heeled over on a long port tack, bound down the wind for
the Gilberts. Gerald stood for a long time at the taffrail, watching
the island grow small in the distance, and finally disappear over the
horizon. The helmsman saw that he was praying, and cautioned
other crewmen to leave him alone.

Chapter 38 –

The Castaway, June 1941

Gerald Gallagher was seasick. He was a poor sailor, always had been, but this voyage on *Nimanoa* had been worse than most for some reason – even though objectively, he told himself, the weather had not been bad. And now this boat trip – not long, but through choppy seas that seemed intent on separating his stomach from the rest of his body.

The ship toward which the lifeboat was pulling was a handsome one – sleek but sturdy, businesslike but yet with something of the yacht about her. And startlingly well armed, with a swivel-mounted three-incher aft, and a smaller gun or two forward. Brand new, flying the High Commissioner's ensign. His Majesty's Fijian Ship *Viti*, only a few months off the ways in Hong Kong, the pride of the Western Pacific High Commission's, and Fiji's, little fleet. Gerald clung grimly to the lifeboat gunwale and flashed a thin smile at Aram, telling himself it would be much more comfortable aboard.

But why was he even going aboard? Why the mysterious wireless message diverting *Nimanoa* – three days out of Nikumaroro, a day or so from Suva – to a rendezvous on the high seas, with no stated purpose other than for him to report to Sir Harry Luke?

The boat bumped the landing stage, and Gerald stood, cursing himself for being shaky, and accepted a crewman's help making the jump across. Up the short ladder to the *Viti*'s deck, and there was the High Commissioner, all smiles in his shorts and starched white shirt, extending his hand.

"Welcome aboard *Viti*, Irish! So glad we could make this work. Come, I'll show you 'round while your boy settles you into your cabin and then we'll get down to business. Suppose you could tolerate a drink, eh? Gin agree with you?"

Gerald wasn't sure anything would agree with his stomach, or vice-versa, but he nodded and smiled, and accepted the frosted glass the steward thrust into his hand as he followed the HiCom forward. There was quite a crowd aboard – Sir Harry's Aide-de-Camp Archie Reid, of course, but besides him Nightingale, a district officer from Fiji, Charleton the Fiji lands director, McGusty from the medical department, Wise from public works, and a young man he had never seen before, named MacQuire, introduced only as being from New Zealand. All Fiji people but MacQuire, Gerald thought; no Commission staff. What "business" did they have with him?

Viti was now underway, steaming south-southwest and rapidly leaving *Nimanoa* in her wake. Fast, Gerald thought, and a blessedly smooth ride. Sir Harry was leading him through a doorway into a very well-appointed conference room, apparently part of the High Commissioner's private suite. Nightingale, Charleton, and MacQuire joined them.

"Are you hungry, Gerald? Thirsty? Need the WC?" Gerald shook his head.

"Thanks, no, Sir Harry; I addressed all my needs before leaving *Nimanoa*. The only thing unsatisfied is my curiosity."

"That we'll satiate at once. Incidentally, for official purposes we're touring Lomaiviti, and giving McGusty and Wise the opportunity to resolve some renovation issues at the Lakemba hospital. All true, of course, but behind us now, so it's all fishing from here in. How's your colonial enterprise coming along?"

"Capital; I'll have my quarterly report to you shortly. I would dearly love to bring in another few hundred colonists, though, and I have a shopping list. But I understand, of course, with the war..."

"Indeed, but we'll see what we can do. In any event, it's the war we're here to discuss – a whole new phase of the war."

"Sir?"

"MacQuire, will you begin? Gerald, MacQuire has just joined us from New Zealand to help with military intelligence matters."

The young New Zealander, who had been slouching at his ease across the table from Gerald, came to attention and tossed back a forelock of dark hair. "Very good, sir." He leaned across the table, looking steadily in Gerald's eyes. "You understand, of course, Gallagher, that what we'll discuss here stays here."

"Indeed yes."

"Very good. Here's the picture, then. In a word, the Japs are coming into the war; we're quite sure of it. Thus far they've been the silent partners in the Axis, biding their time. But we've reasons to believe – excellent intelligence, actually – that they're preparing a major, multi- pronged attack."

"On us."

"On us, and the Dutch, to gain control of the oil and strategic minerals they so desperately need to carry out their imperial ambitions, and while they're about it to take as much territory as they can swallow."

"Surely we're prepared to repulse...."

"Poorly, I'm afraid, which is one of the great secrets we don't want spilled. Singapore's reasonably strong, but our fleet's greatly reduced by the need to patrol the Atlantic sea lanes, and of course much of the army's tied up in Africa and the Mediterranean, to say nothing of needs at home."

"I'd no idea...."

"No. Well, we expect them to strike down the peninsula toward Singapore, and simultaneously to attack us here – in the Gilberts and Ellices. Where, of course, we've no means whatever to resist. We're already evacuating nonessential personnel from Tarawa and Ocean. The great question is whether we can stop them overrunning Fiji."

"Whence," Sir Harry added," the road would be clear to Australia and New Zealand."

"My god."

"Fiji, of course, has precious little in the way of defensive works, though we're building them up rapidly. You'll hardly recognize the place, with all the tunnel digging and battery building underway. And New Zealand has agreed to deploy troops and aircraft."

"No hope for American assistance, then?"

Charleton and Sir Harry exchanged a glance; it was the High Commissioner who answered.

"We've – um – some reason to believe that the Japs just may include some U.S. possessions in their attack plans – perhaps the Philippines. That could be a colossally stupid move on their part – might actually be the only thing that would save us."

"For the moment, though," MacQuire added, "no, no hope for assistance from the Yanks."

"The buggers are all encouraging words," the HiCom growled, "but no chance they'll get off their well-padded arses unless they're forced to."

"In any event," MacQuire picked up the thread, "any forewarning of attack we can get will be in our favour, so as I think you know, New Zealand is deploying coastwatchers throughout the Gilberts and Ellices."

"And this," Sir Harry said, with emphasis, "is where you come in. I want you to take charge of the actual deployment; take the coastwatchers round, introduced them to the natives, get them settled, all under the cover of seeking more colonists for the Phoenix."

"Which in fact it's planned you should do," Charleton added, "and when the deployment's accomplished, you'll return to Gardner and continue as before, with the additional duty of keeping a weather eye out for Japs."

"MacQuire smiled grimly. "We hardly expect an attack on Gardner, or Sydney or Hull, but Canton's another matter. They doubtless know we're preparing to develop a base there, and the Pan American facilities themselves have some strategic value."

The HiCom fixed Gerald with a firm look. "It's a critical job, Gerald, and we think you're the man for it."

Gerald accepted with far more pleasure than his interlocutors could know. It wasn't flying against the Luftwaffe, but it was playing a significant role in the war effort, and a job for which he was, he thought, supremely well equipped. Fluent in Tuvaluan, better with each passing day in Tungaruan, knew many of the chiefs in the Ellices – and he wouldn't have to abandon his people in the Phoenix! He left the conference room feeling more alive than he had in months.

After a rest and a change of clothes, he joined the others on the fantail, where Sir Harry was trailing a deep-sea trolling line.

"Any luck, sir?"

"Not yet. But we're just coming abeam Fotuna, over the horizon there, so I've some hope for something beyond the passing pelagics. Will you join me?"

"Not yet, if you don't mind. I'm still trying to absorb...."

"Don't forget, Gerald, mum's the word. You're in Fiji on leave."

"Very good, sir."

Gerald stood awhile looking at the ship's wake, streaming out toward the horizon. A flying fish zipped across it, a frigate bird hung low looking for food. The other officers had moved somewhat forward to watch a pod of dolphins cavorting off the port beam.

"So, Irish, your little island domain is shipshape, is it?"

"Pretty much, sir. Well as can be expected under the circumstances. We've learned a lot, and I think things should go pretty smoothly from here out, assuming the war doesn't intervene. The coconuts are growing well, the people are pretty happy."

"And no more skeletons in your closet?"

Gerald laughed. "No, thankfully. One's quite enough. Can you tell me what became of those bones, sir?"

"Yes, though we're still keeping the matter under wraps. Got several experts looking at the sextant box – Captain Nasmyth, Harold Gatty, the aviator. There's agreement that's what it is – a nautical sextant box – but some dispute over its origin, I take it – maybe English, maybe French. Steenson looked at the shoe parts and says there are two shoes represented – a man's and a woman's. He thinks the corks on chains are probably from a cask of some kind."

"Ah, and the bones? Does he agree with Isaac?"

"That man! Do you know he quarantined Tarawa because of the bloody bones?"

"No; I knew he was upset I'd not informed him."

"On my orders, and quite properly! Well, he decided they might be a health risk, and slapped a quarantine on the whole harbour, with some five ships in port. You can imagine we put a stop to that without much hesitation."

Gerald smiled, recalling Isaac's amazement at the fuss over the "wretched relics."

"I can well imagine. So when the bones at last arrived, did Steenson and Jock agree with Lindsay's diagnosis?"

"Jock was – um – otherwise engaged, and I sent Steenson back to Tarawa to keep Isaac out of further mischief. David Hoodless was just returned from his training in England, so we gave 'em to him to look at. He said they were the remains of a European or half caste male."

"Ah. Not Polynesian, then."

"Well, possibly half-caste, but what's important is it's a male, not a woman."

"He's certain of that, even with the woman's shoe?"

"Who knows how certain a medical doctor ever is, eh? Anyway, that's his diagnosis, and it's good enough for me."

"Well, it was interesting to think it might have been Mrs. Putnam. I wonder about her navigator –what was his...?"

Sir Harry cut him off. "Yes, puzzling how she got so far off course. If that's what happened. But the woman's undoubtedly dead, eh? Solving the mystery won't bring her back."

"Well, no..."

Sir Harry glanced over his shoulder; the others were out of earshot.

"Let me put it to you plain, Gerald, and then we'll speak no more of it. Things are at a critical juncture with the bloody Yanks. If the Japs don't force their hand, it's doubtful they'll come in, and if they don't, the chances of our survival – of Britain's survival – are close to nil. The PM and Roosevelt are in close communication, and we're assured the President is in our corner, but their legislature is still listening to the pacifists – the 'America first' mob. Among whose leaders is none other than Charles Lindbergh – the pilot, you know?"

"Yes, of course."

"Do you know what they called Mrs. Putnam in the U.S., Gerald?"

"No sir."

"Lady Lindy, Irish, Lady Lindy! Now what do you suppose Lindbergh himself, the fascist bastard, is going to say if it comes out she expired on an island under our jurisdiction?"

"But surely, Sir Harry, we could hardly have prevented it! We had no one on the island at the time! And how petty would the Americans have to be to let freedom and democracy go under because we failed to find their famous flier before she expired?"

"Supremely petty, Gerald, but they've a genius for that, haven't they? It seems ridiculous, I know, but for want of a nail, eh? If a controversy whipped up by Lindbergh delayed America's coming in on our side even a week more than might otherwise be – even a day! – the game could be up."

Gerald's eyes travelled up the *Viti's* wake toward the horizon, and the little island hidden beyond it. Thought about his brother in Malta, the RAF in the skies over Britain. He smiled wryly.

"He works in mysterious ways," he murmured.

"Eh?"

"I was saying, sir, that it's interesting to speculate about that European or half-caste castaway. Washed up from a shipwreck, I suppose."

```
3rd July 1941
Note to file 4439-40 (36) The Secretary,
I have read the contents of this file
with great interest. It does look as if the
skeleton was that of some unfortunate
native castaway and the sextant box and
other curious articles found nearby the
remains are quite possibly a few of his
precious possessions which he managed to
save.
2. There was no evidence of any attempt
to dig a well and the wretched man presum-
ably died of thirst. less than two miles
away there is a small grove of coconut
trees which would have been sufficient to
keep him alive if he had only found it. He
was separated from those trees, however, by
an inpenetrable belt of bush.
GBG.
```

Chapter 39–

The Aeroplane Wreck, July 1941

Keaki liked the way the water poured over the lip of the reef when the tide was low. He could see the reef edge in such detail, the great chunks of coral hanging at odd angles, arrested in their slide into the depths. Creating all kinds of crevices and cracks, caves and tunnels, full of brilliant, colorful, flashing life, and the sparkling cascade of water falling over it all.

"Enough daydreaming, Keaki!" Takena was shouting at him, laughing. "Do you want your mother and sister to go hungry? Will you leave all the work to your poor, weak father?"

Keaki snapped to attention. His father and Baiteke were stalking the reef edge on foot, throw- nets in hand. It was his job, with Takena, to go after the bigger fish that cruised in the surf just off the face of the reef. He forced himself to stop thinking of the fish as brilliant parts of creation; for now, for this moment, they had to be food, and unpredictable adversaries to be outwitted.

Takena straightened up, gently fingering his line and peering down its length, with the studious air of a man fascinated by the ways of fish. The canoe rocked a little as he took hold of the line and began to pull it carefully in, coiling it as he did. Keaki leaned over the gunwale, deciding whether to grab the net or the club.

"Ika na beka" Takena grunted. Keaki marveled at how he could know a fish without seeing it, from the way it moved and tugged on the line. But now he could see it, in brief flashes, then breaking the surface, struggling. *Ika na beka*, of course, a large oily fish, and too big for the net. He picked up the knobby *kanawa* club.

Big one, he thought. Too big, really, for the line; Takena was in danger of losing his hook. He'd have to be quick, and make no mistakes. The fish swerved toward the outrigger side of the canoe and the line slapped against the hull. Keaki seized it and eased the fish up against the side of the canoe, held it there and bashed its head with the club.

Got him! The fish still flopped, but with no real energy, no life. Keaki hauled him up to the gunwale and got his fingers into his gills, but couldn't lift him. Takena jumped nimbly back to help him drag it over the side. Smiled at Keaki, tapped him lightly on the shoulder.

Keaki laughed. "Just one hit, uncle! That's all!"

"That's how to do it. Much better than two or three. Lose him that way."

He didn't mention the one Keaki had lost that way, earlier in the day. Keaki was grateful.

The fish was safely in the bottom of the canoe, rapidly losing colour as the life ran out of him. Takena went back over the outrigger struts coiling the line, running his fingers over it to check for weak spots, making sure the knot was strong attaching it to the hook. He picked a small octopus from the bait bucket. As he re-baited and trailed the line, Keaki went back to watching the streaming reef-edge. He felt very adult, out here fishing with the men along the reef beyond the *Noriti*. But he kept his eyes away from the sparkling piece of creation he had just reduced to a lifeless lump of meat.

Ieiera and Baiteke were picking their way along the brink of the reef, Baiteke carrying a bag of fish so full he staggered. Ieiera raised his net in greeting and called across the water to Takena.

"The aeroplane is out in the air today."

"Yes, the tide's as low as I've ever seen it on this island," Takena called back. "Lots of fish in the tide pools?"

"Enough to burden your powerful young man here."

Baiteke took this as permission to speak, and shouted at Keaki.

"Keaki, have you seen the aeroplane? You should look!"

Keaki had heard about the aeroplane, but not seen it. It had appeared shortly after Mister Gallagher's departure, when a sharp squall had blown through. There was debate among the fishermen as to whether it had been thrown there by the storm or had always been there. Some of the men said they had seen it before, but had thought it was just part of the *Noriti,* ripped off by storms and somehow tossed northwesterly along the reef edge. Others were quite sure they had never seen it. If it had been there, the recent storm had at least flipped it round, settling it back onto the reef so as to show that its metal was far too thin to be from the heavy steel-hulled ship. Bueke and Kirata, who had gone aboard the warship that had startled them right after their arrival, thought it looked like the wing of an aeroplane.

Keaki looked eagerly at Takena. "Can we look at it, uncle?" Takena shrugged. "Why not? Dig in – it's up that way."

Keaki paddled hard and the canoe shot forward, just outside the gurgling water along the reef edge. Takena pointed with his paddle.

"There it is."

The thing was something of a disappointment – a long, twisted piece of some kind of metal, with an odd red stuff all over it. It also looked vaguely familiar to Keaki.

"That's the aeroplane," Takena said, resting with his paddle laid across the thwarts. Saw the question in Keaki's eyes and smiled crookedly. "It can't fly, obviously. It's just part of the wing, you see, and the waves have rolled it all around and twisted it" – he searched for a word, a concept – "made it kind of like a stick with string wrapped round it."

"Why's it all red?"

"It's algae, like on the reef flat, only for some reason it's red. Tumuo tasted it."

Takena paddled gently to keep the canoe still as they looked at the thing. Keaki, sitting on the outrigger boom, tried to imagine it flying, couldn't.

As Takena said, it looked like a twisted stick of some kind, or maybe one of the drills that Mister Kimo used in woodworking. He could see now that the red stuff was indeed a sort of algae growth, and where it didn't grow the thing was a dull gray colour. The thing looked somehow uncomfortable to be resting there on the reef edge, all twisted up into a stick, a log. Something stuck out at one end – a round thing of some kind, black around a gray center.

"How did it come to be here, Uncle?"

"It must have wrecked. Tumuo is quite sure it's an aeroplane – part of an aeroplane."

"Couldn't it be part of the *Noriti*."

"No, it's too thin – the metal it's made of – and the wrong colour. Not the red stuff; that's algae, but the gray stuff underneath. And it's too far; the current flows that way" He pointed back down the face of the reef toward the shipwreck. They all knew how the current flowed, of course, and it made no sense that something so big from the ship could float or be tossed this far north along the reef, against the flow.

"Besides," he said, "Tumuo says that thing on the end is a wheel that aeroplanes land on. I guess they don't always land in the water like the ones that came here. I remember Jack Kimo talking about aeroplanes that land on the ground, on wheels."

"Do you think this is one of the aeroplanes from that ship?" Keaki realized as soon as he'd said it that this was a stupid idea; those aeroplanes hadn't had wheels. They had big bladder kinds of things underneath, so they could land and take off on the water.

Takena only laughed a little bit. "No, it couldn't be. Those aeroplanes didn't have wheels, and they didn't wreck. They landed, and the ship picked them up and took them away.

Takena began to paddle along the reef edge. Keaki gazed back at the aeroplane. "How did it fly?" he asked suddenly.

"Its engine is very strong, and that metal is very light. Alu – alu – like those trays they have in the galley on *Nimanoa*."

Keaki remembered. "Aluminium?

"That's right, aluminium. Ho, that's right, the children of Bueke found a piece just the other day. Bueke made a lure from it, for fishing."

Keaki almost dropped his paddle. That's what that silvery stuff is, he thought, saying nothing but with his mouth hanging open. Recalling how the *co:m* her father had made sparkled in Era's hair. Wondered briefly about his own *co:m,* about Era. Pushed the thought away as his mind took another jump. The big fish-shaped thing he and Baiteke had found the day – so long ago – they went to check the toddy trees. It was made of the same stuff!

In fact, maybe this <u>was </u>the thing they had seen, all twisted up. Yes, he thought, maybe it was the same thing. Or something very much like it.

They started back, paddling for awhile in silence.

"So an aeroplane wrecked here," Keaki finally said, to no one in particular.

"Must have been before we came," Takena observed. "Otherwise we would have seen it wreck." He trailed his baited hook in the water.

Keaki was quiet for the rest of the way home, thinking about the aeroplane. That evening, back in the village, he burst in on Baiteke's tale of struggling with a big grouper in a tide pool.

"The aeroplane..... "Do you think it was that lady?"

Baiteke sighed. No use telling fish stories when his friend got an idea. "That Meela lady Mister Karaka talked about? Maybe. But those bones were on Aukaraime."

"She could've walked."

"I suppose. A long way for a woman, though. And the windward shore. Dangerous."

"Nei Aana used to go there. And anyway, she died."

"Nei Aana hasn't died!"

"No, no, the Meelia lady. Air hard."

"Oh, well, that's so. But wasn't there a man?"

"With her? I think that's what Mister Karaka said."

"Yes, he did. A great navigator, Mister Karaka said."

"Yes. He must have died too."

Baiteke tossed his head. "And we'll die too, if we don't eat some of those fish we caught. I smell it cooking. Race you to your mother's cookhouse!" He sprang up and was gone, scampering toward the village. Keaki followed slowly, deep in thought.

Chapter 40 –

More Bones, July 1941

Sunday, and church services were done. Most of the men were napping, most of the women were busy in the cookhouses, most of the children were playing, climbing trees, sailing toy canoes or real ones. Keaki and Baiteke paddled out the twisting channel from the beach and made for Nutiran.

"I'm going with you only to get fish," Baiteke said, rather stuffily.

"Yeah, yeah...."

"What do you expect to find?"

"I don't know, I just...."

"Maybe another *ata?* Or her other shoe, eh? With 'This is Meelia's shoe' on it in big red letters. Or a bigger box..."

"It's just that if it really is her aeroplane, then Mister Karaka should know about it."

"And you want to be the one to tell him," Baiteke chuckled. Keaki felt his cheeks getting hot. Was it true? Was he trying to –

To what? Trying to look smart for Mister Gallagher? Well, maybe, and what was wrong with that?

It's putting yourself forward, he thought, and that's not the way a person should be. But wasn't it true that Mister Gallagher should know about this aeroplane? And if Mister Gallagher was thankful for the information, well, that wasn't Keaki's fault, was it?

"Wake up, tern poop! Here's the beach!"

Keaki shook himself as they grounded on the reef flat. Baiteke splashed water at him. Keaki mumbled something about octopus urine as he tied off the canoe to a straggly *mao* that was trying to survive in the gravel of the beach.

They picked their way over the slimy shelves of reef, and then along the edge of the steeply pitched coral skree that served as a beach on this part of the island. Before long they were passing the battered bow of the *Noriti*.

"At least there's plenty of fish," Baiteke laughed, slashing the surface of a tide pool with his knife and sending multicolored fish skittering in all directions. "Hoo! Look at them! *arinaimawa! neinei! ikamaura!*[10]"

"Yeah," Keaki said absently, peering ahead for a glimpse of the aeroplane.

---

[10]Wrass, Rainbow Runner, Parrotfish

"Look at this old grandfather!" Baiteke scampered to another pool, where a giant grouper floated, easily five feet long.

"Don't fall in," Keaki smiled thinly. "He'll eat you."

"Ha! I'll eat him first!" Baiteke gnashed his teeth and made claws of his hands. The fish ignored him. Baiteke stood with his hands on his hips, looking the big fish in the eye.

"Why, oh why didn't I bring my spear? I know! Because Keaki the scholar was in such a hurry to go examine the aeroplane."

"I didn't stop you bringing your spear. Why don't you beat him to death with a rock?"

"Maybe I will....."

"Suit yourself. I'm going to the aeroplane."

And the tide, he thought, was just about right. Glancing over his shoulder at the surf, which boomed and threw up a wall of spray, he angled across the rough coral near the shore, toward the outer reef flat

Baiteke shook his head, waved to the grouper. "Well, good bye, grandfather. My silly friend wants to go look at no-fly aeroplanes." Keaki didn't hear him, and if the grouper did, he didn't react.

Close up, from the land side, the aeroplane wasn't any more informative than it had been from the sea. Keaki still couldn't figure it out. A long piece of metal like a pipe, with the black and gray round thing on the end, and the gray stuff twisted all around it. But the gray stuff – was it really aluminium? – did look a lot like the stuff he had used for Era's *c:om*.

"Well, Teng Scholar. Have you solved the mystery?"

"I still don't understand how it flies."

"Flew. It doesn't fly now."

"I noticed that, streaming golden crap of a red-tailed tropic bird."

"Anyway, it's just part of the aeroplane, yes? So of course it doesn't look like it could fly. One stick from a canoe wouldn't look like it could sail, would it?"

"No, I guess not. I guess...."

Guessed what? That whether and how the thing had flown wasn't the point? What, then, was the point? He turned and started back toward the shore, peering into the cracks and tide pools as he went. Baiteke chided him about looking for another skull, and bounced from pool to pool talking to the fish.

Just inshore of the reef flat, Keaki climbed the steep scree and sat down, halfway to the *mao* line. Lying back on his elbows, he looked at the surf crashing on the reef edge, the birds circling above, from time to time plunging headlong into the foam. The aeroplane appeared and disappeared as the waves broke over it. Baiteke was coming slowly toward him, still examining tide pools and cracks in the reef, still chatting with the fish.

"So, what am I looking for, eh?" Keaki asked himself. Was it really all about impressing Mister Gallagher? What would Mister Kimo or his father say to that? Or was he just bored? Finding the skull had been scary, but it had been different from what went on day in and day out. The story of Meela Airhart was sad, but it was interesting, different, a connection with the wide world beyond the reef, beyond the horizon. So many things out there – Ocean Island, Fiji, Germany, *Engiran, Ameriki.....*

Baiteke had reached the edge of the beach, and was standing on the edge of an almost-dry tide pool. Keaki thought he looked agitated, and when an eddy in the wind blew his voice to Keaki's ears, he realized that he was.

"You piece of well-dried chicken shit!"

Baiteke was shaking his fist. What ever could be wrong with him? Now he was stalking up the scree, waving his hands over his head.

"Very fucking clever, friend Keaki. Very funny. Drag me all the way up here to scare me to death."

"What?"

"Don't fuck around with me. You put those things there, didn't you? Just to scare me!"

"What things?"

"Or you knew they were there, and just set me up to see them."

"See what?"

Baiteke picked up a rock, acted as if he was going to throw it at Keaki. "See what? Right, what things, he asks, so innocent...."

"What the shit....?"

"The fucking bones in the tide pool, asshole! Don't you ever get tired of disturbing the dead?"

"What bones in the tide pool? Which tide pool?"

Baiteke tossed the rock up and down, looked at Keaki appraisingly. "The tide pool in your head. You really don't know?"

"I really...."

"You didn't put them there?"

"Who? Where?"

"Come on!" Baiteke grabbed his hand and almost dragged him bodily down the beach to the edge of the tide pool. It had almost no water in it, just drying algae, some puddles, a flopping, gasping fish or two, and.....

Keaki's legs went weak and he almost sat down. Thought better of it, backed away from the edge of the pool. His hands were at his mouth. "Oh no... !"

Takena walked around the edges of the tide pool, looking at the things from different angles. Ieiera crouched on the edge, shading his eyes with his hand. The boys stood waiting for someone to say something. Neither of their fathers had wanted to come when the boys told them what they had found, but they had come, and the boys felt comforted by that, content to leave things to them.

"Well," Takena said, "it's not the same *ata*."

Ieiera continued to peer under his hand. "How do you know?"

"It's bigger, heavier, and it's not missing its – you know, its cheek." Takena patted his own.

"What about the other bones?"

"They're bigger and heavier too."

"So you don't think he swam back here...."

"No, I think it's somebody else."

The bones were jumbled together in the bottom of the tide pool, the skull lying on its side looking blankly toward the shore. Arm bones and leg bones too, and the pieces that Mister Gallagher had called the pelvis.

"How do you suppose they got here?"

Takena gestured toward the shore. "Remember when we were here fishing two weeks or a week ago? I think the sand came out farther – like a big dune. I'll bet they were buried in it, and when that funny squall came through the other day, it blew it away and the bones fell out, ended up in the pool."

"Yes, I remember that dune. But it's always been here...."

"That was a funny squall, almost like *te nakirua*[10]. Those things can – you know –" Takena made circles with his hands – "they can just rip up one place and leave another alone."

"I suppose so....."

"So, brother, the question is, what should we do?"

Ieiera was still peering at the bones under his hand. "What's that shiny thing?"

"Shiny... oh, that thing?" Takena pointed at something small and silvery, almost hidden by some drying algae.

"Yeah, what is it?"

"I don't know. Do you think I should pick it up?"

"It's not among the bones. I think it'd be all right."

"Well, OK....." Takena lay on his belly and reached into the depression, took the thing delicately between two fingers and his thumb. It was rectangular, flat, with little pieces of something soft and flappy hanging off two of its sides. Glass on one side, silvery on the other. Takena held it up as the boys crowded up to look over his shoulder.

"Te tai[11],"* Baiteke said.

"Huh?

"Te tai. Mister Kimo has one. So does Mister Karaka. Those flappy things are like straps that hold it on your wrist. It says what part of the day it is. Those numbers, see? Like a clock, but just small."

"Ah." Takena and Ieiera nodded, looking solemn.

Takena turned it over. "It has words on it."

"Huh," Ieiera squinted at it. "Words in English. Here, boy, can you read this?"

Keaki took the watch gingerly in his hand, wondering if it had belonged to whoever had left his bones here. "P-a-n – pan. That means *te burak-ibaan[12]*, but that's not what this is. You couldn't cook in this little thing, and besides...."

"What else?"

"A-m-e-r-i-c-a-n... Am-ee-ruh-can...? I don't know ...."

"Like those sailors!" Baiteke exclaimed – the guys with the towers. They were *kain Ameriki,* remember?"

"Huh! " Takena scoffed. "A cooking thing from that Ameriki place? You boys are talking out your assholes; doesn't that Babera teach you anything in school? It's obviously *te tai.*"

"Well," Ieiera shrugged, "whatever it is, it probably belonged to that guy" – he jerked his head in the direction of the bones. Keaki dropped the silvery thing like it was hot; it tumbled back into the tide pool. "Let's leave all these things here and report them to Iokina. There'll have to be a meeting....."

---

[11]Wristwatch

Chapter 41–

The Decision of the *Maneaba*, July 1941

Around the sides of the temporary *maneaba,* the families sorted themselves into their *boti* in such silence that Keaki could easily hear the birds making their soft evening settling-down sounds in the trees. Teng Iokina sat in the petitioner's place at the end of the floor closest to the entrance. Teng Abera looked around, smiled a little sheepishly, as though he had just realized that he was entitled by his position to speak first.

"Well," he said, looking around. "Let us begin – uh – with a prayer. Teng Babera, will you please...?"

Teng Babera needed no urging, closing his eyes, raising his hands, and appealing to God to bless the assembly and let them know His will. He spoke on, the Protestants murmuring in response, the Catholics looking uncomfortable but holding themselves in prayerful silence. With Babera's "amen," the *maneaba* fell silent. Teng Abera looked around again, up at the thatch. The silence stretched out and out. The birds cooed softly, the wind moved in the trees.

Teng Beiaruru, sitting just to Teng Abera's right, broke the silence.

"We are meeting," he croaked, "to decide what is the proper thing to do with those things the young men Baiteke and Keaki found up there on Nutiran." Murmurs and nods around the maneaba.

"His Majesty's magistrate, Teng Iokina, has asked us to do this." More nods. Iokina dropped his eyes to the floor .

"As the oldest man here," Teng Beiaruru went on, "it is my obligation to offer the first suggestion, in all humility." Nods, murmurs of agreement; everyone looked at him expectantly. He looked up at the thatch for a moment, then waved his hand – a dismissive gesture, Keaki thought.

"It is really quite simple, I believe. We should respect that person just as Teng Koata did the first one. We should cover him up and leave him in peace."

Murmurs of assent, but some uncomfortable looks, especially from Kirata, Takena, Abera, and Bueke, but it was not their turn to speak.

Eneri was next in speaking order, and Keaki's father after him. Both agreed with Teng Beiaruru. Then it was Kirata's turn. He turned a little red in the face and mumbled.

"Last time we got sick."

Silence. There it was, Keaki thought; it was out. What would the men do now that the fear had been given voice?

Bueke was next. He crossed himself and spoke in a soft voice.

"It is true that some of us got sick. We also must consider that Mister Karaka did not think it was right to bury that – person. He dug it up, and picked up ... and sent them all to Fiji."

Katoi nodded: "And he did not get sick."

Uriam shook his head. "Still, burying the – dead is the right thing to do. We do not want an *anti* to be angry with us.

Now it was Teng Babera's turn. He had clearly been looking forward to the opportunity. He shook his head sadly.

"It is disappointing," he said, enunciating each word clearly and with force, "to hear my brother speak of *anti*. Perhaps it is because he has not yet found Jesus Christ our Savior."

Teng Uriam colored, but could say nothing. It wasn't his turn. Teng Babera went on.

"Last time, Koata and others buried that dead person, and they became ill. Why did they become ill? I will tell you, as God has seen fit to reveal. They became ill because they buried that person with the ceremonies of Tungaru devil worship. This angered the Lord God and he punished them accordingly."

Whispers, frowns, some heads nodding, a few shaking. Kirata looked fixedly at Babera; Takena, Abera, and Bueke stared fixedly at the floor; Eneri examined the thatch above his head. Babera raised a finger, went on.

"Mister Karaka then dug that person up and sent him away to government, and he was not punished. Why? Because what he did was pleasing to the Lord, as well as to government. So I respectfully agree with our elder Teng Beiaruru that the answer is simple, but with respect, it is a different answer. We should put those things in a box and keep them safe until Mister Karaka comes back, or some other representative of government. Mister Karaka will do what is right in the eyes of government, and I believe this will also be pleasing to God."

The next two speakers were Protestants and agreed with Teng Babera. Teng Teiranau, though Catholic, said he respected the wisdom of Teng Babera's words. Takena said he agreed, looking relieved, Keaki thought, perhaps because no one was asking him to bury anyone. Teng Kamarie and Teng Waitabo murmured their agreement.

Every *boti* had now spoken, and it was up to Teng Abera to sum up and either continue the discussion or bring it to an end. He looked around, smiled a nervous smile.

"Well, it appears that most of us prefer to put those – things these young men found in a box or maybe a bag, and keep them someplace safe until Mister Karaka returns. So, Teng Iokina, this appears to be the recommendation of the *maneaba* to government."

Iokina nodded. "Thank you. Thank you all. I believe I agree, this is the right thing to do. I think Mister Karaka would agree if we could speak to him. So – it only remains to be decided who will pack up those ... things, and where they will be kept against Mister Karaka's return.'

This provoked another round of discussion, and gave Teng Babera another opportunity to excoriate the devil worshipers among them. When it was again time for Teng Abera to speak, he looked solemnly round the *maneaba,* letting a full minute of silence go by. No consensus had been reached, Keaki thought; what would be done? Finally Teng Abera looked at Teng Babera, a crooked smile playing across his face.

"Since Teng Babera rightly tells us that there are no evil *anti* that can overcome the love of our Lord Jesus Christ, and since no one is more knowledgeable than Teng Babera in the teachings of Our Savior, I suggest that Teng Babera pack up those things."

Teng Babera was silent for a moment, then waved his hand dismissively.

"Oh well, all right. I will put them in a cloth bag I have, and keep them....." he broke off, perhaps thinking that if he kept the bones in his house no one would come to visit, or worship. Or perhaps, against his will, thinking of *anti.* Eneri, the next in order, rescued him.

"As to where to keep them, why not leave them where they are on Nutiran, but in the bag? No one is going to take them."

Smiles all around. Leave the *anti* up on Nutiran; that should be safe. The thing was decided, and the meeting was soon over, everyone scattering to their homes for the midday meal.

That afternoon, Babera and Eneri went up to Nutiran and collected all the bones in a copra bag, which they put under a *mao* well above the high tide line. Babera said a long prayer.

Chapter 42 –

HMFS *Viti*, September 1941

"Mister Karaka's coming back!" Tirosi was all smiles as he delivered the wireless message to Iokina. "Bringing equipment and stores and even your new wireless operator!"

Iokina smiled broadly. Apparently he was going to get through his time of sole responsibility for the island's governance without major disaster. "So, you'll be leaving us, Teng Tirosi?"

"It's hard. I've come to love this island, you know? But my family... you know."

"Yes, it's difficult to be so far away, for so long. We will miss you, Tirosi, and the exciting messages you bring."

"The new man will bring them just as well, I'm sure. Anyway, Mister Karaka should be here inside the week, and he's coming from Funafuti in the High Commissioner's new ship."

HMFS *Viti* arrived three days later – a bigger ship than any that had visited the island in the last two years, save *Moamoa* and perhaps *John Bolton*. Bigger than *Nimanoa,* anyway, and much prettier.

"Look at the big gun!" Baiteke shouted down from his perch in a *ren* tree. "Yeah," Keaki mused. "And it looks fast, too."

"Maybe that's why it's here at the wrong tide."

"Think they'll be able to unload?"

"Not with our boat." Kirata and half a dozen other men had walked *Nei Manganibuka* out into the boat channel, but now they were all shaking their heads as they looked at the reef that lay between them and the sea.

"Not enough water over the reef?"

"No, not nearly. It looks like they're going to try to use the ship's boats."

The *Viti's* whaleboats were maneuvering alongside, and the crew were unshipping the boom. Soon cargo – mostly building material, Baiteke said – was swinging over the side and being guided into the boats, and the boats were coming in to the reef edge. The men lined up there, legs spread wide, bare feet planted firmly on the coral, to manhandle the stuff ashore.

"Woo, lost one!" Baiteke shouted as a bundle of steel bars slipped out of several sets of hands and hit the water with a splash that soaked the men aboard the boat. But now the boats were headed back for the next load, and the men were dragging and carrying the first loads ashore. The boys ran to help.

Mister Gallagher came ashore in the fourth boat, with Aram and Bauro, who helped him from the boat to the reef, and a big *I-Matang* officer. Mister Gallagher looked tired, and Aram held his arm all the way across the reef.

"I'll be all right from here on, Aram; many thanks." Mister Gallagher smiled thinly at his servant as the other *I-Matang* crouched to pat sand on his face. "And here are Keaki and Baiteke; it's good to see you, young men. Mac, these boys are my wireless mates, Keaki and Baiteke; boys, say hello to Dr. MacPherson."

The boys shook the big man's hand – everyone had heard of Dr. Maffurs. They walked with Aram behind the two *I-Matangs* toward the village. Keaki took Aram's hand.

"It's good to have you back, Teng Aram."

"I'm glad to be here, but today we're going on to Canton. We'll be back in a couple of days. Mister Karaka is –" he hesitated, his voice dropping to a whisper. "He's – I'm afraid he's really sick. Really weak, and so – I don't know, angry and nervous. I've – I've never seen him like this. He's always sick on the ocean, but not – not so much as now."

Keaki looked curiously at the two men walking in front of them. Mister Gallagher did look different, he thought. He didn't seem to walk quite straight, or steadily, and he waved his arms a lot, talking in an unusually loud voice.

"This is where we propose to build the hospital, Mac, if you agree. This is the existing dispensary, which as you can see is quite small. Over there is the convalescent ward – nobody convalescing at the moment, apparently. And there to the right you see our parade ground...."

"Very tidy, Gerald," the big man rumbled. "And that's your happy home beyond, is it?"

"The Rest House, yes. Far too good for me; Jack Kimo truly outdid himself. It's even got running water in the bathroom, and a regular bathtub. Pity there's no time to partake...."

"When we get back, Gerald, and we'll have time for some fishing, eh?"

"Oh yes, Mac; the fishing here is beyond belief. And there's such promise here, truly. I'll be so glad to get back, get on with it. Truly. But enough whining from me. Here's the cooperative store; rather an elegant signboard, eh?"

When *Viti's* whistle sounded and the men returned to the ship, Mister Gallagher was still talking and waving his hands, and still looked shaky. He came close to falling between the reef edge and the boat, which would have been disastrous, but Aram and Dr. MacPherson caught him at the last moment.

Three days later, the weather was overcast and a choppy, sullen swell was running when *Viti* appeared in the lee. Once again the tide was unfavorable – dead low, with water streaming over the reef edge like a waterfall, and a two-meter scramble up from any boat whose crew might be foolish enough to come alongside. The ship steamed back and forth just beyond the reef.

"There's Doctor Maffurs," Baiteke shouted, waving. The big doctor, far beyond hailing range, paid no attention. He appeared to speak sharply to the man next to him at the rail and then walked quickly inside.

"Where's Mister Karaka, I wonder?"

Keaki was wondering the same thing, and wondering why Doctor MacPherson had gone inside so quickly, why no one was waving cheerfully from the rail as usual. Was it just the weather? Was everyone seasick?

The tide rose as evening came on – a gray, dull-colored evening, the birds settling in early, a troubled breeze rattling the palm fronds. Keaki and Baiteke sat on the Rest House steps in the failing light, making string figures. Baiteke disentangled his fingers with a grunt, yawned.

"Shall we go back to the landing? The tide must be almost high enough..."

"Shhh! Look!"

Keaki jumped up, throwing his string away. Someone was running across the parade ground – running like every *anti* on the island was after him.

"Aram!" Keaki started out to meet him, but Aram pushed past him. His face looked wild, and tears were pouring down his cheeks.

"No time! No time! Bauro, Bauro!"

"He's fishing."

"Shit! Help me, then. Got to get the house prepared, and boil some water. Start a fire, will you Baiteke? Come on! Got to make the bed. Oh God, oh God!"

"What's wrong? Why are you..."

"Mister Karaka! Very sick. Come on, hurry!"

It was dark, but they had lamps glowing in the Rest House and water boiling on the kerosene stove in the cookhouse, Mister Gallagher's bed made and turned back, when they saw electric torches coming up the road. Half a dozen men from the ship, and Dr. MacPherson, together with a man Keaki recognized as Native Medical Practitioner Takai. A slender young woman in a nurse's smock followed, with several men and women of the village carrying something on a mattress. They marched up the steps, and Keaki realized that the something was Mister Gallagher, who waved at him weakly.

"Mauri, Teng Keaki. All this fuss.... Really quite all right; just the sea...."

"Do shut up, man!" Dr. MacPherson snapped. "Here, Tafola, his bed's this way. Very well done, Aram. Here, you lot, gently, gently!"

The men – Bueke, Eneri, Kamarie, Abera, gingerly lifted Mister Gallagher into his bed. Some of the women took charge of the cookhouse, while Aram wrung his hands and walked from room to room. The doctor stood for a moment, regarding the man in the bed.

"There, then, Irish. Comfortable? Capital. You're to do nothing but rest, you understand? Nothing, man! And eat when you're told to, drink what you're told to, and in God's name take only the medicines you're given, you understand?"

"Yes, Doctor. I'm sorry to be so..."

"Shut up, Gerald, just shut your great fucking Irish mouth before I forget myself. Boys! You, Keeki is it?"

"Keaki, Sir..."

"Run and find Nei Maria and tell her to come here, on the double." He turned to the young woman. "Tafola, when Nei Maria gets here, put her in the picture and you two take turns watching over him. Tekai, same for you and the local dresser when he shows up; get Bauro to help you if you can find him. I'm to the ship to fetch my – some things I need." He turned on his heel and hurried out the door, pounding down the steps and into the night.

Keaki found Nurse Maria at Tumuo's house, where she was staying with Segalo. The young Beruan hurried to the Rest House after waking Segalo and telling her to take charge of the dispensary. Baiteke naturally volunteered to stay with her there; Keaki didn't wait to see how this worked out. He ran back to the Rest House, where he found everything quiet. Takai and Maria were sitting at Mister Gallagher's table, talking quietly; Mister Gallagher was apparently asleep. Bauro sat in one of the *kanawa* chairs, looking blank. Aram sat on the floor in a corner, his head on his knees, silent.

Keaki stole away to the lagoon beach and sat for awhile on a canoe, unsure what to do with the swirl of thoughts in his head. The clouds had cleared; a shooting star arced across the sky. The moon rose over the trees across the lagoon. Somewhere a *kiakia* cried. Keaki drifted into a troubled sleep, fell off the canoe. The Rest House was quiet; he wandered home and curled up on his mat.

The next day had an unreal quality, everyone in the village very quiet. Things seemed to happen slowly, as in a dream, if they happened at all. Everyone seemed compelled to remain at home, or else to gather together in small groups to talk quietly, or drift silently past the Rest House, listening and watchful. No one worked their *babae* pits; no one went fishing. The women fixed food in silence, or exchanged only an occasional necessary word. Even the babies seem constrained in their play, with or without anyone telling them to be quiet. The hours passed slowly.

Around midday, Aram came down to the lagoon beach, where Keaki and Baiteke were tossing rocks at small sharks. He waded into the water, falling over on his back, and floating awhile. He didn't call to the boys, and they remained on the shore, feeling strangely shy. But as he came out of the water, he smiled at them.

"He's better."

"Ohhh, that's good!"

"Yes, he's eaten a little, and smiled, talked a bit with Dr. MacPherson and Bauro and me."

"Good. What about?"

"I didn't understand. Something about going to Ocean Island, but he doesn't want to go."

"He should stay here!"

"At least till he gets well!"

"I think he will. We can take care of him." Aram lapsed into silence, crouching on the sand and frowning at the trees across the lagoon. Baiteke began rubbing a stick with a stone, making it smooth. Keaki used another stick to draw a picture in the sand. He wasn't sure what he was drawing. The silence stretched out. Finally Baiteke broke it.

"Where have you been – on that *Viti* ship?"

"Oh, everywhere. Fiji, Funafuti, other islands in the Ellices, Beru, Tarawa, Manra, Canton, Orona. In the Ellices we were putting *I Nutiran* ashore – New Zealand soldiers with radios and food and all kinds of stuff. Then we came to Beru and took aboard some settlers for Manra and Orona, and maybe some will come here. Then to Tarawa where Bauro came aboard...."

"Soldiers?"

"Yeah, they call them coastwatchers. Watching to see if the Japanese – uh – do anything."

"Are there Japanese in the Ellices?"

"No, no, but I guess government thinks they might come, and they want to know if they do."

"I hope they don't come here."

"Me too. I'd better get back." Aram clapped Baiteke on the shoulder. "Pretty soon Mister Karaka will be well, and we'll listen to the wireless again. He got a new wireless in Suva; lots of power." He unfolded onto his feet and trotted off toward the Rest House.

The silent day went on, and merged into a silent night. And then it was morning.

It was still dark when Keaki stretched and rolled off his mat, but the colour of sunrise was beginning to seep up over the trees across the lagoon. He stumbled out to the cookhouse where his mother and sister were getting the fire started. He watched them, munching on a piece of dried fish.

"Your friend was here," Taberiki said, throwing back her hair to show him that this information was of no importance to her whatever.

"Baiteke?"

"That lazy boy? No, Aram."

Boikabane carefully put a stick in her small but growing fire. "You better go find him, Keaki. He looked crazy."

"Crazy?"

"Scared, and like he'd been crying. I asked what was wrong, but he wouldn't say; just ran away."

Keaki scrambled to his feet and sprinted toward the Rest House. Where someone large was standing in the darkness that lingered on the veranda. Doctor MacPherson, and he was angry.

"Goddam brainless overemotional Irish bugger!" He said it under his breath, to no one Keaki could see, but Keaki heard him plainly as he ran up the coral-lined path. The doctor noticed him and clamped his mouth shut. Closed his eyes for a moment and seemed to be thinking. Opened them and asked Keaki, pleasantly enough, what he wanted.

"I'm looking for Aram, Sir. He came...."

"Ach, yes, the poor boy. You'll find him in the sunken garden, I think, or therearabouts."

Keaki scampered around the house to the lagoon side, where the coral-lined rectangular *babae* pit was filling up with banana trees. Mister Gallagher had been so pleased that they'd survived the storms with their salt spray, and were on the verge of producing. Aram wasn't there, but Keaki saw him on the beach, on his knees facing the lagoon. He was shaking with great sobs. Keaki came up softly, put his hand on his friend's shoulder. Aram didn't seem surprised, but grabbed Keaki's hand and pulled him down to his knees next to him.

"Keaki, brother, pray with me." He pressed his palms together and launched into a prayer that Keaki only half understood; some of it was English, some Tungaruan, some perhaps Latin. All of it was desperate, delivered in great sobbing gasps. Its gist, Keaki realized, was an appeal for Mister Gallagher's life.

Chapter 43:

Dr. MacPherson's Report

COLONY OF FIJI.
[To:] The Secretary,
Western Pacific High Commission,
SUVA [From:] MEDICAL DEPARTMENT
SUVA, 9th November, 1941.
Sir.

Death of Mr. G.B. Gallagher, M.A.

It is with deep regret that I have to record, for the information of His Excellency the High Commissioner, the circumstances leading up to and terminating with the tragic death of Mr. G.B. Gallagher, Officer in Charge, Phoenix Islands Settlement Scheme. From the telegraphic correspondence you are already aware of the more important of these circumstances.

2. When H.M.F.S. "Viti" left Fiji on her recent cruise, Mr. Gallagher's health had greatly improved as a result of a change of diet and environment. He was, however, suffering from a certain degree of physical and mental exhaustion owing to his complete absorption in the innumerable preliminary arrangements necessary for carrying out so complicated a programme as that marked out for the vessel. On arrival at Niulakita, a boat from H.M.F.S. "Viti" made an attempt to land. Mr. Gallagher and myself were both members of the landing party, and when it was obvious that no landing was possible through the tremendous surf prevailing, Mr. Gallagher prepared to swim through the breakers in order to ascertain the extent to which repairs were required to the existing buildings on the island. He was only dissuaded from this purpose with the greatest difficulty. I merely quote this incident as an example of the intense anxiety and zeal which he exhibited throughout the entire cruise. On arrival at Funafuti (northbound) I noticed that Mr. Gallagher appeared to be suffering a certain amount of facial pain. On examination, I found that one of his molar teeth was abscessed and that several more teeth were in process of decay. I inquired why he had not made arrangements for examination of his mouth by a dentist when in Suva, and was informed that he had fully intended to do so but had

never been able to find the necessary time. I extracted the molar tooth under Evipan anaesthesia, and I then noted that even from an operation of so minor a character his recovery was unduly prolonged, and despite the rapid, complete and very successful anaesthesia induced by the Evipan, he showed some degree of shock.

3. At every stage of the voyage Mr. Gallagher worked unceasingly –often far into the night – and on occasions, when cargo was being loaded, all night. In addition to making arrangements for meetings of the natives on each island, and addressing these, he carried out all the coding and decoding of telegraphic correspondence, the volume of which was considerable. Adverse weather conditions were encountered in the Ellice Group and in the Southern Gilberts, making boat, and even canoe, landings hazardous and attended with anxiety owing to the possible loss of life and of valuable and irreplaceable stores. When such unavoidable delays occurred Mr. Gallagher gradually became obsessed with the necessity for speeding up the vessel's schedule, and finally the saving of even a few hours time became with him a primary objective. I protested vainly, and was consequently not surprised when the vessel reached Tarawa to find that he had not only become noticeably thinner, but was in a state of advanced nervous exhaustion.

4. On our return to Tarawa from the first visit to Ocean Island, Mr. Gallagher was persuaded by Captain Holland to spend a night as his guest at Bairiki. He was brought back to Betio the following morning by Captain Hollandlooking very ill, suffering from a very painful throat, severe headache and disordered stomach. He was put to bed in his cabin on the ship, but after having discovered that he spent most of the time at a typewriter, I had him conveyed ashore to Dr. Steenson's house and placed under the care of Mrs. Steenson and the native nurses at Tarawa Hospital. He was given treatment with Sulphanilamide and made a rapid recovery from the primary condition. Despite all attempts to induce him to remain ashore until convalescence was more advanced, he returned to his duties at the earliest possible moment. He was given a tonic mixture and made some progress, although his appearance was gaunt and it was obvious that he was still suffering from nervous exhaustion.

5. The completion of the tour and his final settlement at Gardner Island now became a complete obsession with him. He spoke of this constantly, and apparently he looked forward to a quiet period which would enable him to read the large quantity of mail which had accumulated for him at Ocean Island, and to take up the threads of his work in the Phoenix Is. For the first time during his residence in

that remote Group he was very well provided with stores of all kinds, and he was particularly anxious to supervise the building of certain new structures on the station, particularly the island hospital, which he had planned to make a model of its kind. On arrival at Gardner Island the weather conditions were far from favourable, and he naturally worried a great deal about the landing of the stores and other material for which he had waited so long. The unavoidable loss of some of these stores, particularly reinforcing iron and timber, was consequently a severe disappointment. He worked incessantly during this time, sparing only an hour in which to conduct me round the Station in order that we might choose finally the site of the proposed hospital.

6. At Hull Island, I accompanied him ashore. He spent a very busy day with Mr. Cookson and the difficulties met with on embarkation again caused him anxiety, particularly as Mrs. Cookson had to be embarked. After leaving Hull Island the following morning (21st September) he informed me that he was certain he had eaten some food which was poisonous, and which had caused him to feel nauseated and finally to vomit. I questioned him minutely as to what he had eaten and could not find that he had partaken of any item different from a number of other persons on the ship. He told me, however, that he had had similar attacks of vomiting at Nikunau and Beru which he had attributed in one instance to tinned mushrooms, and in the other to fish. He had apparently been very ill on both occasions, and this was corroborated by his servant, Aram Tamia. He was given the usual remedies, but the vomiting continued at intervals, and it became apparent that he was suffering from a severe gastritis. I persuaded him to remain in bed while I went ashore at Sydney Island to ascertain the state of affairs there.

7. After leaving Sydney Island on the 22nd the vomiting continued, but as the ship was pitching considerably, and as the stomach was then empty and had been washed out by means of a stomach tube, the vomitus consisted mainly of bile and of fluids taken, which were returned very soon after being swallowed. The bowels were open, although there was a tendency to constipation. Pulse and temperature were within normal limits. There was no rigidity or distension in the abdomen, and no pain on palpation. The patient was by this time quite convinced that the movement of the vessel was exacerbating the vomiting. He was not a good sailor in a seaway and had on several occasions during the voyage been sea sick in the boats. I noted this particularly while the vessel was at Beru for the purpose of embarking emigrants for the Phoenix Group.

8. We arrived at Canton Island on the 23rd September. The weather was then good and the anchorage calm. The sickness had abated and the patient looked brighter. He complained at times of slight colicky pain in the epigastric region. I went into his past medical history very closely and paid particular attention to the fact that he had/an abdominal operation for appendicitis. I also ascertained that he had on occasions during the past two years suffered from colic and nausea, particularly when climbing ship's masts or similar exertion. He had also been ill for the greater part of the journey from England to Australia when he first came out to take up his appointment in the Gilbert and Ellice Islands. He was on that occasion accompanied by Messrs. Wernham and Bevington. Tuberculosis had apparently been suspected by the ship's surgeon, and among his effects I found a skiagram of the chest taken at the British Hospital, Port Said. Apparently no confirmation of the ship's surgeon's suspicions was obtained.

9. Before going ashore at Canton Island, I left instructions with Native Medical Practitioner Tekai, who was on board, that he should be given a special enema. I also forbade him to drink large quantities of iced water, iced mineral waters and fruit juices, which I discovered he had been taking although I had previously given instructions that he was to have broken ice only to suck, and small drinks containing glucose. After going ashore I arranged with Dr. Franklin, Surgeon stationed at the Pan-American Airport at Canton Island, to return with me to the vessel and examine Mr. Gallagher. This Dr. Franklin very kindly did, and he investigated the history most thoroughly and made a most careful examination. Dr. Franklin, I may add, had just completed two years continuous surgical experience in a very large hospital in San Francisco. We both agreed that there had been a gastritis which had probably been made more severe by sea conditions. We both suspected there might be some chronic partial obstruction, but were quite unable to find any corroboratory signs, and decided that expectant treatment was all that could, at that time, be undertaken justifiably. As I felt considerable anxiety about Mr. Gallagher's general condition, and realised that his resistance was exceedingly low, I discussed with him the question of detaining the vessel at Canton until I could make telegraphic representations to His Excellency, or alternatively, that he should remain at Canton Island under the care of Dr. Franklin, who would, if he deemed it necessary, doubtless make arrangements for the Pan-American clipper to take him to hospital in Honululu or Noumea. (Even had he remained at Canton Island, however, I do not consider that he would

have lived to be transported by Clipper to either of these airports.) Mr. Gallagher had been informed that he would receive an important telegram before the vessel left the Phoenix Islands, but, not having received it, as he thought, at Canton Island, he assumed that it would be awaiting him at Gardner Island, the chosen last port of call in that Group. He was, therefore, very agitated by the prospect of remaining at Canton Island. He further assured me that he felt he would only recover in his own house on Gardner Island and amidst his own native people. I, therefore, did not feel justified in pursuing the matter owing to the adverse reaction his mental state was undoubtedly having on his physical condition. I had previously consulted the Commander of H.M.F.S. "Viti" on the question of remaining at Canton Island, but he pointed out that in accordance with the prearranged schedule of the vessel a stay of only twenty-four hours was permitted at Canton Island, and he had received no instructions to vary these arrangements.

10. After leaving Canton Island, your telegram (unnumbered) of the 30th September was decoded by Mr. Hogan, and its contents were communicated to Mr. Gallagher. Its effect on him in his then agitated mental and weak physical state was profound. He told me that he felt that he was "at the end of his tether", and that he proposed to go ashore at Gardner Island and remain there until he was well.

11. We arrived at Gardner Island about noon on the 24th September and owing to tidal difficulties a landing could not be effected until the late afternoon. He was carried on a mattress to his own house, which is at a considerable distance from the landing place. He was more cheerful that evening and passed a more tranquil night than any since the commencement of his illness. Physical signs were still absent. He proved an extremely difficult patient to manage, insisting on trying all kinds of foods for which he had a passing fancy, and refusing to be washed or otherwise nursed in any way. I fortunately had the assistance of two nurses, Nei Maria, stationed on Gardner Island, and Tafola, proceeding on transfer from Tarawa to Funafuti – in addition to those of Native Medical Practitioner Tekai, and Dresser Vaiaga. His condition was, therefore, watched continuously. I had decided that if the apparent improvement was maintained, I would take him to Funafuti.

12. During the night of the 25th September, he apparently contrived to swallow some purgative tablets which he was in the habit of using, and which I had refused to let him have. I suspected that something of this kind had occurred when he began to have renewed

attacks of severe colicky pain. He was given a hypodermic injection of morphia with atropine to relieve this. He also became very excited, declaring that the Government was "letting the settlers down", that he felt himself quite unfitted for secretarial duties, etc. During the forenoon of the next day (26th September) it became apparent that his condition was rapidly becoming grave. Distension appeared in the upper part of the abdomen. There was no movement of the bowels. The tongue which had been remarkably clean hitherto, became heavily furred, the temperature was slightly elevated and the pulse rate became rapid. His colour, however, was good. There was no pain on abdominal palpation. I informed the Commander of H.M.F.S. "Viti" that I feared it would be necessary for me to perform an emergency operation, and preparations for this were immediately begun. Lieut-Commander Mullins sent Mr. Whysall, the Chief Engineer, and several other of his officers ashore to assist in any way possible. Mr. Gallagher, immediately I informed him of the need for an operation, gave me his full sanction to do anything I felt necessary, and further said that he was glad that anything that required to be done should be done on Gardner Island.

13. By the time all preparations for the operation were completed darkness was falling. Signs of intestinal obstruction were now apparent. Mental prostration and exhaustion were marked, vomiting had recommended and was now faecal in type. The question of the anaesthetic gave me much anxiety owing to the persistence of the vomiting. The anaesthetic of choice in such cases is of the spinal variety, and no such was available. The stomach was washed out with sodium bicarbonate solution, and Native Medical Practitioner Tekai anaesthetised the patient with a chloroform-aether mixture. I may say that Native Medical Practitioner Tekai carried out this difficult task with a degree of skill, care, and detachment which would have done credit to a specialist anaethetist in a London Hospital. The abdomen was opened in the middle line. I was immediately struck by the almost total absence of subcutaneous fat. When the peritoneum was opened some fluid was found, but no evidence of pus. The fluid was extremely evil smelling and reminiscent of gas gangrene infection. There was ballooning of the large intestine, and this was followed to the caecum which was bound down by old adhesions. A few inches from the ileocecal valve a mass of adhesions had caused "kinking" of the gut, and must have been productive of a partial obstruction for some considerable time. The walls of the large intestine exhibited a most remarkable appearance, being no thicker than tissue paper, and highly suggestive of the disease, resulting

from malnutrition, and known as Sprue. There was no actual gangrene present, but injection of the bowel walls was marked, and here and there small infarctions producing dark blotches had occurred. Thrombosis of several branches of the mesenteric artery was also evident. I relieved the obstruction and performed a caecostomy. Great difficulty was found in suturing the bowel wall to the peritoneum owing to the extreme thinness of the former. I completed the operation as rapidly as possible, tubes being inserted for drainage of the peritoneal cavity. I was much handicapped by the lack of certain instruments such as large abdominal retractors and proper bowel clamps. H.M.F.S. "Viti", while well equipped for carrying out emergency operation such as amputations and the repair of wounds, etc., in the event of accident or enemy action, does not normally carry equipment to deal with other varieties of major surgery. Artificial lighting presented a problem, but was solved by the Chief Engineer of the ship, who stood near me directing the light from a 5 cell electric torch directly on the operation area. Intravenous saline and glucose were given immediately the operation was completed. Mr. Gallagher's condition was then good, and he made a rapid recovery from the anaesthetic. I realised, however, that his resistance was very low and that toxaemia would rapidly decrease this. He became fully conscious about 8 p.m. He recognised those who spoke to him, talked quite coherently and sensibly, and stated that he felt comfortable. About 11 p.m. he became restless, excited in his speech and semi-delirious at times. He was then given a hypodermic injection of morphia and atropine. It was apparent that he was sinking rapidly, and although capable of being roused and able to recognise individuals he gradually became comatose. The pulse rate was almost uncountable, and I informed the Native Magistrate and others that the end was near. They assembled round his bed, and those who profess Roman Catholicism, led by Mr. Hogan, sat by his bed and offered him the spiritual consolation which the rites of the Roman Catholic Church provide for the dying. His passing at 12.17 a.m. On the 27th September was completely peaceful.

14. While the nurses and other women performed the last offices, Mr. Whysall, Sergeant Corner, Private Burns, Mr. McGowan, and Temou (native carpenter at Gardner Island) proceeded to prepare a casket for the remains. This was completed by 6 a.m. and was a very fine piece of work. The natives kept watch throughout the night, the Catholic members reciting appropriate prayers. At dawn, with the assistance of Mr. Whysall, I pegged out an area at the base of the flagstaff in an east and west direction and a grave was pre-

pared, and lined with coconut fronds. The interment was arranged for 10 a.m. Before that time Lieut-Commander Mullins and such members of the officers and crew of the vessel as could be spared, assembled at the house. The total number of Europeans present was thirteen. The coffin was draped with a new Union Jack and was carried on the shoulders of representative numbers of Europeans, Fijians, Ellice Islanders and Gilbertese. At the graveside Lieut-Commander Mullins read the burial service of the Roman Catholic Church and the hymn "Nearer My God to Thee" was sung by the Europeans present. Lieut-Commander Mullins spoke a few simple and appropriate words (a copy of which have already been given to His Excellency). The Protestant natives sang a hymn in Ellice, and subsequently Maheo, an Ellice Islander, and one of the native wireless operators, paid a simple, eloquent and most touching tribute (in English) to Mr. Gallagher's memory. After the grave had been filled in, the native women on the station placed garlands of bush flowers around it.

15. I have unfortunately during my Colonial service been present at the deathbed and subsequent interment of a number of my brother officers and colleagues, but never have I seen deeper manifestations of sorrow on the part of both natives and Europeans alike, than I witnessed on this occasion. The whole setting of this sad scene was impressive, and to any onlooker would have presented a striking picture. A dense mass of green bush in the background the glistening white coral sand of the Government Station with its careful planning and its wide avenues fringed with young coconut palms, the bright cloudless sky, the infinite variety and gradations of colour in the lagoon in the foreground, the myriads of seabirds wheeling overhead, the group of Europeans wearing Service uniform and natives clad in spotless Sunday garb – all assembled bareheaded beneath the flagstaff where the flag was flying at half-mast.

16. After the funeral, preparations were made to deal with Mr. Gallagher"s effects, and the arrangements regarding these have already formed the subject of separate communications to you.

17. I had decided long prior to Mr. Gallagher's illness that it was incumbent on me on my return to Fiji to write semi-officially to His Excellency the High Commissioner and express my personal admiration of the excellent work which this young officer had accomplished during the short time that the direction of the Phoenix Islands Settlement Scheme had been in his hands. The vision and judgment which he showed in the laying out of the new settlement will be apparent to all who may have occasion to visit the Phoenix

Islands in future, and will remain, I trust, as an enduring monument to a faithful and able officer, and a very gallant gentleman. There is a Gaelic saying that no man is capable of judging the worth of another until they "have burned seven stacks of peat together". I was fortunate in having such a prolonged opportunity in which to assess the fine qualities which the late Mr. Gallagher possessed in full measure, and which he hid beneath so shy and unassuming a manner. It was evident that all those natives who came into contact with him loved and trusted him, and he was devoted to their interests and anxious to do all in his power to secure the betterment of their lot. He was undoubtedly of a delicate constitution and probably suffered much in silence for the cause of duty. I am convinced that, had it not been for the thoughtfulness and care which have invariably been exhibited by His Excellency the High Commissioner towards his young officers serving in remote outposts of the lonely Western Pacific groups and caused him to extend much personal kindness and hospitality to Mr. Gallagher (which were warmly appreciated by him) this tragedy might well have occurred earlier in this officer's service.

18. I have felt compelled to enter into considerable detail in regard to this sad occurrence, and I regret that I also feel it to be my duty to direct attention to the fact that Mr. Gallagher"s death was largely attributable to malnutrition, which undoubtedly resulted from the fact that no steps appear to have been taken by Headouarters at Ocean Island to ensure that he, and other officers serving on out-stations, are at least kept supplied with the fundamental necessities for the support of life and the maintenance of health. The struggle which must invariably exist, for an officer brought up in the generous plenty of a British home to adapt himself to both the climatic and environmental conditions of a remote and relatively barren Pacific Island, must indeed be severe during the early years of his service. Expeditionary forces and exploratory expeditions are planned with the utmost care and forethought by those responsible for their equipment and provisioning. Young officers appointed to the Colonial Service are carefully selected from among the best material provided by great public schools and universities given special training and then posted, with little preliminary initiation, to places where they find themselves suddenly and completely deprived of all the amenities to which they have been accustomed from birth. The results for Government are not infrequently bad from an economic and administrative point of view, and for the officer himself they are often disastrous. I am aware that during the past

few years this point has been fully appreciated by the Western
Pacific High Commission, and particularly by His Excellency the
present High Commissioner, and great improvements have been
effected, such as the provision of refrigerators, etc. I do not consider,
however, that this is sufficient I recently had the opportunity of not-
ing the arrangements made by the New Zealand Government for the
settling of wireless operators and soldiers on various islands. I was
much impressed by the wise and ample selection of stores, medical
supplies and comforts with which these groups had been provided,
and it was to me a sad reflection that after almost fifty years of
British rule in the Gilbert and Ellice Islands, the local Administration still appeared to be indifferent to the necessity for some similar
measures. It is impossible to escape the obvious inferences from the
observed facts. As you are aware, the preventive aspects of medicine,
which would appear to be the obvious ones, and which were in fact
stressed long ago by Moses, have until recent years been neglected in
comparison with the curative aspects. Similarly, a measure of care,
foresight and planning would, I feel, do much to prevent the physical and mental deterioration which has on occasions manifested
itself in those who at the outset of their official career showed
marked promise and ability.

19. From the result of conversations in the past, I feel certain
that His Excellency the High Commissioner and yourself will be in
substantial agreement with the foregoing paragraph.

20. In conclusion, I wish to express my very sincere appreciation
for the great help and support for my actions under very difficult and
trying circumstances so promptly given by telegram by His Excellency the High Commissioner and officers of the Western Pacific
High Commission; also my great indebtedness to Lieut-Commander
Mullins, Flying Officer Hogan (who kept a continuous wireless
watch for 92 hours), Mr. Whysall, Chief Engineer, Sergeant Corner
and all the officers and crew of H.M.F.S. "Viti".

> I have the honour to be,
> Sir,
> Your obedient servant,
>
> D.C.M. MacPherson,
> Assistant Director of Medical Services, Fiji

Chapter 44 –

The Deep Sea, September/October 1941

No one had lit a lamp in the *maneaba*. Sitting in the darkness seemed right, Keaki thought, squatting on his haunches behind his father and mother in their *boti*. No one was speaking, and that too seemed right.

But the *maneaba* is designed for discussion, and finally – after an assenting nod from Abera – Beiaruru cleared his throat and began.

"This is an extraordinary time," he said slowly in his creaky voice. "We are confronted with a deep mystery, and the way we respond to it may determine whether we live or we die."

"Eng!" the guttural affirmative came out of the darkness on all sides. Teng Beiaruru continued.

"Let us take our time. Let us not rush. Let us take a measured decision. And let every *boti,* every person who wants to speak, be heard, whether man or woman or even child."

"Eng!"

"As is customary, the *boti* of Teng Abera will begin."

Abera started, cleared his throat, paused. A shuffling sound ran around the building as people settled themselves to listen.

"First," Abera began, "those boys found the *ata* at Aukaraime, down at the other end where the *kanawa* were cut, and where there are turtles. Our magistrate at the time, Teng Koata of Onotoa, buried that *ata."* He fell silent and Eneri picked up the thread.

"Teng Koata and others then got sick, with boils and lesions, and very tired and weak. There being no NMP on the island at the time, and since – the dresser did not have training in such an illness, they were treated with native medicine by the woman Nei Aana, wife of Teng Koata the magistrate."

Iaiaera raised his eyebrows, glancing around the *maneaba.* "Which seemed to be effective, and confirmed some in the belief that perhaps burying the *ata* had been wrong, or that touching it had been unhealthy."

"Eng!"

"Then" Kirata said sadly, "Mister Karaka, the administrator of the Phoenix Islands, may God rest his soul, came to live on Nikumaroro, and when he learned about the *ata,* he became determined to dig it up."

"It must be remembered," Bueke added, "that Mister Karaka also found other bones at the *ata* place, and he thought they might be someone he knew. He determined that they should be kept together and returned to that woman's family. This, most of us felt, was correct, both for government and for God."

"Eng! Eng!"

"So the bones – Mister Karaka gathered those things together, and Tumuo built a box to contain them. And Mister Karaka gave them to Doctor Isaac and Captain Harness to take to Fiji, where the High Commissioner, Sir Harry Luke, wanted to look at them."

"And so the bones all went to Fiji," Uriam said in a stately voice, "and Mister Karaka did not get sick."

"At that time," Katoi added. Uriam nodded his acceptance of the interruption and went on.

"Then Mister Karaka went away to Fiji, and those boys found more bones, up on Nutiran. These are the bones with which we are now concerned. We felt it would be best to put those bones in a bag and hold them until Mister Karaka came back."

"So I, Babera, minister of God, obedient to the will of the congregation, placed those bones in a bag and put them carefully under a large *mao* up on Nutiran, where they have remained from that time until this time."

"And then," Teng Mereke murmured, "Mister Karaka came back, and..... died, and is now buried under that little concrete house at the base of the flagstaff." Somewhere in the darkness there was a great sob. Aram, Keaki thought.

"So, this brings us to the question we must answer. What shall we do with those bones? What will keep us safe from....."

"The wrath of the Lord God," Babera put in, out of turn, drowning out Mereke's "the *anti.*"

"Let us consider," Teng Beiaruru creaked, "the remarkable fact that both discoveries were made by the same two young men, Takena's son Baiteke, and Iaiaera's boy Keaki. That is a great coincidence, a mystery."

The *maneaba* fell silent. Keaki wanted to become very small, and crawl under something. But his father spoke.

"Teng Beiaruru, since a question has been asked about my family, may I be permitted to speak before it is my turn?"

"Eng!"

"Of course, Teng Iaiaera."

"I am prejudiced toward my son, of course, but I do not think there is fault in him, or in Takena's son either. Both are curious, active, hard-working boys. In the first instance, they were helping with the work of the community when they quite accidentally found the *ata*. They did the right thing; they didn't touch it, they reported it to adults. And notice that they have not become ill."

"Which may mean," Babera threw in without permission, "that they are the tools of the Evil One."

Utter silence. Then Takena's voice came out of the darkness, dripping irony.

"So, if my son is possessed, Teng Babera, do you Protestants have an exorcism ritual you want to perform...?"

Baiaruru cleared his throat. "With respect, you gentlemen are both out of order. Does the *boti* of Iobi have anything to say?" Iobi made a negative grunt and tapped the shoulder of Teiranau, the next in order.

"In my opinion," Teiranau began, slowly, "there is no point in trying to fix blame for what has happened. We are only human beings, and cannot know the ways of the Almighty. With all respect for our LMS teacher, it would be well for us to remember the lesson of Job, and not assume for ourselves wisdom that is not ours. I see no fault in these boys, and no reason to discuss it further. It is a distraction from the question of what to do with those... things. Teng Takena?"

"Thank you, Teng Teiranau, for myself and on behalf of my son. I have nothing to add at this time."

It was now Teng Kamarie's turn to speak, but for a long moment he was silent.

"I think," he said at last, "that it is time to take a decision in this matter, and it seems to me that the best course of action is to be found in the beliefs of our ancestors."

Teng Babera snorted, but didn't interrupt. Keaki peered through the darkness toward where Kamarie's voice had gone silent. Kamarie was a quiet man, but when he spoke, people paid attention. What could he mean about the ancestors? What had the ancestors done in such a case? Whose ancestors? Different islands had different customs.

Kamarie coughed quietly and continued. "As you all know, my family and I came to this island from Temaraia, in Nonouti. But my mother came to Nonouti from way up north – Butaritari. She was a schoolteacher in the mission school, and my father was the groundskeeper, and... Anyway, her village was Kuma, and her *utu* was a lineage of great navigators and porpoise callers." Whispers all round the room; people were impressed, Keaki thought. But what did this have to do with the bones?

"There at Kuma there is a hole in the rock near the shore, and this is where the dead are put – feet downward, as though standing up. And the ocean comes, and takes them away. This is how the Kuna people honor their dead, as their navigator ancestors taught."

Silence again. Kamarie seemed to be finished, but what did he mean? Teng Baiaruru cleared his throat.

"Excuse an old man's ignorance, Teng Kamarie, but I do not understand what direction to take from your words."

"No one has greater honor than a navigator. "

Silence again. Everyone weighing options, Keaki thought. Perhaps the bones were those of a navigator, perhaps not, but if they treated him as one, would his *anti* not be pleased? Perhaps at least go away? Was this what the adults were thinking?

"Those things..." Teng Baiaruru murmured, as much to himself as to the *maneaba*. "Those things were in the water, in a hole."

Several voices responded — "*eng.*" Then Kamarie's voice, in a whisper.

"With respect, elder, I believe we should treat that person as a navigator, and return him to the sea."

Silence again for some time before Waitabo – the next in speaking order, Keaki realized with a start – whispered: "I agree. This is the wise thing to do."

The cycle was complete and it was Abera's turn to speak. He did so with such forcefulness that Keaki jumped. "Of course! This navigator has been unable to catch his canoe; his bones have been rattling around in that hole in the reef. "

"So true!" The exclamation was from the end of the building, someone speaking out of order in an excited hiss. "His spirit will be pleased and peaceful if we take them out to sea."

Teng Babera started to say something about devil worship and blasphemy, but he was drowned out. *"Eng! Eng! "* Guttural affirmation came from the darkness on all sides.

Baiaruru waited awhile and then asked: "Is this, then, the decision of the *maneaba?"*

"Eng! Eng!"

"Very well, then, who will do this thing?"

Silence, stretching out and out. Keaki realized that he was holding his breath. Should he volunteer? Could he? And what might happen if he did? He imagined his arms and legs breaking out in ugly pustules, dripping noxious fluids, swelling up. Teng Eneri operating, cutting into him...

Baiaruru tried to break the impasse. "Teng Iokina, does government have a recommendation?"

Iokina said nothing. The silence was as thick as curdled coconut toddy. Then someone cleared his throat, and Baiaruru turned unerringly toward the sound.

"Teng Eneri, is that you?"

"It... it is, Teng Baiaruru. I believe.... This is a medical matter, and it is my duty..."

"Thank you, Teng Eneri, but please remember that being a government person did not protect Mister Karaka. And in any event, we cannot send you out on the deep sea by yourself; this navigator's remains should be taken well out of sight of land. Teng Kamarie, do you agree?"

"*Eng, eng.* Away from the influence of the land."

"So – a strong canoe, and someone to sail it."

"With respect, Teng Baiaruru?"

"Teng Ieiera?"

"Thank you. Since it was my son who found these things, I believe it is my responsibility to take them to the deep sea."

"Teng Baiaruru?"

"Teng Takena."

"With all respect for my good friend Teng Ieiera, it was my son who actually found the things, so I will take this responsibility."

There were chuckles in the darkness, including a brief one, snapped off, from Baiaruru.

"You gentlemen can both paddle canoes, yes?"

"*Eng.*"

"Could you both, perhaps, be attentive enough to paddle or sail one canoe together, in a common direction?"

Chuckles, then laughter, the tension breaking all around the *maneaba*.

"*Eng!*"

"*Eng!*"

"Then I suggest, gentlemen, that you cooperate with Teng Eneri to perform this task."

"Far enough, you think?"

Takena stood up on the outrigger platform and peered under his hand to the east. "I can't see the island."

"Then it's far enough. Eneri?"

Teng Eneri, the only one to touch the bag of bones – now weighted with a heavy coral rock – lifted it with a grunt out of the canoe's prow and set it gingerly on the platform. Paddling gently to keep the canoe steady, Keaki and Baiteke looked at their fathers uncertainly.

Takena peered up at the cloudless sky. A frigate bird sailed overhead. "I wish we had Teng Koata to say the right thing."

Ieiera grinned crookedly. "But we do not, brother, so it's up to us."

Keaki peered over the side. He had never been this far out on the open ocean in a canoe. How deep was it, he wondered. It looked very dark, very empty. What lived down there, if anything? Would the bones fall all the way to the bottom, or stop someplace part-way down, caught up in some thickening of the water? What was at the bottom? If he fell overboard, could he swim to the island? How would he get there? How had the old navigators known where to go? How had Koata known?

Takena was stumbling through a Catholic funeral prayer of some kind, trying to remember Latin words. He ended, and Ieiera said a short prayer in Tungaru – much more elegantly, Keaki thought. They all looked at each other. Takena looked around a little sheepishly, then nodded, and Eneri opened the bag. Gingerly, he pulled out the skull and set it on the outrigger platform. Keaki noticed for the first time that it was rather bigger than the first one, and somehow thicker seeming. More teeth, too.

Takena lit his pipe, puffed on it for awhile, and then blew tobacco smoke in the skull 's face – a final gift from the living to the dead. He looked the skull in the eye sockets, and spoke solemnly.

"You who have gone before us, please understand that we are mere, foolish, still-living men, who stumble along and do the best we can in life. Sometimes we do wrong, perhaps occasionally we do right, who but the Lord God can know? We are putting you in the ocean from which we suppose you came, in the hope that this is the right thing to do, and that you will find your canoe and continue your journey to whatever spirit place is right for people of your kind. We pray to God that he will guide you and keep you on your journey, and we pray that you will understand what we do, and carry on with your journey rather than remaining with us to trouble our dreams and our lives, and those of our children and babies. We ask all this in the name of Jesus Christ Our Lord. Amen."

"Amen," the others nodded, sat quietly with hands folded.

Eneri gently put the skull back in the bag, tied it up and hung it over the side. He let it go, and they all watched as it sank, a white shimmering in the dark depths of the sea, soon out of sight.

Chapter 45 –

War Talk, November/December 1941

"There will be war, fighting, in these islands; I've no doubt." Mister Kimo took a long drink of toddy, wiped the bottle's mouth and passed it to Tumuo. "On that ship *Viti* the wireless goes nighttime and daytime, and Mister Ian and Sir Harry Luke spend all their time decoding messages and looking solemn."

It felt to Keaki like time was swirling around and backing up on itself. Just like a year or more ago, here they all were in Tumuo's house – Tumuo and his family, Mister Kimo, Aram, Baiteke, with Edwin and John snoozing in the corner. Comfortable, just like old times. But everything was different, and the future seemed unimaginable. Were the Japanese, or the Germans or those other guys, the Italians, going to be dropping bombs here, on Nikumaroro?

A few days earlier the *Viti* had hove to off Nikumaroro, but a high westerly swell was running and neither boats nor canoes could get across the reef; she had finally blown her horn and gotten underway, rounding the north cape headed east. Now she was back, and Mister Kimo, John and Edwin had come ashore for a quick visit while Iokina and some of the senior men got the new settlers into their assigned places, and others finished unloading the stores. Still others were preparing to depart, going back to the Gilberts or Ellices, or to Ocean or Tarawa or even Fiji. And the High Commissioner himself was on the island, Sir Harry Luke, being shown around by Doctor MacPherson..

Aram had the toddy bottle now; he was getting quietly drunk. He had wept uncontrollably when Sir Harry and his aide-de-camp, Mister Ian, stood at attention at Mister Gallagher's grave, and the flag – held at half-mast this last month – was hauled back to the peak. Sir Harry – a short but very distinguished *I-Matang,* and his much taller aide had both been very kind to Aram, but Sir Harry had insisted that the time of mourning was past, and life must go on.

"So, brother," Tumuo was saying, "The High Commissioner went on to Canton when he couldn't come ashore here, and tomorrow he's going back there again?"

"Yes," Mister Kimo laughed shortly, "around and around – Nikumaroro, Manra, Orona, Canton, then back here, now to Enderbury and I think that little island, Phoenix, then back to Canton. So I played truant from my team, eh? Went with them from Manra to Canton and left them there while I came to see my favorite island."

"Left them to drink beer and gamble, eh?"

"Oh, it's a simple job, and they don't really need me till it's time to put on the finishing touches. Then we can all drink beer and gamble together. " Mister Kimo slapped his knee and laughed his great laugh.

Tumuo looked at him with level eyes. "It's good of you to come visit your family, brother."

Mister Kimo was silent for a while before responding, looking at the ground. "Who knows when we'll see each other again, eh? This trip isn't really about building the new administrator's house on Canton."

"Is it not, then?"

"Seriously, brother, for me and my team it is, maybe, but does Sir Harry Luke build houses? Does he make his new ADC, Mister Ian Thompson, build houses? Do they just wander around on their ship visiting little islands? Like I say, war's coming, and that's why Sir Harry's here – or rather, why he's going to Canton. Has to talk with the Americans, I think. Maybe they're going to join the war on our side; I don't know. But Sir Harry is really worried about the Japs. If there's war with the Japs....."

He shook his head and accepted the bottle from Keaki. Keaki had only tasted it to be part of the group; he didn't much like coconut toddy. Baiteke, of course, had taken a big swig.

"They're very strong, the Japs." Tumuo didn't make it seem like a question.

Mister Kimo kept shaking his head. "Very strong. I talked with a guy from Jaluit, a Marshallese guy I know. He said it's amazing what they're doing there, building huge concrete buildings and landing places, flying in monster aeroplanes. He says they have ships with guns like this!" He made a circle with both his arms.

He handed the bottle to Baiteke and watched him without expression as the boy tipped it high. Keaki felt shy of him; looking so solemn, but the silence brought a question bubbling up inside him.

"Mister Kimo, you say there are Americans on Canton?"

"Oh yes, there are the Pan Americans.... "

"Pan Americans?"

"The people who fly these huge aeroplanes that land and take off in the lagoon, fly clear across the ocean. They've built a landing place and machine shops on Canton, and they even have a hotel – a sort of rest house for people who fly on the aeroplanes. I don't know if they're the ones Sir Harry is meeting, or if somebody's flying from America to talk with him, or what. There's a lot that's secret, and I'm just a simple handy man, you know? A brown handy man." He laughed, a short bark.

"Sho," Baiteke mumbled, "that'sh where that *te tai* came from."

No, Keaki thought, kicking Baiteke; let's not talk about those bones. Mister Kimo raised an eyebrow.

"Te tai? Wristwatch?"

Baiteke started to open his mouth. Keaki looked at him fiercely and spoke quickly to fill the gap. "Yeah, we found a wristwatch, but it – uh – got lost. It said "Pan American" on the back."

"Huh, that's interesting. I wonder if one of their aeroplanes has been here."

"Mebbie sho," Baiteke mumbled, "remember, Keaki, that shtuff you made into the comb for Era?"

"Shut up, Baiteke."

"Beeootiful Era...!"

"Shut up!"

Mister Kimo laughed, reaching for the bottle. "Keaki, boy, we all do stupid things for love, eh? What's this stuff you found?

"Oh – uh — Silvery-gray stuff kind of like shell but softer, more flex- ible. It shows up now and then on the reef flat up at Nutiran. I think it's alum..."

"This stuff, eh?" Tumuo reached up to a shelf on the wall behind him, fished a piece of the gray stuff out from under a *Noriti* turnbuckle. Keaki's eyes went wide; it was the same colour as his piece but bigger, rectangular, with long skinny pieces attached around the edges. Tumuo handed it to Kimo.

"I found five or four of these just the other day; they were nailed along one edge to a piece of thin lumber, and floated up on the beach. I thought they'd make good patchs or something. Aluminium, I think."

Mister Kimo turned it over in his hand. "Yes, aluminium, and those are rivets. And those things are called Timmerman nuts; I don't know why. I'll bet it's from an aeroplane. Maybe one of the big Pan American planes...."

"I've never seen such an aeroplane here – though there is that piece of an aeroplane up on Nutiran, with the wheel..."

"Gone now," Baiteke threw in, opening his drooping eyelids for a moment. "Not there after lasht shtorm."

Keaki felt things click together in his mind, and a strange sense of regret, almost shame, spread over him. He could almost hear Mister Gal- lagher, down there at the skull place. Had he or Baiteke seen anything – shiny, two engines. He'd got so confused thinking about engines pulling against each other....

Even drunk, Baiteke reached the same conclusion. "Prob'ly that lady's aeroplane," he mumbled, but no one was paying attention. Mister Kimo and

Tumuo had turned to discussing how well the aluminium might work as inlay in wooden boxes.

Baiteke slept late in the morning. Which, Keaki thought, was a good thing; he didn't have to confront the fact that Segalo was leaving. It had been decided for some time that she would go to Fiji to be trained as a nurse, and the *Viti*'s visit provided the opportunity for her to travel in comfort, with Mister Kimo and his boys for protection at least as far as Canton.

"Nobody told me!" Baiteke moaned when he finally did wake up and found the love of his life gone, the big armed ship already just a memory. Keaki felt little sympathy.

"I don't think Tumuo realized he needed your permission."

"She didn't even get to say goodbye!"

"Why should she? She'd never said hello."

"What will I do, Keaki? My heart is breaking!"

"Carve a box. Climb a tree. I don't know. Put her out of your mind. Think of all the other girls...."

"There's no other girl for me! Shut up, fish-fucker; leave me alone!" He stormed off across the village toward the lagoon. Hours later, Takena found him passed out under a canoe, an empty toddy bottle next to him. Takena shook his head and chuckled as he gathered his son up in his arms and took him home.

A week later, as the sun began to set, Keaki was startled to see the new wireless operator, Fasimata, sprinting from the wireless shack toward Iokina's house. Before long Iokina was pounding on the bell outside the *maneaba*, summoning the people to a meeting. The Japanese, he announced, had dropped bombs from aeroplanes on ships from *Ameriki* at a place called Pearl Harbour.

Excerpt from Sir Harry Luke, *From a South Seas Diary*, 1938-1942, Nicholson & Watson, London, 1945

Sunday 30th November. By this time the westerlies had abated and we were able to get ashore. Gerald Gallagher had made Gardner the model island of the Phoenix and we walked for the best part of a mile along the broad and well laid out "Sir Harry Luke Avenue" to the station on the lagoon side of the island. In the middle is Gallagher's grave, lovingly constructed by the natives to

McPherson's design, and beyond it his house, built entirely of native materials like Holland's and Steenson's at Tarawa, airy, spacious and far and away the best type of house for Europeans in this part of the world. Here we lunched off delicious grey mullet, caught fresh for us by the natives in the lagoon, where I had a swim while the fish were being cooked by Gallagher's faithful servant Aram. Aram has vowed to remain in Gardner for twelve months to watch by his master's grave. At present the natives number only about forty, but the next lot of settlers are coming to Gardner (native name Nikumaroro), which is to be the headquarters of the Phoenix group.

When Gallagher died, Aram wrote to his mother in England a letter which both in feeling and in form is the most perfect letter of condolence I have ever read. In conveying restrained emotion with classic beauty of composition this Micronesian native has nothing to learn from us. This is the letter:

Nikumaroro
(Gardner Island)
Phoenix Group
Gilbert and Ellice Dear Mrs. Gallagher,
    It is with great regret and sorrow that I, Aram Tamia, Mr. G. B. Gallagher's servant, write this letter.
    I have lost the most wonderful, kind, good and thoughtful master that any servant ever had. He took me from school on the island of Tarawa and I have been with him ever since; he has never taken any journey without me.
        I was married last year and I have a son who is named Bernard after my late master.
    Mr. Gallagher is laid to rest at the foot of the flag-mast, and the flag he taught us to love and respect waves over him every day.

We, the people who dearly love him, are going to tend his resting place. It is also for that reason, and a custom of my people, that I am remaining here for some time with my master.

Please will you, his mother accept from me, his sorrowing servant, my deepest sympathy in your sad loss of such a good son and man.

Your obedient servant Aram Tamia

I was handed several petitions. One was addressed to "the famous and High Commissioner who has called to hear our troubles."

Another began:

"Greeting. We are happy at your arrival, you, our father who looks after our lives in these strange places."

Another, from two native mission workers, ran as follows:

"The High Commissioner

Greetings.

We are happy for you have come, you who is our father gives us blessings when we are in trouble.

We ask about the works that are done on the Sabbath. If the ship leaves the island and the things are on shore, we are told to work, and church services canceled. The people have all been punished for 'damage' and the keeper of the law here told us that we were to be in the punishment also.

We ask about our position as Jesus's servants"

I thought I could not answer this one better than by reminding them that the Sabbath was made for man, not man for the Sabbath.

Sailed in the evening for Hull Island (native name, Orona).

Chapter 46 –

Beer Belly Batkey, May 1946

"That is one fine box."

Kilts turned it around in his hands. Dark, fine-grained wood, reddish, with a neatly fitted top. All carved from a single log. A floral pattern inlaid around all four sides, in shiny silvery metal – maybe aluminum?

"Three beer," the artisan grinned through missing front teeth.

"That's Beer-belly Batkey," Smith chuckled. "Sopko says no trading booze, but he's real persistent."

"Four Coke," Kilts offered. The native grimaced.

"No, sorry, Coke no good. Beer."

"My girl would really like that box," Kilts mused.

"So offer him three beers, and you drink the Cokes."

"Shit, what about the CO?"

"We're here, Sopko's at the Station. We're on liberty; we got five hours. How's he to know who drinks the beer ration?"

"Four beers," Batkey grinned and nodded enthusiastically.

"Three." Kilts held up fingers.

"Three beer, one coke."

"OK, done." Kilts reached into the back of the truck and fished out the bottles, passed them to the grinning native, and stashed the box in their place. "Say, Batkey, you got any more boxes?"

"Yes, yes. You come my house. I show."

"Why not?" Kilts shrugged. "I bet I could sell these suckers for twenty bucks each back in San Diego."

The U.S. Coast Guard had been on Gardner Island – the natives called it Nikumaroro – since 1944. Twenty-odd very bored sailors with a lieutenant in charge, manning Loran Station 92 at the south end of the island. Every couple of weeks some of them would drive the station's truck up to the village to eat and trade with the natives; they were strictly forbidden from giving them any of the station's beer, and from engaging in what the C.O, Lieutenant Sopko. called "push- push." Occasionally they paid attention.

Now in 1946 the war was over, and the Coast Guard was going home. Kilts had arrived from Canton a few days earlier to start dismantling the station and filling the Quonset huts with the parts. This was his first opportunity to visit the village up at the north end, and as fast as they were going with the dismantlement, it might be his last.

As they walked toward the shore the neatness of the parade ground faded into disorder. The roads were pretty clear, but the dispensary grounds were grown up in low brush, littered with coconut fronds and the odd medicine bottle here and there. Batkey's house, when they reached it, was just as disorderly, with thatch needing to be replaced and the ground strewn with beer bottles and other detritus – washpans, pails, pots, pieces of aluminum. Kilts picked one up. A roughly rectangular piece with some rivets.

"So that's where the inlay comes from," Smith said.

"Yeah, I guess."

Batkey shouted toward the cookhouse and a woman emerged, carrying a mat that she spread on the ground. Kilts and Smith sat.

"Tea?" Batkey inquired.

"No, thanks. Got coffee?" Batkey looked uncomprehending.

"Never mind. What about the boxes?"

Batkey ducked into the house and emerged with two boxes, neither quite as fine as the one Kilts had already bought.

"Five beers."

"Both?"

"One."

"Each," Smith interpreted.

"Hmm. Have to think about it. I sure like this aluminum inlay."

"Very nice aluminium," Batkey agreed. "From aeroplane."

"Lifted off a PBY, I s'pose," Smith guessed.

"No, no. Not PBY!" Batkey interjected. "From reef – out there." He gestured toward the reef flat beyond the shore.

"Doesn't want to admit lifting it."

"No lift! No steal! Found! Fishing, by ship, *Noriti*. Found!" He pantomimed pulling the aluminum out of a crevice.

"Jap, I guess," Kilts guessed.

"No, not Jap," Batkey said authoritatively "Jap never come here. U.S. woman, and man."

"Oh yeah?" Smith smirked. "Woman flying a U.S. plane? One of those pussy pilots the PB4Y yokels paint on their noses, prob'ly."

"Before war come. Woman, man. Mister Karaka tell us."

"You don't say? Rosie the Riveter, maybe." Smith chuckled at his own wit. Y' know, Floyd, I still have beers waiting back at the truck."

"Air... Air..." Batkey was holding his head, trying to remember, and wrap his tongue around the unfamiliar syllables. "Air-hard! Meela!"

"Oh man," Smith rolled his eyes. "This gets better and better."

"Uh... not Amelia Earhart?" Kilts inquired, looking intently at Batkey, who nodded energetically.

"Floyd, if you wanta listen to this bullshit, you go ahead. I want my beer."

"Go ahead, Smitty. I'll just sit and talk with Batkey for awhile."

"Suit yourself. Remember we gotta start back at 1500. Amelia Earhart. Oh man..." Smith strolled off toward the parade ground with his hands in the pockets of his shorts.

Kilts tapped a Camel out of his pack and offered it to Batkey, who accepted it happily. Kilts lit it for him, and lit up himself.

"So, Batkey, what about this airplane, and Meela Airhard?" Batkey looked apologetic.

"My English....." He brightened. "You wait. Back, just moment."

He motioned to his woman and hurried off. She brought Kilts a drinking coconut, with a graceful bow and a smile. Kilts accepted both with pleasure. A couple of little naked kids were peeking at him from the ramshackle thatched house. He wiggled his fingers at them; they shrieked with laughter and disappeared.

Here came Batkey with another villager. As they approached, Kilts speculated about their ages. Batkey, he guessed, was in his early twenties, but looked older – probably from drinking and hard living.

"As hard as an asshole can live in paradise," he snorted.

The new guy – Kilts had seen him around, but always hanging back, never part of the crowd that jostled for candy and smokes –he looked younger, maybe late teens, but hard-muscled, strong. Hard to tell ages, though, with these natives.

"This my friend Keaki," Batkey grinned. "He good English."

"OK. How d'you do, Kiyki. I'm Floyd."

"Froyd. G'day."

"Batkey was telling me about this alum – aluminium."

"Yes?"

"He said it came from an airplane?"

"Yes, on reef near *Noriti* – big shipwreck – after storms, we find pieces.

"He says it was a woman's plane?"

"Yes, we think."

"Amelia Earhart?"

Kiyki smiled cautiously. "You know this lady?"

"Well, not exactly. That is, everybody in America knows about her. Why d'you think it was her plane?"

"Mister Karaka tell us, maybe, when we find – find – bones."

"Bones?"

"Yes But he say not talk about."

"Why not?"

"I don't know. Just not."

Kilts thought fast. This guy knew something, and if he really knew about Earhart... There could be a book in this, movie rights....

"I – I'm a friend – Miss – Nei Amelia's nephew. We've all been looking for her."

"Nephew?"

"Yes – er – her father's sister's son." He wondered if Earhart's father had a sister. Didn't matter; if he didn't know, Kiyki sure as shit didn't.

"So it's OK to tell me. And I can pay...."

"No, no pay." Kiyki was emphatic; Batkey looked crestfallen. Kiyki was clearly in charge, and had made a decision. "We will tell you."

"Thank you very much. The family will be real grateful."

They all settled on the mat, and Batkey shouted to the woman to bring tea. One of the little naked kids – Batkey's daughter? — stood looking at them, leaning in the door, finger in her mouth. A chicken strutted across the yard.

"When we first came here," Kiyki began, "first there were just men."

Take notes, Kilts thought, and flipped out the pocket notebook he kept for listing needed supplies. As always he had several pencil stubs in his pockets. He made a note: "just island men."

"Later more people come. Batkey and I come. About twenty-three people here when we found bones, maybe."

Twenty-three men, Kilts scrawled. "Where did you find these bones?"

"Near end of island. Cutting *kanawa* trees. Just near end. Found – skull. Then Magistrate find bottle, and Mister Karaka find more bones."

"Back in the bush?"

"Yes, skull was by edge of *mao* – bush. Mister Karaka say it might be that lady. Said had to go to Fiji, to Suva, to High *Komitina.*"

"Who was this Mister Karaka?"

"Administrator, boss, captain – of these islands."

"Magistrate?"

"That was Koata, yes. Mister Karaka was...."

"How d'you spell that, do you know?"

"G... A... L... It's on his grave – on parade ground."

"Oh, that guy with the plaque. Gallagher. Irish fellow, eh?"

"Some people – Doctor Mafurs called him that."

"So why did Mister Karaka think it might be – Aunt Amelia?"

"Woman's shoe with the bones. American kind. Mister Karaka said maybe size nine, I think. We don't wear shoes, you know." Kiyki held up one of his broad, callused feet.

"Right. So he took the bones to Fiji?"

Kiyki hesitated. "Yes. He did"

"To the government authorities?"

"Yes, to *Komitina.*"

"I wonder what they did. When was that?"

"Before War."

"1939? 1940?"

"Yes."

Kilts puzzled over this, drawing on his cigarette. If Earhart's bones had gotten to Fiji it would have been big news. Why hadn't it been? Maybe....

"How did he get to Fiji?"

"On *Nimanoa,* I think."

"What's that?"

"Boat."

"The colony's boat?"

"Yes, Colonial boat."

Wow! Kilts thought. All that distance in that dinky little whaleboat – *Nei* something or other, must be *Nimanoa.*

"So he rowed all the way... ?"

"No, no, other men rowed."

"What happened then?"

Kiyki looked pained. "He died."

"Gallagher?"

"Yes. He go to Suva. Then he die."

"In Suva?"

"No. He get very sick on boat outside Suva, on sea. He die."

"But he's buried here – on the parade ground."

"Yes, they bring him back. Doctor Mafurs bring him. He die. We bury him. All very sorry, sad."

"Was it a disease?"

"That made him die?"

"Yes"

Kiyki looked at the ground, mumbled. "Maybe. Some say ghost sickness."

"What did Doctor – the island doctor say?"

"Doctor Mafurs?"

"Yeah."

"I don't remember. Something like – Ruu..."

"Nu? Pneumonia?"

"Maybe."

"What happened to the bones?"

"I don't know."

"The – doctor didn't bring them back?"

"No."

"Prob'ly threw 'em overboard, scared of ghosts," Kilts murmured to himself.

Kiyki started, stared at Kilts. A long moment passed. Kilts thought furiously; how could he take back what he'd said? Stupid of him not to know that Kiyki would understand, and be offended. But Kiyki didn't really look offended. He looked troubled, and thoughtful, and then like he'd made a decision. He looked Kilts in the face, solemnly.

"Scared. Yes. Didn't want *anti* – ghosts – here. So put bones in the ocean."

"You did? I'm..."

"Yes. We find bones. Then Mister Karaka die. We think spirits, you know? We were afraid. So we ... we take bag with bones in it and our dresser – island doctor – drop that bag in ocean." A faraway look came into his eyes. "Those bones not come back."

"My God," Kilts said, more to himself than to anyone else. "So the word never got out."

He scribbled for awhile, as Kiyki looked thoughtfully into the distance and Batkey pulled the last puffs out of his cigarette. Kilts picked up the piece of aluminum. "What about this?"

"Like I say, on reef by *Noriti,* shipwreck. You want see?"

"Sure, if it's not too far. And where you found the bones, too."

"OK, you come."

"Wait, let me check..."

"We tell your friends. Only two or one hour."

Kiyki's canoe carried them swiftly across the channel, and then they walked on shelving coral past the hulking wreck of the *Norwich City.* The tide was low. North of the wreck, Kiyki and Batkey led the way out onto the reef flat – first jumping over holes and wide cracks, then walking on smooth wet coral. Kilts looked at the flat surface, stretching away to the northwest.

"Like a fucking landing strip," he muttered.

Kiyki was pointing to the reef edge, where the surf was crashing. "There was – aeroplane wreck there. Gone now."

"Washed away?"

Kiyki shrugged. "Yes, must be."

"But this is where you got the – aluminium?"

"Different parts reef. After storms, big waves. Big pieces, little pieces. Not many, but sometimes. I stop after find bones, but others still pick up, time to time."

"And where were the bones?"

Kiyki pointed toward the gravelly beach, topped with brush. "Over there, and at end of island."

A week later, Kilts leaned on the *Myrtlebank's* taffrail as the cutter sliced eastward for Canton. The treetops of Gardner Island sank quickly behind them.

So this was what happened to Amelia Earhart, and in all the civilized world only he knew. It was a big responsibility, he thought, and a big opportunity. He could go to the newspapers, or to Earhart's family – that Putnam guy. Or he could.... He really could write a book.

"Writing lessons," he murmured. "Take writing lessons. Write a book. Make something of myself. Make a fucking fortune."

San Diego Tribune—July 21, 1960
(San Diego, California, U.S.A.)

SAN DIEGAN BARES CLUE TO EARHART FATE

by Lew Scarr

Gardner Island is a five-mile hyphen of coral punctuating a million square miles of nowhere and nothing in the Central Pacific.

If a San Diego man is right, it is where Amelia Earhart crashed and died 23 years ago.

The water slapping the short, sharp Gardner shoreline is as warm as your bath and as blue as your baby's eyes.

Coral Looks Smooth as Silk From Air

At low tide the smoothest coral in the world is exposed for 200 yards. From the air it looks as if you could dry your nets there, fly your kite, or, alas, land your plane.

Actually, this smoothest coral is slashed with canyons six to 10 feet wide and 40 to 100 feet deep. At the ends of the 200 yards, the hard beach drops deceptively, 100 feet or more at one spot.

A plane attempting a landing there would be dashed to pieces.

And in the warm, blue water slapping the Gardner shore, Floyd Kilts says, Amelia Earhart's airplane, the Flying Laboratory, lies in a crust of shells.

Islands Base for Coast Guard Unit

Kilts, 68, of 3615 Oleander Dr., is on leave from his job with the state Department of Veterans Affairs after suffering a heart attack. During World War II he was a chief carpenter in the Coast Guard for four years.

He was stationed on 15 islands in the Pacific installing and dismantling loran stations (navigational aids). One of the 15 was Gardner.

That was March, 1946, nine years after the world's greatest woman pilot and her navigator, Fred Noonan, flew the twin-engine Lockheed Flying Laboratory from here to eternity.

No satisfactory, documented explanation of the disappearance has been accepted. Even after the navy officially listed Miss Earhart and Noonan as dead, there was the nagging feeling among some that the tousle-haired aviator lived.

Recently a story that she was captured and executed by the Japanese was scotched. Kilts said the story was impossible anyway because it held that Miss Earhart turned up on Saipan, a 90-degree error from take-off at New Guinea to Miss Earhart's announced destination to Howland Island, more than 2,000 miles away.

Amelia Reported Flying Line to Island

But Gardner is on roughly the same longitude as Howland and only 380 miles south. The final authentic message from the Flying Laboratory said Miss Earhart was running north and south, perhaps on the line between Howland and Gardner.

Kilts knows this bit of reasoning is hardly enough, but there is more. Here in his words is the rest of the story:

"A native tried to tell me about it. But I couldn't understand all of it so I got an interpreter. It seems that in the latter part of 1938 there were 23 island people, all men, and an Irish magistrate planting coconut trees on Gardner for the government of New Zealand.

"They were about through and the native was walking along one end of the island. There in the brush about five feet from the shoreline he saw a skeleton.

"What attracted him to it was the shoes. Women's shoes, American kind. No native wears shoes. Couldn't if they wanted to—feet too spread out and flat. The shoes were size nine narrow. Beside the body was a cognac bottle with fresh water in it for drinking.

"The island doctor said the skeleton was that of a woman. And there were no native women on the island then. Farther down the beach he found a man's skull, but nothing else.

"The magistrate was a young Irishman who got excited when he saw the bone. He thought of Amelia Earhart right away. He put the bones in a gunnysack and with the native doctor and three other natives in a 22-foot, four-oared boat started for Suva, Fiji, 887 nautical miles away.

"The magistrate was anxious to get the news to the world. But on the way the Irishman came down with pneumonia. When only about 24 hours out of Suva he died.

"The natives are superstitious as the devil and the next night after the young fellow died they threw the gunnysack full of bones overboard, scared of the spirits. And that was that."

This same account was related by the doctor to New Zealand officials.

Kilts knows that there are those who never will believe absolutely that the skeleton was that of Amelia Earhart, not without a dental identification or something. But Kilts believes it.

He is sure that Miss Earhart crashed on the coral trap of the Gardner beach and crawled into the brush and died.

He thinks that Miss Earhart thought that Gardner was Howland. Or even if she realized it wasn't Howland she tried to bring the fuel-empty Flying Laboratory down at any old port in a storm—in this case, the treacherous Gardner Island.

So, there you are. Kilts knows there have been many Amelia Earhart theories and may be many more.

Next month he will fly to the Philippines to visit his daughter and, perhaps, stop off at Gardner in the middle of nowhere and nothing to hunt for an airplane and do a little theory proving of his own.

Chapter 47–

A White Coral "G", 1948

Following Aram, whose bare feet move easily over the sand while we break through and flounder in the land-crab holes, we reach the area toward the landing place where bush has been allowed to encroach on and choke the growing coconuts, and here we find the working party, engaged in hacking it clear again under the burly Tem Buake, Island Chief of Police. It is tough discouraging work in the heat and we laugh with them at their feckless neglect which has made it necessary. .... Further east from the end of Aukaraime the atoll rim narrows, the soil is less fertile, supporting only buka, and that reaching no great size. At the eastern tip the wedge-shaped area is taken up partly by great pools, set in the coral and rain filled. The buka trees rise here sixty feet high, and were partly cleared to accommodate the neat grey iron Quonset huts of the U.S. radio installation, neatly sealed, awaiting dismantling and transportation. Turning the tip to return along the northern rim, narrow, thundering with surf driven by the north-east trade winds, the path ends in a house built for Gallagher on a strip of land cleared from lagoon to ocean beach so that the fresh winds blow easily through. Beyond this there is no path, save along the steeply sloping, sandy ocean beach.

Paul Laxton, "Nikumaroro."
Journal of the Polynesian Society June/September 1951

"For Mister Karaka." Aram swiped his arm over his sweaty forehead, and went off up the surge ridge with his shovel.

Baiteke grimaced at Keaki over the piece of sheet metal they were maneuvering onto the roof of the little house.

"For Mister Karaka, for Mister Karaka. Does he forget that man's dead?"

Keaki took a nail from between his teeth and began hammering it through the corrugated steel into the roof beam. "He knows."

"So why rebuild that man's house?"

Keaki shrugged, watched Aram struggling to push his shovel into the rubbly ground and uproot a small *kanawa*. Baiteke asked the question every time they came down here. Every time, he answered it the same way, wondering why he couldn't think of any better reason.

"It makes him feel better. He's doing what he thinks Mister Karaka wanted him to do." He tossed the hammer to Baiteke, who caught it and began nailing down his side of the metal.

"Well, I'm not helping him again." He banged the last nail emphatically.

Keaki leaned over the roof with a piece of wire, and attached the small piece of bent metal that would direct rainwater into the big square Tarawa Police tank. Straightened and sat for a moment, pondering. He couldn't blame Baiteke – didn't blame him. Wasn't sure himself, really, why he was helping Aram. Except there was nothing else to do. Just tend his farm, fish, tend his farm, fish. They had been down here – what, six times since the Coastguards had left? Rebuilt the little house, re-cleared the land, planted coconuts, tended them, watched them die. His eyes wandered along the rows of neatly-dug holes, some still containing the remains of dead, rotting trees, others now completely empty. Even Aram had finally had to concede that this land just wasn't any good for coconuts. But he still wanted to keep it clear from the ocean to the lagoon, with only nice shade trees and that big *ren* where the bones had lain. Still wanted the house to be usable, even though no one used it.

Keaki sighed, shook his head and twisted the wire tight. Baiteke tossed his hammer to the ground, grabbed the edge of the roof and flipped down, landing lightly. Considering how plump he'd gotten, Keaki thought, Baiteke still moved pretty gracefully. He tested the tightness of his wire, was satisfied, and jumped down to stand beside his friend.

"We shouldn't have to help him again, till maybe five years or six years."

They stood looking at the house. About the same as it had been all those years ago, when Mister Gallagher was doing his searching, except now it was roofed with metal from the abandoned Coastguard station at the place they called Ameriki. The old canvas roof had long since rotted to shreds.

Up on the surge ridge, Aram threw down the *mao* he'd uprooted and moved on to another. Baiteke chopped the end off one of their drinking coconuts, took a long drink and handed it to Keaki.

"No years. Fuck this, I'm through. Come on, let's shoot some birds."

"You shoot them. I'm going to help Aram."

"Crazy Aram, crazy Keaki. Keep that *komitina* land clear, keep that house nice and clean for the *anti* of Karaka." Baiteke took the old .22 pistol out of his carrying basket and stumped off into the trees. It was Aram's pistol, part of his magistrate's gear, but Aram never used it, and let Baiteke carry it around.

Keaki climbed the surge ridge toward where Aram was ripping up another *mao*. Wondered again why he was here. Sure, it was a nice place, and it was good to be away from the village, but why come down here and sweat in the sun? Or if he had to sweat, why not work his own land? The land he thought he'd get, that is, when government finally got around to formal allocations. Maybe that was it; everything was still so uncertain. The war was over but there was still no real *I-Matang* government, no decisions about who owned what.

But still, why this? What power did Aram have to get people to do such pointless things in memory of Gallagher? Even before he'd become magistrate, but especially now. Sweep the parade ground, mend the flag, rake the gravel on the roads, and now clear out the little bushes and trees that were once again reclaiming the cleared *komotina* land, and repair the little house there. Why?

The crest of the ridge was growing thick with *mao;* Aram had no chance of clearing it all and keeping it clear. There were other changes – storm winds had picked up many of the sheets of corrugated iron that had formed the slipway for the *kanawa* logs, scattered them around the clearing, and piled many of them up along its southeast side. The remains of the campfire where they had found the bird and turtle bones had disappeared under the *mao*. But the *ren* tree was still standing tall, full of nesting birds.

Aram was leaning on his shovel near the top of the ridge, looking at the ground. No, not the ground – at that pile of *te aubunga* — shells of giant clams – that Mister Karaka had pointed out the first day they had been there. The tar paper Aram had laid over it later was long gone – just tattered little fragments of black fabric with bright green speckles on it – and the shells were once again shining in the sun, though the *mao* was growing up to shade them. Aram glanced at Keaki, but didn't move. He shook his head.

"Who do you think that was?"

"Who?" Keaki asked, though he knew.

"Those bones. Do you think it was that woman?"

Keaki sat down next to the pile of shells, picked one up and turned it over in his hand. Its hinge side was chipped and broken, as though someone had tried to pry it open.

"Maybe it was that woman," he said neutrally.

"I wonder what she did with these *aubunga*."

"Ate them, I guess – like the birds and the fish."

"I wonder what Mister Karaka thought."

The pop of the .22 interrupted them, and a whoop from Baiteke, some-where off in the bush. "Must've got a bird," Keaki said, to change the subject.

"Why bring them up here?"

Keaki sighed. "Maybe she had no knife, couldn't just take out the meat and leave the shell."

"What a lot of work! *I Matang* work all the time. I remember Mister..."

Another pop, another whoop. "Baiteke is doing pretty good."

"Yeah." Aram threw a rock at a coconut crab, who scuttled back into the mao. "What do you think killed her?"

Keaki was getting irritated. "Everybody dies," he snapped.

"Bad side of the island, I think."

That was what Keaki thought, too, but he didn't want to say it. "Maybe not for *I-Matang*. Probably just got sick."

"Like Mister Karaka."

Keaki looked into the *mao,* its fleshy light green leaves glistening in the sun. Spirit side of the island. Whatever else had happened, someone had died here, and when Mister Gallagher collected those bones....

The old question – what spirits were here on the windward side? The *anti* of the bones, or something more – more a part of the island, more like the island itself? Nei Manganibuka? Or something that was here even before Nei Manganibuka? Something as much a part of the island as the coral itself, the *mao,* the *buka,* the thunder of surf?

Aram turned over a shell with his stick. "What do you think happened to them?"

"She ate them."

"No, the bones."

"Well, Mister Karaka sent them to Fiji, to government...."

"And then he died, and then the war came. I wonder if they ever got back to her family."

"You're the magistrate now. You could ask."

"Who would I ask? Everybody's gone. Dead or sent away somewhere. What would I say?"

"I don't know. Maybe it's best to just forget it."

"Maybe. It's all just so.... incomplete."

Keaki stared at the empty eastern horizon. So incomplete. Yes indeed, the story of the bones was so incomplete. But was anything ever complete? What made something complete? When would he be complete? What would make him so?

Down below, Baiteke came out of the bush with three big frigate birds. He laid them on a log and chopped off their wings, tossed the wings into the tops of the *mao* bushes where they hung among the leaves.

"Why's he doing that?" Aram wanted to know.

"It's a trick he's trying. He thinks the crabs will smell the blood and come running, try to climb into the *mao*. Then he can grab them."

Aram looked at him, a little wildly, pleadingly. "We shouldn't take crabs from here!"

Keaki didn't ask why not. He knew why not. He didn't know what he knew, but he knew he didn't want to eat crabs from here. Not birds, either, but Baiteke could worry about the birds; he'd already shot them. He shuddered slightly, took Aram's hand, and led him down the slope. The young magistrate came along, unprotesting.

"Baiteke!" Keaki called out as they went. "Leave the crabs alone! They belong to government! Let's go home!"

He led Aram toward the waiting canoe. Baiteke came along behind, grumbling.

At the canoe, Aram dropped Keaki's hand. "Oh shit," Keaki thought, "he's going to do it again."

"Thank you, Keaki," Aram spoke formally, almost mechanically. "Thank you, Teng Baiteke. You go on back to the village; I'll walk around there when I'm finished here."

"Finished here," Keaki knew, could mean many hours from now, and a long walk home around the ocean shore of the island – past the Ameriki station, up the road the Coastguard had built to the village. Aram had always got home safely, but leaving him alone – leaving anyone alone with night falling on the windward shore – was risky business, seemed wrong.

He knew what Aram would be doing, though Baiteke did not. Aram had revealed it to him, and to him alone.

He was writing Mister Gallagher's name.

Carefully, on the ground in a protected spot not far from the canoe landing. Writing it in pure white staghorn coral – thousands and thousands of little pieces, finger-sized, picked up one by one and carefully sifted down through cupped hands onto the algae-blackened rubbly ground to spell out the dead man's name the way the *I-Matang* did: "G-A-L-L-A-G-H-E-R." He had the letters on a piece of paper he kept in the pocket of his shorts, to guide him. He had been almost through the second "L" when he showed Keaki what he was doing.

"So people will always know," he had said, nodding. "His name will always be here."

Keaki stood up to his knees in the pungent water of the lagoon, holding the side of the canoe and looking at his friend. Remembering the nights around the wireless, the search, the horrible time when Mister Gallagher... He shook his head, driving the thoughts away.

"You shouldn't stay. Or I should...."

"No, you go along. I like to be just alone here for awhile, and you know.... there are things I have to do." He nodded toward the coral shelf at the edge of the *mao;* for the first time Keaki noticed the small canvas bag sitting there. Filled with staghorn, no doubt.

"It'll be dark..."

"The moon is almost full, and there are so many stars. And the coast-guard road makes it easy."

"Come on, Keaki," Baiteke grumbled. "He's the fucking magistrate; do as he says."

The wind was on their quarter and the canoe sped through the light chop. The sun was still warm, the breeze cool. Puffy piles of white cloud drifted across the endless blue sky, darkening now in the east, and bright *kiakias* swooped over the trees. Little sharks raced out of their way, their fins leaving intersecting V-shaped wakes.

Baiteke opened a bottle of sour toddy. By the time they wove through the coral heads to the lagoon beach, he had passed out, lolling on his back on the outrigger platform. Keaki had abstained as usual, but he felt an inexplicable urge to drink till he lost consciousness. Instead he sat for a long time on the beach, and watched the trees across the lagoon turn green-gold, and the *kiakias* come home to roost.

Chapter 48 –

Digging Up Mister Gallagher,
Early October, 1968

"Bloody Hell!" The bos'n ran calloused fingers through his thick mop of curly black hair. "How the fuck we get fucking bones outa there?"

Keaki and Baiteke leaned on their shovels. William, the pudgy fireman from Bettio, dropped the coffin on the ground and sat on it.

"Big piece of concrete," he said in Tunguran.

The bos'n, who spoke Pidgin and his native Dayak, scowled and ignored them all. "Fucking shit," he said. It was his favorite expression.

The four men stood in what had been the parade ground, almost unrecognizable for the coconuts and pandanus that had sprung up. They smoked cigarettes and looked at Mister Gallagher's grave monument. About seven feet long, over two feet wide and high, pointed at the top like a house. All built of coral blocks cemented together, and covered over with cement plaster. Underneath, a low platform of coral, lined with coral slabs. A mature coconut tree at the head end – Keaki vividly remembered watching Aram place the seed nut there, tears pouring down his face – and the brass memorial plaque at the other. The bos'n gave the plaque a hostile stare, as though he hated it.

"What dat fucker say?" The bos'n didn't read English very well. Keaki read it to him, the almost-memorized words. Feeling a tightness in his chest that he had almost forgotten.

In affectionate Memory
Of
GERALD BERNARD GALLAGHER, M.A.
Of the Colonial Administrative Service.
Officer in charge of the Phoenix Islands Settlement Scheme
Who died on Gardner Island, where he would have wished to die, on the
27th September, 1941, aged 29 years
His selfless devotion to duty and unsparing work on behalf of
The natives of the Gilbert and Ellice Islands
Were an inspiration to all who knew him, and to his labours is largely
Due the successful colonization of the
PHOENIX ISLANDS.
R.I.P

Erected by his friends and brother officers.

"Big man," William observed, noncommittally.

"But fucking dead," the bos'n observed. "You fellah know he got dis big rock on top him?"

Baiteke stubbed out his cigarette on the flagstaff. "Yeah, we helped build it."

"Why you not tell me?"

Keaki shrugged. "Nobody asked."

"Fucking stupid savages."

"Why we got to dig him up?" William wanted to know.

"Orders, shithead, got orders."

They were alone in what had been the government station, abandoned now to the crabs, the birds, the rats, the few cats and chickens that had escaped the departing colonists and survived the subsequent poisoning of the dogs. No sounds but the rustling of crab claws and the whisper of palm fronds in the wind, the distant boom of surf.

An hour after coming ashore, Keaki still felt disoriented, almost dizzy in the dappled light under the trees, where once everything had been open to the sky. The place was the same, the place was different; time had passed, time had stood still, time had circled around and around.

He and Baiteke – though signed on as seamen aboard RCS *Ninikoria* – had been hired as guides to their old home, to lead the way to Mister Gallagher's grave. Swabbing decks and polishing brightwork on the colony's new ship with its high foc'sle and grumbling engine, they had steamed out of Tarawa and clear across to the Line Islands, to Fanning and Washington and Kirimati, and then down into the Phoenix, to Enderbury and Manra and Orona – all those islands he had heard of for so long but never seen – and now this morning, there had been the darkness on the water, the sun rising, the white birds circling like sparks. He had shut his eyes and almost expected, when he opened them, to turn to his father and ask him about the *Noriti,* watch him hail Jack Kimo in his canoe.

But his father was dead, not at the rail. Mister Kimo was on Tarawa, not in the canoe. Thirty years had flowed past since that morning. Six years since they had all been bundled off Nikumaroro and shipped to the little village in the Solomons, to which they had given the familiar name. Four years since he and Baiteke – restless and broke – had gone up to Tarawa looking for work, and found it at the Catholic mission, and in the ships.

All that time. What was time? How did it happen, why did it pass? He had opened his eyes and found – the sun had leaped into the sky – that the island wasn't quite the same as the one he had awakened to back then. Much of the *buka* forest was gone, replaced by coconut and pandanus. And there was the landing channel the Navy men had blasted through the reef flat when they came to take the people out – looking almost natural now, its raw edges smoothed by algae. There was the tall concrete monument at its head, still shining white but almost lost now in the *mao*.

The four of them had left the ship in the whaleboat with the strange English ladies who were among the *I-Matang* passengers. One of them had babbled happily about taking their pictures digging up the grave, but it had been easy to pretend they didn't understand her, and then lose her at the landing. She had gotten in the shade of the knocked-down water tank by the cooperative store to do something with her picture machine, and they had just melted into the bush. They'd laughed about it as they stumbled through the fallen coconuts and fronds up the "Sir Harry Luke Avenue" toward the Government Station.

The almost invisible avenue. Punctuated with coconut palms and pandanus, and sometimes walls of *mao* they had to chop through or work their way around. Waving their knives ahead of them to fend off the spider webs that draped everything. It had been easy enough, though, to follow the curbs of standing coral slabs that lined the avenue, and keeping track of direction had been a welcome distraction from –

Well, from really seeing the place, Keaki thought. It felt like some kind of *anti* place, where spirits might live in their own fragments of disconnected time. No living people, no pigs; just the occasional chicken or cat. Houses – well-remembered houses – falling down into piles of thatch around stark standing corner posts, leaning gables. Household goods – cans, bottles, pans, a bicycle, tilly lamps – scattered and piled where people had dropped them.

And then they had come to the parade ground – realized they were walking into it, but only because they passed through the gap in the wall that bounded the Government Station. Confirmed their guess by seeing the flagstaff standing straight against the curving lines of the coconut trees, and Mister Gallagher's monument at its foot.

"What if we didn't do it?" Baiteke asked, an aside to Keaki in their own language. .

"Your nun women would be angry."

"What if we didn't tell them?"

"Talk English, fucking savages!" The bos'n barked.

Baiteke shifted from one foot to the other. Keaki did nothing. William laughed and slapped his thigh.

"Baiteke, man, you one smart fellah!"

"Why smart?" the bos'n growled.

"He say, 'what if not do it?' Not dig up that fellah, hey?"

"We got orders, you lazy cannibal, from Cap'n Ward."

"Yessir, but Ceptin Ward, he ain't here!"

"Bos'n," Keaki started to speak up, was cut off.

"Got orders."

"Bos'n," he persisted. "Captain Ward didn't order us get killed, OK? What we do, hey? Dig big hole – two metres deep, maybe more, right next that great heavy concrete monument..."

"Then dig in sideways, hey?" Baiteke continued, "like crabs, hey? Scratch around for them fellah's bones and drag 'em out....."

The bos'n smacked the flagstaff with his thick hand, making it shiver. "And then that fucking rock fall over on us and squash us flat. Fuck that; we'll just bust up the fucking rock."

"With what, bos'n?" William asked, wide-eyed. "These shovels? Coconuts?"

"Why you shitheads not tell me this thing here? Now we got go back to ship, get sledgehammers, unless we can find...."

"Wait, bos 'n, think. Why we s 'posed dig this fellah up?"

"I dunno, orders."

"It's because his mama asked the government to get him," Baiteke said with authority.

"How you know?"

"He was Catholic, I'm Catholic. The Sisters told me."

The bos'n stared at him, silent for a moment. He might or might not have been Christian, but he certainly wasn't Catholic.

"His mama," Baiteke went on, "she's in *Engiran,* and she Catholic. Find out nobody live on island any more, hey? Wrote letter to government and mission. 'My little boy be lonely; you get him, bring him to graveyard....'"

"Catholic thing, hey?"

"Yeah," Keaki said, "and a government thing. *I-Matang* thing, you understand *I-Matang.*"

"O'course; not stupid. *I-Matang* mean white man."

"They think he ought to be in a graveyard on Tarawa, but ..."

"So make stupid black men and brown men dig em up."

"Yeah, that's....."

"And mebbe die when big fucking rock fall on 'em."

"Right, and..."

The bos'n stood silent for a moment, rubbing his chin. Then he laughed – a short, loud bark, and slapped his thigh. "OK, fuckers, here's what we do, hey? We fill up dis coffin with rocks an' stuff, nail her up, and dose sisters never know what dey be burying!"

Baiteke caught Keaki's eye; they both feigned astonishment.

"Oh man! What an idea!" Keaki shouted, slapping Baiteke on the back. "Bos'n, you are one smart fellah! They be all solemn, burying that coffin, and never know...."

"Huh! Put up gravestone, hey? Say dem prayers all serious, sing songs."

"All for a box of rocks."

"We better take off metal fellah, take it with box."

It was quickly done. They pried off the plaque, filled the coffin with coral and pieces of wood to approximate the weight of a skeleton, and nailed it firmly shut. Sat down to admire it, and have a smoke.

"So," William said, eyes going round. "Now what?"

"Too soon go back ship," the bos'n declared. "Not even middle of day. Dey know take long time dig up dat fellah. Say, Baikey, what about dose crabs?"

"Sure," Baiteke said, "lots of crabs, all over. Especially across the passage, there to the north." He gestured toward Nutiran, unseen through the mass of vegetation. "You know how to catch?"

"Hey, I champion crabber, man. Let's get some!"

Keaki crushed his cigarette in the coral. "You guys go on; I think I'll look around the village for awhile. Three-four hours, then I'll take the coffin back to the landing, meet you there."

"OK, suit self. You come, Baikey?"

"Yeah – no, I think I'll stay here with Keaki. I ate enough *ai* to last a lifetime, when we lived here."

"More fool you." The bos'n picked up his knife and strode off into the bush, with William trailing behind.

Silence fell over the parade ground – but for, as always, the sound of wind in the fronds, bird calls, and the dull roar of surf on the windward side. Keaki sat cross-legged on the ground; Baiteke sat on the coffin. They both smoked awhile, looking at the monument.

"He wouldn't want to be moved," Keaki said at last.

"No, and he wouldn't want his monument busted up."

"We all felt good about making that monument."

"Yeah, just like he wanted, like that guy in Samoa."

Keaki smiled wryly, remembering. "Stevenson, the writer. He really liked Stevenson. "

And so did I, he thought, even if I never did figure out why Uncle Erasmus said hoot.

What had happened to Mister Gallagher's books, he wondered, and what was in all the ones he hadn't read? They'd all been packed up and sent to Fiji when *Viti* had visited, way back then, and taken Segalo away. He smiled at that, at how crushed Baiteke had been at her disappearance.

He'd recovered soon enough, made Bueke's daughter Tebaono pregnant and married her, gotten his farm, made toddy, gotten drunk, made boxes for the Coast Guard, farmed, fished, gotten fat.

And he, Keaki? With his daydreams, his puzzles?

"Pretty much the same."

"What?" Baiteke asked. Keaki started; he hadn't realized he had spoken aloud.

"Oh – the government station – looks pretty much the same."

"Are you crazy? There's nobody here."

"Well, aside from that."

Baiteke threw a stone, hit the flagstaff with a loud crack. "I still don't understand why they made us leave."

"It was a vote, remember?"

"I didn't vote to leave. Neither did you."

"No, but enough people did. That's how voting works."

"Whale shit. They lied to us, saying there wasn't enough water.

"Maybe."

"Maybe? You know there was enough rain to fill the cistern. Shit, it's still full."

"Maybe because nobody's drinking from it."

"Look how healthy these trees are."

Keaki lay back on the ground, watched the *kiakias* circling above the palms, against the sky, wondering how many books there were in the world, and what was in them all. And why *had* they had to leave Nikumaroro?

"I don't think the problem was really with the island, or even with the Phoenix."

"What, there was really no rain in *Engiran*, so they moved us off Nikumaroro?"

"No, I think there was no money in *Engiran,* or not enough to do all the things *Engiran* used to do before the war, and they couldn't afford to keep supporting us."

"But we were making money! More copra every year!"

"Yeah, but you know what's been happening to the price of copra."

"Well, yeah. So we had to make choices, like Mister Laxton said, and we all just nodded our heads like boobies and...."

Keaki grimaced. Mister Paul Laxton had come to the island in 1949, charged, he said, with making hard choices, or rather, insisting that the people make them. Those who were willing to stay permanently could do so, but they would have to live on their farms and devote themselves to the coconut crop, make the colony economically self-sufficient within a few years. Those who weren't willing to do this could go back to the islands they had come from, or perhaps find work elsewhere. Most of the people had elected to stay – himself included, because he had nothing else to do, no place to go. Mister Laxton had overseen the final allocation of lands, including lands up on Nutiran, where Keaki had established his farm. They had cut and planted, marked boundaries, torn down their houses in the village and moved them to their farms. Only the bare bones of the government station had been left, and even the parade ground had been planted to coconuts.

That had been the end for Aram. Faced with the choice of watching Mister Gallagher's grave disappear amid the coconuts, watching the Rest House slowly decay, he had gone on a government ship to Canton Island to look for a job. He hadn't even said goodbye.

"Yeah, choices. I wonder what happened to Aram."

"Somebody told me he was on Kiritimati, working for government on those bombing tests." Quite a few people had gone to work on that island where the government had tested bombs like those the Americans had dropped on the Japanese to end the war. Mister Kimo had worked there for quite awhile after being reunited with his family. Edwin and John and their mother had been imprisoned by the Japanese on Ocean Island, and were lucky to have survived. Now they were all on Tarawa, and Mister Kimo didn't work any more.

"We should have looked for him when we stopped at Kiritimati," Keaki mused, but wondered whether Aram had known they were there, and avoided them. "It looked like a pretty nice island."

"Better than rotting Tarawa." People said that Tarawa had been a nice place before the war, but even now, twenty years later, it was a mess. Trees just beginning to mature, replacing all those that had been blown up and rooted out. Still lots of unexploded bombs and mines, the bones of dead Japanese turning up every time someone dug.

"Well, at least there's work on Tarawa."

"I'd rather stay here."

"Our wives would miss us."

"True. Poor ladies."

"Well" – Keaki stretched, scratched his back on the gravel – "So what are we going to do?"

"About Mister Karaka?"

"Yeah."

"Nothing, now. We've decided. The bos'n and William are gone."

"We could still dig him up; we have the shovels. You're the Catholic, who'll go to hell if we do the wrong thing."

"I'll risk it. "I can always do *bure.* Let's go look at the Rest House"

Keaki unfolded himself from the ground and followed his friend through the trees. The Rest House was distinguishable from its surroundings only by being brown, and more angular than the coconut forest. Up close though – the veranda roof had collapsed all along the front, and there were gaps in the thatch of the roof, but otherwise the house looked very much as it had six years ago. Except empty, lonely, somehow fragile, somehow threatening.

"Shall we go inside?" Baiteke started up the walk.

"I don't know..."

"*Anti?*"

"Something like that."

But he followed Baiteke up the steps and into the house. The floor-
boards creaked. Rats scurried across the floor, and a couple of crabs.
Baiteke shook his head.

"Aram – this would break Aram's heart."

"It breaks my heart. How long do you think it'll last?"

"What?"

"The Rest House."

"Pretty much falling apart already. Thatch is all brittle and dry, probably a lot of rot in the posts." Baiteke sat gingerly in one of the *kanawa*
chairs. It creaked threateningly.

"You're going to fall on your ass."

"Yeah," Baiteke sighed, standing up and fumbling in his shorts pocket
for a matchbook and his cigarettes.

"Tumuo put a lot of skill into those chairs."

"It was a good place for Mister Karaka."

"And now look at them."

Keaki shook his head. "Ashes to ashes...."

He walked out onto the lagoon-side veranda, which creaked and shifted
under his weight. In the sunken garden, the bananas were being over-
whelmed by *mao* that had seeded itself there, and a young coconut was
coming up. Behind him the sun was getting lower, gilding the trees across
the lagoon. The birds were beginning to circle, thinking about roosting.
Shark fins rippled the surface of the water. Dust to dust, he thought. *Buka*
to *buka,* except the *buka* weren't coming back, nor the *kanawa.* Instead it
was all feral coconut and pandanus, and *mao, mao, mao.*

A crackling sound behind him. Baiteke, cigarette hanging from his lip,
was leaning against a doorpost, watching a tongue of fire climb the woven
mat wall. Smiling crookedly, Keaki joined him, put his arm around his
shoulder and gave it a squeeze.

They walked together out of the burning house, back to Mister Gallagher's grave monument. Sat on either side of it and watched the flames
sweep up into the thatch. Watched the tall peaked roof explode, twist, and
fall, pulling the water tank with it off the top of the concrete bathroom. It
didn't take long, didn't even make much smoke.

Keaki lit a cigarette, blew smoke at the front of the grave marker.

"*Ao k na toua Manra,* " he whispered, "*ma kanoa ni wam te ungira ma
te taitai...* "[13]

---

[13] And you will tread Manra, and the contents of your canoe will be pandanus...

From Seven Years' Island Hopping, by Roddy Cordon, Volume II, pages 45-4 7, 1998.

Tuesday found us early at Gardner. The purpose of this visit was to disinter the body of a District Commissioner named Gallacher who had died – of appendicitis, I understood, while on duty there. His mother had learned that the island had been evacuated, and she had appealed to the Government to bury him in a populated area such as the headquarters island. So a party of sailors armed with spades, carrying a spare coffin in case of need together with a clean sheet also in case of need, landed and set off for the cemetery. I had just run out of film and I wanted to record this incident, but the sun was so bright that I had to look around for some shade in order to unload and reload the camera. All the shade there was was inside a large broken tank which stood on the shore. I popped inside and effected the change, and when I emerge there was no sign of the landing party. I appealed to Heather Smith, the girl guide leader, who was inspecting shells on the beach, but she hadn't been looking in the right direction, and in spite of our casting around we found no clues except for one wild hen scurrying about.

When we had exhausted this lead we had to give up the idea of following the now invisible party and being in at the recovery scene, so we set out to explore. It seemed that we had the whole island to ourselves, and the atmosphere which pervaded the area was inexpressively peaceful.

The sun was so powerful that we struck into the coconut jungle and came upon a deserted village, once again showing evidence of good planning and careful attention to water storage....

We then struck inland to find the lagoon, and intended to paddle in the clear water, but that intention quickly evaporated as we saw that even in the shallowest water at the edge the lagoon was crowded with small pink triangular fins. We were not brave enough to venture any nearer acquaintance with even one baby shark, let alone a trillion so we just walked along the lagoon side...

Back at the landing stage there was quite a time to wait before we eventually saw a sailor appearing from the north bearing a coffin aslant his shoulder. That was the signal for the boats to come out from the ship, and we were soon on deck, to be met with dark prognostications of rain and heavy weather because we had now a corpse aboard. It did rain, too, that very night.

Notes

Fact and Fiction

Thirteen Bones is constructed around real events that occurred between 1937 and 1950. My descriptions of the places where the events happened, particularly on the now-uninhabited island of Nikumaroro, are based on my own experience and on archaeological evidence. With the exception of a few supporting characters all named individuals are real – or were, virtually all now being deceased. In describing them and their actions, I have tried to be as truthful as allowed by the character of written and oral historical and ethnographic data.

Here are some of the facts I used in imagining *Thirteen Bones*. For details see *Amelia Earhart's Shoes* (King, Jacobson, Burns and Spading 2004), *Finding Amelia* (Gillespie 2006), and updates at www.tighar.org.

The Mystery

On July 2nd, 1937, aviation pioneers Amelia Earhart and Fred Noonan, attempting to circumnavigate the globe at the equator, went missing over the central Pacific Ocean. A vigorous search by the U.S. Navy and Coast Guard yielded no trace of them. Many radio messages were received after the disappearance that were initially thought to be from the Earhart plane, including several that radio direction finding indicated came from the vicinity of the Phoenix Islands in the central Pacific. When floatplanes from the USS *Colorado* flew over the islands several days later and did not locate the lost fliers, the radio messages were dismissed as hoaxes. Earhart's and Noonan's fate remains a mystery that has generated vast speculation and many hypotheses, most of them impossible to test. An exception to this rule is the proposition that Earhart and Noonan landed and died on Nikumaroro.

The Islands

The night before their disappearance, Earhart and Noonan flew over a portion of the Gilbert Islands. The Gilberts, which now make up the bulk of the Republic of Kiribati, are inhabited by people of Micronesian ethnicity and language. Southward lie what were then called the Ellices, now Tuvalu, inhabited by Polynesian speakers. Kiribati and Tuvalu became independent in the late 1970s, and are members of the British Commonwealth. In 1937 they comprised the Crown Colony of the Gilbert and Ellice Islands, overseen by the Western Pacific High Commission (WPHC). The WPHC was responsible not only for the Gilbert and Ellice Islands Colony but for the Solomon Islands Protectorate, Pitcairn Island, British participation in the condominium government of the New Hebrides and New Caledonia, and relations with the Kingdom of Tonga.

Its High Commissioner also served as Governor of Fiji. The WPHC also exercised British sovereignty over the Phoenix and Line Islands, scatterings of mostly uninhabited atolls east of the Gilberts.

The PISS

Some months before the Earhart disappearance, Harry Maude, a young officer in the Colonial Service of the United Kingdom assigned to the Gilbert and Ellice Islands Colony, conceived an idea for relieving growing population stress on some of the colony's islands. He proposed that the WPHC create new coconut-growing communities in the Phoenix Islands. No doubt wondering whether his supervisors would balk at the acronym, he called it the Phoenix Islands Settlement Scheme (PISS).

The PISS was not without a geopolitical rationale. Their mid-Pacific location made the Phoenix Islands strategic assets in the then-anticipated intercontinental aviation industry, and some of them possessed economically important phosphate deposits – derived from millennia of accumulating bird dung. As a result, control of the islands had been for some years the object of more or less desultory competition between the United Kingdom and the United States. In June, 1937, hostilities between the two nations were narrowly averted after both landed colonizing parties on Canton, the largest of the Phoenix Islands. The PISS would be a vigorous assertion of British control.

Nikumaroro

In October of 1937, Harry Maude and his colleague Eric Bevington undertook a voyage of exploration to the Phoenix Islands to assess their suitability for colonization. Accompanying them were ten delegates from the Gilbert Islands, among them Koata, native magistrate of the island of Onotoa. A Roman Catholic, Koata was well known for his role in putting down a 1930 uprising by radical Protestants on his home island, in which he narrowly escaped death before Harry Maude arrived to get matters under control.

One of the islands on which the party landed was then (and occasionally is still today) known as Gardner Island. Finding it imminently suitable for settlement, Koata and his fellow delegates named it Nikumaroro. In the traditions of the Gilbert Islands, Nikumaroro was an island lying under the lee (downwind) of Samoa and richly endowed (as was "Gardner") with *buka* trees (<u>Pisonia grandis</u>). It was the home of Nei Manganibuka, an ancestress who brought the *buka* tree and the art of navigation to the Gilberts. Deeply revered, Nei Manganibuka has a dark side; in one tradition she kills her parents once they have taught her everything she needs to know, and in others she takes several forms of vengeance on her brothers after they abandon her at sea.

Nikumaroro is a coral atoll, about four miles long and a mile and a half wide including its central lagoon. It rises only some ten meters out of the sea at its maximum elevation. Heavily wooded, it was inhabited in 1937 only by a host of seabirds, rats, and crabs, including the giant coconut crab <u>Birgus latro</u>. The center of its lagoon is at latitude 4 30'46" south, longitude 174°31'06" west; the reader can navigate to it by name on Google Earth.

Gallagher

On 5 July 1937 – three days after Earhart went missing – Gerald Bernard Gallagher was accepted as a Cadet in the British Colonial Service, and assigned to the WPHC. On 17 July he sailed for the Pacific. At the time, the High Commissioner was Sir Arthur Richards; in late 1938 he was succeeded by Sir Harry Luke, a long-time colonial official with deep roots in the Middle East. The WPHC was headquartered in Suva, Fiji, but Gallagher was assigned to the Gilbert and Ellice Islands Colony; he reported for duty at that colony's headquarters on Ocean Island (now Banaba) on 14 September.

Gallagher was of Irish ancestry and a devout Roman Catholic, described by one of his contemporaries as "the most Christ-like man I have ever met." His father, Gerald Hugh Gallagher, served as a colonial medical officer in west Africa; his mother, Edith, was a Londoner. His younger brother Terrence was (at the time of his death in 1942) a lance corporal in the Royal Irish Fusiliers. Before joining the Colonial Service, Gerald worked for a time in agriculture, attended Stonyhurst College, Cambridge University (Downing College), and St. Barthomew's Hospital Medical School, and – about the same time he joined the Service – learned to fly and obtained a private pilot's license.

The Settlers

In December 1938 the PISS was launched, with settlers established on Sydney Island (under its new name of Manra) and Hull Island (whose name became Orona). A ten-man working party was landed on Nikumaroro/Gardner under Koata's supervision, to clear brush and plant coconuts preparatory to settlement. Over the next two years the population of Nikumaroro grew modestly as settlers and relatives were landed. Among these were Ieiera, from Arorae atoll in the southern Gilberts, his wife Boik-abane, their 10-year-old son Keaki, and 8-year-old daughter Taberiki. Another immigrant family was Takena from Onotoa with his wife Karirea and his children Merina, Tarema, Beia, and Baiteke. The settlers established a village and a government station toward the northwest end of the island, along the shore of the main channel connecting its lagoon with the sea.

Gerald Gallagher became Maude's second in command of the PISS, and when Maude was reassigned to Pitcairn Island in mid-1940, Gallagher became the scheme's administrator. He resided at first on Sydney/Manra, but in August or September of 1940 he moved his headquarters to Niku-maroro and embarked on an ambitious development program – intending, it was said, to make the island "the model island of the Phoenix". He was ably supported by Jack Kimo Petro, the colony's public works officer. Petro was descended from a shipwrecked Portugese mariner in the Ellice Islands, now Tuvalu, who had married into an island family. He was renowned for his ability to design and build virtually anything, and to make any mechanized equipment run.

The Skeleton

Sometime in early to mid-1940, the colonists on Nikumaroro discovered a human cranium near the southeast end of the island. The subsequent history of this skull and its associated bones and artifacts are the subjects of considerable WPHC documentation.

TIGHAR

Since 1989, Nikumaroro has been the focus of historical, oral historical, archaeological and other research by The International Group for Historic Aircraft Recovery (TIGHAR). It is this research that motivated and equipped me to undertake this novel, but I alone am responsible for any errors of fact or interpretation.

The Island In 2009

At this writing, in 2009, Nikumaroro is as devoid of human inhabitants as it was in 1937, though a good deal of its aboriginal buka forest has given way to feral coconut and pandanus, and to tangled masses of mao (Scaevola frutescens). The ruins of the colonial village and Government Station can still be detected near its northwest end. On the opposte end are the remains of a World War II-era U.S. Loran Station. Not far away is a peculiar archaeological site – called the Seven Site – that features evidence of cooking fires, the consumption of birds, fish, sea turtles, and giant clams, and an enigmatic set of activities involving a small house roofed with corrugated steel and many sheets of corrugated iron scattered on the ground. Nikumaroro today retains an ethereal beauty, a mystic quality that tempts some visitors to imagine spectral shapes among the trees, supernatural forces at work. In a few decades, however, it most likely will be gone, lost to the inexorable rise of the world's sea levels. Already erosion is chewing at the shoreline of Karaka village, and house sites are disappearing steadily as the ocean advances on the central parade ground with its well-marked grave.

Chapter Notes

Prologue

<u>Earhart's passing:</u> My account of Earhart's death is entirely imagined, of course, but is consistent with the archaeological and historical evidence; see *Amelia Earhart's Shoes* for details.

<u>The crabs:</u> Nikumaroro supports a large population of coconut or robber crabs, <u>Birgus latro.</u> <u>B. latro</u> is probably the largest living arthropod in the world, with a body that can be almost the size of a basketball and pincer arms that can extend two feet or more out on each side. In its juvenile form it is a hermit crab, taking up residence in a discarded gastropod shell that it carries around with it, changing shells as it grows. As an adult it develops a hard, dark brown-to-purple exoskeleton. It is an omnivore, famous for being able to open a coconut and capable of reducing a mammalian carcass to a skeleton in a matter of days. See www.coconutcrab.co.uk/ for details. Nikumaroro is also home to a huge population of strawberry hermit crabs <u>(Coenobita perlatus)</u> and other land crabs of all sizes.

<u>Koata and Mautake:</u> Harry Maude, who as a British colonial officer conceived of and organized the Phoenix Islands Settlement Scheme (PISS) of the Western Pacific High Commission (WPHC), wrote of his exploratory expedition to the islands in *Of Islands and Men*, (Oxford, London), which was published under his editorship in 1968 (See www.tighar.org/Projects/Earhart/Documents/Maude.html). He writes: "The mainstay of the expedition was undoubtedly my own personal staff, consisting of Tem Mautake, the First Assistant to the Native Lands Commission and an acknowledged expert on all aspects of native custom; Teng Koata, the Magistrate of Onotoa, whose exceptional qualities of loyalty and leadership had been proved in the Onotoa religious troubles of 1931...." Paul Laxton, a subsequent Phoenix Islands administrator, writes of the colony's founding in his 1951 *Journal of the Polynesian Society* article, "Nikumaroro" (www.tighar.org/Projects/Earhart/Documents/laxton.html), says: "The old men and the people named the island. Home of Nei Manganibuka they called it, the tall fair-skinned goddess who came from Samoa to teach canoe-craft and the lore of ocean navigation...."

<u>Mister Mauta, Mister Eric:</u> Eric Bevington, Harry Maude's colleague in the 1937 expedition, wrote in his journal for 13th October 1937: "After breakfast I made an easy landing across the reef end walked across the shallow inner reef- lagoon. It was teeming with fish, undisturbed for years by

humans. Coral fish and animals were visible everywhere, of colours varying from bright oranges, and reds, to blue and greens of the richest hues.
There was truly the most amazing romantic feeling – an uninhabited coral
island. Everywhere were fish, birds, and teeming life. Overhead thousands
of sea birds wheeled and soared – there were terns, frigates, boobies, and
many other. The natives added to the general excitement; here were their
own natural foods, in masses and easily caught. Maude' s lumbago was bad,
so I was to take the Gilbertese round the island, walking so we could see
everything of it" (See www.tighar.org/Projects/Earhart/Documents/ Bevington Diary.html).

Naming the island: Maude, in "The Colonization..." pp 328-9,
describes Nikumaroro and his visit of 13 October 1937, saying: "Gardner
(Island) was ... inevitably called 'Nikumaroro,' after the home island of a
Gilbertese ancestress, Nei Manganibuka, who swam from her home *i-an
Tamoa* (under the lee of Samoa) to Nikunau in the Southern Gilberts, bear-
ing the branch of the first *buka* tree in her mouth."

Chapter One

Teng Beiaruru 's story: Beiaruru's tale is loosely derived from one told
by H.C. and H.E. Maude in *An Anthology of Gilbertese Oral Tradition,*
"The First Voyage of Te Kaburtoro," (Maude & Maude 1994:120-22).

Poop-talk. Some sources on the colloquial use of language in Kiribati
report that *kang butae,* "eat shit," is a common bantering greeting among I
Kiribati (Tungaru) teen-age boys. Having (with some regret) not spent
much time with I Kiribati teen-age boys, I cannot testify that this is cur-
rently the case, and given the volatility of adolescent and subadolescent
humor I certainly cannot say with any authority that it was the case in 1939.
The boys would hardly have been boys without some means of teasing one
another, however, and since even by the permissive standards of Oceania
they were a bit young for sex, I have guessed that their humor was scato-
logical.

Arrival at Nikumaroro: Harry Maude, in a memorandum report on the
April 1939 settlement expedition to Phoenix Islands, wrote: "Gardner
Island was reached on the 27th and, to the general relief, smoke was seen rising from the site of the new settlement, there having been no opportunity of
getting into touch with the island since February, when the British Pacific
Airways Survey Party left with their wireless set." (Maude memorandum of
29th November 1939). The survey party to which Maude alluded was from
New Zealand, and was on the island from late 1938 until early February
1939, studying its suitability as an aerodrome. The ten-man working party
left by Maude on the island arrived in late December 1938.

Chapter Two

The shipwreck: The SS *Norwich City* was fighting a storm on the night of 29 November, 1929 when she ran full tilt onto the Nikumaroro reef. At the time, the island was misplaced by several miles on nautical charts. The ship caught fire and burned, and eleven men died — five British sailors and six Arab firemen. The remainder of the crew got ashore and remained there for five days, much tormented by rats and coconut crabs, before rescue ships were able to take them off. They found the bodies of three of those lost, and buried them; they also left a cache of excess supplies against the needs of future castaways. A photo labeled "wreck survivors' camp," taken by a survey party from New Zealand in late 1938, shows what presumably is this cache, reduced to a litter of containers, as though someone had dismantled it and consumed whatever was edible. See www.tighar.org /Projects/Earhart/Documents/Documents index.html#20 for copies of original documents.

Asbestos: The dangers to public health posed by asbestos were of course not known in 1939. The corrugated asbestos on Nikumaroro has held up remarkably well, and remains scattered about the village in considerable quantity.

Returnees: In his first progress report on the PISS, Harry Maude wrote: "With one exception, however, the Arorae workers have not adapted themselves as successfully as was hoped to the very arduous conditions on the island and it has been found necessary to select further workers from other islands. .... (I)t is proposed to return 5 of the working party on Gardner to their homes, carefully selected substitutes having been chosen" (Maude, , First Progress Report, Phoenix Islands Settlement Scheme, p 18). In his subsequent memorandum on the 1939 settlement visit (cited in the last chapter), he reports that "(t)he ship was boarded by Mr. J. Pedro, Artisan in Charge of work on the island, who gave a glowing account of the progress made since I had left the island on the 15th January and the way in which the whole community had, without exception, maintained their health and spirits." Nevertheless, the Arorae workers were apparently returned to their home islands; as of 30th June 1939, in the first full census we have of Nikumaroro residents, only five members of the original ten-man working party were present (Koata, Abera, Kirata, Takena, and Babera).

Chapter 3

The *Swan's* crew: Mr. Ron Bright kindly supplied me with copies of entries from U.S.S. *Swan's* deck log for 28th April 1939, together with the names of Lt. Greenslade and his officers. The log, signed by Lt. JG Thomas Griffin, notes that at "1800 Mr Gerald B, Gallagher, Territorial Representative of the British Government at Sydney arrived on board for dinner," and that he departed at 2100. At 2321 the ship was underway for Orona, whence it sailed on to Nikumaroro. In a telegram dated 29th April, Gallagher reported to the Resident Commissioner on Ocean Island (now Banaba) that "U.S.S. 'Swan' and 'Pelican' visited Sydney Island with two seaplanes on the 28th . April for the purpose of taking aerial survey pictures." He went on to say that his wireless had been down so he had received no instructions, but that since the ships' work had been allowed on Canton and Enderbury, he had raised no objection (Gallagher, 29th April 1939).

Gallagher's lack of shoes: Harry Maude arrived at Manra aboard *Moamoa* on the 29th (which probably allowed Gallagher to send his telegram to Ocean Island). In his *Of Islands and Men* chapter on the PISS Maude comments that Gallagher's "shoes... had long succumbed to the sharp coral rock and his feet were bound up in layers of rags. If I remember rightly, he wore size thirteens, so the provision of shoes for him was a perpetual difficulty. (Maude 1968:337).

Chapter 4

The sky canoes: The aerial photographs taken by the planes can today be accessed at www.tighar.com.

The visit of the New Zealanders: The report of the New Zealand Pacific Aviation Survey Expedition of 1938-39 can be accessed at www.tighar. org/Projects/Earhart/Documents/Documents_index.html#25, together with a report and a journal by two members of the expedition. The group camped on the northwest end of the island, which came to be known as "Nutiran."

Islanders' reaction to Americans: The U.S. and Great Britain had been in competition for the Phoenix Islands since the mid-19th century, first because of their value as sources of phosphates in the form of semi-fossilized bird guano, then because they were seen as potentially useful in transpacific aviation. Hence the New Zealand survey of 193 8-39, and the interest of the U.S. Navy in obtaining airphotos. In 1939, Pan American World Airways was planning to establish a base for its transpacific Clipper service on Canton Island, about 200 miles northeast of Nikumaroro. For details of the competition see Maude 1940 and MacDonald 2001.

Mister Kimo's visit to the American ships: The deck log of the U.S.S. *Pelican* documents that "Mr. Jack Pedro, foreman of Gardner Island and two natives came aboard" at 1120 hours. At 1240 one of the planes was hoisted on board. Between 1405 and 1513 the three island residents left the ship, Jack Petro being the last to leave (See King et al 2004:311). It is not clear whether they departed in separate canoes or if one canoe came and went several times.

Chapter 6

The cistern: The cistern with its corrugated asbestos roof was still shedding and collecting water in 2007.

Chapter 7

Nei Aana's religion: I imagine Nei Aana as a vigorous traditionalist because of her self- described encounter with Nei Manganibuka (See Chapter 10). In the Gilbert and Ellice Islands as elsewhere in the world, the Catholic Church was relatively tolerant of traditional spiritual beliefs. The London Missionary Society (LMS), the primary Protestant institution in the area, was much less so.

Chapter 8

Protestant revolt on Onotoa: Harry Maude, who with the Protestant mission leader Reverend Eastman brought this event under control, described it in detail in a 1967 *Journal of Pacific History* article; see Maude 1967).

Coconut toddy: One tiny part of the vast archive of information on Kiribati contained in the web pages of Dame Jane Resture (who was born on Manra) is a discussion of the making and drinking of coconut toddy; see www.janeresture.com/kiribati_food/index.htm. My personal experience with toddy is from a 1978 boat trip to the island of Ramung in Yap, where a seemingly unending supply of bottles was passed around continuously. I recall Ramung as a lovely and fascinating place, but my memories are extraordinarily vague.

Chapter 9

Scavenging from the shipwreck: Archaeological work at the carpenter's house site in the colonial village – almost certainly Jack Kimo Petro's residence when he was on the island – has yielded an array of machine parts and fittings, many of which appear to be from the *Norwich City*. Artifact #2-4-V-17, found in 1997 at another house site in the village, was once a brass clock, subsequently used as a tar pot.

Chapter 10

Aubunga: There are hundreds of fist-sized giant clam – genus *Tridacna* – valves on the shelving coral shore next to the peninsula called "Kanawa Point" by the New Zealand survey party, and mapped at the time as covered with the tree called Cordia subchordata by biologists. The embayment formed by the shoreline and the peninsula was and is home to large schools of *baneawa* fish.

Nei Aana's encounter: In his 1951 article "Nikumaroro," Paul Laxton writes of the "lagoon peninsula, (where) Ten Aram showed the site of the 'ghost *maneaba.*' The wife of Teng Koata, the first island leader, had been walking one afternoon and saw a great and perfect *maneaba,* and sitting under its high thatched roof, Nei Manganibuka, a tall fair woman with long dark hair falling to the ground about her, with two children: she conversed with three ancients, talking of her island of Nikumaroro, and its happy future when it would surely grow to support thousands of inhabitants. Nearby, on either side of the peninsula two large pools form on the lagoon flats, filling on the high springs, when tens of thousands of tiny young *baneawa* fish take refuge in them from the ravenous *ulua* which prey on them in the deep water" (Laxton 1951).

Chapter 11

The wreck: The grounding of the *Nimanoa* was the subject of a board of inquiry held aboard HMS *Wellington* at Funafuti on 18th July 1939. The report of the board, in the WPHC files, concludes that "the cause of the grounding was that the engine failed to go astern owing to a seized master air control valve."

Gallagher's Tungaru language ability: Since his arrival in the western Pacific in 1937, Gerald Gallagher had spent a considerable time in what were then called the Ellice Islands, and learned the Polynesian Tuvaluan language spoken there. According to Western Pacific High Commission records now in the Kiribati National Archives, however, he did not pass his lower standard government language examination in "Gilbertese," the language of the people long known as Tungaru and now called I Kiribati, until 20th July 1941.

Chapter 12

The voyage of the cement mixer: In a 2005 conversation with TIGHAR's Van Hunn and me in Majuro, Republic of the Marshall Islands, the late Edwin Petro assured us that his father had conveyed his cement mixer from island to island on a raft towed by canoes. Aside from this assurance, this chapter is wholly an invention.

Taberiki's treasure. In 1991, TIGHAR researchers found a piece of plexiglass at a house site in the ruins of the colonial village. Its thickness and curvature were consistent with that of the windows in Amelia Earhart's Lockheed Electra 10E. It had been cut up, perhaps to make goggle lenses. See *Amelia Earhart's Shoes,* p. 157.

Chapter 13

The remarkable Rest House lavatory: As of 2007, the concrete lavatory still stood – all that remained standing of the Rest House – complete with claw-footed bathtub.

Chapter 14

Maneaba and boti: The *maneaba* and the *boti* have been widely described and discussed in the ethnographic literature on Kiribati/Tungaru. See for instance pages 197-254 of *Tungaru Traditions* (Grimble 1989), and *The Gilbertese Maneaba* (Maude 1985).

USS *Bushnell's* visit: The key dates, events, and American personnel described in this chapter – including the conflict over work on Sunday – are based on a number of reports, memoranda, and journals maintained or produced at the time aboard USS *Bushnell,* photocopies of which are in TIGHAR's files and scheduled to be available on TIGHAR's "Ameliapedia" via www.tighar.org.

Chapter 15

Towers, etc.: Like the preceding chapter, this one is based primarily on TIGHAR's files of documents produced by USS *Bushnell* during her survey.

Nikumaroro for Catholics: Apparently on at least one occasion, Koata proposed that the island be reserved entirely for Catholics. An 8th July 1940 telegram in Tungaruan from Gallagher to Koata says (in rough translation: "Tell people on Gardner that the High Commissioner does not agree with the application made by them for settling only Catholic members on Gardner - tell them not to worry about this" (From file KNA 11, Kiribati National Archives; photocopy in TIGHAR files).

Chapter 16

Arrival of Tumuo: See *Amelia Earhart's Shoes,* pp 27 8-79 regarding arrival on Nikumaroro of the future Mrs. Emily Sikuli, then known as Segalo, and her family. In 1999 Mrs. Sikuli told us that her father, Temou Samuela, was an accomplished canoe builder, carpenter and fisherman.

The *kanawa* grove: Aerial photos taken by aircraft from USS *Pelican* in April 1939 appear to show a small grove of large trees at what today is referred to as the "Seven Site" near the southeast end of the island. These trees are not visible in later air photos, and are not there today. There is archaeological evidence at the Seven Site that we believe represents logging activities. Gerald Gallagher, in his report to Suva quoted in Chapter 33, mentions that at least one *kanawa* tree had been cut in the vicinity.

Chapter 17

Corrugated iron: In the 1880s, the entrepreneur John Arundel placed a crew of Nieue Islanders on what would become Nikumaroro, to begin a coconut plantation. Records of his enterprise now in the Kiribati National Archives reveal that he imported corrugated iron to build structures in support of the effort, which failed. At the time the PISS colony was established, all that remained of Arundel's plantation were scattered groves of coconuts and, presumably, the remains of a building or two, which we think would have been on Nutiran. Today, the rusted remnants of corrugated iron sheets litter the "Seven Site" at the southeast end of the island, where Arundel's men are not known to have planted any coconuts.

Chapter 18

Koata's considerations: My imagining of Koata's thoughts and decisions about the dead are based mostly on Arthur Francis Grimble's *Tungaru Traditions,* pp. 65-80 – a section fittingly titled "Death." Also see H.C. and H.E. Maude's *An Anthology of Gilbertese Oral Tradition.* As for the Benedictine bottle : The Sisters of the Good Samaritan, a Benedictine order, established a girls' boarding school near Brisbane, Queensland, in 1916; it continues in operation today as Lourdes Hill College. Onotoa had (and has) a substantial Catholic population. Beyond these facts and sources, my reconstruction of Koata's thoughts is pure fantasy.

Chapter 19

Koata's treatment of the skull: The ceremony described is based on depictions of Tungaru mortuary ritual by Grimble in *Tungaru Traditions.* His chant is based on one quoted by Grimble on pages 65-66 of the same book.

Catching his canoe: According to Grimble (*Tungaru Traditions* pp. 76-77), the passage of a light rain shower while someone lay dying was regarded as a sure sign that his or her ghost would have a smooth passage to the next world, and was associated with a safe voyage by canoe.

The slipway: As of 2007 when we recorded their distribution in detail, some of the corrugated iron sheets at what we call the Seven Site were still aligned, forming a row starting at the crest of the surge ridge and running downslope toward the lagoon. A few others were embedded in the lagoon-shore, roughly aligned with those on the ridge.

The men's song: This song is adapted from one recounted by Harry Maude on pp. 332-33 of his book, *Of Islands and Men,* sung by some of the Phoenix Island colonists before leaving their home islands.

Chapter 20

The sickness: In his second quarter PISS progress report (5th July 1940), Gallagher notes that: "(t)here is evidence on Gardner Island that the European food on which the labourers are living is beginning to have ill effects. Several natives are suffering from boils and minor skin complaints, whilst one case of incipient scurvy was noticed" (apparently during his short visit to the island, mentioned in the same report).

Chapter 21

Round object in the water on which Eddie sits: Greg Stone of the New England Aquarium, who first visited the island in 2002 (See "Phoenix Islands: a Coral Reef Wilderness Revealed," *National Geographic Magazine* February 2004), reported seeing what appeared to be the axle of a wheel, similar to those on Amelia Earhart's Lockheed Electra, embedded in the coral on the shore of Tatiman Passage not far from the site of the house where Teruio and his family once lived. A careful search for this "wheel of fortune" by a small TIGHAR team in 2003 revealed nothing, but a large storm had recently gone through, possibly moving it (See King et al 2004:358-66).

Jack Kimo's return: It is difficult to reconstruct Jack Kimo's movements, but it he seems to have returned to Nikumaroro around this time, and Gallagher's travel to the Gilberts is documented both in his quarterly reports and in *Titiana,* Kenneth Knudson's 1964 report on the Manra colony.

Chapter 22

Thatch from Orona: In his third quarter 1940 PISS progress report, Gallagher says that houses on Nikumaroro were built using "materials obtained from the demolition of the old islanders' dwelling houses at Hull Island."

Koata's navigational prowess: Eric Bevington tells this story about Mautake, Koata's fellow elder delegate on the 1937 expedition (Bevington 1990: 15-16; I've taken the liberty of putting it in Jack Kimo's mouth and applying it to the Onotoan.

Gallagher's request for *kanawa:* In an 18th June 1940 telegram found in the Kiribati National Archives, Gallagher (apparently on Beru) asked Jack Kimo Petro on Nikumaroro "whether there are forty kanawa trees on Gardner good enough to send to Rongorongo to be sawn into planks." Jack replied: *"kanawa* trees over hundred on Gardner." See King et al 2004:33 8).

Chapter 23

Keaki's method of *co:m* delivery: The "love stick" is a traditional courtship device in Chuuk, and a popular handicraft item with tourists today.

Chapter 24

The uprising: Like the mention of the event in Chapter 8, Koata's recollection of the Onotoa uprising as recounted here is based on "The Swords of Gabriel. A Study in Participant History" (Maude 1967).

Chapter 25

Mister Gallagher's arrival: Gallagher describes his relocation to Nikumaroro in his eighth progress report; see www.tighar.org/Projects/Earhart/ Documents/Gallagher_Report2.html.

The bathtub: The bathtub was still there as of 2007.

Aram's earlier time on Nikumaroro: In 1989, we found a small, broken patch of hardened cement not far from the ruins of the Rest House. While it had still been fluid, what appears to be the name "Aram Tamia" and the date "10/2/39" (10th February 1939) had been scratched into it. Though Maude, in his PISS progress report, says the staff had been withdrawn from the island before this date (water having been found), I can think of no other reason for Aram to have been on the island so early, and speculate that he simply did not have a firm grip on the date.

Gallagher as pilot: "Flying helmet" is listed in the inventory taken of Gallagher's effects after his death; see www.tighar.org/Projects/Earhart/ Documents/Gallagereffects.html. Gallagher's nephew, Gerard Gallagher of Edinburgh, has told TIGHAR that his uncle learned to fly and was licensed to do so while at Cambridge.

What the wireless said: Based on contemporary broadcasts available in textual and/or audio form on various websites (for instance at
http://news.bbc.co.uk/onthisday/hi/dates/stories/july/10/newsid_35160 00/3516193.stm and www.authentichistory.com/ww2/index.html)

Chapter 26

Stevenson's monument: Robert Lewis Stevenson's grave monument is a concrete structure in the shape of a small, peaked-roofed house on a concrete base; it stands on Mt. Vaea in Samoa (See for instance
http://en.wikipedia.org/wiki/Robert_Louis_Stevenson#Monuments_and_commemoration).

Chapter 27
Telegrams: The complete text of all correspondence about the bones discovery can be accessed at www.tighar.org/Projects/Earhart/Documents/ Bones Chronology.html.

Chapter 28
The windowscreen: We have found many small cut fragments of copper windowscreen on the Seven Site during archaeological investigations there. We now think they may have been left by the castaway, perhaps in trapping fish on the reef.

Arundel: The late Harry Maude was fascinated by Arundel, and was researching his career shortly before his death in 2003. He discussed Arundel on Nikumaroro in *Of Islands and Men,* p. 326 (www.tighar. org/Projects/Earhart/Documents/maude.html).

Kirata's embarassment: A telegram by Gallagher on 28th April 1941 says that part of what was probably an inverting eyepiece was found but "thrown away by finder." See www.tighar.org/Projects/Earhart/ Documents/Bones Chronology4.html.

Telegram: Text and discussion at www.tighar.org/Projects/Earhart/ Documents/Bones Chronology.html.

Chapter 29
Telegrams: Text and discussion at www.tighar.org/Projects/Earhart/ Documents/Bones Chronology.html.

Chapter 30:
Telegrams: Text and discussion at www.tighar.org/Projects/Earhart/ Documents/Bones Chronology.html.

Chapter 31
Moving the houses: Gallagher's ninth (fourth quarter 1940) PISS progress report (See www.tighar.org/Projects/Earhart/Documents/ Gallagher Report.html) describes the work done to relocate the village and construct the government station.

Chapter 32
Tank and tarpaper: The tank, identified from an aerial photograph, was what first drew TIGHAR to the Seven Site in 1996. The roll of asphalt siding was soon discovered on the nearby surge ridge. Both remained on the site in 2007.

Progress report: The complete text is at www.tighar.org/Projects/
Earhart/Documents/Gallagher Report.html

Chapter 33

Covering up the _aubunga:_ In archaeological work at the Seven Site in
2001, we found a layer of fiberglass flecks from asphalt roofing paper –
obviously the decayed remnants of material pulled off the roll that lies
nearby – extending out to the southeast from the vicinity of the Tridacna
clam scatter we called Clambush 1.

The casket: We do not know what the casket actually looked like. My
description is based on a _kanawa_ box shown to us by Mr. Foua Tofiga of
Suva, a Tuvaluan retired civil servant who served on the WPHC staff with
Sir Harry Luke, and who received the box in Tuvalu as a wedding present.

Gallagher's letter: Text and discussion are at www.tighar.org/Projects/
Earhart/Documents/Bones Chronology2.html. This document was apparently not telegraphed but was transmitted as a hard paper copy with the casket and sextant box to Suva.

Chapter 34

German raiders: The sinking of the _Rangitane_ and the subsequent
attack on ships off Nauru are described at www.thebells.btinternet.
co.uk/rangitane/story.htm, among other sources.

Dr. Isaac's interest in the casket: I am grateful to Ms. Denise Murphy
of Hong Kong, who played in Dr. Isaac's (then Verrier)'s home in Suva as a
child, for the information that he collected boxes.

Chapter 35

Isaac's note: Text and discussion at www.tighar.org/Projects/Earhart/
Documents/Bones Chronology2.html.

Gallagher's attitude toward Isaac: Distaste for Isaac, often with allusions to his homosexuality, has been commonly expressed by former colonial officers with whom my colleagues and I have spoken or corresponded.
Those acquainted with him in non-official capacities have expressed far
more favorable opinions of him, and he is remembered in Fiji with considerable respect and fondness as a kind, generous, and productive – if eccen-
tric – intellectual, writer, and political figure. See for instance Mara
1997:18-19, 21, 80-81).

Correspondence regarding Isaac's handling of the bones, etc.: For test
and discussion see www.tighar.org/Projects/Earhart/Documents/Bones
Chronology3 .html.

Gallagher's deleted offer to Isaac: It was in this crossed-out form that
we found Gallagher's note in the Kiribati National Archives. Apparently the
file was one brought from Nikumaroro in hard copy after Tarawa was re-

taken from the Japanese, since all files on Tarawa at the time of the Japanese invasion were destroyed.

Isaac's response to Gallagher. See www.tighar.org/Projects/Earhart/Documents/Bones_Chronology3.html for text and discussion. It is Isaac's reference to a "guillotine conversation" – that is, a conversation cut off in some manner – that makes me suspect that Isaac and Gallagher had occasion to converse, and hence leads me to imagine Isaac aboard *Nimanoa* when she made her circuit of the Phoenix Islands and collected the bones. Since Gallagher's wireless did not give him voice communication with Tarawa, he and Isaac could hardly otherwise have had a "conversation," guillotined or otherwise.

Solving the *boti* problem. In *Titiana,* Kenneth Knudson (1965: 51) recounts the story of how Gallagher dealt with this problem on Manra. Laxton (1951; see www.tighar.org/Projects/Earhart/Documents/laxton.html) describes how the permanent *maneaba* on Nikumaroro, when it was finally built in 1949, was named *Uen Maungan i Karaka,* "an idiomatic phrase which may be equally translated 'Flower to the Memory of Gallagher' and 'The Flowering of Gallagher's Achievement.' Thus they commemorate the English gentleman whose devotion and leadership made their new home possible."

Land demarcation. Galagher's first quarterly PISS report for 1941 mentions that "(w)ork was also commenced on the demarcation of land-holdings on southwest side of the island."

Allocation of the skull place. Gallagher's own map of land plots on the southeast end of the island has not been found, but an undated (but post-1943) map found in the Kiribati National Archives (reproduced on page 337 of *Amelia Earhart's Shoes*) shows the only plot in the area, at approximately the location of the what we now call the Seven Site, assigned to "Komitina" (Commissioner). A 1954 map (shown on page 338 of *Amelia Earhart's Shoes*) shows what appears to be roughly the same parcel assigned to "Karaka."

Viaiaga and Maria. Both are mentioned in Dr. MacPherson's report (Chapter 43); it is not clear, however, precisely when they arrived.

Chapter 37

Tirosi's telegram: We do not have this telegram, but think it likely that one like it exists or at least existed (many records were lost during World War II). We know the bones arrived in Suva by late March of 1941, when Gallagher's transmittal letter was added to the files and Drs. Hoodless and Steenson at the Central Medical School began examining the bones and the artifacts respectively.

Gallagher's instructions to Iokina: This note is in the Kiribati National Archives; a copy is in TIGHAR's files. A rough translation into English indicates instructions of a routine nature.

Chapter 38

Gallagher's seasickness. MacPherson (see Chapter 43) describes Gallagher as prone to seasickness. Susan Woodburn, in *Where Our Hearts Still Lie,* her 2004 biography of Harry Maude and his wife Honor, mentions the corkscrew motion that *Nimanoa* made when under power, which made Mrs. Maude dread travelling in her.

The *Viti:* HMFS (or RCS) *Viti* is described at www.nzmaritime.co.nz/viti.htm.

The meeting: I have no documentation to prove that this high-seas rendezvous actually occurred, but suspect that something of the kind did. *Nimanoa* is documented as departing Orona, apparently after stopping at Nikumaroro and collecting Gallagher, on 14th June. Sir Harry, in his *From a South Seas Journal* (1945:195-96) says he sailed from Suva in *Viti* at midnight on 15th June, accompanied by Charlton, McGusty, Wise, Nightengale, MacQuire, and Gallagher, "who has arrived today from the Phoenix Islands in the *Nimanoa.*" It is impossible for *Nimanoa* or any other vessel afloat at that time (or this, as far as I know) to cover the thousand miles between Orona and Fiji in two days. It may be simply that the records of *Nimanoa's* movements are wrong, or that Sir Harry misremembered dates in compiling his journal, but it is also not impossible that *Viti* intercepted *Nimanoa* at sea so Sir Harry could bring Gallagher aboard and explain his mission in private. My premise that MacQuire was an intelligence officer is based only on the fact that I have not found him identified as anything else, in Sir Harry's book or in the WPHC files we have examined.

Putting a stop to Isaac's quarantine: See the 14th February 1941 telegram at www.tighar.org/Projects/Earhart/Documents/Bones Chronology3 .html.

Examination of the bones. The fact that MacPherson, who served as the forensics instructor at the Central Medical School, was not the one who analyzed the bones remains an unexplained peculiarity. David Hoodless had more recent medical training, but is not documented to have had any particular expertise in forensics or osteology. See *Amelia Earhart's Shoes,* Chapter 21 (King et al 2004) for discussion of Dr. Hoodless's analysis and our reasons for thinking the bones may nevertheless be Earhart's.

Gallagher's "castaway" memo. Text and discussion are at www.tighar.org/Projects/Earhart/Documents/Bones Chronology5.html. Gallagher's allusion to the impenetrable brush is odd if not disingenuous, since all one would have to do to get around the *mao* between the southeast end and Arundel's plantings on the northwest would be to walk along the beach.

Chapter 39

The aeroplane: This description follows one given us by Mrs. Emily Sikuli of Suva, formerly known as Segalo, the daughter of Tumuo Samuela. She said her father had shown her the aeroplane wreck. See www.tighar.org/Projects/Earhart/Bulletins/15_Carpentersdaught/15_Interviews.html for details. As of 2007 there was a patch of red algae at the approximate location where Mrs. Sikuli said the wreck had lain.

Chapter 40

Bones on the Nutiran reef: Veterans of the Nikumaroro colony now living in the village of Nikumaroro in the Solomon Islands told Dr. Dirk Ballendorf that human bones had been found at both ends of the island (See www.tighar.org/TTracks/12_1/solomon.html). Emily Sikuli was more explicit about the northern bones, though she seemed (to me) to conflate the story with that of the bones on the southeast end. In any event, she said the northern bones were found in the water on the reef near the *Norwich City*. See www.tighar.org/Projects/Earhart/Bulletins/15_Carpentersdaught/15_Interviews.html for details. Beyond these reports, I have no factual basis for thinking that Fred Noonan's bones were ever found by the colonists – other than that it is the only way I can make complete sense of Floyd Kilts' account; see Chapter 46.

Chapter 41

This chapter is entirely my own invention.

Chapter 42

This chapter is based largely on MacPherson's report; see Chapter 43.

Chapter 43

This chapter is a verbatim transcript of typewritten text found in the WPHC files, Hanslope Park, England; since transferred to Aukland, New Zealand. Published by TIGHAR at www.tighar.org/Projects/Earhart/Documents/MacPhersons_Report.html . My colleague Dr. Daniel Postellan, a medical doctor, tells me that Evipan, which Dr. MacPherson reports using as an anesthetic, is a poor one, also known today as hexobarbitol. The "skiagram" Dr. MacPherson reports examining was probably an x-ray film; "skiagram" is a general term for an image made up of shadows or outlines.

Chapter 44

This chapter is entirely my invention, designed to account for some aspects of the Kilts account (See Chapter 46). The account of burial practices at Kuma is derived from Grimble, *Tungaru Traditions,* pp. 69-70

Chapter 45

Jack Kimo's visit: In an interview in 2005, the late Edwin Petro told TIGHAR's Van Hunn and me of awakening one night and overhearing his father talking with Teruo, Aram, and Keaki about Keaki's discovery of aluminum on the Nutiran reef, and what its origin might be. Such a conversation could have taken place, of course, only at a time when all four plus Edwin were on the island, and it seems implausible that someone would not have told Gallagher about such a discovery had he been there. But when would Aram have been there and Gallagher not? Only sometime after the latter's death, but Edwin also told us that his family relocated to Ocean Island shortly after the attack on Pearl Harbor, which occurred only days after the High Commissioner's visit to Nikumaroro. The *Viti's* passenger and messing records do not indicate that Jack Kimo Petro and his family were transported to Nikumaroro, but both these records and Sir Harry Luke in his *From a South Seas Diary* say that the ship transported a "public works team" to Canton to construct a new house for Fleming, the British resident there. It is at least plausible that the resourceful Mister Kimo arranged the short passage to Nikumaroro without leaving explicit record, and it is the only way I can find to place all the characters Edwin mentioned together at the same time without word of their discussion reaching Gerald Gallagher.

Sir Harry Luke's visit: This voyage of the *Viti,* including the visit to Nikumaroro, is described by Sir Harry Luke in his *From a South Seas Diary 1938-1942,* pp. 2 17-30.

The rectangular aluminium objects: TIGHAR has recovered three such objects from the vicinity of the carpenter's house. They are not stock parts of any known airplane, but are thought perhaps to have been specially fabricated heat shields to insulate auxiliary fuel tanks from heater ducts. See *Amelia Earhart's Shoes:*363-66 and www.tighar.org/Projects/Earhart/ Bulletins/55_HeatShields/55_DetectiveStory.html for details.

Excerpt. From Sir Harry Luke, *From a South Seas Diary,* pp 220-23

Chapter 46

Sopko: Lt. Charles Sopko was the CO of the Loran station for most of its life. I am grateful to veterans of Loran Unit 92 and others, and to the late Lt. Sopko's son Steve Sopko, for information about life at the station.

Kilts: Floyd Kilts passed on before we could interview him. He apparently never got back to Nikumaroro. His daughter, Dorothy Josselyn, told me that he had in fact written a book about the bones story, but the manuscript had been lost. See *Amelia Earhart's Shoes* p. 281.

San Diego *Tribune* story: Verbatim transcript; see www.tighar.org/ Projects/Earhart/Documents/KiltsStory.html.

"Coral looks smooth as silk:" Kilts may have flown to or from Nikumaroro in one of the PBYs that serviced the Loran station, so would have seen the reef flat. TIGHAR has mapped an extremely smooth stretch of reef flat off Nutiran, where Emily Sikuli (Segalo) reported aircraft wreckage, that is easily long enough to accommodate landing an airplane. See also "An Aerial Tour of Nikumaroro," video available from TIGHAR.

Chapter 47

Laxton's account: For full account see www.tighar.org/Projects/Earhart /Documents/laxton.html.

Re-roofing the house: Archaeological evidence indicates that a small structure, roofed with galvanized corrugated steel (not iron like the sheets on the surge ridge), once stood near the still- open hole where we think the skull may have been exhumed. It was rigged to drain water into the Tarawa Police tank. There is evidence of unsuccessful coconut planting in the same vicinity.

Aram's markings: Not far from the remains of the house, the tank, and the hole, in 2001 we noted and recorded a rough "G" shape made of staghorn coral on the ground. By 2007 it had disappeared under encroaching *mao,* which discolors the coral and makes such markings indistinguishable from their surroundings.

Chapter 48

Text of the plaque: The text is as given by Sir Harry Luke in *From a South Seas Diary* and in WPHC records. In 2001, before learning that Gallagher's remains had been – we were assured – relocated, TIGHAR had a duplicate plaque made up and affixed it to the grave marker, in a small ceremony paying our respects to Gallagher's memory. The original plaque is in the cemetery on Tarawa. Gallagher's bones may be there, too, but the fact that his monument still stands, with no evidence that it has been moved to permit removal of his body, leads me to speculate that Mister Karaka may still lie in Nikumaroro's gravelly coralline soil.

Surviving domestic animals: Dogs were systematically exterminated by government after the island was evacuated. Roddy Cordon (quoted in text) mentions seeing a chicken in 1968. There was a desiccated cat in the still-standing (but since blown down) cooperative store near the landing when we first visited the island in 1989.

The channel and monument: The channel, connecting the natural boat channel to the open sea off the reef, was blasted in 1963 during preparations for removing the people of the Nikumaroro colony. Very suitable for rubber boat landings, it is routinely used today by the very few vessels that visit Nikumaroro, including TIGHAR archaeological expeditions. The concrete and coral- block tower marking its landward end was still standing tall at the time of our first visit in 1989, but by 1991 it had been completely destroyed, apparently by a very serious storm out of the west.

Reasons for abandoning the colony: Dr. William Stuart, an ethnographer who worked with the Nikumaroro colonists shortly after most of them relocated to the village of Nikumaroro in the Solomon Islands (I assume for the sake of the story that Keaki and Baiteke went to Tarawa instead), wrote in his dissertation: (Stuart 1971: 196-97): "The Phoenix Islands suffered, as did the rest of the Gilbert and Elice Island Colony... from droughts during the two and a half decades the Phoenix colony was viable. By the late 1950s, however, Pan American Airlines and other commercial endeavors housed at Canton Island, and which had used the labor provided by Hull and Gardner had become obsolete. Because of this fact which was coupled with the rather severe drought of the early 1 960s and the attendant expense of aiding the Phoenixes, (and, it should be recorded, the general retrenchment of British Colonialism everywhere), the British decided to evacuate the Phoenixes and to resettle the inhabitants elsewhere, in the western Solomon Islands."

Laxton's demand for change: Laxton's own account is at www.tighar.org/Projects/Earhart/Documents/laxton.html

Mister Kimo's fate: TIGHAR's Van Hunn and I were given the story of the Petro family's wartime trials by the late Edwin Petro when we interviewed him on Majuro in 2005. Jack (Mister Kimo) was not captured by the Japanese and went on to help build the facilities for the British nuclear tests on Christmas (Kiritimati) Island. His family, however, had relocated for uncertain reasons from Canton (now Kanton) Island to the Gilbert and Ellice Islands colonial headquarters on Ocean Island (now Banaba). They were imprisoned by the Japanese, but unlike many of their friends they were not massacred. Jack died long after the war in Tarawa. To our great regret, Edwin passed on in 2007.

The fate of the Rest House: We recorded the archaeological remains of the Rest House in 1989. The cookhouse still stood (It has since taken a serious hit from a falling coconut tree), as did the concrete bathroom, but beyond these there was nothing left but the concrete slab on which it had been constructed, and a number of fallen, burnt posts and rafters. In 2007 we used the slab as a dumping place for coconuts and fronds cleared during archaeological study of the wireless site and the site of the "carpenter's house" occupied by Jack Kimo Petro's and Tumuo's families.

Roddy Cordon: Ms. Cordon went to Tarawa from England 1965 as a Women's Education Officer. She remained there, with a few trips home and to Australia and New Zealand, into the early 1970s, and traveled widely throughout Kiribati and Tuvalu, including one visit to the Phoenix Islands. In 1996 she published *Seven Years' Island Hopping*, whose second volume includes her description of the visit to Nikumaroro. She says nothing about Keaki and Baiteke, but someone aboard her ship must have known the way to Gallagher's grave, so I have taken the liberty of assigning this role to our protagonists.

Acknowledgements

I am solely responsible for the way this novel portrays the fate of Amelia Earhart, the island of Nikumaroro, the Phoenix Islands Settlement Scheme, and the thoughts, words, and actions of the people portrayed. But I have had a great deal of help in acquiring the knowledge and opinions on which my portrayal of them all is based. There are many people and institutions to whom I'm indebted.

First of all, I'm thankful to The International Group for Historic Aircraft Recovery (TIGHAR) for getting me involved in the search for Earhart and for taking me to Nikumaroro to do fieldwork in 1989, 1997, 2001, and 2007 (Another expedition is planned in 2010). And I'm grateful to all my TIGHAR friends and colleagues for their help, collegiality, and comradeship. I'm especially grateful to all the TIGHAR members who reviewed drafts and offered helpful comments and criticisms.

I'm grateful to the Republic of Kiribati for permission to visit Nikumaroro and conduct research there, and to the many individuals in Kiribati, Fiji, New Zealand, Tuvalu, Australia, the United Kingdom, and the United States who have helped with and facilitated our work.

I'm especially grateful to Foua Tofiga, Emily Sikuli (Segalo), the late Edwin Petro, the late Sir Ian Thompson, the late Harry Maude, and all the other veterans of the Phoenix Islands Settlement Scheme, who have with great generosity shared their recollections of the period.

And finally, I thank all my friends, colleagues, and correspondents throughout Micronesia, who over the decades have given me glimpses into what life is like on those beautiful, dangerous, threatened islands.

Bibliography

Most of the original documents I used in imagining this story are available, or will soon be available, via the "Ameliapedia" – a wiki under construction on TIGHAR's worldwide web site, www.tighar.org. Following are relevant traditionally published sources.

Baraka, Tione

   1991   *The Story of Karongoa.* Narrated by an Unimane of the Boti of Karongoa n Uea on Nikunau in 1934, transcribed by Tione Baraka of Taboiaki on Beru, translated by G.H. Eastman, edited, annotated and revised by H.E. Maude. Institute of Pacific Studies, University of the South Pacific, Suva

Bevington, Eric

   1990   *The Things We Do For England – If Only England Knew.* Acorn Bookwork, Salisbury, Wilts, UK.

Cordon, Roddy

   1998   *Seven Years' Island Hopping.* Cordon and Wood, Eagle, Lincolnshire, UK.

Gillespie, Ric

   2006   *Finding Amelia: the True Story of the Earhart Disappearance.* U.S. Naval Institute Press, Annapolis MD.

Grimble, Francis

   1989   *Tungaru Traditions.* Edited by H.E. Maude. Melbourne University Press, Melbourne

King, Thomas F., Randall S. Jacobson, Karen R. Burns, Kenton Spading

   2004   *Amelia Earhart's Shoes.* Altamira Press, Walnut Creek, CA.

Knox-Mawer, June

   1986   *Tales From Paradise: Memories of the British in the South Pacific.* Ariel Books, BBC Publications, London.

Knudson, Kenneth E.

1964 *Titiana: a Gilbertese Community in the Solomon Islands.* Report on the results of a field study for the "Project for the Comparative Study of Cultural Change and Stability in Displaced Communities in the Pacific. Department of Anthropology, University of Oregon, Eugene.

Laxton, Paul

1951 "Nikumaroro." *Journal of the Polynesian Society* 60:134-60, Honolulu.

Luke, Sir Harry

1945 *From a South Seas Diary 1938-1942.* Nicholson & Watson, London

Macdonald, Barrie

2001 *Cinderellas of the Empire: Towards a History of Kiribati and Tuvalu.* Institute of Pacific Studies, University of the South Pacific, Suva.

Mara, The Right Honorable Ratu Sir Kamisese

1997 *The Pacific Way: A Memoir.* University of Hawai'i Press, Honolulu

Maude, Henry Evans

1940 *Report on the Phoenix and Line Islands With Special Reference to the Question of British Sovereignty.* F.W. Smith, Printer to the Government of His Britannic Majesty's High Commission for the Western Pacific, Suva, Fiji.

1967 The Swords of Gabriel: A Study in Participant History. *Journal of Pacific History* 2:113-36.

1968 *Of Islands and Men: Studies in Pacific History.* Oxford University Press, Melbourne.

1980 *The Gilbertese Maneaba.* Institute of Pacific Studies and Kiribati Extension Centre, University of the South Pacific, Suva.

1991 *The Story of Karongoa* (edited). Institute of Pacific Studies, University of the South Pacific, Suva

Maude, Honor C. and Henry E. Maude

    1994   *An Anthology of Gilbertese Oral Tradition.* Institute of Pacific Studies, University of the South Pacific, Suva.

McQuarrie, Peter

    2000   *Conflict in Kiribati: A History of the Second World War.* MacMillan Brown Centre for Pacific Studies, University of Canterbury, Christchurch.

Stone, Greg

    2004   "Phoenix Islands: a Coral Reef Wilderness Revealed," *National Geographic Magazine* February 2004

Stuart, William

    1971   *Cultural Ecology: Prolegomena to a Natural Science of Anthropology.* PhD dissertation, Department of Anthropology, University of Oregon, Eugene.

Woodburn, Susan

    2003   *Where Our Hearts Still Lie: A Life of Harry and Honor Maude in the Pacific.* Crawford House, Adelaide.

CPSIA information can be obtained at www.ICGtesting.com
Printed in the USA
LVOW041602030712

288726LV00005B/131/P